"Flora Speer opens up new vistas for the romance reader."
—*Romantic Times*

FOR LOVE AND HONOR

Tearing his mouth from hers, Alain put his hands on Joanna's upper arms and pushed her away from him, holding her back when she tried blindly to reenter his embrace.

"Dear God," he whispered, seeing her bruised lips and tear-filled eyes. "Joanna, what have I done to you?"

He watched her breath shudder through her body, the sweet, delicate vessel into which he yearned to pour himself. His hands tightened on her arms.

"This was not your fault," he said, still whispering. "You are but fourteen and completely innocent. I am seven years older than you. I am the one who should have known better than to start this."

"I am a woman," she wept. "This time tomorrow I shall be a married woman, with a husband who is also seven years older than I."

"Aye, and tomorrow night you will go to Crispin's bed, not mine." When she gasped at the cruelty of that flat statement, he added, "Tomorrow night I shall die of grief and longing for what I can never have."

D0324714

Other *Leisure* and *Love Spell* Books by
Flora Speer:
LOVE JUST IN TIME
CHRISTMAS CAROL
A LOVE BEYOND TIME
NO OTHER LOVE
A TIME TO LOVE AGAIN
VIKING PASSION
DESTINY'S LOVERS
MUCH ADO ABOUT LOVE
VENUS RISING
BY HONOR BOUND

FOR LOVE AND HONOR

FLORA SPEER

LEISURE BOOKS NEW YORK CITY

A LEISURE BOOK®

July 1995

Published by

Dorchester Publishing Co., Inc.
276 Fifth Avenue
New York, NY 10001

If you purchased this book without a cover you should be aware that this book is stolen property. It was reported as "unsold and destroyed" to the publisher and neither the author nor the publisher has received any payment for this "stripped book."

Copyright © 1995 by Flora Speer

All rights reserved. No part of this book may be reproduced or transmitted in any form or by any electronic or mechanical means, including photocopying, recording or by any information storage and retrieval system, without the written permission of the Publisher, except where permitted by law.

The name "Leisure Books" and the stylized "L" with design are trademarks of Dorchester Publishing Co., Inc.

Printed in the United States of America.

Prologue

St. Justin's Abbey, England
A.D. 1152

Father Ambrose, the abbot of St. Justin's, was seventy-three years old. The sharpness of his eyes remained undimmed by his great age, but the once fierce features of a peerless warrior had softened over the years. Ambrose was now famous not for his feats in battle but for his great learning, and for the kindness and concern he showed to those who came to him with their problems, from within the abbey and from the outside world. On this late November morning he was particularly interested in what the newly arrived travelers in his receiving room had to say.

They were three in number, two richly dressed men and a girl not quite sixteen. In the courtyard a few servants and the men-at-arms who had come with them were awaiting Ambrose's decision on where they were to spend that night.

"You will need my help," Ambrose said to his three guests. "You cannot do it alone."

"True, but you must not join us until the moment is right," replied the taller of the two men. "If we move too quickly, all will be lost. The castle is too strong to take by frontal assault, which is why we ask you to shelter our men until we need them."

"They are welcome to stay here. And you, my dear?" Ambrose's eyes rested on the young woman. "Will you also remain at St. Justin's until this scheme is concluded?"

"By my own wish, I am part of the plan," she responded. "I cannot stay behind, nor would I want to. If it were necessary, I would go disguised as one of the squires."

"You are your father's own child, brave and perhaps a little too clever for your own safety." Ambrose smiled at her. "I dare to say that, because 'twas I who baptized you. I will also make free to say you have grown up to be beautiful, with a spirit much like your lovely mother's."

"Scandalous priest," teased the second of the two male guests. "What would your fellows here at St. Justin's say to hear you pay such compliments to a lady?"

"They'd say what they have so often," Ambrose replied, his blue eyes twinkling; "that I lived too long in a foreign land and have not recovered from it even so many years after my return.

2

"Very well, dear kinsmen and friends," he continued, sobering. "Tell me all you plan to do and how I can help you. There is a lady who has needed rescuing for far too many years, a murderer to be brought to justice, and men falsely proclaimed outlaws to be proven innocent and restored to honor once more. We have a difficult task ahead of us. I include myself most willingly in whatever you plan to do for the sake of justice and the righting of wrongs, so the dead can rest in peace at last."

"For honor's sake," said the tall man, nodding agreement with the priest's words.

"For love," declared the second man with barely restrained emotion.

"For love and honor both," murmured the young woman.

Part I

Joanna
England, A.D. 1134

Chapter One

Early in the year, Baron Radulf of Banningford decided the time had come to marry off his daughter. Joanna was fourteen, the proper age to wed, and others told him the girl was beautiful, though Radulf could not see it himself. But then, he seldom looked at Joanna. He was too preoccupied with his own problems to bother with her.

For years Radulf had successfully navigated his way among the competing ambitions of his neighbors, the great Marcher lords who held vast estates along the border between England and Wales. So far, by a combination of guile toward those lords and friendship with King Henry I, he had maintained his independence and kept his holdings intact, but now the times were changing and Radulf felt himself in danger. On his last visit to court he had seen that King Henry was aging and unwell. Radulf did not think the King would live much longer—a year or two, perhaps three. Henry's heir was his arrogant daughter Matilda, to whom he had forced his nobles to swear allegiance. Sacred oaths or no, few Norman nobles wanted to be ruled by a woman, and there were many who would prefer to see Henry's nephew Stephen on the throne. Radulf feared a period of civil strife and lawlessness would follow Henry's death, until a new ruler was decided upon. During that perilous time he would need staunch allies if his lands were not to be swallowed up by some greedy earl.

Radulf was greedy himself. He wanted more lands. He wanted power. Most of all he wanted a strong male heir whom he could train as he wished and to whom he could relinquish both lands and power when the time came for him to lay aside earthly concerns.

Radulf had no sons. His first wife had produced only the one girl, Joanna, dying even as her child came into the world. His second wife had repeatedly miscarried before succumbing to a wasting disease. And his third wife had given him no children at all in spite of Radulf's nightly attempts to rectify her barren condition. Having now reached the advanced age of forty-eight, Radulf had come to the reluctant conclusion that his most likely hope for an heir lay in a grandchild.

Haughston, the barony that bordered Radulf's lands to the east, belonged to an old comrade-in-arms who had recently died, leaving his estate to his only son, Crispin. The boy was doubtless inexperienced in worldly affairs, and therefore, Baron Radulf reasoned, he would be willing to be guided by a well-seasoned father-in-law. An alliance between Joanna and the lord of Haughston could only be advantageous to both parties.

It seemed the young man's advisers felt the same way, for the suggestion of a match between Baron Crispin of Haughston and Lady Joanna of Banningford was accepted with flattering promptness. Over the next two months the clerks met to discuss terms, Joanna's dowry was decided upon, the marriage contract was drawn up, and the wedding date was set for Midsummer's Eve. Only then did Radulf appear in the solar where the women of his castle spent much of their time, to inform his daughter of the arrangements he had made for her. He arrived at the door of the solar accompanied by his personal guard Baird, who seldom left his side.

"Do you know Baron Crispin personally?" Joanna asked her father after hearing the news. "Is he young or old? Ill-favored or fair?"

"What difference does any of that make?" demanded Radulf. "You will marry as I order you."

"Yes, Father." Joanna knew better than to challenge her formidable parent. She had been afraid of him for as long as she could remember.

"I did not meet your father until my wedding day, and ours has been a satisfactory marriage," said her stepmother, Rohaise, trying as usual to be helpful and to mollify any sign of anger in her husband. "My lord, perhaps if you would mention Baron Crispin's age to us, that will be enough for now. And if you could tell me how many guests he will bring with him, it would be of great assistance to me in planning meals and sleeping arrangements. I do want the festivities to reflect your importance, yet I would not waste provisions unnecessarily."

"The boy is twenty-one. He was knighted only last week," said Radulf, grumbling a bit at being thus pressed for information by a woman, while at the same time appreciating his wife's admirable frugality. He reflected that he had little to complain of in Rohaise, save for the galling lack of a son. Still, she was only eighteen; she might yet give him what he wanted most. Recalling the previous night and how cheerfully she had manipulated his aging body into renewed vigor, Radulf gave her a benign look and almost smiled. Rohaise was the best of his wives; he would continue trying to get her with child. In the meantime he had a healthy daughter to use as a pawn in his quest for more land and a dependable ally. He was feeling pleased with himself; the marriage was a brilliant stroke on his part, and Rohaise would delight in planning the week of wedding feasts. He could afford to be generous in answering her question.

"You may have a new gown, and Joanna, too, as well as the linens and other household goods stipulated in the marriage contract," he told Rohaise. "As for the company, I'd say fifteen to twenty extra mouths to feed on the bridegroom's account. Add to that the other people I'll want to invite. Plan for at least a hundred guests, including servants."

"So many?" Joanna's voice quavered at the thought. She was nervous already. She had no experience of crowds. Her father had kept her at home, refusing to let her foster at some other castle as was the custom with young noblewomen. And all of this crowd of strangers—a hundred or more!—would be staring at her.

"I am a man of importance," Radulf declared, flushing with the rise of his easily disturbed temper.

"Joanna and I know that, my lord." Rohaise hastened to placate him. "Neither of us was expecting your announcement, so we are both greatly surprised. And I think Joanna may be just a bit intimidated by the change that will soon occur in her life."

"Hmmm." Radulf regarded his daughter as if she were a brood mare, ignoring the tumbling golden curls and blue eyes, skipping quickly over her chiseled features and slender wrists and hands, to linger on her squared shoulders and nicely rounded hips. She was not tall, but she would probably grow a few more inches in the six years before she turned twenty. For all her youth she looked like a girl who could give birth easily. That pleased him.

"Teach her what she needs to know," he ordered Rohaise. "Instruct her to be a welcoming and compliant wife, serving her husband's needs in the marriage bed. When you have finished, and when the time is nearer to the day, I'll have a few words with her myself, to be certain she understands the purpose of this alliance." With that, Radulf motioned to Baird to follow him and took himself off to the bailey, leaving his quaking daughter in her stepmother's care. When the solar door had closed upon the men Rohaise opened her arms and Joanna went into them.

"What did he mean?" Joanna whimpered, her sapphire eyes wide. "Oh, Rohaise, I've heard the servingwomen whispering about men, but they always stop when they see me approaching. Has it anything to do with the monthly bleeding that began last summer? You said then that it meant I was old enough to have children. That's what he wants, isn't it? Grandchildren. But I don't know how," she finished on a sob, feeling utterly incompetent in this most important area of a noblewoman's life.

"Your husband will teach you how," Rohaise said, and launched into a brief explanation of the physical intimacy between husband and wife.

"Do you mean I will have to let a stranger touch me like that?" Joanna cried, deeply shaken by the information. "I have accidentally seen men unclothed once or twice, and I've noticed that they are made differently from women. He will put that—*that*—into me? I do not think I want to wed. I will tell my father so," she ended on a note of rising panic.

"It is a noblewoman's lot in life to be married at her father's bidding," Rohaise reminded her. Rohaise knew that Radulf would not allow any change in his carefully laid plans, and she wanted to spare Joanna the punishment she would certainly receive if she refused to wed now. "It happens to all of us except for those who enter a convent. When you are alone with your husband he will do what I have described."

"Oh, Rohaise." Joanna's face was pale, her eyes huge and dark with fear. "It must hurt so much."

"Only a little, and only the first time." Rohaise pulled Joanna's head down to her shoulder and spoke softly, quickly, refusing to allow her own embarrassment to stop her from doing what she could to ease Joanna's terror. "It can be very pleasant, especially as the man grows older and thus less hasty and fierce. I have learned not to dread Radulf's attentions each night."

"But Lord Crispin is only twenty-one," Joanna whispered. "It will be many years before he is less hasty and fierce."

"Perhaps," Rohaise said, reaching for a shred of comfort, "perhaps he will learn to love you. I do believe, if the man were to love the woman, what he did to her in their bedchamber might be the most beautiful thing in the world."

That night, alone in the tiny chamber that was accorded to her as the daughter of the lord of Banningford, Joanna lay in her narrow bed and thought about the unknown man who would soon take possession of her body. She had no mirror, so she could not tell if she was fair to the eye or not, but when she ran her hands up and down the length of her body she knew her skin was smooth and soft. He, this stranger who would be her husband, would lay his hands on her bare breasts—*so*—and perhaps slide his hands gently across her abdomen—*in this way*—to the place between her thighs where golden curls grew, before he spread her legs and—*no!*

"No!" She turned in bed, flinging herself face-down, burying her sobs in the straw mattress so no one passing her door would hear her. Lord Crispin would hurt her. He would be rough and coarse as her father and his men were. Night after night he would do *that* to her.

She had seldom in her life asked for anything for herself when she prayed. Her entreaties to heaven had been filled instead with pleas for the repose of her mother's soul, or for the souls of her first stepmother and that poor lady's stillborn babes, or for Rohaise when she was sick; for rain during a draught or forgiveness for some trivial girlish sin. On that night, for the first time in her fourteen years, Joanna prayed for herself with terrified fervor.

"Please," she whispered into the darkness, "let the man to whom I am to be bound be good and honest, clean and healthy, and fine-looking. And please—oh, please—let him love me with all his heart until the day he dies, so that he will always be gentle with me and never strike or bruise me, and not hurt me when he does *that* to me. . . . "

So distressed was she at the thought of her coming marriage and so unaccustomed to thinking of what she wanted for herself was she that she neglected to specify that the man who would love her so enduringly should be Lord Crispin. And she was far too young and innocent to know that prayers are sometimes answered in strange and unimaginable ways.

Chapter Two

Many of the invited guests had already assembled ere the bridegroom came to Banningford Castle two days before the wedding. He brought with him only a small company. Standing between Rohaise and her father in the narrow entry hall, Joanna watched them come up the stairs and into the castle keep, leaving brilliant sunshine and warmth outside.

As always the great hall at Joanna's back was damp and chilly, though the air smelled relatively fresh thanks to the thorough cleaning Rohaise had ordered and the new rushes and sweet herbs strewn across the floor at her behest. But nothing could alleviate the cold and darkness of a place built with arrow slits instead of windows; not the fire roaring in the hearth or the torches set in sconces along the walls, or even the dozen tall, branched silver candelabra burning the finest beeswax candles. These candelabra Rohaise had set upon the long tables, and they cast pools of golden light that caught the jewels and shining silks worn by men and women alike, shattering the colors of fabrics and furs, precious stones and gold, into glittering shards of brilliance that danced against the dark background of shadowed gray stone walls, heavy tapestries, and faces seen in half light.

In the alternating areas of dark and light, Rohaise's wine-red gown glowed like a somber flame and her gold necklace sparkled. Joanna's midnight-blue silk dress reflected a deeper radiance, and the simple gold bracelet on her left wrist, her only remembrance of her dead mother, was almost unnoticeable except when she touched it. In her present nervous state the bracelet was like a talisman to her, its smooth surface soothing beneath her trembling fingers.

The first of the party from Haughston was a priest, Father Ambrose, who was Lord Crispin's uncle, his late father's brother and, until a few weeks previously, Crispin's guardian. While Radulf and Rohaise courteously greeted the clergyman just inside the arch of the door, with the ever-present Baird on guard beside them, Joanna allowed her eyes to stray toward the others who had crowded in behind Father Ambrose and who now stood waiting to speak to their host and hostess. There were a few servants and squires in the entry hall, but these Joanna dismissed as unimportant at the moment. She wanted to see her betrothed. It was difficult to decide who he might be, for three young men, distinguishable as nobles by the fineness of their dress, stood together.

They had come to the wedding in the highest of spirits, in radiant health, and with all the brash assurance of newmade knighthood. Joanna had seen her father's men stand so confidently and walk with that same slight swagger. She was accustomed to new knights who glanced boldly about the hall, their eyes challenging the older men or resting on every pretty serving maid they encountered. These three were familiar types to her, and in beholding that familiarity she lost some of her fear.

Radulf was still talking to Father Ambrose, guiding him toward the hall with Rohaise a step behind them and Baird as usual following Radulf like a bulky shadow. The tallest, largest of the three young men merely nodded to her before, at Father Ambrose's signal, he hastened to catch up with the older folk. The second man, a lean, sharp-featured fellow with straight black hair, winked at Joanna, then grinned in such a mischievous way that she could not be offended.

It was the third man who captured Joanna's fascinated attention. He was remarkably good-looking, with a firm, square jaw, a straight nose, and crisply curling dark brown hair cut close about his ears. His level gray eyes held hers, making her think he was weighing her value. The other people around them passed on, moving out of the entry and into the gloom of the great hall, but this man remained, pausing to speak to her.

While she gazed at him the motions and sounds of the hall faded away until it seemed to her that they stood alone together in some far-distant and secluded part of the world, linking eyes and hearts and lives in silent communication. Surely, oh surely, this was her betrothed, this tall and handsome youth whose cool look softened into silver-gray warmth as they stood regarding one another. How glad she was; she could marry him with no qualms, for she had at once recognized in him a kindred soul. How she knew it, she could not tell, but know it she did, and her heart rejoiced.

"My dear lady." His mouth curved into the beginning of a smile, and Joanna found herself smiling back at him. How thoughtful of him to wait until her family and his friends were gone so their first words to each other could be spoken in relative privacy.

"My lord." She made him a curtsy and was about to put her hand into his when the gesture was forestalled by her father's loud voice.

"Joanna, come here and be presented to your betrothed!"

With a glance at the handsome man, Joanna obeyed, wondering at herself as she did so. Where had she learned that flutter of her eyelashes or the swift and quickly repressed smile that only he could have seen? She had never flirted before in her life, but it had come so naturally. And now she knew he was watching her. Indeed, he was close on her heels, following her across the hall. She could feel his presence at her back. She imagined she was leading him, and he would go wherever she desired. It was a powerful, heady sensation. She looked up at her father with shining eyes, wishing she dared thank him then and there for the husband he had chosen for her.

Then Rohaise gave her a frightened look and her father frowned at her. Brought back to reality with a sudden gasp of understanding, Joanna knew she had made a mistake. Her heart stopped its dancing and began to sink.

"Daughter, you forget your duty to our guests," Radulf said sternly.

"It is no doubt an overly exciting time for a maiden. She ought to be excused her nervousness." Father Ambrose appeared to be kind, yet somehow he gave Joanna the feeling that he understood what had just happened to her and did not approve.

But what *had* happened to her? Why was it so hard to breathe; why did her heart beat so painfully? She dared not even glance at the gray-eyed young man. She could only stare at the stone floor with one hand clasped over the bracelet on her other wrist, praying silently—and with a last stubborn flicker of hope that refused to be quenched by the growing despair of certainty— *please, let it be him,* while her father made the introduction.

The hand that reached for hers, that lifted it away from her mother's old bracelet and held her fingers with gentle strength, was large and bore blond hair upon its back and wrist.

"My lady Joanna." Her hand was borne upward and she was forced to look at Baron Crispin of Haughston while he pressed his lips upon her fingers and then bent to kiss her cheek.

He was nice enough looking to please any girl. Tall, big-boned, and muscular, blond with blue eyes and a ruddy face, from his expression Crispin looked to be a kindly man. Under other circumstances she would have been delighted with him. It was just that for an instant she had dared to dream, to hope . . .

"Here are my best friends," said Crispin, turning to them. Indicating the slim, black-haired man, he added, "This is Piers, the third son of the Baron of Stokesbrough. Since he has to make his own way in the world, Piers is about to become one of my household knights, so you will know him well before long. And this curly-haired lad is Alain, heir to the Baron of Wortham. He'll be riding north when we leave Banningford, to help his father hold Wortham against the Scots and the wild Cumbrians."

"So far away?" She could not help it; the words slipped out, sounding as lost and desolate as she felt. She saw a flash of something in Alain's eyes, a response to the cry that had come from her heart. She prayed her father had not noticed.

"That's just what I said when I learned of it," Crispin told her, apparently oblivious to her pain. "But then, you and I are going even farther away."

"How can that be?" Radulf snapped out the

question. "Your principal seat is at Haughston."

"So it is," Crispin responded mildly. "But I also have lands in Normandy, which my father had not visited for years before he died, and which now require my attention. I'll take you with me, Joanna, as soon as the wedding feasts are over at this week's end. I have also a wish to make a pilgrimage to Compostela in Spain, and again, I'd have my wife by my side."

"I have never been away from Banningford," Joanna said, intrigued in spite of her heartache. "I think I would like to see more of the world."

"I'm glad to hear it." Crispin smiled at her, a touch of warmth breaking through his bland exterior. "You will find I am a religious man. When we return to Haughston in a few years I plan to build a new chapel there, finer and larger than the present one. Perhaps you would like to embroider an altarcloth for it. I have been told that you are a skillful needlewoman."

"A few years?" exclaimed Radulf, visibly upset by this news. "What of your wife, sir? Would you have her miscarry your heir while you force her to endure rough roads and dangerous sea voyages? A newly wed couple ought to stay at home until the wife has produced at least two sons!"

"I do assure you, Lord Radulf, that I will take the greatest care of the lady Joanna," Crispin said. "I, too, understand the importance of a healthy heir."

"I'll undertake to guarantee that your daughter is well cared for," added Father Ambrose, "for I am to travel with the couple to London first, and after that at least as far as Normandy."

"I suppose you are on your way to Compostela too?" grumbled Radulf rather rudely.

"No, to Sicily," Father Ambrose informed him. "I go in the footsteps of Adelard of Bath, that remarkable scholar of blessed memory. If God grants me a safe journey, like Adelard, I, too, shall study at Palermo for a few years."

"My goodness," said Rohaise, a bit too brightly and with an apprehensive glance in her husband's direction, "so much travel. So interesting. Joanna, I shall want to hear all about it when you return. Radulf, my dear, won't the tales of Joanna's journeys make wonderful entertainment when we are all gathered together on a cold winter's evening? Sir Alain, you may visit us, also. I'm sure my lord Radulf would enjoy hearing about your battles against the Scots and—what was it?—the Cuthbrians?"

"The Cumbrians," Alain corrected gently. His eyes met Joanna's with laughter that melted into wistful longing.

"I don't hold with travel," Radulf said. "Except for his forty days' service to the king each year and the needs of warfare, a baron ought to stay at home and guard his castle. I thought that's what you intended to do, Crispin. It's not right to go off like that, not when the Earl of Chester and his friends are growing ever more powerful. As for the other Marcher lords, who knows what will happen in the next year or so?"

"That's exactly what my seneschal in Normandy says about my estates there," Crispin responded with unbroken good humor. "His concern and yours, too, I think, is all because the king is old and ill." They went on in that way, talking at cross purposes, with Crispin remaining polite while maintaining that he *would* leave Haughston, and Radulf becoming increasingly annoyed that he could not convince the younger man to give up his plans.

Joanna stopped listening to them. After kissing her hand when they were introduced Crispin had tucked it into his left elbow, placing his right hand over it, so she had to remain by his side, but she let her glance roam about the hall. All was in readiness for the midday feast, the tables covered with snowy linen cloths, the silver cups and plates arranged on the high table gleaming in the candlelight. At the lower tables wooden trenchers or plates made from hollowed-out slices of day-old bread awaited the diners. The servants were bringing in pitchers of wine and cider and tall silver water ewers with basins and linen towels, so the guests could wash their hands before eating. She noted these details with the almost unconscious efficiency of a well-trained chatelaine. With the same detachment she saw that Rohaise had gone to instruct one of the servants, and that several of the other male guests had joined the group around her father and Crispin, but a portion of her mind remained separate from what was going on in the hall. In that separate part of her thoughts she was trying to adjust to what had happened to her that morning.

If she had been given a choice, she would have taken Alain of Wortham as her husband in a heartbeat. But the choice had not been hers to make, and she must live with her father's decision. Trained as she had been through all her life to obey him, the thought of defiance barely crossed her mind before she rejected the idea. She had seen often enough the kind of punishments meted out to those who interfered with Radulf's plans. She would marry Crispin and make no protest about it.

At least they would travel. She had long dreamed of foreign lands, and now she would see them. She would cross the Narrow Sea to Normandy and follow the pilgrim route into glamorous, mysterious Spain, where Saracens lived. She might even see a Saracen in flowing robes, mounted upon his fleet steed, or gaze upon the fabled cities of Moorish Spain. Bedazzled by the prospect, she almost convinced herself that she *wanted* to marry Crispin, until she saw Alain watching her. Then her heart constricted with a painful twist, and all thought of travel and an interesting life beyond the gates of Banningford Castle crumpled downward into ashes.

"Art moonstruck?" Piers clapped a hand on Alain's shoulder.

"Does it show?" It was no use trying to keep anything from Piers. His eyes were sharp and his quick thoughts went to the nub of every problem.

"To me it shows," Piers said. "But I think Crispin has not noticed yet. At the moment he's divided between concentrating on his lady and paying respectful attention to her father's rantings."

"I'd hide my feelings from both of them. I'd not hurt Crispin or Joanna, or make either unhappy for my sake."

"If I were you, I'd watch the lady's father too," Piers advised. "I think he has noticed your interest in his daughter."

"Thank you." Alain forced a smile. Trying to sound like his usual carefree self, he said, "Let's eat and drink; let's celebrate Crispin's coming nuptials."

"Don't drink too much, lest you speak amiss when the wine fills your head and say something you ought to keep to yourself."

"You were not always so cautious before you became a knight, old Sir Piers," said Alain, laughing now.

"All's not as it should be in this place. There is something strange about Radulf's determination to keep his daughter and son-in-law at home. I think he is truly angry about Crispin's plans to travel to Normandy and to stay away for several years. From what I've seen of Radulf so far, I doubt if it's because he loves his daughter too much to part with her for long."

"Who would not love her?" Fortunately, Alain's voice was too soft for anyone but Piers to hear him. He watched Crispin lead Joanna to the high table. "What a sweet and lovely lady she is. See how gracefully she moves, how her face lights

25

when she smiles. And her hair—dear God, that wondrous golden hair!"

"Have a care." Piers's voice was as quiet as Alain's own, but the note of warning was sharp and clear, and it sobered Alain at once.

"Aye," Alain said, linking his arm with Piers's and pulling him toward the tables, "I have always found your advice to be well-spoken. I'll heed it now."

But for the immediate future heeding Piers's excellent advice was clearly going to be difficult, for at that instant Crispin saw them, and at his insistence extra seats were brought so they could both be placed at the high table among the most favored guests, with Piers next to a pretty young noblewoman and Alain beside Joanna.

At first she did not look at him. She could not bear to. Fearing he would see how her hands trembled, she ate little, but sat with her right hand tightly covering the bracelet on her left wrist, hoping thus to keep them still. She averted her eyes, looking toward Crispin, who ate meat pie and a large slice of roasted ox with healthy relish and without seeming to notice her discomfort.

"I hope Lady Rohaise did not mind the change in seating," Crispin remarked between bites of meat. "I could not let my kinsmen sit at the lower tables."

"Of course not." Then, realizing what he had said, she added, "I did not know they were related to you. I thought they were but friends."

"They are friends, and much more besides."

Crispin lifted his silver goblet for a servant to re-fill it, then drank deeply before he went on in the serious, solemn way she was beginning to think was his natural manner of speaking. "We three are cousins in various degrees. The mothers of Alain and Piers were sisters; Alain's grandfather and mine were brothers. We are all but a few months apart in age, and as it happened, we were fostered at the same castle. After being pages and later squires together, after living together for so many years, we are more like brothers, and I for one fully expect that we will remain on the same good terms for the rest of our lives."

"I pray it may be so," Joanna said, silently vow-ing never to do anything to damage that precious friendship. She forbade herself to think about Alain with longing. She would think only of Cris-pin, her betrothed, who seemed to her even on such short acquaintance to be an honest, serious-minded young man. She could respect him, and she owed him her allegiance.

But during the feast she could not avoid talk-ing with Alain, and it would have looked strange if she had tried to ignore him. When Rohaise ex-cused herself from the table in order to see to some domestic matter, leaving only an empty seat separating Crispin from Radulf, and Radulf claimed Crispin's attention once again by extoll-ing the benefits of a baron remaining at home where he would be readily available to attend to any emergencies on his lands, good manners forced Joanna to converse with Alain.

"Crispin's a fine man," Alain said, looking hard

at her. "He will treat you well. Be equally gracious to him."

"I intend to be the wife he wants." Her chin was up, her expression cool and distant. "Nor will I interfere in his friendships."

"It's odd that Crispin should be the first of us to wed," Alain mused, "when it's Piers and I who have always chased after the ladies, while Crispin never seemed to care about them at all."

Wondering if he was deliberately trying to irritate her to see if he could elicit a heated response, she kept her voice crisp and cold.

"I do not consider continence a defect in my betrothed," she said, "nor will I find it a fault in my husband."

"I did not think you would." Intensely aware of her pain and confusion, which he sensed matched his own, Alain ached to touch her, or at least to say something to commend her gallant attempt to hide the distress of her spirit. Thanks to her self-control he did not think anyone in the great hall had noticed the immediate and overwhelming flare of attraction between them except Piers and, possibly, Father Ambrose. And her watchful father, of course; but after the marriage ceremonies she would no longer be under Radulf's jurisdiction but Crispin's, and thus she would be safe from Radulf's ire. Alain wanted her to be safe. He wanted—ah, God in heaven, he wanted her! He had known lovely women before and had enjoyed the favors of several, including one very highly placed lady, and he had cared deeply for at least two of those women, but never in all his twenty-one years had he experienced the devastating certainty of knowing within moments of meeting a woman that she was the other half of his soul. And with the same pure and absolute certainty, as though she had spoken the words aloud in her precise and beautifully modulated voice, he knew Joanna had experienced the same blinding revelation of enduring and passionate attachment.

Bitterly he reminded himself that on the day after next Joanna would belong forever to Crispin, his kinsman, his friend. Hearing Radulf's loud voice raised even higher in dispute with Crispin, Alain felt a peculiar chill go down his spine, a premonition of he knew not what unlucky occurrence. The sensation made him take a risk he otherwise would not have chanced. As far as he dared, before he and Joanna could be interrupted, he said what was in his heart.

"My sweet lady, I know not how it happened so suddenly and completely that I should be irrevocably attached to you, but I do swear that I am your servant until I die. If you ever have need of me, if aught goes wrong in your life, you have but to send word and I will come to your aid."

"I will have a husband to protect me." She spoke sharply so as to hide what she felt. Ah, how she wished he had kept silent. His words were a temptation, feeding a dream she should not treasure, just when she had promised herself to think no more of him.

"I meant the promise for Crispin as well as for you," he said quietly. "He's more than kin; he's a dear friend, too, and after your marriage, through him you will be my kin as well. The times are difficult, Lady Joanna. Who knows what may befall us in the years to come? We keep a large garrison at Wortham. I have already said the same words to Crispin, but I wanted you to hear them too. If you need me, alone or with my men-at-arms, you have but to ask."

The feast had ended; the guests began to drift out of the hall. There was to be a hunting party that afternoon that would last well into the long twilight of midsummer, and men collected in groups, calling to each other that they would meet at the stables or in the outer bailey. Alain stood, putting his hand to Joanna's elbow to help her rise. On her other side Crispin pushed back his chair, still talking—or rather, listening—to her father. Alain's eyes were on her, and some recognition of his promise of aid seemed appropriate. In a few days he would be gone, out of her life for years and possibly forever. Until then she could keep her feelings hidden.

"I thank you for your loyal friendship," she said, giving him her hand. He held it a bit over-long, until her father stepped to her side, frowning.

"Alain has promised support to my husband and me in time of trouble," Joanna said to him, hoping thus to allay the almost certain explosion of Radulf's temper.

"Armed support is a man's business and no affair for a woman to concern herself with," Radulf growled, unappeased. "If he has something to say on that matter, he ought to say it to Crispin."

"So I have. And I promise the same support to you, my lord," said Alain. With a bow he left the table, joining Piers and heading for the outer door.

"Young fool," grumbled Radulf, staring after him with a calculating look.

"He is occasionally impetuous," Crispin said, "but he is an honorable man, Radulf. You can always depend on Alain to do what is right. My lady Joanna, will you ride next to me in the hunt this afternoon?"

"Gladly, my lord." Joanna took his hand and let him lead her into the entry hall, to the foot of the staircase that curved along the inside of the western tower, where her chamber was.

"Put on your hunting garb," Crispin said in his serious way, "and I'll remove these extravagant silks and also don more sensible clothes. Do you enjoy the hunt?"

"I like to ride," Joanna responded, "but I have no taste for the kill. I always feel sorry for the poor trapped beasts." She ended the words with a guilty laugh, for after every hunt her father always scolded her about her queasiness at the sight of a dying animal.

"I perceive that you are a kind and gentle-hearted lady," Crispin said, pulling her hand upward to rest it against his broad chest. "This pleases me greatly, since I am not overfond of hunting myself. I've seen too many lords take unseemly pleasure in the cruelty of it. I know hunting is necessary—we need the meat it provides to feed our people—but I will never burn with passion for the spilling of blood."

He opened her curving fingers, pressing them flat over his heart, and she could sense its steady beating. She looked up at him with troubled eyes, wishing she could feel for him just a small part of the dangerous emotion that flamed in her for Alain. How had she come to this torment within a mere instant of seeing Alain and in such opposition to what she ought to feel? How could her heart be so divided and she yet live?

As she stared up at Crispin, seeing him while not seeing him at all, he bent his head and touched his lips to hers. His mouth was warm, soft, tender against her own. It was a pleasant kiss, the kiss of a dear friend or a close cousin, or even a brother. Straightening again, Crispin smiled at her. Still she stared at him, unable to speak.

"Have I shocked you?" he asked. "I'm sorry if I did, but there is no harm in a man kissing his betrothed. And you are more lovely than I dared to hope."

"No, my lord," she whispered, leaving him to decide, whether she meant that she was not shocked, or if she saw no harm in what he had just done.

"Are you going hunting or not?" demanded Radulf, coming up to them with Baird right behind him. "Either way, the kissing is best left until your wedding night."

Joanna could feel the color flooding her face. For a moment she had forgotten what Crispin would do to her once they were wed. For a short time she had let herself consider him as just a pleasant young man, with whom she could be friends. After her father's words she could no longer look at Crispin.

"I'll change my gown," she muttered and, lifting her heavy skirts, she ran up the steps to the privacy of her tiny room.

Later, when they were mounted and making their way through the forest surrounding Banningford Castle, Crispin approached her again. But this time Alain and Piers were with him.

"I'd like you to know my dearest friends as I do," Crispin said. "I'd have you love them too."

Joanna could not answer him. A tense and drawn-out silence followed Crispin's well meant but distressing words, until Piers spoke.

"We are easy enough to love, Lady Joanna," Piers informed her. "We are the most delightful fellows you are ever likely to meet."

Hearing the humor in his voice, she chanced looking directly at him. She found in his eyes and his face such an expression of understanding and warm admiration that she was able to relax a little despite Alain's presence.

"I feel certain I will soon consider both of you as brothers," she replied. Then, deliberately and with a touch of arrogance learned from years of watching her father, she included Alain in her haughty regard.

"Any man would be deeply blessed to be related to you, Lady Joanna," Alain said, nearly destroying her composure with the implication, clear to her if not to his companions, that *brother* was not the relationship he had in mind.

"The horns are sounding," Piers said, his dark eyes showing sympathy when they rested on Joanna's face. "Alain, let us join the hunt. Crispin, you'll bring your lady along with you?"

"I will, in a moment." Crispin put out one hand to Joanna's reins, holding her horse in its place. "You two go on. I'd speak with my lady alone."

When the others had disappeared into the screen of trees and underbrush Crispin moved his horse closer to Joanna, his hands still on her horse's reins.

"I'm glad that you like them both," he said. "You please me well, Joanna. I think in time you and I will grow to care deeply for each other."

"I pray it may be so," she said fervently. "I would love you, and you alone, my lord."

"If you have no objection, I would like to kiss you again," he said. "I have no wish to offend you, but I would not have you come to me all unfamiliar with a man's touch. I think it would be a good idea to begin gradually, for I doubt if you have ever been kissed before this day."

"That's true, my lord. I have been well guarded." Hoping to erase the image of Alain's handsome face that lingered still in her mind, she looked at Crispin's well-shaped, sensitive mouth. "I wish with all my heart that you would kiss me again. If you wish, you may put your arms around me too."

He must have felt how violently she trembled; she thought she would fall off her horse from the quaking of her slender frame. His arms were a source of strength and comfort to her, holding her firmly in her saddle. Once again his mouth was gentle on hers, stirring in her no terrifying desires but only peace and calm and a blessed sense that he would take care of her and keep her safe from feelings she ought not to have. She could rely on Crispin. His mouth pressed a little more firmly on hers, and under that pressure her lips parted. His breath was fresh and warm.

When the kiss ended she put up one hand to touch his face, noticing the contrast between the smooth skin of his upper cheeks and the roughness of his chin, where a golden stubble grew. With one finger she brushed his lips, then, hearing him catch his breath, she withdrew her hand.

"I'm sorry. That was too forward of me, but I wanted to touch you," she confessed.

"You are so innocent," he said. "My dearest lady, I am very happy. I hope you are too."

"Oh, yes, my lord," she responded. "I know now that my father chose the best and most honorable of men for me. I will be proud to be your wife."

"Too much pride is sinful," he cautioned, "but I believe I understand what you mean, and I thank you for the compliment. And now I think we should ride on and join the others, or your father will think I have been misusing you."

Joanna went with him, firmly convinced that after such a tender interlude she could not possibly think of any other man. She stayed close by Crispin's side throughout the hunt. She was

grateful to him when he urged her away from the
site of the kill, where Baird stood proudly with
his long hunting knife and his clothes bloodstained, grinning up at the mounted Baron Radulf, who called out his hearty approval. On the
way home from the hunt Crispin rode next to
Joanna in such a way that over the combined
bulk of him and his horse she could not see the
slaughtered animals being carried along to the
castle to be dressed and cooked for the next midday feast.

She was content to sit with Crispin at the light
evening meal of cold meats, bread, and cheeses
while he once again refuted her father's claims
that he ought to remain at Haughston and forget
his planned journey. She scarcely heard her father's words, but sat with her right hand nestled
into the crook of Crispin's elbow, with his hand
over hers. She was beginning to like the sensation of his warm flesh in contact with her own.

Ignoring the games the younger guests were
playing in the open square edged by the banquet
tables, or the dancing that came later, or even the
late-evening entertainment of the minstrel whom
Rohaise had hired to sing of love and high adventure, Joanna remained with Crispin. She
studied his features while he conversed with
Radulf and Father Ambrose. Her future husband
was so large-boned that she feared he might easily become corpulent as he grew older. She
would see to it that he avoided such a fate by
gently urging him not to eat or drink too much,
as Rohaise did with her father. Joanna suspected

that she would be more successful with Crispin than Rohaise was with Radulf. Crispin was a milder man than Radulf; he would be kinder to his wife than Radulf was. She would make Crispin happy; she would go with him anywhere and would order his household exactly as he wanted. When he turned in his seat to smile at her, his light blue eyes warm, she smiled back and for just an instant rested her cheek upon his shoulder, while in her sweet, youthful ignorance she imagined spending a long and contented future with him.

And when, with her father's permission, Crispin conducted her to her chamber door at evening's end, and tilted her chin upward, she responded to his gentle good-night kiss with genuine tenderness. Nor did she flinch when he allowed his hand to drift downward so that it skimmed over her shoulder and came to rest briefly on her breast. She felt nothing but a faint embarrassment, quickly squelched when she reminded herself that he had the right to touch her in any way he wanted. He did not take unfair advantage of that right, nor did he force himself upon her in any way. He merely opened her chamber door, saw her safely inside, and, after murmuring a hasty good night, closed her door again and went away. He left behind him a girl so confused and bewildered by her own emotions and by her reactions to two different men that she could not move, but stood trembling and dry-eyed for a long time before she found the strength to remove her gown and crawl into bed.

Chapter Three

At midmorning on the day before the wedding, the men directly concerned discussed the final terms of the marriage contract. At the time the meeting seemed no very important matter; the details of Joanna's dowry and the manner in which the future children of Crispin and Joanna would eventually inherit Radulf's lands had already been settled.

"I have no doubt that there will soon be strife in England," Radulf said to Crispin and Father Ambrose, having taken them into the lord's chamber to speak with them in private, while Baird stood guard outside the door to keep any intruders away. "We all know that in warfare young men are the ones most likely to be seriously wounded or killed. Crispin, I suggest that in the event of your early death I be made guardian of your minor children and administrator of your lands in their behalf. I want this written into the marriage contract so it will have the force of law behind it."

"Uncle Ambrose is my closest kin, and he has been a fine guardian of my interests," Crispin said with a warm look at the priest who was listening intently to this conversation. "I have assumed that he would take up the guardianship of my children if it should become necessary."

"I do not question Father Ambrose's worthiness," Radulf hastened to say. "He has done his duty by you once, and done it well. But let us be honest; he's an older man than I am and therefore less likely to live until your children come of age. Furthermore, he plans to leave England for some years. Whereas I am younger, a proven administrator of my own lands and castle, well able to defend Haughston with force if it becomes necessary. And I will be right here at Banningford."

"Then Alain is my next nearest relative to Ambrose." Crispin responded to Radulf's eager intensity with the measured thoughtfulness that was characteristic of him. "Alain is young and vigorous. He would make a good guardian for my children."

"It's but a distant connection," Radulf scoffed. "You and Alain had the same great-grandfather, which will make him only a cousin to your children, while I will be their grandfather and they the direct heirs of my own lands. And, Alain lives far north of here, but my lands border yours, so

I would be nearby to keep a watchful eye on them. Indeed, should ill fortune befall you, I would take your children into my household, to live with me until they are old enough to be on their own."

"What you say is true, and it's kind of you to think of this." Crispin appeared to be considering Radulf's arguments most seriously.

"I could do no less for my own flesh and blood." Radulf replied to Crispin's comment with a frank and open attitude. "Who could be more concerned for my own grandchildren's welfare than I myself?"

"Though we have King Henry's agreement about the inheritance of the lands in question," said Father Ambrose, "who is to say what will happen once he is dead? Radulf, you are right; a strong hand will be needed to protect Crispin's children, not only in the event of his death, but should he be away for a long time fighting, which could easily happen. Allow me to make a suggestion: Let us have an agreement that in the event of Crispin's death or extended absence, Radulf will be guardian of any minor grandchildren and their lands. In return, should Radulf die first, Crispin will take direct control of *his* lands with the understanding that they will be passed on to Radulf's grandchildren when they come of age, in the manner already written into the contract. What say you to that, Radulf?"

Radulf considered the proposition, hesitating for only a few moments.

"Agreed," he said.

"I'll tell the clerks," said Ambrose. "They'll write out this new clause and we can read it over this evening. I think this was a fine idea, Radulf, a good way to protect your grandchildren."

"I have tried to think of everything," Radulf replied.

Later, Crispin told Piers about the new arrangement.

"I don't understand," Piers said, frowning in perplexity. "Radulf is the older, so it's more likely that he will die before you."

"He honestly believes there will be a war when the king dies, and that I'll be fighting in it," Crispin replied. "Anyway, it's only a precaution, and Uncle Ambrose agreed to what Radulf suggested, and even added to it."

"There is more to it than that, I'm sure," Piers insisted.

"Well, I don't think Radulf likes Alain much," Crispin said. "Perhaps he had it in his mind to cut out Alain as a possible guardian of my children. But, you know, his reasoning was good. It is better, I think, to have a grandfather who is a near neighbor to watch over the young ones than a cousin who must live far away in order to tend to his own responsibilities. Ambrose saw the sense in Radulf's idea, as well as I did."

"Then Ambrose is as innocent and guileless as you," Piers replied.

While her father and her husband-to-be discussed the terms of her marriage contract, Joanna was busy in the enclosed herb garden set next to the inner bailey wall. It was one of her favorite spots. There the air was always fresh, perfumed in summer by the roses, lavender, thyme, and other herbs that had been added over the years since her great-grandmother had planted the first rosebushes and lilies. In a castle dominated by warriors who cared little for beauty the herb garden was a uniquely lovely and feminine area. Joanna had spent many pleasant afternoons there, alone or with Rohaise, weeding or pruning or, as she did today, gathering the herbs the cook would need to flavor the dishes even now being prepared for the next day's banquet.

Her visit was also in the nature of a lingering farewell to the plants and flowers she had helped to nurture throughout her girlhood. After the events of the following day she did not think she would have time before she left Banningford to spend another quiet hour cutting parsley or rosemary or mint to heap into the basket she had slung over her arm. She would miss the herb garden. It would be several years before she could start her own garden at Haughston. She wondered if there was such a garden at Crispin's Normandy estate.

The thought of Crispin, coupled with the sensuous fragrances of roses and lavender and lilies, forced her to consider her unruly emotions. Drawn to Alain while at the same time frightened and deeply distressed by her chaotic emotional response to him, she told herself now as she had done at least twenty times since meeting him that she could not allow herself to think of him. She ought to think only of Crispin, whom she genuinely liked and admired. In any case, her personal feelings did not matter. She had to obey her father's wishes and marry Crispin. Radulf would not allow her to refuse at this late date. Were she to try, she did not doubt that her punishment would be swift and terrifying, and, if Radulf was angry enough he might include Rohaise in the punishment as well, if only as a means of relieving his rage.

From behind her she heard the garden gate creak open, followed by the crunch of a footstep on the gravel walk, a tread heavier and firmer than that of Rohaise. Thinking it might be Crispin, come to tell her his business with her father was finished, she made certain she was smiling before she turned to greet him. She would invite him to sit upon the little stone bench in the corner and talk with her while she worked. He could tell her more about his plans for the long pilgrimage to Spain. But the welcoming smile died on her lips when she saw who it was that had intruded upon her solitude, as if she had conjured him up out of her forbidden dreams.

"My lady. Sweet Joanna." Alain drew in a deep breath. "Forgive me. I should not have come here. I will leave." He made no move to go. Instead, his eyes locked on hers, silently speaking words she knew he should not allow to pass his lips. She instinctively understood that he was doing battle with himself, wanting to stay while

43

honor required him to go before he did something unforgivable.

"Why did you come?" she cried, then bit her lip, wishing she had not asked.

"You know why." *Because I cannot stay away from you.* The words lay between them as surely as if he had spoken them aloud.

"I cannot—you must not—" She stopped, fighting tears.

"Not ever," he agreed.

They stood with half the herb garden separating them, simply looking at each other. She memorized his face and form, letting his presence burn itself into her mind beyond all hope of forgetting. Without realizing it they leaned forward, unable to withstand the force that urged them toward each other, and while Alain kept his arms stiffly at his sides, Joanna put out one hand, reaching toward him as if she were grasping for life itself.

"Why did it happen?" she cried, unable to tolerate for another moment the anguish that was tearing her apart. "Why then, just before I met *him?* If I had known and loved him first, it might not have happened at all."

"Ah, no, there you are wrong," he said, taking a single step along the path. "It would have happened all the same, and it would have been a thousand times worse. If we had met when you were already wed, no longer an innocent maiden but knowing, as I do know, the passion and tenderness that can lie between a man and a woman, then nothing could have kept us apart.

It's only the combination of your sweet innocence and the love I have for Crispin that keeps me from you now. Were you not a maiden, I am not certain I could resist what I feel for you. As it is—" He gestured with one hand and fell silent.

"I know that what you speak of is wrong," she whispered. "No man should want to touch another man's betrothed or wife. Nor should a woman want to be touched by anyone save the man who is bound to her. And yet what I feel here, in my heart, is pure and true." With one clenched fist she struck her bosom.

"I know," he said sadly. "It's the same for me."

"I like Crispin," she went on, as if he had not spoken. "He will be a kind and gentle husband."

"That he will. Crispin will never stir your heart or heat your body as I would, but he will be a good husband, and a fair lord to you—and to your children." His voice broke on that last phrase. "Your children," he repeated.

She could not help herself. Too young and inexperienced to fully understand her own emotions, she could no longer withstand the compulsion to feel his arms around her. She dropped the basket of herbs and put out both her hands to him.

"Please," she whispered. "Please."

He stepped closer, so close she could feel the heat of his body. She gulped back a sob and tried to catch her breath. Her chest ached so badly she thought it would burst with pent-up tears and half-understood needs and anger at the unfairness of life—and in that bursting kill her and end her pain.

And then she was in his arms and his mouth was on hers, and it was as though a blinding flash of lightning had struck her, followed by a roar and a crash of thunder that would never stop.

Alain had repressed desires of his own that had mounted steadily over the past two days, and now those desires flamed out of control. He savaged her mouth, forcing his tongue between her teeth and plundering the sweetness he found in her. She responded eagerly, clinging to him, trying to match the stroking of his tongue with innocent thrusts of her own, at the same time molding her body against his.

It was her inexpert reaction to his driving passion that finally brought him to his senses. Tearing his mouth from hers, he put his hands on her upper arms and pushed her away from him, holding her back when she tried blindly to reenter his embrace.

"Dear God," he whispered, seeing her bruised lips and tear-filled eyes. "Joanna, what have I done to you?"

He watched the breath shudder through her body, the sweet, delicate vessel into which he yearned to pour himself. His hands tightened on her arms.

"This was not your fault," he said, still whispering. "You are but fourteen and completely innocent. I am seven years older than you. I am the one who should have known better than to start this."

"I am a woman," she wept. "This time tomorrow I shall be a married woman, with a husband who is also seven years older than I."

"Aye, and tomorrow night you will go to Crispin's bed, not mine." When she gasped at the cruelty of that flat statement, he added, "Tomorrow night I shall die of grief and longing for what I can never have. But I tell you now, Joanna, I will never again touch what rightfully belongs to Crispin. Nor will you see me at Haughston until long years have passed, not until I am able to greet you as a friend, and only a friend."

Abruptly, he took his hands from her arms. Without his support she stood drooping like a rag doll. Neither of them said anything. There was nothing more to say. He just backed away from her, one foot after the other crunching lightly on the gravel path until he reached the gate. He stood a moment longer, devouring her with his eyes, while she remained limp and lost, with tears coursing down her cheeks.

"You are my only love." The whispered words hung on the herb-scented air long after he had left her.

It was Rohaise who provided Joanna's salvation during that last afternoon and evening before the wedding day. She could not prevent Joanna from having to sit beside Crispin during the banquet that lasted from late morning until well into the afternoon, but once the men began to rise from the table, Rohaise stepped in, exercising her right as lady of the castle.

"My lord," she said to Radulf, "there is still some last-minute sewing to be done on Joanna's wedding gown. Then it will be time to bathe and prepare her for the morning. I ask you to excuse her, and me, from the hunt, and Joanna from the evening meal. She ought to seek her bed early tonight."

The tone in which she made this last suggestion appealed to Radulf's deepest concern and averted the angry exclamation he had been about to make.

"Aye," he said in his coarse way, "she looks too pale and weary for a young man's liking. Give her some herbal potion to make her sleep well tonight, for I doubt she'll sleep at all tomorrow, not with a strong young bull like Crispin between her thighs. And you, girl," here he caught Joanna's chin in one hand, making her look at him, "remember what I've told you. I want no squeamishness from you tomorrow, no weeping or trembling when your new husband approaches you. You'll do what he wants, and you'll give me a grandchild as quickly as possible."

When his womenfolk had left the hall Radulf and his personal guard, Baird, began to walk toward the outer door, through which the guests were now passing on their way to mount for the hunt.

"That fellow Alain does not love you," Baird said, very low. "He looked at you just now as if he'd like to run you through."

"So you noticed, did you?" Radulf sounded pleased. "Did you also mark the lustful way in which he regards my daughter?"

" 'Tis well she's to marry so soon," Baird mused. "In a few days the feasting will be over and we can say farewell to Alain of Wortham and send him off to where he belongs."

"Aye," murmured Radulf, "to where he belongs. And glad I'll be to see the last of him. He's the one person who could upset all my plans."

In fact, there was no sewing at all left to do on Joanna's bridal clothes; that had been only an excuse to get her away from the men. Rohaise was wise enough, and knew Joanna well enough, to understand that something was seriously disturbing her stepdaughter.

They spent the afternoon in Joanna's chamber with a pitcher of spiced and sweetened wine. After seven years of marriage to Radulf, Rohaise was well skilled in the art of coaxing information from someone unwilling to reveal anything at all. It did not take her long to have the entire story out of Joanna.

"Perhaps what you feel for Alain is only your way of rebelling against what will happen to you tomorrow night," Rohaise suggested. "If all your thoughts are fixed on Alain, who is unattainable, you need not think of Crispin and what he will do to you."

"But I like Crispin very much," Joanna cried. "I am so confused. If Alain had not come to Banningford, I would marry Crispin with joy, and I think we would be content with each other for the rest of our lives. When Crispin kisses me it's warm and gentle, and he is not at all repulsive to me. But when Alain kissed me—"

"He kissed you?" Rohaise exclaimed, interrupting.

"This morning, in the herb garden," Joanna confessed, glad to tell someone about the deed that had weighed heavily on her conscience.

"He dared?" Rohaise was so horrified by this revelation that Joanna began to fear she would report it to Radulf.

"It was but one kiss." Joanna could not decipher the expression on Rohaise's face, but her concern about her father's possible reaction was quickly dissipated.

"I should not have left you alone for a moment," Rohaise cried. "If Radulf were to learn of this—"

"He won't unless you tell him," Joanna said, fairly certain now that Rohaise would not tell. "After the kiss he did not touch me further. Indeed, he swore that he would never touch me again."

"What was it like?" Joanna had never seen her stepmother look the way she did just then, appalled, entranced, excited, all at once.

"It was a burst of blinding beauty," Joanna said, reliving the kiss for a moment. "It was as though our hearts had blended and could never be separated again."

Rohaise rose from the stool where she had been sitting and went to stare out the arrow slit that served as a window. To Joanna's amazement, she began to cry. Joanna had never seen her stepmother weep before.

"Oh, I am sorry to upset you so," Joanna cried, flinging her arms around Rohaise. "I should not have told you."

"How I wish," Rohaise murmured, still looking at the wooded landscape below the tower wall, "that someone would come along the road down there, a man who would kiss me like that, and set my heart afire. To be treated with tenderness just once—just once in all my life . . . to be loved . . ."

"What I wish," Joanna murmured, opening her heart completely and speaking what she had barely dared to think, "is that Alain would kiss me like that again and put his arms around me, and hold me as close as he did in the herb garden. But I know he never will."

"I wonder which of us is the more unfortunate?" asked Rohaise. "You, at least, will be able to leave Banningford Castle." With a visible effort she stopped her tears, wiping them from her cheeks with a determined gesture. "We must cease our foolish dreaming and be sensible women. I'll tell no one of your secret; have no fear on that account. Now, I have ordered the servants to prepare a great tub of hot water, so let us go down to the bath house and soak away our sadness and wash our hair. With everyone gone out to hunt we will have complete privacy. When we have finished we'll come back here and I'll brush your hair until it's dry. Then I'll have a tray sent up for you for the evening meal. I will have to sit by Radulf's side, but you can be excused for this one night, so you need not see any of those men who trouble you so deeply, not your father or Alain or Crispin, either. After a good night's rest you will be strong enough to do what you must tomorrow."

"You are so good to me." Joanna kissed her stepmother and brushed away her own tears.

Later, at day's end, when the serving girl was about to leave the kitchen with the tray for Joanna, Rohaise prepared the pitcher of wine herself. Into it she put the herbs she knew would give Joanna a dreamless and refreshing sleep on a night when, unaided, she might well have lain wakeful until dawn. Later still, in the great hall, when Radulf began to complain to her about Joanna's absence, she whispered to him what she had done, and he nodded his approval.

"You are a good girl, Rohaise," he said, relaxing back into the lord's chair. Putting out a big, callused hand, he patted her upper thigh, then pushed his hand down into the crease between her thighs, mussing her silk gown and not caring who saw him fondle his wife in public. "Aye, a nice girl. I'll sleep in your arms tonight."

And Rohaise smiled at him as she always did, and tried to look as if she thought his words and vulgar gestures were a great compliment.

Chapter Four

Joanna's wedding finery was well chosen to show off her blond, sapphire-eyed beauty. Her long-sleeved undergown was made of soft, flowing silk in a shade of gold so pale it looked like winter sunlight. Over it she wore a heavier silk pelisse, a garment introduced to England some six years earlier by King Henry's daughter Matilda, the widow of the Holy Roman Emperor, who had returned to her father's court, bringing with her the latest fashions from the continent. Joanna's pelisse, made of greenish-blue silk, was knee-length and had short sleeves. All its edges were trimmed in gold embroidery, and it was drawn in tightly at her slender waist with a gold belt, making the stiff folds flare out over the softer fabric of the undergown. She wore a sheer veil of pale gold and it, together with the thin gold circlet around her brow, barely controlled the torrent of golden curls that fell to below her waist.

Rohaise, who was taller and thinner than her stepdaughter and who had brown hair, was robed in similar style, with a green undergown and a brilliant gold pelisse. Beneath her gold circlet, Rohaise's hair was braided and then confined in a gold mesh net, as befitted a married noblewoman.

Many of the women guests also wore undergown and pelisse, though some of the older women still favored the loose-flowing gowns and shawls that had been the style of Henry's first queen. Most of the men were in tunic and hose, and all wore as many jewels as they could afford. Crispin's tunic was a shade of blue-green that almost exactly matched Joanna's pelisse—a happy accident, according to Rohaise—while Piers wore dark red and Alain a deep shade of green. Even Father Ambrose was resplendent in green and gold vestments. Altogether the company assembled in the shadowy great hall for the reading and signing of the marriage contract, which was the most important part of the day's ceremonies, presented a brilliant, glittering picture of shifting colors and forms.

For most of her wedding day Joanna was numb and unable to think clearly. She had allowed Rohaise and the servingwomen to dress and adorn her as if she were some inanimate doll. She went where they told her to go, walked and sat and stood as she was ordered to do. Only later did she realize that she had experienced none of the nervousness she had expected to feel upon becoming the object of so much sustained attention. Only dimly did she afterward recall the slow, measured way in which Father Ambrose had read out the marriage contract so all the guests could hear and understand the terms. She did not remember signing her own name to the contract or watching Crispin, Radulf, or any of the other witnesses sign or seal it, though she later saw the contract with her name upon it. Nor did the moment stay in mind when, with the contract triumphantly held up by Radulf for all to see, she officially became Crispin's wife. But always thereafter, for the rest of her life, she could relive the comforting way in which Crispin held her hand and smiled at her while they walked from the great hall to the castle chapel to hear mass and have the marriage blessed.

Once the mass was over there was only one more deed necessary to make the marriage completely legal, but the time for it would not come until after long hours of feasting and drinking and entertainment. Joanna sat beside Crispin at the high table and let him hold her hand and smiled when she ought to smile—and all the time she thought about the night to come and the consummation that would be the final act of the marriage ceremony.

As the day slowly passed and evening drew near, she gradually lost her initial numbness and became more aware of what was going on around her. She saw Alain and Piers talking to two young ladies. She noticed Rohaise directing the servants. She even heard her father giving advice to Crispin.

"Just blow in her ear once or twice to excite her," Radulf said to his new son-in-law in a voice louder than it should have been, "and then have at it. I want a grandchild and you need an heir."

When someone spoke to Radulf, diverting his attention, Crispin glanced at her. He must have seen her embarrassed reaction to her father's crude remark, for his hand tightened over hers.

"I believe all husbands and wives are nervous on their first night together," he said. "You need not fear me, Joanna. I have no desire to hurt you."

"I am not afraid, my lord. I have been told what will happen. And after Rohaise told me my father gave me a lecture. I know my duty," she said wryly. "I am to bear a son as soon as possible and, after him, as many children as I can, to make certain there will be at least one surviving heir to reach manhood and inherit your lands and my father's."

"It sounds so cold-blooded when you say it like that." Crispin's clear and remarkably pure blue eyes met hers. His voice was low and kind. "I have often thought it must be difficult for a woman, to have no choice of her husband."

"I cannot quarrel with my father's choice for me," she said, not adding that if she *had* been given a choice, she would be spending this night not with Crispin but with his cousin and friend, Alain. She could not be that honest, so she confined herself to words she believed Crispin would want to hear. "I will try my best to be a good wife to you, my lord. I want to please you in every way."

"You already do." He put an arm around her shoulders and kissed her softly on the lips, the action raising a cheer from the guests. She responded with naive eagerness.

But when Crispin drew away, freeing her to look elsewhere, the first person she saw was Alain, standing not far from her beside one of the tables, his face sharply illuminated by the light of the candelabra just in front of him. His mouth was drawn into a tight line of pain, his eyes dark pools of grief and longing. He was staring directly at her.

Joanna wanted to scream, to weep out her own misery, to pound her fists on the table, displaying all the anguish of her painfully divided heart. She did none of those things. She was too well trained to let her emotions loose before her father and his guests. What she did was turn to Crispin and kiss him full on the mouth, as hard as she could. Then, embarrassed by her own act, she buried her face in his wide shoulder. She heard laughter and applause. She felt Crispin's arm around her once more, holding her close, his large hand smoothing her hair.

"It's all right," he whispered. "My poor, frightened girl, it will be all right, I promise."

"You are so good and kind," she said, ashamed at her inability to go to his bed with a whole and open heart.

*   *   *

The ritual for the bridal night proceeded as it had been planned. The ladies took Joanna to the chamber where she and Crispin were to begin their life together, and there, led by Rohaise, they stripped all her clothing from her and quickly bathed her. They had barely finished before there came a knock on the door. Rohaise opened it and the men entered, pushing before them a naked Crispin. Father Ambrose, still in his green and gold vestments, was among the men. He made short work of blessing the marriage bed and saying a prayer to ask for children of the marriage. Taking Crispin's hand and Joanna's and linking them together, Father Ambrose instructed Crispin to kiss his bride. This Crispin did, in a perfunctory way, managing to touch no part of her except her lips.

"You'll have to do better than that, lad," cried Radulf, in high good humor at the culmination of his carefully laid plans. "Remember my advice."

With much laughter and more than a few jokes of the sort that would have been considered most unseemly at any other time, the newlyweds were bundled into bed and the curtains drawn about them.

For Alain, this scene was the worst part of the long, unhappy day. He could not avert his eyes from Joanna's naked form, so smooth-skinned, girlish, and slender, with her budding, pink-tipped breasts—and her hair, that long, waving glory of pure gold that streamed down her back to well below her waist. That first sight of his love unclothed would stay with Alain until he died.

She saw him looking at her and blushed, but he kept his eyes on her while the heavy blue bed-curtains were pulled closed, gradually shutting her away from his view. At the last instant Joanna's eyes met his, and in them he imagined he saw a plea, saw fear, and a wish for something other than the lot her father had arranged for her.

He told himself he was a fool; any innocent girl would be frightened on her marriage night, and the more so when her bedchamber was crowded with inebriated folk making crude jests. He hoped Crispin would be gentle with her. Alain rather thought he would. His cousin was not a passionate man where women were concerned, and so he would most likely feel no need to force himself upon his bride too hastily. Crispin was not a man to terrorize a young girl. Crispin's kind-hearted character was the only thing Alain could find to be grateful for.

As for himself, there was nothing Alain could do now but wish them well—and leave, before he said or did something they would all regret. It seemed the other guests would leave too. At many wedding celebrations the revelers remained in the bridal chamber, eating and drinking while the marriage was consummated on the other side of the bedcurtains. The small size of the rooms in Radulf's castle prevented this, for not everyone could fit into the chamber, and would-be witnesses to the bedding were stuck on the stairway, jammed together and unable to move. Having seen the couple properly bedded, the guests trouped out to continue their feasting in the great hall, where there was more space to move around.

That was when Alain left the party, during the confusion of getting everyone out of the bridal chamber and down the crowded stairs. Alain simply jumped off the open side of one step to the floor below. Then, taking a large jug of Radulf's best wine along, he made his way to the stable, where he sat upon a pile of straw and drank steadily until the jug was empty. The wine did nothing to ease his pain. Drunkenly angry when there was no more, he threw the jug against the nearest wooden post, smashing it into pieces.

Sinking farther down into the straw, he buried his head in his arms, wishing he could get out of his mind the picture of Joanna, naked and heart-stoppingly desirable, and his cousin and friend Crispin, also naked, locked together in a passionate embrace behind those damnable blue bed-curtains. The imagined scene aroused him to an even more painful state, his own desire for Joanna rapidly becoming an unbearable ache that tortured not only his spirit but his youthful, ardent body as well.

"Why?" he groaned. "Oh, God, Joanna, why couldn't it have been me?"

"You know why. Crispin holds the bordering barony." Piers sat down beside him. "Here. I brought another jug of wine. It's the only thing that will help you tonight. Tomorrow we'll have to think of something else."

"You're a good fren'. The bes' fren' of all," Alain declared with drunken solemnity. Taking the offered jug, he upended it, pouring wine down his throat.

"You're going to be sick in the morning," Piers observed.

"I'm sick now. An' I'll never be cured. You know that, ol' Sir Piers? Never cured. Never. Love her till I die."

"Never is a long, long time," said Piers, catching the jug just as Alain dropped it and rolled over in the straw. He had brought Alain's cloak along, as well as the wine, and now he covered the sleeping man, pausing with one hand on Alain's shoulder. Out of sympathy with his cousin's pain, Piers took a few swigs from the jug himself before he rolled up in his own cloak and lay down to sleep.

Within the blue dimness of the marriage bed, the new-made bride and groom lay stiffly, not touching each other. In all her short life Joanna had never been so embarrassed or so frightened.

"You did say that Lady Rohaise told you what I will do?" Crispin's voice beside her startled her.

"Yes." Joanna's own voice was just above a whisper. "I will not fight you, my lord. Do what you must."

"I'd have you find it pleasant, too, Joanna." He moved beside her, his hand brushing across her breast. She jerked in surprise at the contact of bare flesh with bare flesh, and Crispin took his hand away.

"It would be better if I could see you," he said.

"I am glad you cannot," she replied. "I'd be ashamed to have you look at me again without clothing."

"There's no need for shame with your husband," he told her. "You have a lovely body."

He put his hand on her breast again, and this time she stayed still, letting him stroke her skin. Gently he teased at her nipple. She caught her breath, parting her lips just as his mouth found hers and pressed softly. It was not at all like being kissed by Alain. There was none of the lightning-bolt fire of Alain in Crispin. Thinking to warm his excessive gentleness and at the same time to please him, she touched the tip of her tongue to his lips. Immediately he pulled away, and she could sense his displeasure.

"Where did you learn to do such a thing?" he demanded. "Only whores do that."

"I didn't know," she stammered. "I heard the servingwomen talking. I thought you would enjoy it."

"Joanna, you will please me best by behaving like the innocent maiden you are now, and after this night by always acting like a proper wife. There are certain things that good women do not do."

"I did not know." It crossed her mind that Alain thought she was a good woman and still had kissed her in that way. Alain had said he loved her, which Crispin had not done.

"Of course you did not know," Crispin said tenderly, bestowing another gentle kiss on her lips. "In your innocence you allowed yourself to be led astray by the gabbling of foolish servingwomen. You must not do it again; it is not becoming to the wife of a baron. I will teach you everything you need to know in these bedroom matters."

"Yes, my lord." With firm resolution she banished every thought of Alain and made herself concentrate on Crispin.

She soon found there was nothing to fear in him. He was by nature a gentle man, perhaps better suited for a cloistered life than for the part of a strong and warlike baron. His treatment of her was scrupulously polite. He kissed her repeatedly, always with his mouth closed. While he kissed her, he stroked her breasts and her shoulders and arms until she began to experience an aching sensation deep in her belly that made her put her arms around him and press herself against him. He held her closely, with one hand now stroking along her back and down to her hips and outer thighs until she began to moan and twist in his arms. Then, as if in response to her cries, his male hardness rose in a swift rush against her thigh, startling her.

Someone had left candles burning on a table in the bridal chamber so they would not be in complete blackness, and by now Joanna's eyes had adjusted to the semidarkness behind the bedcurtains. She could see Crispin's shape when he rose beside her, and she saw the outline of his stiff manhood. She whimpered, but it was not in fear. His persistent, gentle wooing of her body was having its desired result. He put both hands upon her breasts, kneading her nipples, and the heavy ache deep inside her began to focus on one particular spot.

Crispin drew his hands slowly down across her abdomen and on to her thighs. Then he began to pull her legs apart. At first she wanted to protest, but all she could do was utter a soft, helpless cry. Remembering Rohaise's instructions, she voluntarily adjusted her position, allowing him access to the most private part of her body. He knelt between her thighs, and a moment later she could feel him pushing against her.

"I will be as gentle as I can," he promised.

"I understand." She took a deep breath. Preparing herself for pain, she placed a hand on each of his shoulders.

It was more like a stretching sensation than actual pain, and it was only briefly uncomfortable. Crispin slowly pushed himself into her, pausing once when she cried out, and then continuing until he was completely inside her. He slid his hands around to her buttocks to pull her closer still, and he began to move. She was already partially aroused by his prolonged attentions, and there was in his steady, continuing motions a friction that began to warm her still more. He was being as gentle as he had promised, and the heavy ache in her belly had changed into a sweet, warm hunger that gnawed at her. She threw her head back, gasping for air.

"Does it hurt?" he asked, apparently misinterpreting her movement.

"No, my lord." She sounded as if she was in pain, but it was not pain; it was something else, something just beyond her reach. "It is pleasant," she assured him, wishing he would continue what he was doing indefinitely.

"Good." He kissed her cheek. "I hoped you would find it so." He moved twice more, pushing harder and deeper now, and then expelled a long breath. When he withdrew from her and rolled to one side she clutched at his shoulder as if to keep him where he was.

"Please don't stop, my lord."

"I must, for now. And call me Crispin." Putting an arm around her shoulders, he pulled her close, kissing her brow.

"It was so sweet and gentle," she said. "Not frightening at all. Could we do it again soon?"

"We will," he promised. "Every night until I get you with child."

"I hope you will not stop then," she said. "I think with practice I might enjoy it even more."

He did not answer, but only chuckled and held her a little more tightly.

And when, later that night, he knelt between her thighs again and touched her in places he had not stroked the first time he had taken her, she warmed to him even more. When he buried himself in her and held her buttocks, pushing her against him, she grasped him in the same way, so that they were firmly fused, and the tight fitting together of their bodies stirred her into a sudden and brief explosion that shook her for an instant, making her cry out softly. Again he kissed her and held her tenderly afterward.

"I think you and I will do very well together," he said in a satisfied voice.

"Oh, yes, my lord—I mean Crispin," she responded eagerly.

During the rest of that night she did not think of Alain at all.

Chapter Five

"It's time to rise." With those words, Piers dumped a full bucket of cold water onto Alain. Alain groaned and rolled over. He sat up for a moment, wiping moisture from his eyes, then flopped backward into the straw, lying there like a dead man.

"Come, Alain, it's growing late. Our absence will be remarked, and you will have to answer questions."

"I want to sleep." Turning onto his side, Alain burrowed deeper into the straw.

"All right; in that case, I'll just have to try again." Piers took the bucket back to the stone horse trough outside the stable door. There he refilled it and, returning to Alain once more, doused him a second time. By now Alain was not so deeply unconscious as he had been at first. He sat up, yelling his outrage at Piers's treatment of him, just as one of the ostlers appeared.

" 'Ere, wat's this?" demanded the ostler. "Don't wet the straw, ye'll rot it! Out o' my stable, ye young bandits!"

"Your stable?" Piers said in a haughty tone. "We are Baron Radulf's guests, and I do not like the way you speak to your betters."

"Guests, eh?" The ostler laughed, not at all concerned by Piers's claim. "Radulf keeps a good stable, 'e does, and when I tell 'im wat ye two 'ave done, throwin' water all over the straw, 'e'll side wi' me, 'e will. Now, where's yer wimmin? Get 'em out o' the straw and clear off. There'll be no fornicatin' near the 'orses."

"There are no women here." Alain was on his feet by now, holding himself upright by keeping one hand on Piers's shoulder. "I have renounced women," he said solemnly.

"In that case ye've learnt a bit o' wisdom in yer short life," observed the ostler. Apparently softened by the sight of the wet and bedraggled Alain, he added more kindly, "If yer young lordships will be good enough to leave now, I'll 'ave the stableboys clean up the wet straw ye ruined."

"I'm sorry about the straw." Thinking it a good idea to appease the man, lest he make a complaint to Radulf about them, Piers pulled a coin out of the purse he wore at his waist. "My friend wasn't feeling well last night and needed a quiet place to rest."

"Drunk, was 'e?" said the ostler, tucking the coin into the folds of his clothing so quickly that

Piers wondered if he made a habit of accosting folk who spent the night in the stable. There were probably a fair number of such people; privacy was hard to find in a castle, and a stable, with its partitions and dark corners, was a good place for a lusty man-at-arms to bring a serving wench or a pretty kitchen maid. Piers had taken a few women into the straw himself in the days when he had been a squire.

"We thank you for your courtesy, sir," said Alain to the ostler, bowing low. Piers caught his friend just before Alain fell on his face, pulling him upright again.

" 'E's still drunk, if ye ask me," remarked the ostler. Spying the pieces of the wine jug Alain had broken, and looking from it to the whole jug Piers had just picked up, he asked, " 'Ow much did 'e drink?"

"More than enough," said Piers, at the same instant that Alain said, "Not nearly enough."

"Aye, it's a wench, all right," noted the ostler, watching Piers lead Alain out of the stable.

Alain stopped in the stableyard, blinking in the bright sun of a midsummer day.

"Come on," Piers urged. "We'll visit the bath house first. I'm sure it will be full of other men in your condition. Then we'll see the castle barber, and afterward, with fresh clothes and some solid food in your belly, you'll find you feel a lot better."

"I meant it," Alain said, walking beside Piers. "I have given up all women."

"That's your aching head talking. You don't

look like a monk to me," Piers said with his usual good sense. "In any case, if you care enough for her to make yourself this miserable on her account, then there is one women whom you will not give up."

The hot water and steam of the bath house did wonders for Alain's sore head, and by the time he had been shaved and had changed his soiled clothing he felt much better. He entered the great hall with Piers, anticipating food for his growling stomach and a single small cup of wine.

The first person his eyes lit upon was Joanna, in a green gown and with her hair caught up high into a golden net like the one Rohaise often wore—Joanna, smiling and looking into Crispin's eyes as if she was deep in love with him. And Crispin looking back at her with a possessive warmth that nearly shattered Alain's composure.

"Damn," he muttered. "Did they have to rise so early?"

"It's past midmorning," said Piers. "Let's greet them. It can't be avoided, so let's have it over and done."

"Here you are," called Crispin, having caught sight of them. "Where have you been hiding?"

"In the stable," Alain replied, looking at Crispin because he didn't dare to glance at Joanna.

"Ha!" Crispin laughed. "With a wench, I suppose?"

"With a jug," said Piers. "Actually, with two jugs. I brought the second one."

"How are your heads?" Crispin was still laughing at them, clearly unaware that anything was wrong.

"My head is fine," Alain responded, adding in a whisper, "It's my heart that's broken."

Crispin did not hear him, but Joanna did. Alain saw her startled expression, saw her blanch to waxy paleness and then turn rosy-red.

"Will you hunt with us?" asked Crispin, still oblivious to the tension between Alain and Joanna.

"We will, if our breakfasts stay down," Piers said cheerfully. He put one hand on Alain's back to push him away from Crispin and Joanna and toward the trestle table, where bread and cheese and cold meats were laid out for those who wanted a morning meal. Detaching himself from Joanna's side, Crispin followed them.

"I haven't deserted you, you know," Crispin said. "My marriage won't change our friendship."

"Nor will it change the fact that we are cousins," said Piers before Alain could speak. "But having a wife does change a man."

"For the better, I think," Crispin said with great seriousness. "Joanna is lovely, sweet and affectionate and not as shy as I feared she would be. I'm a happy man this morning."

"Now, those are words I am glad to hear." Radulf had come up behind them. "Good day to you, lads. Crispin, if you have a moment, I would speak with you. It occurs to me that while you are in Normandy there may be something I can do in your name at Haughston. Now, I wonder—" He drew Crispin away, leaving Alain and Piers standing alone by the breakfast table.

"If there is one thing that is going to change our close friendship with Crispin," Piers observed, looking after them, "it's Crispin's father-in-law."

"He does seem oddly reconciled to Crispin and Joanna going abroad," said Alain. "Yesterday he was still angry about it."

They watched Crispin and Radulf walk across the hall, saw Joanna hurry to Crispin's side and take his arm and gaze up at him.

"I can't stay at Banningford." Alain set his wine cup down hard on the bare table. "It's killing me."

"You can't leave right now," Piers said. "Crispin will want to know why you've changed your plans, when you are promised to remain here until he and Joanna leave."

"What do you advise, dear old Sir Piers?" There was no humor in the familiar joking title. Alain sounded infinitely weary, and Piers understood that he was close to the breaking point. Alain could not long tolerate the sight of Joanna hanging on Crispin's arm and mooning over him with the eyes of a lovesick calf. Something would have to be done.

"Stay just today and tomorrow," Piers suggested. "That will satisfy Crispin and won't insult Radulf, as our early departure would do. It will be easy enough to avoid those you don't want to see during the hunt, and hunting will consume the better part of each day. We'll think of something to keep us out of the great hall in the evenings. Tomorrow night I'll say I want to begin my duties at Haughston at once, that I'm bored with feasting and drinking. Crispin knows me well enough to believe that story. You can tell him you want to keep me company and that you'll spend the first night of your homeward journey at Haughston with me. Crispin will easily accept such an excuse."

"Two more days?" Alain shook his head. "I don't want to stay so long. I'm not sure I can."

"Do it for friendship's sake," said Piers. "It's the best way to handle this situation."

"All right." Alain gave in. "Once again I'll take your advice. But I have an uneasy feeling. I've had a premonition of misfortune ever since I came to Banningford. Piers, if you see me drinking too much, stop me. I want all my wits about me for the next two days."

In later years, Alain was to wish many times that he had left Banningford Castle on the day after Crispin's marriage. So many lives would have been different if he had followed his own inclinations. But stay he did, and thus condemned himself to play out the long tragedy that was even then beginning to unfold.

He took deliberate care to stay away from Crispin and Joanna when they were together. With Crispin, alone, he had no problem. He loved Crispin as he loved Piers, and the three of them had their own memories and jokes and ways of doing things stemming from the time when they had first met as lonely pages and discovered that they were related. Crispin's mild and thoughtfully measured responses to life made a good foil for the clever intensity of Piers and for Alain's own more volatile spirits. They had never quarreled, and Alain would see to it that they did not quarrel now. For this reason he kept his tongue in check, drank little, and was scrupulously polite to everyone, including Radulf and his henchman Baird, neither of whom Alain liked. He did his honest best not to think about Joanna. And he counted the hours until he could leave Banningford Castle.

While Alain drank his wine with caution, Radulf was not so abstemious. Enormously pleased that Joanna's marriage had been consummated and hopeful that she would soon produce the grandchild he wanted so badly, Radulf drank a bit too heartily.

"Weddings are lusty celebrations," he said to Rohaise, who sat on his left side for the feast. "I feel like a bridegroom myself." As if to prove the truth of this statement, he grabbed her hand, pressing it hard against his bulging groin.

"My lord, please," Rohaise exclaimed. "What will your guests think?"

"The men will think that I will make my own heir before Joanna and Crispin give me one," Radulf replied, leering at her. "Don't be so damned prudish, woman. No one can see what happens beneath the tablecloth."

Rohaise kept tugging at her hand until Radulf released it, but almost immediately he began to grope at her breast. She sat stiffly, staring straight ahead, wishing she had the courage to strike his hand away and demand that he treat her with respect, in public at least. Crispin's friend Sir Piers was sitting on her left side, and she knew he must have noticed how Radulf was pinching and rubbing her. How could anyone avoid seeing what Radulf was doing? When Baird came to stand across the table from Radulf and ask him a question about the night watchmen Radulf finally took his hand away. Rohaise knew her face was flaming. She thought she would die of shame, especially after she noticed a few ladies at the lower tables casting sympathetic glances in her direction.

"My lady," Piers said, "this sauce is delicious. Did you devise the recipe yourself?"

"I learned it from my mother," Rohaise replied, understanding what he was trying to do. She risked looking at him, fearing to find pity in his eyes, but he only gave her a friendly smile.

"Then, Lady Rohaise, your mother is to be complimented, and her daughter as well."

"I leave most of the cooking to the kitchen staff and only supervise them," she told him, greatly relieved to be discussing a neutral subject, "but this sauce I always prepare myself. When you marry, Sir Piers, you have only to send to me, and I will see to it that your wife has the instructions so she can make it for you."

"You are charitable as well as gracious," he replied, letting his hand rest on her elbow for just a moment, in a way that Radulf could not see. The kind gesture almost made Rohaise cry.

"Piers, do you remember?" Crispin called

along the table, and launched into a story about their boyhood days as pages, to which Piers supplied the humorous details.

Rohaise sat back in her chair so Piers could lean forward and see Crispin while they talked. On Crispin's other side, Joanna smiled and laughed at the amusing tale. Being careful not to let Radulf see her observing Piers, Rohaise took the opportunity to look more closely at him. She liked what she saw. His face was long and narrow, and though it was obvious that he had shaved that very day, still, he looked as if he ought to do so again. His beard would be thick and black, like his hair, and his eyes were so deep a brown they were almost black.

She knew his behavior toward her meant nothing. Piers was only being polite to her because he was a gentleman, but she savored the pleasure of being treated like the lady she had been raised to be, when Radulf was always so coarse and crude with her, even before guests. Sir Piers of Stokesbrough would never be rude to a woman; he would always be kind, even if he cared nothing at all for her. Still, his gentlemanly treatment of her lit a tender glow in her heart that lasted until the feasting was done and it was time for the daily hunt to begin.

That afternoon Crispin was thrown from his horse while hunting. Laughing at his own clumsiness, he got up and remounted, assuring his companions that he was unhurt. But by the time he returned to the castle that evening he was feeling the effects of the tumble. Piers and Alain went with him to his chamber, where they quickly divested him of his clothing to see how much damage had been done.

"It is a nasty bruise," Piers said, touching the blue spot that had formed across Crispin's chest. He pressed a little harder, testing the bones. "I don't think you've broken any ribs, but you ought to have hot compresses on it, and perhaps an herbal poultice. And on your knee and elbow, too, if you intend to hunt tomorrow. Where's your squire? I'll send him to the kitchen for a basin of hot water."

"He's helping to bring in the game," Crispin said. He tried to stretch the muscles in his shoulders. "Ow, that hurts. I can feel the results of my lack of real exercise in the past few days. I need to get back to the practice yard."

"You've had other matters on your mind," said Piers, picking up a shawl and draping it over Crispin's bare shoulders.

It was Joanna's shawl, a deep blue that matched her eyes. Alain had seen her wearing it one cool evening. He turned away from the sight of it wrapped about Crispin's skin.

"I'll get the water," Alain offered, wanting to remove himself from the chamber Crispin shared with Joanna. The very air was fragrant with the rosewater scent she wore, and a pair of her shoes sat beside a clothing chest that must be hers.

Alain had almost reached the kitchen when he met Joanna, who was carrying a basin and a pitcher from which steam was rising in curly wisps. Steeling himself to reveal no emotion, he met her worried look.

"You've heard," he said, taking the heavy pitcher out of her hand and retracing his steps beside her.

"I wish I had been there to help him, but my father told me not to ride. He fears," she stopped, swallowed hard and then went on, not looking at him. "My father fears that if I ride in the hunt, I may miscarry."

"Shouldn't your riding, or not riding, be Crispin's decision?" Alain tried hard not to think about Joanna bearing Crispin's child.

"My father overruled Crispin," she said.

"And you obeyed Radulf?" Alain immediately answered his own question. "Of course you did. You always have, haven't you?" The sarcasm was not lost on her. She would have protested, no doubt pointing out to him that women had little opportunity to decide anything for themselves, but Alain went on, venting a small part of the rage he felt at their predicament. "Who in the name of all the saints does Radulf think he is, countermanding a husband's wishes? Whose rule are you under, Joanna, your father's or your husband's?"

"I wish to heaven I were under my own rule," she snapped. "Then I could tell you overbearing men what a woman really thinks, *and* how she feels!"

"Overbearing?" Eyebrows raised, he regarded her with amused surprise. "Aye, we must seem so to you. I'm sorry, Joanna. I did not mean to scold you, but I'm a bit worried about Crispin."

"My father said his injuries were not serious."

"It's not his physical condition I was thinking about. All day I've had the strangest feeling about Crispin, and when I saw him falling off his horse, I thought that must be why. But it was only a foolish premonition. He's not badly hurt. Here, see him for yourself." Opening the chamber door, Alain ushered her inside.

Radulf was there, and Father Ambrose, both of them examining Crispin's bruises, while Piers stood to one side, watching them. Seeing Joanna, Crispin took a step toward her, but Radulf stopped him in order to bend his elbow up and down a few times, assuring himself that it was still in working order.

"Oh, Crispin," Joanna cried, "are you all right?"

"Leave us, daughter," Radulf growled over his shoulder. "We'll tend to Crispin's injuries and call you later."

Joanna's face betrayed her disappointment at this command, but after setting the basin down on the clothes chest she went to the door. There she stopped, looking toward Crispin with concern. Seeing her hesitate to remain with her husband because her father had ordered her to go, Alain lost his temper.

"God in heaven!" he exploded. "Crispin is a man, Radulf, not a prize stallion for you to mate to your favorite mare. And Joanna is a human being, too, whatever you may think."

"Alain!" Father Ambrose turned a shocked glance in his direction.

"I think we should go," said Piers, moving toward Alain.

"I'm staying," Alain announced.

"You may please yourself." Dismissing Alain's outburst, Radulf returned his attention to Crispin. "I think we should bind up your ribs. Joanna, find Rohaise and tell her to give you some of the linen strips we use for bandages."

"I know where the bandages are, Father."

"Then do as I tell you, and get them. Crispin, sit down on the bed and take off your hose and let me see your knee. We can't have a limping bridegroom, can we? Joanna, I told you to get the bandages. Don't just stand there, girl; do as I say. Never mind; here's Crispin's squire. I'll send him instead, since you can't seem to follow a simple order, you stupid wench."

Radulf gave an order to the squire, then greeted his own man, who had come to the chamber door.

"Baird, you've arrived at last. Take Joanna away, will you?"

Now it was Joanna's turn to explode. The chamber was full of men—her father, Father Ambrose, the squire—who had brought two friends with him—Baird, whom she heartily disliked, Piers, and, most of all, Alain. Alain who looked at her out of eyes filled with such love and grief that his pain threatened to join with her own unrelenting anguish to destroy her. She was trying so hard to be a good wife to Crispin, but every time she looked away from him she saw Alain watching her. It was too much. She could bear no more.

"I am not a girl!" she shouted at her father. "I am no longer under your command. Thanks to you, I am a married woman, and this is my bedchamber, that I share with my husband. Get out and leave us alone, all of you. Leave me alone with my husband. I will care for him. *I*, his wife, the woman he beds at night. Get out! Get out!"

"Daughter." Signaling to Baird to assist him, Radulf moved toward Joanna in a threatening manner. Father Ambrose stopped him.

"Lady Joanna is right," the priest said. "There are too many of us here, and Crispin's injuries are far from serious."

"I'm glad to hear that at least one of you has some sense," Joanna snarled, only slightly appeased by this support. "Now go away, every man of you."

She stalked them toward the door, glaring at Alain when he paused to set down the pitcher of hot water on the clothing chest next to the basin Joanna had brought. Piers was the last man to go, and she shoved at his shoulders to force him through the door, then closed and bolted it.

"How fierce you are." Crispin was watching her with a bemused expression. She flew across the room to him, putting her hands on his bruises, bending to kiss the sore spot over his ribs. "Joanna, my dear, this passion is not necessary."

"You could have been killed." Consumed with guilt over her recalcitrant feelings for Alain, worried by Alain's words of a premonition having to do with Crispin, she pressed her lips to her husband's face, kissing him over and over while she talked. "You must promise to be more careful. Now, let me help you. I put herbs in the pitcher, and I'll use a cloth dipped in the water to bathe your ribs and take away the pain. I can make you feel better. Oh, Crispin, Crispin."

In that instant when she ran her hands over her husband's sturdy body all of her confused and tormented emotions came together; her desperate yearning for Alain's embrace, anger with her father for what he had unwittingly done to them by marrying her to Crispin, and rage at the way he had tried to send her out of the room when Crispin was hurt and needed her. All of these feelings combined with her real tenderness and growing affection for Crispin himself to create a violent hunger that forced her in a surprising direction.

"Come to bed, Crispin," she said, the inflection of her voice making it clear that she was not speaking of nursing care.

"What, now? In daylight?" Crispin looked startled but not angry.

"Yes, now." She caught his hand, pulling him toward their bed.

"Joanna, this is most unseemly."

"I don't care. I am angry. I am frightened. I am terrified at the thought of what might have happened to you, and I not there to comfort you. I am your wife and I want—I want—" Still holding his hand so he could not leave her, she climbed onto the bed and lay down. With her free hand she pulled her skirts up to her waist, revealing her lower body to him. She opened her legs, exposing herself. She heard him catch his breath and saw his immediate phsyical response to what she was offering. Not certain that he would accommodate her even now, fearing that his natural reticence and sense of what was proper might keep him from her, she did not release his hand. When she reached for the cord that held his hose she had to use her left hand. She was awkward, and he did not help her. In fact, he made a strong effort to reestablish himself as master in their marriage.

"Joanna, take away your hand. I will tell you when and how we will—oh, Joanna." Crispin broke off, closing his eyes and gritting his teeth, for she had freed him and put her hand upon him, rubbing hard.

"You *are* a stallion," she murmured, watching him grow larger beneath her fingers. "A huge, beautiful stallion."

"You should not do this." It was his last protest.

"I want you inside me." Rage and loss and grief had brought her to this. There was no other balm for the bitter wound that had torn open her heart. In Crispin's arms she would find forgetfulness and at least a few moments of peace. Still holding him, she guided him forward. "I want your child, Crispin. Give me your child."

He entered her in a hot, slippery rush, and she wrapped her legs around him, pulling him deeper, and deeper still. Being Crispin, he could not give her what she craved, could not be wild and fierce with her until she was completely satisfied. Being Crispin, he could only be gentle, so that the explosion inside her, when it came, was gentle, too, and much too brief to relieve the clamoring need that drove her. When he withdrew from her she dissolved in tears and frustration.

Crispin sat on the edge of the bed, shaking his head at her. She made no move to adjust her clothing, but lay in the disorder of her crumpled gown with the golden net on her hair askew.

"I never imagined a gently bred girl would behave in such a way," he said sternly.

"Don't be angry with me," she begged. "When I heard you had been hurt I was so afraid for you that I was overcome with joy to see you whole and only bruised a little."

"I did not realize you cared for me so much," he said. Reaching out in his slow, deliberate way, he placed one hand on her thigh. "Does this offend you?"

"No, my lord." She shifted her legs a little, allowing him to move his hand higher.

"If I were to remove my hose completely and lie on the bed, then you could bathe my knee with your marvelous herbal water, as well as my ribs and elbow," he noted.

"Yes, my lord." His fingers were edging higher along the sensitive skin of her inner thigh.

"But your gown would soon be dampened."

"I can remove it, my lord. And my coif."

"That would be . . . more convenient."

"Yes, my lord." Smiling at his solemnity, she slid off the bed to remove all of her garments.

"Such dedication to my welfare does you credit," he murmured when she returned to him with a wrung-out cloth in one hand. "I believe you ought to start with my knee and work your way upward."

He said nothing more but lay quietly, letting her sit beside him and apply the cloth to his knee. When she bent forward her loosened hair spread across his legs. With both hands he brushed it back, tucking it behind her ears.

"I did not know having a wife could be such a pleasant thing," he said.

"I thank you, my lord." She rose to dip the cloth into the basin again, pouring more hot water over it from the pitcher, knowing all the time that he was watching her every movement, and she wearing no clothing at all. It made her blush to think of it, the two of them naked in the daylight, yet it was exciting too. She placed the hot cloth on his knee again. He sighed deeply.

"Is it too hot?" she asked. "It did not burn my hands."

"It's not the heat of the cloth, Joanna."

"I can see now you have serious need of my tender ministrations," she told him, looking up from his knee to a spot that plainly throbbed with eagerness for her touch.

"You called me a stallion," he said. "Ride me."

With no further touching or caressing, without even kissing her first, he lifted her, setting her down hard on top of him. Her eyes went wide.

She had not known a man and woman could come together in this way. His hands were on her hips, holding her firmly in place.

"You will have to move," he said. "I am in too much pain to help you."

"You lie, my lord." But move she did, though awkwardly at first, not knowing how to do what he wanted. Still, her enthusiasm grew until she cried out in astonished delight, "Oh, Crispin, Crispin," before she fell across his chest, resting there in panting exhaustion while he groaned and thrust beneath her.

"I did not know you would be like this," he said when they lay peacefully once more, "funny and passionate and most endearing."

"Nor did I know you had a sense of humor," she told him.

"I never show that part of myself to strangers," he said. "My dearest friends know it. Alain and Piers and I have had some amusing times together."

Alain, who looked at her with haunted eyes. *I will not think of him*, she vowed yet again. *We will part soon. He will go home. It will be easier then.*

Aloud she said, "Crispin, I like you so much."

"Dare I hope that, in time, it might be more than liking?" he asked. "I want you to care deeply for me, Joanna."

"I do care already," she said, "and I'm sure I will care more as time goes on."

"I would not have you think me a nuisance," he murmured a while later, "but do you think we could—just once more before we rise?"

"Of course," she responded. She opened her arms to him, telling herself that her marriage would prove to be a good one. Love would come later, when she knew him better. For now, the warm tenderness he evoked in her was enough.

Though they were to make love once in the far reaches of the night when the banqueting was over, and again in haste when morning came and he was late for an appointment with Radulf, forever after Joanna firmly believed it was during that June evening, when she first began to reach beyond Crispin's reserve and to truly know his kind and gentle soul, that their child was conceived.

Chapter Six

"So, you're leaving, are you?" Radulf could not bring himself to play the genial host, as if he meant what he said. Not with these two guests. His words rang false. "My dear young friends, why not stay for the entire week of feasts?"

Listening to Piers explain why not, Radulf looked from him to Alain and back again, his eyes hard.

"Well," Radulf said, the mask of pleasantry slipping a bit more, "if you care so little for your precious Crispin, then of course you must go before his wedding celebrations are done. But not until tomorrow. You will spend one more night beneath my roof, I hope?"

"That was our plan," Piers said.

With an abrupt nod, Radulf moved away, calling to the waiting Baird to follow him.

"I expected he'd be eager for us to leave," Alain remarked, puzzled by Radulf's insistence that they should remain for another night. "I don't think he likes either of us."

"His feelings for us won't matter after tonight," Piers said. Seeing Alain cast an apprehensive look about the great hall, he asked, "What's wrong?"

"Does the hall seem unnaturally dark to you?"

"All of the candles and torches are not yet lit," Piers noted, "and the outer door is wide open, so there is bright light coming in through the entry hall. That makes the shadows seem deeper."

"Perhaps." Alain sounded unconvinced. "For a moment everything went dark. It must have been my imagination."

"You are tired after the long hunt this morning. Late nights and early mornings, long hunts and longer banquets; it's enough to drive a man to his knees. Give me the honest life of a hard-fighting knight, I say, and forget these interminable celebrations."

"Especially this one," Alain agreed.

They were not the only guests who would be leaving the following morning and, publicly at least, Radulf professed to regret each departure. Two barons were due at court to begin their forty days of yearly service to the king, while a third would return home for his son's marriage. In acknowledgment of this diminution in the number of his guests, Radulf ordered Rohaise to set forth an especially fine feast on that last day when all of them would gather together in his hall.

Once more Alain and Piers were at the high table. Piers was given the seat beside Rohaise, but Alain was farther along, between a stately older noblewoman and a plump, middle-aged lady who kept putting her hand on his thigh when she talked to him. At another time he would have been amused by her open interest in him; a month ago he might even have responded to her blatant invitation, but on this night he could think of no woman but Joanna. From where he sat he could not see her; Crispin's body blocked his view. He knew he should not try to speak to her alone, but he wanted desperately to tell her once again that he would come to her aid if ever she needed him. Good sense told him it was not necessary to repeat what he had already said, but his heart and his growing unease told him otherwise.

"Here is special wine." A servingwoman poured out the ruby liquid for each of the ladies, emptying the pitcher in her hand. "Here is more," she said, reaching for a fresh pitcher from the tray Baird was holding.

"I'll do it," Baird said to her. "Take the tray and the empty pitcher to the kitchen. I'll be along in a moment and give you more."

"Baird, why are you doing this service?" Alain asked.

"It's Baron Radulf's best wine." Having finished filling Alain's cup, Baird straightened, smoothing down his green wool tunic with his free hand. "Radulf ordered me to make certain the servants don't steal it to drink for themselves, while giving his guests the vinegary, lesser stuff."

"A wise precaution," remarked the elderly noblewoman. "The kitchen folk will eat and drink everything if you don't watch them."

"Servants are so untrustworthy," said the plump woman on Alain's other side. Resting her hand on his upper thigh, she continued, "I knew a lady whose personal maid stole her jewels. Can you imagine such a thing? Stole her jewels right out of her bedchamber and ran away with them!"

"Shocking," said the elderly lady.

Amused and mildly diverted by them, Alain sipped his wine. He did not care for the taste of it, but he thought he ought to drink it rather than insult Radulf by leaving the cup nearly full. Radulf might be looking for an excuse to start a quarrel with him. He'd be glad to get away from Banningford Castle on the morrow. The atmosphere of the place set his nerves on edge, or perhaps it was just his longing for Joanna. Either way, he looked forward to the next day's dawn. At least the feasting was almost done.

He saw Crispin rise and leave the table, with Piers following him to the outer door. Crispin was weaving a little, as if he had taken too much wine. Piers looked around, met Alain's eyes, and tilted his head in a way that told Alain his assistance was needed. Alain set his nearly empty wine cup on the table and began to rise.

"Forgive me," he said to his two companions, "but I must leave you. It looks as if the bridegroom needs my help." He found it hard to stand upright; all at once his head began to spin and he was shaken by a wave of nausea.

"You've had a bit too much yourself, I think."

The elderly woman gave him a disapproving glance.

"Only two cups since the feast began," Alain reported.

It was a long way to the door, and he traversed the distance with growing uncertainty. He was finding it increasingly difficult to focus his eyes. He hung on to the wall, hoping his dinner would stay in his stomach where it belonged until he had found Piers and Crispin. Then, hearing Piers's voice, he followed the sound.

Joanna saw the three of them leave the great hall and shook her head in exasperation. How foolish men were to drink too much when they must know they would be sick the next day. Or that night, if they consumed enough. Poor Crispin.

She glanced around the hall. Her father sat alone for once, staring down into his wine cup in gloomy contemplation. Farther down the table, Father Ambrose was chatting with a nobleman and his lady. Rohaise was, as usual, out of her seat and busy with the servingwomen. The guests seemed to be enjoying the banquet, and no one else looked more than routinely drunk. Piers, too, had appeared to be sober. It was odd that only Crispin and Alain should be overcome by wine. Leaving her chair, Joanna followed the men into the entry hall, intending to help them if she could. At the very least she could hold Crispin's head and wipe his face with a refreshing cool cloth after he had finished being sick.

The entry hall was empty. Not even the man-at-arms who should have been guarding the entry was in his place, though she caught a quick glimpse of someone on the top step outside the open door. Whoever it was had vanished, most likely heading down the steps into the inner bailey. This outer door was on her right; on her left the stone staircase wound upward to the private rooms of the west tower. Beneath the curve of the staircase, in the far corner of the entry hall, was a door leading into a room where the men-at-arms who guarded the west tower could gather between their watches, and where they could leave their heavier battle gear, to have it nearby in case they needed it. The door to this room stood partially open.

For the convenience of the men-at-arms a small garderobe had been built into the outer wall of the guards' room, from where it could empty directly into the moat. Joanna thought it likely that Crispin and Alain had gone there, as the nearest place to relieve themselves. A sound from behind the door appeared to confirm that impression. She hurried to the door and pushed it all the way open. She was inside the room before she fully appreciated the horror of what she beheld.

That Piers had just emerged in haste from the garderobe was evident from the disorder of his hose. He and Alain were supporting Crispin, who was drenched in blood. A long hunting knife lay on the floor. There was blood on the floor, too, and blood on Alain's clothing—blood everywhere—red—red—and Crispin ghostly pale, his head lolling.

"Put him on the floor," Piers said.

Joanna was there before they could lower him, not caring if her fine silk gown was ruined, kneeling in the sticky wetness to lift Crispin's tunic and expose the dreadful wound that would surely mean his death. She did not flinch from the blood. She had seen enough blood in the few years since she had been old enough to help Rohaise bind up the wounds of various men-at-arms whenever there was an accident or a battle in or near the castle. But never before had anyone who had been so intimately associated with her been so grievously wounded.

"Crispin! Oh, my dear." She gathered him into her arms, knowing there was nothing she could do to help him. His wound was too terrible, the loss of blood too great.

He was aware of her. His eyes were open and he was looking at her. His lips moved.

"Why?" Crispin whispered. "He—he—*why?*"

"Who did this to you?" Piers demanded, kneeling beside the fallen man. "Crispin, tell us. We'll see him punished."

"Father," Crispin said, looking at Joanna and then at something over Piers's shoulder. "Father . . ."

"Piers, move aside, please." Father Ambrose was there. "Thank God I followed Joanna to see what the trouble might be. Crispin, my beloved boy, can you hear me?"

Crispin drew a short, rasping breath. When he exhaled the light went out of his eyes. Father Ambrose made the sign of the cross over him.

"Time enough later to finish what I must do for Crispin," Father Ambrose said. "Crispin is dead, and my first concern must be for the living."

A low, heartrending moan issued from Joanna's throat. She still held Crispin's body in her arms, his head on her shoulder, rocking him as if he were a child.

"Hush, my dear," Father Ambrose said, his hand resting briefly on her bowed head before he straightened and began to deal with the consequences of murder. "Try to postpone your grieving for a little while yet, until I ask a few questions. Joanna, did you see what happened?"

She could not speak. She tried, but the words would not come. She was numb, all her emotions frozen. Knowing Crispin was dead, but as yet unable to accept that fact, she was barely able to shake her head. But she could see and hear with unnatural clarity, and the events of the next hour seared her heart and her memory so deeply that she could never forget them.

"Piers, tell me quickly: did you see who did this?" Father Ambrose asked.

"I was behind the screen then, using the garderobe," Piers said. "I heard a noise, and Alain called to me, and when I came out he was holding Crispin."

"Alain." Father Ambrose turned to him, and Joanna looked at him too. Alain's blue tunic and hose were soaked with Crispin's blood; his face was white and haggard. He looked as if he might burst into tears at any moment. Father Ambrose put a hand on his shoulder, steadying him. "I must ask you this, Alain, because I recognize that hunting knife. It is yours. Did you stab Crispin?"

"I loved him," Alain choked. "I was sick—still sick—head splitting—"

"Did you have your hunting knife in the great hall?" Father Ambrose's voice was sharp.

"I—I don't know." Alain rubbed at his forehead, his bloodstained hand leaving a path across his pale skin. "Can't remember. Perhaps later."

"There may be no later for you." Father Ambrose returned his attention to Piers. "Why are you not sick?"

"I don't know, unless it's because I only ate a little roast beef and drank but a sip of the wine. It tasted bitter to me, and since I ate and drank too much last night and felt the worse for it this morning, I resolved to be more careful today." Piers looked toward the door. "Where are the men-at-arms? Why hasn't anyone else come in here?"

"An excellent question," said Father Ambrose, walking to the door and closing it.

"There was no one on guard. And no one else is ill." Joanna spoke so suddenly that she surprised even herself. The others stared at her; then Piers and Father Ambrose looked at each other. Alain dropped to his knees beside her, his movements clumsy.

"Crispin," he said, stroking Crispin's face. Joanna pulled her husband closer to her breast.

"Don't touch him!" she cried.

"Joanna—please . . ."

"Piers," Father Ambrose said, picking up both the hunting knife and the cloak some careless man-at-arms had tossed over a bench, "I want you to take Alain out of the castle. Go now, before Radulf orders the gates closed."

"I can't leave." Alain was still looking at Joanna, who would not look back at him.

"You *must* leave, and at once." Father Ambrose lifted the younger man to his feet and set the cloak about his shoulders, covering his bloodstained tunic. "It's your knife that killed Crispin. You are drenched in his blood. Baron Radulf does not like you, in large part because he is aware of your interest in Joanna. He will welcome the chance to blame you for this murder. You must go quickly. It is my duty to inform Radulf of what has happened, and I cannot delay much longer, or someone may discover us and raise the alarm."

"He's right, Alain." Quick-witted Piers had understood the danger at once. He took the hunting knife Father Ambrose handed to him and stuck it into his belt. "Radulf will never give you a chance to prove your innocence, Alain, especially since you can't remember what happened. Damn! If only I had stayed out of the garderobe."

"Don't blame yourself. None of this is your doing, of that I am certain. I'm depending on you, Piers," said Father Ambrose. "Get Alain safely away from here. I will not tell you before Joanna what to do next, lest Radulf find a way to force the information out of his daughter, but I believe you understand my intent."

"Yes," said Piers, "I do understand. But even for Joanna to hear this much could prevent our escaping to safety."

"I will give my father nothing!" The violence in Joanna's voice made all three men look at her again. "I will say nothing to my father."

"Joanna . . ." Alain began, reaching toward her.

"You cannot keep your promise to aid me," she said, still with that same barely repressed violence. "Go. Save yourself from my father's vengeance. Prove your innocence later if you can. Leave me with my dead husband."

"I swear," Alain said, "that as soon as I can, I will return. I'll come back for you, Joanna."

That much she heard and remembered later, but she did not hear what else he said; the storm of grief that had been building inside her broke and the tears she had been fighting overwhelmed her. She did not know it when Alain and Piers left, nor did she feel Father Ambrose's comforting hand on her shoulder while he waited, hoping to give them time to escape before he was forced to report Crispin's murder. Too much had been done to Joanna in the few days just passed; too many people had demanded more of her than she could give. Too many conflicting emotions had assaulted her. Now she could think of nothing but her own pain and the loss of Crispin. She retreated far inside herself, to a place where pain and loss no longer mattered.

But she could not completely remove herself from what was going on around her. She was aware of the clamor of Radulf's entrance into the guards' room, with Baird and a group of his men-at-arms behind him. She screamed and fought the men when they tried to take Crispin's body from her, giving him up only into Father Ambrose's caring hands. She heard Rohaise's voice, and knew it when Baird picked her up from the floor and, holding her against his old brown tunic, carried her up the stairs to the room she had shared with Crispin. It was Rohaise who pulled off her blood-soaked gown and washed her arms and hands and then her body, where Crispin's blood had seeped through her clothes. Rohaise tucked her into bed and put heated stones at her feet to stop the shivering that racked her, and Rohaise gave her herb-scented wine to drink. And then, mercifully, Joanna slept, knowing nothing more.

Below, in the great hall, Radulf was once again arranging his daughter's life.

"I have sent out search parties to locate those two knaves," he said to Father Ambrose. "When we find them Alain and Piers will hang for what they've done."

"You might do well to search elsewhere for the killer," Father Ambrose suggested.

"Why?" Radulf looked hard at the priest. "Do you know of anyone else who wished harm to my son Crispin? Aye, that's how I think of him, as my son, for his fine character endeared him to me as soon as I met him. And to my daughter. Poor Joanna is completely undone by this tragedy."

"I would like to see her, to offer what words of solace I can," said Father Ambrose.

"She's sleeping now. My wife is sitting with her. It's a kind thought on your part, Father Ambrose, but you need not concern yourself. Rohaise and I will take care of Joanna. I see no reason not to have the funeral at Haughston, as you wish. Let's do it tomorrow; then you can leave at once on your journey to Sicily."

"I think now that I ought to postpone my voyage," said Father Ambrose. "With Crispin gone, Haughston will need an administrator."

"But the task is mine," Radulf said, "and glad I am that we had the arrangement written into the marriage contract. Upon poor Crispin's death, I became the administrator of Haughston, and guardian of Crispin's child."

"Child?" Father Ambrose repeated, astonished by this idea. "Crispin had no children."

"We don't know that yet, do we? Joanna may be with child."

"Dear heaven." Father Ambrose let out a long, sad sigh.

"The marriage was well and truly consummated," Radulf went on with satisfaction. "I went myself to see the bloody bedsheet the next morning, after Crispin and Joanna had left the bridal chamber. Then, of course, they had several more days and nights together."

"Two," said Father Ambrose. "Only two days and two nights after the wedding night."

"Well, it's enough, isn't it?" Radulf smiled at the thought. "Even now, Crispin's son may be growing in my daughter's womb: an heir to his estates and mine."

Father Ambrose crossed himself and murmured a prayer for Joanna's continued good health and safety.

"Aye, Father, I'll keep her safe," Radulf said. "Joanna means much to me, and all the more so if she's with child. Well, what is it, priest? You don't look happy. Did you want Haughston for yourself, so you could give it to the Church? Do you think I gained control of those lands by a trick?"

"What I think," said Father Ambrose, "is that you are as honest as you know how to be."

"Well, then, there's no problem," said Radulf. "You can leave for Sicily immediately after the funeral tomorrow."

"Before I go I would like to see Joanna," Father Ambrose insisted. "I would join her in prayer for Crispin's soul."

"Why don't we wait until tomorrow," Radulf suggested, "until we learn how she's feeling then?"

But on the morrow he informed Father Ambrose that Joanna was too ill from shock and grief to have any visitors. He saw no reason to tell the priest about the scene that had taken place at dawn between his daughter and himself, with Rohaise looking on.

"I *will* go to Crispin's funeral," Joanna announced.

"You will stay in this room until I say you may leave," Radulf told her.

"I am no longer under your rule," she cried. "I am a married woman."

"You are a widow, returned to her father's care, and too grief-stricken to leave her chamber," Radulf said.

"I will obey you no more!" She did not flinch

101

when Radulf raised his hand as if to strike her. After a moment he lowered his hand.

"I have spent long years of my life protecting my lands against the Marcher lords," he said. "I'll not strike you and take the chance of making you miscarry if you are with child. I'd not risk losing any chance to have a rightful heir who will protect my lands when I am gone."

"That's all I am to you," she said, torn between joy at the thought of giving poor Crispin a posthumous child and anger at her father's coldness toward anything but his own interests and ambitions. "It's all I've ever been, isn't it? Just a vessel to carry your heir. You don't love me. I don't think you love anyone."

"Rohaise," Radulf said to his wife, who had been watching and listening to this quarrel with growing distress, "call a servant and order brought to this room whatever you will need for Joanna and yourself until I return from Haughston."

"My lord?" Rohaise sounded as if she did not understand.

"Do as I say, woman," Radulf snapped.

"But, my lord, I have much to do today," Rohaise protested. "We have guests who must be fed and entertained."

"Whatever guests are still here after last night's murder," Radulf said, "will go to Haughston with me for the funeral. I've sent a man to command the servants there to prepare a funeral feast for us. When it's over the guests may go home or to the devil, for all I care. You, my dear and obedient wife, will spend today in this room, with

Joanna. I'll post Baird outside the door to be sure you are not disturbed. Now, call that servant, for I am impatient to be on my way."

"I want to see Father Ambrose," Joanna declared.

"You will see no one but Rohaise and myself," Radulf told her. "And don't think to coerce Rohaise into carrying messages for you. She knows better than to defy me, don't you, Rohaise?"

After a quick glance at Joanna, Rohaise nodded. "Yes, my lord," she said.

"You are mad," Joanna told her father.

"I know of no man who would say so," he replied with perfect calmness, "though there are many who would count you maddened by grief for making such an accusation, so watch your tongue."

* * *

At the end of the funeral service Radulf rose to speak.

"I do entreat all of you, dear friends," he said to the congregation assembled in the tiny chapel at Haughston, "that if any of you should learn the whereabouts of those two miscreant knights, Piers of Stokesbrough and Alain of Wortham, you will capture and hold them under close guard and at once send word to me of what you know of them. I would not have Crispin's murderers go unpunished. I have this morning sent a message to King Henry, asking him to declare Alain and Piers to be outlaws. I want to see both of them hanged for what they have done—yes, hanged for all they were noblemen born! Beheading is too good for men who would murder their own kin.

"Now, let us bury Crispin in the crypt below this altar; let us lay him to rest with his forebears. I do solemnly swear that I will have a memorial effigy of him carved in finest marble and placed upon his tomb. I also swear to be a faithful administrator of his lands, holding them in trust for the son I pray his widow will bring forth to carry on his line."

It was a speech that was admired by all the men present, for though the murder of kin was not unknown to some of them—and was occasionally deemed necessary in the interests of self-preservation—still they had their notions of rough justice, and on that morning Radulf's declarations exemplified all that was finest among the Norman barons. Whether King Henry decided to pronounce them outlaws or not, Alain and Piers would not last long if either was captured. As for Joanna, any man there would have done the same, would have insisted that his daughter might—just might—produce the child who would justify his usurpation of lands that had once belonged to another.

All the guests had gone and Banningford Castle was quiet once more. Baron Radulf, now the ruler of twice as much land as he had held a week previously, was totally confident in his new powers when he confronted his daughter and his wife in the bridal chamber where Joanna had remained after Crispin's death.

"Stop your weeping!" he shouted at Joanna. "You may have enjoyed Crispin's lovemaking, but it was nothing more than physical pleasure. You did not know him at all, not any better than Rohaise and I did. Will you stop that sniveling?"

"He was kind to me." Joanna tried her best to obey her father's irritable command. "Given time, his kindness and my gratitude that he was not rough with me might have grown into mutual contentment. We might have learned to care deeply for each other." Seeing the disbelieving way her father was looking at her she fell silent, knowing he was incapable of understanding her tender fondness for Crispin.

"It is my dearest wish to keep you safe," Radulf announced. "Therefore, you will remain in this chamber."

"What are you saying?" Joanna cried. "Am I a prisoner? If so, why? I have done nothing wrong."

"Let us hope not. You will stay here, under guard, until we know if you are with child."

"But that will take weeks," Rohaise protested. "I can understand if you do not want her to ride, or to engage in strenuous activity that might lead to a miscarriage, but, surely, my lord, you will allow Joanna to spend part of each day in the solar, as she is accustomed to do. Her needlework—"

"She can do her needlework here," Radulf said. "There is light enough."

It was, in fact, a lovely room, the best guest chamber in the castle, high in the west tower, safe and private. Because it was so high, situated out of arrow's reach on the level just below the lord's own chamber, the windows could be larger than the mere arrowslits that broke the gray stone walls of the chambers on lower levels. In this room there were two windows set close together in the thick walls, so they formed an alcove. Directly beneath the windows a wide stone shelf was padded with pillows to make a seat. For greater comfort the windows had not only wooden shutters but heavy woolen curtains that could be drawn across the alcove on winter nights to keep out the cold. Crispin's belongings and his clothes chest had been removed from the room at Radulf's direction, but all of Joanna's possessions remained.

"I see nothing wrong with this room," said Radulf, eyeing the two braziers that would in winter burn charcoal for heat. "This is unusually comfortable. You ought to be perfectly happy here."

"I cannot remain in one room every day for months," Joanna cried.

"But that is just what you will do," Radulf replied. "I cannot allow you to converse with, or even to see, any man but myself until I know if you are with child by Crispin. Thus, there can be no doubt of the father's identity."

"What if she is not with child?" asked Rohaise.

"Why, then," said Radulf, flexing his large fingers as if he would wind them about his daughter's slender throat if she should prove barren, "I shall marry her to someone else once her mourning is over and we are certain she carries no child. I must have an heir. I must!"

"My lord, this is overly cruel treatment of a girl who has only obeyed your wishes," Rohaise persisted.

"Need I remind you that if you had given me children, this treatment of Joanna would not be necessary?" Radulf turned on Rohaise with the relish of a man who enjoyed browbeating those who could not strike back. " 'Tis a grievous fault in a wife, and if you prove disobedient in addition to being barren, I will feel justified in casting you off and sending you to a convent."

"But if Joanna is with child and she takes no exercise," Rohaise declared, risking her own welfare for Joanna's sake, "she will grow weak and ill, and thus able to bear only a sickly babe for your heir. I am thinking of your interests, my lord, when I say that if you allow Joanna to walk on the battlements each day, and occasionally visit the herb garden, I will go with her to be certain she speaks to no one."

Radulf looked from his wife to his daughter, indecision written plain on his face, while Joanna held her breath.

"Joanna may walk on the battlements and you with her," he said to Rohaise, "but only with Baird to guard you both. *He* will make certain no man approaches Joanna."

This was not what Joanna wanted to hear; there would be no pleasure in walking with Baird, whom she disliked. But she reminded herself that she was fortunate not to be confined to her chamber at all times.

"Thank you, Father," she said, as meekly as she

could, considering the rebellion festering in her heart.

"Baird will guard your door, too," Radulf decided. "In addition to the bar on the inside, I'll have a strong lock installed on your door to better protect you from intrusion. Baird's woman, Lys, will clean your room and bring your meals. You will not try to make a friend of her, and Baird will guarantee to me that Lys will carry no messages for you."

"I have no wish to speak to Lys at all," Joanna said. "She is a dreadful woman."

"Nor will *you* carry messages to or from Joanna," Radulf said to Rohaise. "Not if you value your life."

"I will obey your wishes, my lord."

"For the present Baird and I will hold the only keys to this room once the outside lock is on the door," Radulf went on. "Speak to one of us when you want to enter here."

"Yes, my lord." Rohaise bowed her head in acceptance of her husband's orders.

When Radulf had gone Joanna sank down upon the window seat, leaning her head against the stone wall.

"Is this all I am to be allowed to see?" she asked. "Just the view from these two narrow windows? I will go mad."

"Don't lose hope." Rohaise sat beside her.

"Thank you for trying to help me," Joanna said.

"I wish I could have done more. Without your company my life would be loveless as well as childless. I will do anything I can to ease your imprisonment, for that's what this confinement is. I would help you escape if I could find a way, though where you might flee, except to a convent, I do not know."

"Don't put yourself in jeopardy with my father for my sake," Joanna cautioned. Smiling ruefully, she added, "If he were to send you away, what would I do? We have only each other, Rohaise."

"I will be careful," Rohaise promised. "I'll take care to please him in bed each night, and try to soothe his temper when it flares."

"It would be a great joke if you were to get with child after all this," Joanna said.

"I begin to think the fault for my barrenness lies not so much with me as with Radulf," Rohaise told her. Then, changing the subject, she asked, "What of Alain? Do you believe Radulf's claim that he killed Crispin?"

"No matter what my father or anyone else says," Joanna replied, "I know in my heart that Alain could not commit murder."

"That is what I think, too," Rohaise said, "nor Sir Piers, either. But I wish I knew who did do it."

Chapter Seven

Father Ambrose left Haughston early on the morning after Crispin's funeral. He traveled alone. It was safe enough to do so; even in that part of England, so near to the Welsh border, under King Henry I there were precious few who would dare to attack a priest. Father Ambrose rode a gentle mare and had, in addition, two other horses; a spare mount for himself and a pack animal that carried his few belongings, along with a surprising amount of food for one traveler. Since he had made no secret of the fact that he was going to London and then on to Hastings, from where he would cross the Narrow Sea to Normandy, he took the road leading in that direction. This road, which was little more than a track in the wilderness, wound through a deep forest. As the day was bright and warm, Father

Ambrose went bareheaded, his freshly shaven tonsure a shining symbol of his holiness for all the world to see. But his thoughts were not on matters spiritual, and as he rode along he repeatedly sent searching glances into the greenwood on either side of the road. When, in late morning, a figure muffled in a dark cloak stepped into the road before him, he pulled hard on the reins, stopping his horse at once.

"Thanks be to God," he exclaimed. "I feared I had missed you, or that you had been taken during the night and I not told of it."

"You had best come into the trees," Piers said. "Alain and I have found a spot that should be safe for a while, at least until we have decided what to do next." Taking hold of the bridle, he led Father Ambrose's horse off the road. Since their reins were attached to the priest's saddle, the two extra horses could only follow.

"I'm surprised you were let out of Haughston with these animals," Piers remarked, looking at the horses with admiration for their fine quality.

"I was surprised, too, so much so that I wonder if I'm being followed, though I have seen no sign of pursuit." At that point in their progress through the dense greenery Father Ambrose swung lightly to the ground; the underbrush had become too thick for him to ride without being seriously hindered by large bushes and low-hanging tree limbs. "You will forgive me for saying that, having forsaken my knightly vows for holy orders only five years ago, I find it a pleasure to be so well mounted once more and to be riding

111

out on a quest for justice on so fine a day."

"Did you steal them?" Piers asked, looking toward the horses again.

"Certainly not, my son," the priest replied with just the trace of a twinkle in his eyes. "They are but a donation from Baron Radulf to Holy Mother Church, in partial penance for his sins. Ah, Alain, there you are. Thank God you are safe."

"I would not be even this safe without your help and Piers's quick wits," Alain said, leaving the cover afforded by a thick clump of bushes and coming toward the priest. "Somehow we have eluded an army of searchers and the dogs Radulf ordered set on our track. We spent the whole of that first night standing in a pond with cold water up to our necks while the hounds yapped and yammered too close for my ease. In spite of the cold and the uncertainty, still I thank you both for my life."

"If only we could have saved Crispin's life, too," Piers murmured. "If only we were four here together, instead of just three."

"Aye. Crispin's death angers me and pains me sorely." Ambrose bowed his head, crossing himself. "I shall never cease to pray for my nephew's dear soul. It's all any of us can do for him now."

They stood in a rough circle, each man close to tears at the thought of their lost kinsman and friend, while Ambrose said a prayer.

"Having consigned Crispin to the care of our most blessed Lord," Ambrose said, "it is my next duty to care for the living. And it seems to me that at least one of you is in sore need of my care."

The Alain of Wortham whom Father Ambrose

regarded in that forest glade was a very different man from the openhearted, cheerful young fellow who had arrived at Banningford Castle less than a week earlier for his cousin's wedding. Alain's face was pale and drawn, his every movement taut with tension, as if he were poised for flight at an instant's notice.

"Have you been ill again?" Father Ambrose asked, much concerned.

"No, the sickness passed quickly. I have been worried for your sake," Alain explained. "And I have been afraid that Piers and I would be caught before I could remember everything that occurred on that terrible night and thus prove that I did not murder Crispin. That's what Radulf is saying, isn't it? That I did the deed? We knew he would. Uncle Ambrose, I want you to convince Piers to separate from me. Tell him it's the best thing for him to do. He won't listen to me."

"It has been a long time since I've heard you call me uncle," said Ambrose. "The word is sweet to my ears, even if it is only an honorary title. My dear boy, I cannot advise Piers to leave you. What would he do—return to Haughston, where he was to become a household knight for Crispin? Go where Radulf now rules? How long do you think Piers would survive there? Radulf will claim—indeed, he is already claiming—that Piers is as culpable as yourself."

"It was a foolish idea." Alain rubbed both hands across his face. "I can't seem to think clearly right now."

"Perhaps that is because you haven't eaten recently," Ambrose said. "My lads, will you share my midday meal with me and listen while I give you good advice?"

"More than that," said Piers. "I, for one, will promise to follow whatever advice you give."

"Now those are the words of a wise man." With the easy movements of one who had once been a fine knight and who was still in remarkably good physical condition, Ambrose pulled a package out of his saddlebag and tossed it to Piers. There was a wine jug fastened to the packhorse's back, and this Ambrose removed and gave to Alain. Then, hoisting his priest's robe up to his thighs, Ambrose sat cross-legged on the ground.

"Leave the horses as they are," he said when Piers made a motion toward unsaddling the mount he had ridden. "We may have to leave this charming spot in haste. You may drink freely of the wine, Alain. There is no poppy syrup in it."

"Poppy syrup?" With the wine jug at his lips, Alain paused to stare at the priest. "Is that what made me sick?"

"I think it most likely," Ambrose said. "Poppy syrup mixed with certain herbs will produce the symptoms we saw in you. The ingredients are easily available. Any good chatelaine will have them in her stillroom, ready to mix together to ease the pains of wounded men."

"Surely you don't think the lady Rohaise is involved?" asked Piers. "Or Joanna, either?"

"No," said Ambrose firmly, "I do not. Having no proof of anyone's guilt, I leave the choice of culprit to your imaginations. But I would wager, Piers, that had you taken a full cup of wine with your meal instead of a mere sip on the night when Crispin died, you would have been sick also. Though such speculation means little without incontrovertable proof, I believe that you were both meant to be blamed for Crispin's death."

"Who did it?" Alain demanded.

"I do not know," said Ambrose.

"But you suspect," Alain persisted tensely.

"I will not speak a name and thus cast doubt on any man's character without proof," Ambrose replied.

"But I am being blamed without proof!" Alain cried. "And, heaven help me, if I had to prove my innocence, I could not do it, for I still cannot remember exactly what happened when I left the great hall that night."

"You were not meant to remember," Piers put in. "That's what the poppy syrup was for, to confuse us."

"Is Joanna well?" Alain asked suddenly.

"I have not seen her since that night. Her father has locked her in her bridal chamber." Ambrose went on to tell his companions all that he knew about Joanna's situation and of Radulf's search for the two men whom he had loudly proclaimed to be Crispin's killers.

"We must find a way to release Joanna." Alain rose as if he would start at once for Banningford Castle.

"Do not even think of it," Ambrose advised. "One man, or two, cannot hope to conquer Banningford. You would be captured, and I don't doubt that Radulf would torture both of you into madness, and confessions, before hanging you from the battlements. Sit down, Alain, and listen to me. I want you and Piers to travel with me to Sicily."

"No," Alain protested. "I won't leave England. Justice must be done for Crispin's sake. I have to find proof of who is the true murderer and clear my name. I have to rescue Joanna from that tower room."

"In time I believe you will," said Ambrose. "But there is nothing you can do for now except save yourself."

"I won't leave Joanna!" Alain's face was dark with anger, his fists clenched.

"Perhaps I should have put poppy syrup in the wine after all," murmured Ambrose.

"Alain, keep still and listen to him," Piers urged. "We may not have much time before the searchers Radulf has sent out after us reach this part of the forest." As usual Alain listened to Piers when he would heed no one else.

"All right, old Sir Piers, I'll hear what Uncle Ambrose has to say."

"Sit down, then," Ambrose ordered, and Alain obeyed.

"I am known to be traveling to London, and then on to Normandy," Ambrose said, "which means that Radulf's men will most likely concentrate their search south and east in that direction, in the belief that I will try to aid your escape."

"They will more surely think so when they learn that you have taken three horses to speed our journey," Piers noted.

"Exactly." Ambrose nodded. "That was my intent: to make them think so. But while Radulf looks for two knights with a priest heading for London, three priests will ride north for a day or two and then turn westward into Wales. I have robes for you in the saddlebags there."

"Wales?" Alain repeated. "Why to Wales?"

"From Wales," said Ambrose, "it's easy enough to get to Ireland."

"A fine idea," Piers noted approvingly. "That ought to put Radulf off our trail. And from what I've heard of the Welsh, they won't be very helpful to him even if he does pick up our scent."

"Aye." Alain did not show much enthusiasm, but he did keep quiet while Ambrose went on, telling them the rest of his plan.

"Once in Ireland we can easily find a ship bound for Bordeaux, since there is a thriving wine trade between the two places. From Bordeaux we will travel southward overland to Narbonne and thence to the Middle Sea, where we can take ship for Sicily."

"It is a long journey," Alain objected. "It will take months, especially if the weather is bad and the winds against us while we are at sea, or waiting ashore for a ship to leave."

"All the better," said Ambrose with a touch of mischief in the glances he gave to both his companions. "There will be time for me to further your education while we travel. You will need to learn more Latin than the little you know now. A fair knowledge of Greek would not be amiss. Then there is Arabic, of course. I have been

117

studying it for several years in preparation for my second visit to Sicily."

"It's all well enough for a learned man like yourself, but why should I want to speak a heathen tongue?" Alain asked scornfully.

"The question betrays your ignorance of the land to which we are going," Ambrose told him. "In addition to the languages, I will teach you what I know of the remarkable kingdom of Sicily, so that you will be able to make your way at King Roger's court. I want you to avoid the foolish mistakes I made while I was in Sicily on my way home from the Holy Land. When I was still a knight I did not appreciate the learning or the other opportunities that were available to me if only I had cared enough to take advantage of what was offered. Now I return in search of the learning I missed on my first visit, and I would have you take advantage of the opportunities I once ignored."

"If I leave England with you, which I have not yet agreed to do," Alain said, "I will go only as far as Ireland, or possibly Bordeaux, and only for a short time. I will admit, a sea voyage might do much to clear my thoughts and make it possible for me to remember what happened when Crispin was killed. I can see that leaving England might be a good idea until the furor dies down. But as soon as I can, I will return, to prove my innocence and to rescue Joanna from her father."

"I thought I had made it plain to you," Ambrose said. "Radulf will see to it that you are proclaimed an outlaw. Once King Henry signs the proclamation, any man in England may kill you without fear of retribution. When your father dies you will not be able to inherit his lands. They will escheat to the crown instead."

"Then I will be a landless knight, like Piers," Alain said, trying to accept a truth he had refused to acknowledge until that moment.

"However," Ambrose went on, "in Sicily a knight with intelligence and skill in battle can earn lands and a high title."

"Which will do me no good in England," Alain responded.

"In one thing only do I agree with Radulf," Ambrose told him. "King Henry will not live much longer, and when he dies I believe there will be great confusion in this land, for like Radulf, I do not believe many nobles will follow a woman ruler. In that very confusion lies your best hope. Writs of outlawry are sometimes forgotten or rescinded during times of civil strife. Go to Sicily with me, Alain, and there gain lands and wealth and power. Then you can choose your best time to return and claim what is rightfully yours."

"You are talking about years," Alain objected. "What about Joanna?"

"There is nothing you can do for Joanna." It was Piers who answered the question; Piers, who had been listening to Ambrose with ill-concealed and growing excitement. "Radulf will keep Joanna under such close guard that no one will be able to reach her. He must keep her confined, for she is his best means of consolidating his control of Crispin's lands. If Joanna bears Crispin's heir—"

"I know all of that." Alain was on his feet once

more. "Don't go over it again. I can't bear to think of what has be done to Joanna. I am sick once more—sick of your reasonableness. Neither of you knows what it is to love until your heart breaks and your mouth goes dry and you would dare anything for her sake—anything!"

"Do you really think I do not know?" asked Ambrose, still sitting on the bare ground with his robe hiked up to his knees and a crust of bread in one hand. "Why do you think I laid aside my chainmail and put on this coarse priest's robe instead, if not for the sake of One I love more than life itself? For Him whom I love, I, too, would do anything, even die a martyr's death if I must."

"It's not the same as loving a woman," Alain declared.

"Perhaps not." Ambrose maintained his calm in the face of Alain's impatient anger. "I have loved a woman or two in my time, while I was yet a knight. I understand what you are feeling now, and how hard it is to be rational when your thoughts are in turmoil and all of your body aches for her touch, her presence. I ask you to consider that you cannot help Joanna; but in trying to do so you may waste your life while bringing even greater harm to her. If you wait, and think, and plan carefully, then in some later day you may succeed where today you would surely fail."

"Wait? I cannot!" Alain flung away from his companions, heading into the forest. Behind him, Piers made as if to follow, until Ambrose caught at his arm.

"Let him go," Ambrose said. "Give him time to

think it through. Alain is no fool. He will reach the right decision."

Alain crashed through the underbrush, pausing only to swing one fist at the thickest tree he could find. He did the tree no harm, but he sorely bruised his knuckles, and the pain of torn skin and aching bones brought him to his senses.

He knew Ambrose was right. If he could have rescued Joanna and taken her along to Sicily with him, he would have done so and never looked back at England. But he could not save her, not without forfeiting his own life, and he could see now that in doing so he would not help his love. If ever he might hope to save Joanna from her father, he would have to leave England as soon as he could. He had sworn over Crispin's body to return to Joanna, and return he would, but not yet.

He pounded at the tree again, almost enjoying the pain in his hand, which helped him to forget the ache in his heart. *That* was a pain that would not leave him until he held Joanna in his arms once more.

Nor would he show his pain. It was unmanly to be so open, and he was a boy no longer. He would hide what he felt. He would do as Ambrose suggested: make himself wealthy in Sicily, and so powerful that Radulf would be but an ant beneath his boot. Then he would return, to destroy Radulf and claim his love.

"I will be back," he whispered, his forehead now against the tree bark, his bloodied fist at his mouth. "Wait for me, Joanna. I will come back to you."

Chapter Eight

One hot mid-August night while he was undressing for bed, Radulf's dearest wish was given new promise.

"My lord," Rohaise said, "Joanna and I are certain that she is with child. Since you have not visited her for several weeks, she asked me to tell you." When Radulf turned to stare at her, forgetting that he still held his sweat-soaked tunic in one hand, Rohaise went on. "Twice now Joanna's monthly bleeding has not appeared, and lately she is sick each morning. There are other indications, but those are the sure signs."

For a few moments Radulf knew true happiness, until he began to consider adverse possibilities.

"There is no promise that it will be a boy," he said, "or that Joanna won't miscarry, or that the child will live once it's born."

"Oh, my dear lord, can't you just be hopeful?" Rohaise asked. "Joanna's spirits are vastly improved. She is so grateful to be given this opportunity to provide one last service for poor Crispin. She will welcome his child whether it is a son or a daughter."

"Joanna can indulge in womanish fancies; she does not need an heir." Radulf looked at his pretty, brown-haired wife, who had just climbed into their bed. Her pink and white shoulders showed above the green coverlet; her throat was long and slender. Radulf frequently wanted to put his hands around that elegant throat and press the life out of her in punishment for her barrenness, but he had sense enough to know he needed Rohaise to manage his household for him and to see to it that Joanna was properly cared for, at least until his grandchild was born.

And there was still the chance that Rohaise might give him a child. If he had a son as well as a grandson, how fine it would be. Then he might begin to feel safe from the ever-encroaching Marcher lords. Thinking about the possibility of his own child always increased his interest in Rohaise. Reaching out, he grabbed the coverlet and pulled it back, revealing all of his naked wife, from her small, high breasts to her slender waist and long legs. He pulled those legs apart and knelt between them, a tall, big-boned man, fair of hair and blue of eye like his daughter. He had been handsome in his youth, but in middle age his face was florid and his body heavy from too much food and drink. It was the drink, along with his constant worry about not having an heir, that too often made it impossible for him to take Rohaise as he wanted to take her. He did not love her, but it had always been pleasant to hear her moan and sigh beneath him before he enjoyed his own release. She had never refused him and she seemed to like what he did to her.

At the moment he could not do what he wanted, for his body was not responding to his desire; his manhood hung limp and shriveled. He took Rohaise's hand and placed it on himself.

"Make me hard," he ordered.

She had an amazingly supple body. With her legs still spread wide and Radulf kneeling between them, she sat up to kiss him, letting her tongue flick in and out of his mouth.

"You needn't do that," he muttered, pulling away. "Just concentrate on what's important."

"You liked this the last time, my lord." She tickled his nipples with one hand, while with the other hand she stroked him below. He remembered well the last time, when she had lain beside him and caressed him for what seemed like hours, even putting her mouth on him and sucking until he was hard enough to push her onto her back and take her as a man should take a woman, and she had cried out and held on to him, begging him not to stop.

Thinking about Rohaise's lips and tongue on him on that other night, while in the present her skillful fingers fondled and stroked and strayed into places where they should not be, Radulf finally felt his body harden.

Rohaise moved, straddling his thighs and then settling herself around his hips so that he penetrated her swiftly and deeply. With a stab of pleasure, Radulf pushed against her, before he realized that no man worth the name would allow his woman so much freedom in bed. There was only one way for a real man to take a woman; with her flat on her back and the man pounding into her from above. The sole question in Radulf's mind was whether he could lay Rohaise down without disengaging from her, because if they separated he might go limp again. But when Rohaise began to swivel her hips against him with increased enthusiasm, he decided it was worth the risk. Clasping her buttocks tightly, he pitched forward, forcing Rohaise onto her back where she belonged and driving himself deeper into her.

The damned woman kept moving and wriggling, but it no longer mattered what she did, because now Radulf was where he was supposed to be—on top of her—and he felt like a much younger man, hard and vigorous, thrusting into her again and again, powerful, potent, the way a man should be, until with a loud cry of relief his body gave up its seed. He went limp again at once, but that was of little concern to him; Radulf had just proven his manhood to himself. Rolling off Rohaise, he waited, expecting her voice.

"Thank you, my lord," she said, as he had taught her to do.

"You are a good wife." Radulf patted her shoulder, feeling expansive after his sexual success. A compliment now and then would help to keep Rohaise docile. If only she would bear a son!

When Radulf lay snoring on his side of the bed Rohaise curled up facing in the opposite direction so she could watch the broken shafts of moonlight filtering through the closed shutters. Once again, largely by her own insistent efforts, she had found physical release with Radulf. It had been a hollow pleasure. It always was. She had learned within a few weeks of her marriage to him that she was a much more sensual creature than her husband. She needed the kisses and caresses, the stroking and tenderness that Radulf would never give her. Sometimes, when he required her help to become hard, he would touch her, but it was never enough to satisfy her need for emotional warmth and tenderness.

Feeling utterly alone in the bed she shared with Radulf, Rohaise longed for a man who would kiss her and put his hands on her with gentle skill while he led both of them to a closeness that would last beyond his immediate physical desire. She had only a vaguely imagined picture of this man in her mind. He would be honest and kind, and always polite to her. She would not allow herself to put a name to the man, for to do so would be to admit to adulterous thoughts. But all the same she fell asleep dreaming of someone who would treat her with the affection she craved, and knowing in her heart that if ever he came to her she would do anything at all for him. Anything.

*   *   *

In her own room, one level below the lord's chamber, Joanna was also wakeful. The memories she forced out of her thoughts during the day loosed themselves upon her at night. Stricken by a hopeless passion for one man, married to another man, widowed within days, imprisoned by her father, and now pregnant, she saw all that had happened to her as the result of her meek obedience to Radulf's wishes.

Her obedience had harmed others as well as herself, causing Crispin's death—she was more and more certain of that—sending Alain out into the world as a fugitive, and catching innocent Piers in the same snare as Alain, for Radulf claimed that Piers was Alain's accomplice.

She wondered whether Radulf would tell her if Alain was dead. She decided he probably would, as a way of letting her know that he, Radulf, had triumphed. Thus, so long as she did not hear otherwise, she could assume Alain yet lived. She prayed each day for his safety, and for Piers, too.

At night, alone, lying in her bed or sitting wakeful in the windowseat, she nursed her sense of injustice over what had been done to her and encouraged the flame of rebellion that had begun to grow in her bosom. She would be careful, for she had a duty to protect Crispin's child, but somehow she would find a way to make things right—for herself, for her child, for Piers, and, most of all, for Alain. He had promised to return to her. She would see him again . . . she would.

She was certain of it. She would wait for him.

If Joanna had known how many years it would be before Alain came again to Banningford Castle, she might well have given up all hope and, in spite of her duty to her unborn child, might have flung herself from the battlements in utter despair.

Conceived in early summer, Joanna's child was born on the first day of spring in the Year of Our Lord 1135.

In advance of the great event Radulf brought a midwife from Chester to Banningford to see to the safe birth of his grandchild, but Joanna took one look at the dirty crone and begged Rohaise to be the one to receive the child from her body instead.

"I don't trust her," Joanna whispered, "because she is my father's hireling. Rohaise, you have helped several of the wives of Father's knights, so you are not without experience. Please, I want only you in the room."

"I'm not sure," Rohaise began, but Joanna clutched at her arms in near panic at the thought of the midwife handling her baby.

They were walking on the battlements, as they did each day, with Baird just a pace or two behind them. Joanna's body was so swollen in the last stages of her pregnancy that if she wanted to get up the steps to the top of the castle wall she was compelled to allow the detested Baird to help her. She hated having him take her arm, but she had no choice, and the walks were vital to her, providing not only exercise but the only contact she had with the busy life of Banningford. By her father's orders no one was permitted to approach or speak to her, but she could see people going about their business in the bailey and observe the men-at-arms who stood watch on the walls. There were one or two of the men who always made a point of smiling and nodding to her while Baird's attention was elsewhere, which made her feel a little less isolated.

"Rohaise, you must promise me." Joanna linked her arm through her stepmother's elbow. "Swear that when my time comes you won't leave me alone with that filthy creature."

"I'll see what I can do," Rohaise said, her voice too low for Baird to hear. "I noticed how much the midwife drank last night. Perhaps she can be bribed."

"Whatever you do, do it soon," Joanna begged. "I don't think I have much more time."

In fact, her labor began an hour after she returned to her chamber, the water breaking in a great gush and her pains coming hard and close together from the very beginning. Rohaise never left her side, but the midwife was in the room, too.

"Please make her leave!" Joanna cried, seeing the woman's dirty face and toothless grin. Rohaise waited until Joanna's most recent pain had subsided before explaining.

"Radulf insists on her presence," Rohaise said, "so she must be here. But I have made a bargain with her. For a large pitcher of wine and some

129

coins I had saved, she will sit in the corner and leave us alone. She has ordered Lys to bring up two buckets of boiling hot water and has agreed to send Lys away immediately afterward, so that we can be alone."

"Thank you. I'm glad to be relieved of the presence of Baird's woman, too. I know what I am asking of you, Rohaise. If something goes wrong and this child is born dead or imperfect in any way, my father will punish you as well as the midwife. And he'll punish me, too," Joanna finished, bracing herself against the next pain.

"I would never leave you alone," Rohaise said, taking Joanna's hands and holding them tight. "Hold on to me, now."

"It shouldn't be coming so fast," quavered the midwife, putting down her wooden winecup to come closer and look at Joanna. "It's a first child; ye should struggle for hours yet, perhaps days." She would have put a grubby hand on Joanna's abdomen, but Joanna shrank back.

"Leave me alone. Don't touch me."

"Have yer own way, then. Ye'll be screaming for me to help ye soon enough." With that, the midwife went to the door to admit Lys with the water. True to her bargain with Rohaise, she quickly shooed Baird's woman out of the room, then bolted the door.

"No one else will disturb us," Rohaise said to Joanna. Pointing to the corner, she told the midwife, "Sit down and stay there until I call you."

"Do what ye will. 'Tis naught to me so long as I'm well paid," said the midwife.

Now began the hard work of bringing forth new life, for as the midwife had noted, Joanna's body was not dawdling through the usually slow first hours of labor. It seemed to Joanna that her womb was as eager to expel the child as she was to hold it in her arms. And through every grinding pain and all the exhausting effort Rohaise was with her, holding her hands, wiping her brow, encouraging her. Rohaise made her walk up and down the chamber, and when she could no longer walk because her legs were trembling so badly, Rohaise ordered her to squat on a straw pallet on the floor and held her steady while Joanna pushed and pushed until she thought she would die of weariness. Rohaise kept her so concentrated on the task at hand and the child came so quickly that though she grunted and groaned and even cursed once or twice with the effort she was making, Joanna did not cry out until, toward the very end, she felt something hot and wet sliding out of her body. Then it was a shout of triumph, not pain, and Rohaise cried aloud, too, catching the child and lifting it while Joanna sank back onto the pallet. Quickly Rohaise cleaned the baby and wrapped it in a soft cloth.

A thin, determined wail came from the tiny mouth, and Rohaise turned the baby, holding up a corner of the cloth so Joanna could see it was a boy. Joanna stretched out her arms and Rohaise put the baby into them. Joanna held him against her breast. The baby nuzzled at her and she laughed, the first happy sound she had made in nearly a year.

"Help me to take off this dirty shift," she said to Rohaise. "My son Crispin is hungry." A moment later the baby suckled contentedly, but he soon drifted off to sleep.

"Well," said the midwife, leaving her corner and drawing near in an aura of wine fumes, "ye've birthed a fine son, haven't ye? I'll tell ye wot; let me inform Baron Radulf and I'll keep yer secret: that ye did it yerselves, without my help."

"I have already paid you," Rohaise began, but a happily relaxed Joanna stopped her.

"It's all right; let her be the one to tell my father, and let him give her the midwife's fee. It's nothing to us so long as little Crispin is healthy and whole. But, woman, give us a little time alone before you go down to the great hall."

"That I can do, for ye've not been unkind to me as some folk are, and ye gave me good wine. Ye birthed it so soon, girl, that the folks below won't be expectin' any news for hours yet." The midwife peered over Rohaise's shoulder, watching her wash the blood off Joanna's thighs and body. "At least she ain't torn. Ye'll heal quickly, girl, and soon be ready to receive a man again." Pouring herself yet another cup of wine, she retreated to her corner.

"I have no interest in any man but this one," Joanna murmured, kissing her baby's soft flaxen hair. "How fair he is."

"So he should be, with two golden blond parents," Rohaise said. "How sad that Crispin cannot see him." But she could tell that Joanna did not hear her. All Joanna cared about just then was her son.

Radulf was ecstatic. As soon as the midwife had relayed the good news, he bounded up the stairs and burst into Joanna's room.

"A boy!" he exulted. "At last! Unwrap him, Joanna, and let me see with my own eyes."

Joanna did as he ordered, and Radulf gazed down at his heir. The baby trembled at first in the cool evening air, but then he stretched out his little legs and opened huge deep blue eyes. Delicately, almost reverently, Radulf put out one thick finger and for an instant touched the tiny male organ.

"Good. Good," he said, now rubbing his hands together. "Baird says there is a woman on one of my farms whose child has died, leaving her with huge breasts full of milk. I'll order her to the castle tomorrow to be the wet nurse."

"No." Wrapping up her son again, Joanna held him closer, as if to protect him from her father's plans for him. "I will nurse little Crispin myself."

"Crispin? Never!" Radulf glared at her. "My grandson will be called William, after the great conqueror who granted these lands to my family."

"Crispin," Joanna repeated, giving Radulf hard look for hard look. "He will be named for his father."

"I said *William*."

She could tell he was angry. It never took much to raise Radulf's temper, but on this occasion

Joanna had a weapon and she was prepared to use it. Her months of isolation had changed her. She would never again be cowed by her father. On the surface she might appear to obey his wishes, but in her heart rebellion was now permanently lodged.

"He will be christened William Crispin," she said. "I will agree to the William, and you will agree not to call that wet nurse to care for him. After all, do you want your grandchild nourished on a villein's milk when I can provide noble food for him?" She knew her father's pride and saw that she had judged him correctly. With a growing sense of power, she watched him consider and accept her argument.

"Very well," he said, as if he was conferring a great honor upon her. "You may nurse your son."

"And I will attend the christening," she told him. "I have given you the heir you wanted and no one can doubt his parentage. Now my most unfair confinement is at an end."

"Do you think so?" Radulf's eyes narrowed, his lips twisted in a cruel parody of a smile. "Perhaps you do not yet understand the lengths to which I will go to protect my daughter and my grandchild. You, and the baby, will remain here, in this room, where I can be certain that you will be safe."

"I will attend William Crispin's christening." Never had she been so determined. "Even Baird could not prevent me."

"Baird." Radulf stared at her for a long time, his eyes cold, his face hard. She looked back at him, matching his coldness, until she saw understanding come into his eyes. Then he laughed, and it was not a pleasant sound. She thought he was surprised at her, and his next words proved she was right, though he did not say what she thought he might. "Truly, my blood runs in your veins. You should have been a man, Joanna, for you are as stubborn as I am. Very well; I will grant this one concession. You may attend the christening. But not the feast afterward; you and the child will return to this room directly from the chapel. Baird and Lys will escort you."

"*I* will carry my son." There was a peculiar sense of freedom about bargaining with him as an equal. "William Crispin will go to and from the chapel in my arms."

"I will choose the godparents." It was Radulf's counteroffer. He named the Earl of Bolsover and his lady, and added the name of a priest of nearby St. Justin's Abbey, a man renowned for his holiness. Joanna had no objection to any of these people, but she pretended to consider Radulf's selections for a while before nodding her head.

"I agree to those godparents," she told him. "Now, if William Crispin is to be healthy, he will need more fresh air and sunshine than you have granted me. In addition to one hour upon the battlements each afternoon, I will take him for a second hour in the morning, beginning the day after tomorrow."

"Do not press me too far," Radulf warned, but he did not refuse her demand.

"And Rohaise will attend me as she has been doing," Joanna finished, hiding a smile, for Radulf was looking at her with a new respect.

"Very well," he said. "Perhaps your fertility will prove contagious to Rohaise. But ask me for nothing more, and see that you take good care of my grandchild." Turning on his heel, he left Joanna's room.

"How did you dare to face him down like that?" Rohaise cried. "I cannot believe he gave in to you."

"Not to me," Joanna replied. "He did it for his grandson's sake. And I did not get what I want most; I did not win my freedom. He will never let me go. He will keep me here and use me to gain his own ends and not care that he ought to love and cherish me because I am his daughter and because I am a decent and honorable person who until recently has always followed his direction. My daughterly obedience has led me to this, to a tower room from which there is no escape."

Joanna did not add what else she thought: that her nine months of confinement had been in part a blessing, for they had given her uninterrupted time in which to consider the events surrounding Crispin's death. As the months had passed and the lingering shock and horror had receded, she had found she was able to recall more and more of the details of that night, until she remembered everything that had occurred. She wondered over and over what the killer's motive might be, until she reached her own conclusion. She knew who, and she knew why, but she could not tell

Rohaise, for such knowledge would endanger her stepmother's life, and Joanna would not put anyone else in jeopardy for her sake. It was enough that three good men had seen their lives destroyed.

Looking down at little William Crispin, she reflected that now she had two reasons for enduring and surviving whatever Radulf might do to her. The first reason was her son, whom she loved with an all-consuming passion. She would see to it that he grew up to be a different kind of man from her father. Perhaps he would be gentle and thoughtful, as Crispin had been. Her second goal was to bring Crispin's murderer to justice. She did not know yet how she would do it, how long it would take, but she was determined to find a way, and that determination strengthened and hardened her.

One week after her son was born Joanna celebrated her fifteenth birthday.

Part II

Yolande
Sicily, 1135–52

Chapter Nine

On March 21, the same day on which Joanna's son was born, Alain, Piers, and Father Ambrose arrived at Palermo. It had been a lengthy, and in many ways a painful, journey.

After successfully avoiding Radulf's searchers long enough to cross the border from England into Wales, they had headed westward toward Bangor, where Ambrose knew several monks at the abbey named for St. Deiniol.

"There we can rest in safety for a few days," Ambrose said, "while we arrange to take ship for Ireland."

They never reached Bangor. Along the way they were intercepted by Welsh tribesmen, who took them as prisoners to Gryffyn, the local leader. In a wooden hall set behind a tall log palisade, Ambrose, who as a priest was the member of their party most likely to be believed, recounted a simplified version of the events at Banningford Castle that had caused them to flee England.

"You speak well," said the dark, wiry Gryffyn, "but how do I know you are not spies, sent to learn if we Welsh are plotting against the wicked Normans? I cannot let you leave me without first confirming your story. You will remain here, as my guests, until the scouts I will send across the border have heard the latest gossip from our friends along the Marches."

"And when you learn that Father Ambrose has not lied, what then?" demanded Alain, who was much irritated by this delay.

"If it's truth you speak," Gryffyn retorted, "I'll see you on your way with my blessing, for I have no love for our neighbors to the east, who would dearly like to hold all Wales in the same tight grip that has strangled England for the past seventy years. But if I discover that you have lied, by the next sunrise your heads will decorate my gateway."

"We have not lied," Ambrose told him calmly, before Alain could give vent to the anger that rose in him too swiftly these days.

It took Gryffyn's spies more than a month to verify the tale. Having heard the report his men brought, Gryffyn informed his increasingly restless guests that Radulf was still seeking information about Alain and Piers, and Father Ambrose, too.

"He calls you a horse thief," Gryffyn told Ambrose. "Radulf says you rode into his castle on a mule and left it with three of his best mounts. 'Tis a shameful thing, Father, that a man of God should commit such an offense." By the twinkle in his eyes it was plain that Gryffyn was highly amused by the story, and that he admired Father Ambrose's cleverness.

"It was my plan to give the horses to the monastery at St. Deiniol." Ambrose looked not the least bit ashamed of what he had done. "I thought they could be sold and the silver used to feed the poor."

"What did you imagine would happen if simple monks were known to be selling stolen horseflesh?" Gryffyn asked. "Those horses, fine though they are, will cause trouble for St. Deiniol's. Give the horses to me instead. I'll see that they are smuggled into South Wales and then into England, to a location where their discovery and identification, if it ever occurs, will only confuse Baron Radulf as to where you have gone. As for the monks of St. Deiniol, out of admiration for your wit and your courage I will present six Welsh ponies to them, to use as they see fit. Just leave it all to me; my greatest joy is found in teasing and tormenting those border barons."

"He has probably stolen the ponies he'll give to St. Deiniol," Alain muttered afterward, but Piers and Ambrose both accepted Gryffyn's arrangements, so he made no protest. He did not really care what Gryffyn did. His heart was not in Wales, but at Banningford Castle. He longed to see Joanna, to put his arms around her and comfort her, to tell her he would love her always. He wanted to free her from her father's cruel imprisonment.

And he knew that Piers and Ambrose were right when they told him, each time he raised the subject, that there was nothing he could do that would not end in his death and, probably, in even stricter confinement for Joanna. Each night before he slept he repeated his vow to find a way to return to Joanna. But after Gryffyn freed him and his companions and found them a ship bound for Ireland, Alain set his face each day in a direction that took him ever farther from his love.

Once in Ireland, it was ten days before they found a ship sailing to Bordeaux, and their vessel was storm-tossed and mightily uncomfortable, but Alain was much relieved to discover that, unlike Piers and Ambrose, he did not become seasick; he did not need the few days they spent resting in Bordeaux once the ship had berthed there.

From Bordeaux they traveled overland, following the course of the River Garonne to Agen, where Ambrose fell ill, with vomiting and a severe flux of the bowels. At first Alain teased him, saying Ambrose had eaten too many of the luscious plums for which the area around Agen was famous, but when on the following day he and Piers also became ill, it was no longer a laughing matter.

In the difficult weeks that followed Alain began for the first time in his life to think seriously about his own death, and the possibility that he might not live long enough to see Joanna again. A deep, quiet sadness descended upon him, and with it a dignity and reserve that hastened the transformation from the boy he had recently been to a man of dignity and maturity.

It took them six weeks to recover enough from their illness to travel again, and by then it was late October. Still not in the best of health, they pressed on by easy stages to Toulouse, to Carcassonne, and finally to Narbonne, where an exhausted Ambrose insisted that they all must rest before undertaking the rigors of another sea voyage.

They spent the Christmas season in Narbonne, and it was not until mid-January that they set out again, only to encounter more of the difficulties that routinely plagued all travelers. They were within sight of Sicily when a storm blew them far to the northwest, driving their ship aground in Majorca, where they were forced to spend weeks waiting for it to be repaired. Finally, in mid-March, they approached Sicily a second time. Again they were battered by one of the severe storms that can strike suddenly in that part of the Middle Sea, but this time they were more fortunate. In a driving rain their captain brought his vessel around the jutting end of the breakwater into the harbor, where the rolling waves of the open sea were immediately replaced by calm water. To Alain's amazement, as the sailors cast out the lines and secured the ship at wharfside, the rain stopped and the sun broke through the clouds.

"A good omen for your arrival," the captain said

to Alain, glancing skyward.

"I hope so," Alain replied, his own eyes on buildings made of pale gold limestone, on a huge cathedral in the process of construction, on the spire of a minaret beside a gold-domed mosque. So strange, all of it, and so oddly beautiful. The streets in the vicinity of the harbor were thronged with folk in a variety of dress—Norman knights dressed in chainmail, Jewish merchants wearing dark robes and curly beards, Moslems in turbans and cloaks, smooth-shaven Greeks with dark eyes and high-bridged noses—for on this island, ruled by a tolerant and cultivated king, all religions and all conditions of men lived together in a state of peace. So Ambrose had told him, and now Alain saw the evidence of that claim.

Throughout their seemingly endless journey and despite his long illness, Ambrose had done his work well; Alain was able to understand a few words of the Arabic that drifted up to him from the dock, and he caught also the rapid sounds of Greek being spoken. Drawing in a deep breath of exotically odorous spring air, he looked westward, toward the royal palace that sat apart and a little above the city.

"At last." Having recovered from his seasickness enough to rise from his pallet belowdeck, Ambrose joined Alain at the rail, with Piers not far behind. "After so long a voyage I hope you are not disappointed by your first view of Palermo."

Alain did not answer. He was too busy watching the activities along the wharf to speak. Beside him, Piers squinted against the sudden brilliant sunshine so he could see better.

"The city looks dry," Piers said, "and dusty in spite of the rain. Not at all like England."

"There will be so much for you to see and to do," Ambrose told him, "that you will soon forget to be homesick."

"I am not at all homesick," Piers replied, looking around with great interest. "I am fascinated."

So was Alain, but not in the same way. While Piers, during the next days and weeks, embraced Sicily with the enthusiasm of a man who has left nothing behind to regret, Alain found that amid the colors and sounds and smells of this warm and sunny land there remained a corner of his heart that held the picture of cool, misty greenness. The central image of the picture was a girl with long waves of golden hair and eyes like finest sapphires.

Not that Sicily was all hot sunlight and brilliant color. They all three found cool oases where flowers bloomed and fountains played and green leaves sparkled with drops of breeze-blown water. But that was later. First, before they were allowed to explore the city and find lodgings, they had to undergo the examination required of all travelers who put in at Palermo.

This took place in a small building just off the wharf where their ship was docked. It was cool inside the thick walls, and the shade was welcome to eyes not yet accustomed to Sicilian sunshine. They were welcomed by a splendidly dressed man in a spotless white turban and a blue-and-white-striped robe. His dark beard was neatly trimmed, his black eyes searching and intelligent.

"I am Abu Amid ibn Amid, the royal commissioner in charge of gathering information." With a graceful wave of one hand, the man indicated that they should be seated upon a bench softened by pillows and a layer of thick carpets. In front of the bench a brass tray rested on a carved wooden stand, and on the tray were several pitchers and silver goblets, a plate of dried fruit, and a second plate piled high with pastries. Abu Amid seated himself opposite his guests. "Allow me to offer you refreshment while we talk."

The pitchers contained cooled fruit juices; the pastries were dripping with honey and crunchy with almonds; the dried fruits were dates and figs and apricots, all so intensely sweet they made Alain's teeth hurt. But the juice tasted wonderful. He emptied his cup and accepted more from the servant who silently glided about the room, seeing to their needs. When they had all been served Abu Amid began to speak, his carefully phrased Norman French giving Alain the impression that he had spoken the same words many times. As Abu Amid continued, it became clear that this was indeed the case.

"Our great and honored king, Roger II, being interested in all manner of knowledge, has formed a commission to gather from visitors to our land whatever geographical information they can provide. From what land do you come, good sirs, and how did you voyage here? Was it entirely upon ship, or overland for part of the way? Will you describe to me the rivers, mountains, cities along your route, the weather, the storms you encountered, the appearance of the skies at night?" He went on and on, asking question after question, until Alain felt completely drained, as if the journey itself had been drawn out of his memory to be recorded by the secretary who sat at a nearby table, writing down every word in flowing Arabic script.

They answered Abu Amid honestly; they had nothing to hide, and Alain at least had the feeling that the royal commissioner would have known if he had spoken one false word. Never was the questioning less than courteous, but it was persistent, and for their honest answers they had at the end of several hours a reward that was to change all their lives.

"Because you have knowledge of a land still unfamiliar to us," Abu Amid said, "you ought to have an interview with King Roger. But he sees no one at present. Only a month ago our beloved Queen Elvira died, and the king has withdrawn into seclusion to mourn her loss, for she was the very light of his life. However, there is another man who will be interested in what you have to tell of distant lands and uncharted seas. Especially the seas. Yes, you must meet the Emir of Emirs, Emir-al-Bahr, George of Antioch."

"Emir-al-Bahr? Ruler of the sea?" The title roused Alain from his sympathetic consideration of a king who had lost the woman he loved.

"You speak Arabic?" Abu Amid looked surprised.

"Only a little," Alain admitted. "Father Ambrose

has tried to teach Piers and me, but I fear we have been indifferent students."

"Father Ambrose." Abu Amid regarded the priest with glowing eyes. "This information makes you even more interesting. May I hope that you have come to Sicily for further study?" As he spoke, Abu Amid signaled with one hand, and within the blink of an eye two servants awaited his bidding just inside the chamber door. One of these servants was dispatched with a message for George of Antioch, informing him of the arrival of the three Englishmen, while the other servant was sent to collect the two small bags that had been left on the ship, all the belongings the travelers possessed. Before the day had ended Alain, Piers, and Father Ambrose were housed in sumptuous apartments in the home of George of Antioch, chief minister of the realm, second only to King Roger in power and influence.

"If this is not a palace," said Piers, looking from the open windows with their wide view of the harbor and the sea to the silk-draped walls, his glance then moving on to contemplate more furniture than he had ever seen in one room before, "then, in heaven's name, in what kind of place lives the king of this land? How can any man be richer than this?"

"I believe it would be possible for you to earn similar wealth," Ambrose told him. "Other men have done so. King Roger is said to be generous to those who serve him loyally."

"How many ships in the navy?" asked Alain, his gaze fixed upon the numerous craft in the harbor.

"Do they truly fight ship to ship and not just use the vessels to transport men and supplies? I know too little of such things."

"Those," said Ambrose, "are questions you must ask of our host when you meet him this evening. In the meantime I ought to be at my prayers, which I have neglected too often during our journey."

"I am going back to the harbor," Alain decided. "I want to look at those ships again. Piers, will you come with me?"

"Until I recover completely from the lingering effects of seasickness, I'd rather stay as far from the water as possible," Piers replied. "The garden I see below looks inviting. I think I'll walk there and try to accustom my legs to solid ground once more."

They separated, Piers making his way down an outside stairway to the garden. Seen at ground level, it was even more delightful than it had seemed from above, and for a time he wandered in peaceful contentment among artfully arranged trees and shrubbery. The flower gardens that would later in the season bloom in riotous exuberance were in full bud. Gravel paths led through the garden and strategically placed fountains delighted the eye and ear with the sight and soft sounds of falling, sparkling water.

Beyond the cultivated area near the house, Piers found a more natural space that offered shade and coolness in a day grown surprisingly warm. He brushed between two bushes and found another gravel pathway leading into the distance. Piers followed it to a tiny round structure. The walls of this building were carved in an open fretwork design, and there was no door, only an open, pointed arch. Inside he could see a wooden table, a patterned carpet, and some bright pillows on a low platform that was also covered with carpet. The whole was lit by several glowing brass lanterns. From within this pavilion came the sound of a low, rumbling snore. Wondering if perhaps he had inadvertently stumbled into a trysting place kept by George of Antioch, Piers stopped walking. Another snore issued from the pavilion.

"Sir, will you help me?" The words were spoken in accented Norman French. The soft female voice came from directly behind him. Piers whirled to confront the speaker.

At first he thought she was unreal, a figment of his imagination or some creature conjured up by a magician. Her hair was covered by a black scarf, and the robe that shrouded her from throat to toes was also black. Her eyes were dark, too. She looked as if she might melt back into the shadowy greenness from which she had emerged. Then whoever was in the pavilion snored again, making the mysterious creature giggle. The illusion was broken, and Piers saw she was just a very young girl.

"You want my help?" he asked.

"If you please." She caught at his arm. "Come with me. It's not far."

She led him off the path, into a thicket where untamed brambles grew. She knelt, pointing through the twining vines and leaves. Piers knelt beside her, not knowing what to expect.

"In there," she said. "There is a wounded bird. My arms are too short to reach it, but I think yours are long enough."

"You expect me to rescue a bird from that mess of thorns?" he asked. "Why don't you just leave it alone?"

"We can't do that." Her words made them companions in the rescue effort. "Please, sir, bring it out before the cats get it."

"The cats," Piers repeated, wondering what he had gotten himself into. All he could see of the girl was the pale shape of her face, her large, shadowy eyes, and two delicate, slender hands. From within the tangle of vines came a faint rustling.

"Please," the girl said, her glance sweet and trusting.

Reluctantly, Piers slid his right hand into the place, wincing when a thorn scratched him. His searching fingers closed around a trembling, feathered thing. He could feel the frantic beat of a tiny heart. Taking care not to hurt it, using his left hand to widen the passage, he drew the bird out of the thicket.

"Oh, thank you." The girl was on her feet. "Will you carry it, please? It's better not to move them too much, so if you will just keep it in your hand as you are doing now."

"Carry it where?" Piers asked.

"Back to the pavilion, of course." Once again she led the way. "Set it down gently, there on the table."

Piers did as she wanted. Upon looking around the pavilion, he discovered the source of the snores he had heard. On the platform extending around the wall of the pavilion, an elderly woman lay upon the silk pillows, her head and overweight body covered with dark clothing similar to the young girl's.

"Shh." The girl put a finger to her lips. "That's Lesia, my nurse. Let her sleep."

"What are you going to do?" Piers saw several strips of narrow white fabric on the table near the injured bird. On the platform sat a bird cage.

"I am going to bind up its wing as best I can," the girl said, "then keep it safe until it is healed and can fly again." She was working as she spoke. The bird sat still beneath her fingers and soon the job was done. Gently she placed the bird into the cage and closed the little door.

"Will it heal?" Piers asked, watching the girl's delicate face and her beautiful hands.

"Once it recovers from its fright, I think it will," she said.

"Not another injured bird?" Lesia the nurse had awakened. With a healthy yawn she heaved herself into a sitting position and swung her feet to the floor.

"Another?" said Piers. "Does she do this sort of thing often?"

"She has always been like this," the nurse said. "One day it's a stray cat, the next day a bird, or a dog, or a horse that needs her attention. I vow, if a poisonous viper were hurt, she'd try to heal it, too."

"Of course I would," said the girl. "All are God's creatures."

"Not snakes." Lesia was on her feet, glaring at Piers as if he were a serpent. "You, sir, must leave. At once."

"Lesia, please," said the girl, her dark eyes on Piers. "He may be a wounded creature, too."

"There are guards within sound of my voice," Lesia told Piers. "Out. Now. Leave."

"I stumbled in here by accident," Piers said, trying to pacify her. "I did not mean to intrude upon your privacy, and I offer my apologies for doing so."

"If you mean well, then leave us," Lesia ordered.

Her fiercely protective demeanor gave Piers no choice but to withdraw as quickly as he could. With a last look toward the girl, he left the pavilion. Her image went with him, making him wonder who she might be. He grimaced, recalling her words. A wounded creature? Not Piers of Stokesbrough! He had no hurts a girl like that might cure.

There was a balustraded white stone terrace along one side of the house, where George of Antioch liked to sit in the evenings, watching the light change on the sea and the ships leaving and entering the harbor. There were few sights more pleasing to George than a view of tossing waves with the sky arching above. It was there, on the terrace overlooking the sea, with the sky turning orange and gold and the shadows lengthening toward the purple of twilight that Yolande saw the stranger again.

She was sitting on the little stool placed next to the chair in which her Uncle George was relaxing, and she had just been teasing him that he was secretly longing to give up his honors ashore and go to sea again, when she heard footsteps.

"Here are our guests." George rose to greet them. He was a tall, impressive man in his mid-forties, with prematurely white hair and beard. A Levantine Greek by birth, who had fought for the Moslems in Tunisia before transferring his allegiance to Roger of Sicily, George was renowned as a brilliant naval leader. He was also broad of shoulder and he was blocking Yolande's view of the newcomers. She stepped to one side just as the man she had been expecting came through the arched windows and onto the terrace.

He was so thin. She saw again the telltale signs she had noticed earlier and knew he was emaciated and pale from illness. She had met other travelers who arrived in Sicily in a similar condition after a long sea voyage. A little rest and food would cure him and his two friends. They would require new clothing, too. She could tell they were all freshly bathed and barbered, but their garments were travel-stained and in sad need of repair or replacement.

"My niece, the lady Yolande." George drew her forward.

Waiting politely while he introduced her to each man in turn, Yolande noted every detail of their appearance. The priest was about ten years older than her uncle, brown of hair, kind of face, a man anyone would trust. Alain was tall and handsome, but enveloped in a sadness that set him apart from ordinary life. Instinctively she knew that Alain of Wortham would not look with delight upon the famously beautiful ladies of Palermo.

"So this is who you are, my lady. How fares the bird we rescued?" Sir Piers of Stokesbrough took Yolande's hand and laughed at her when she tried to say his full name.

"The bird does remarkably well, sir. I believe you will fare well also." She laughed back at him, marveling at his good looks. His eyes were dark brown, sharp and clever, deeply searching when they met hers. His straight hair was black as a starless night, his face narrow, his finely arched nose a miracle of human flesh. And his wide mouth was so beautifully shaped that Yolande had all she could do not to touch it with her sensitive fingertips. That she was able to restrain herself had more to do with her respect for her uncle and a desire not to embarrass him before strangers than with her own inclinations.

In the society of Norman Sicily, with its strong Moslem influences, it was rare for a woman to have as much freedom as Yolande. The ward of George of Antioch for the past ten years, she was not really his niece, but the term described their relationship so aptly that by now they both believed in it. In George's house there were innumerable servants to do his bidding, or Yolande's, and a head steward who ran the household, but at seventeen Yolande fancied herself the chatelaine. On this night, as she often did when foreigners came to visit, she wanted to play the great lady with George and his guests, sitting with them at table and listening to their conversation about distant lands.

Except that she could not pay attention, not after the talk had veered onto the subject of the Sicilian navy and the way it was used to suppliment King Roger's land forces during warfare. These were men's concerns. Yolande was interested in people and, at the moment, in one particular person. Happily, Piers had been seated at her left hand.

"You do not find the strategy of sea battles as interesting as do your friends," she said to him. It was not a question, just a statement of obvious fact, and she feared it was rather an inane opening, but it got her Piers's full attention.

"I am not fond of ships," he said. "I get seasick."

"So do I." Yolande laughed. "I remember too well my only sea voyage. When I was very small my mother brought me here from Salerno. I was so sick that she thought I would die before we landed. Since that time I have never again set foot on a ship."

"I wish I could do the same." Piers sighed ruefully, knowing the time would come when he would have to go to sea once more. Liking the musical sound of Yolande's soft laugh and the way she had centered her attention on him to the exclusion of the other three men, he looked more closely at her. There was more of her to see now that she had discarded her head scarf and the all-enveloping black robe. She wore a shimmering green dress, and her luxuriant dark red-brown hair was drawn up into a knot and decorated with thin gold ribbons. There was a loose end of ribbon that curled just behind her left ear. Piers thought if he tugged on it, all the intricately wound ribbons would come loose and her hair would tumble down around her shoulders. Or perhaps it would spill to her waist or below. Startled by his own imaginings, he looked into her eyes. They were as dark as her hair, with flecks of an even darker shade when she turned toward the light. They were soft eyes, warm and melting, set in a remarkably expressive face with a firm, almost square jaw.

"You said you came to Sicily as a child," Piers remarked, to keep her talking to him while the others still discussed naval affairs. "Was your mother George's sister? Or was it your father who was his brother?"

"Oh, no, we are not closely related at all. *Theo*," she spoke the Greek word with a charming accent, "does not just mean *uncle*. It is also a title of respect, for a young person to use when addressing an older man. In my case, it was my late stepfather who was distantly related to Theo Georgios."

"Then you are not Greek?"

"By adoption only." Yolande's lips curved in a bewitching smile. "My real father was a Norman baron who held lands in Apulia under our present king's father. He died before I was born. My mother was a Hungarian noblewoman. I am named for her." She delivered these last pieces of information with a lifting of her head and an expression that conveyed to Piers her delight at such an unusual heritage.

Piers looked at her more closely, noting the way the slight upward tilt at the corners of her eyes and the high cheekbones combined to give her a vaguely exotic appearance. This woman would never look old; she would only grow more beautiful with the passing years. Gazing at her, Piers knew he wanted to see her at age fifty, or sixty, or even older, when the soft flesh of youth had given way to the purity of fine bone structure and elegant bearing.

And yet he did not desire her with the sudden hot flare of passion he had from time to time known with other women. What he felt for Yolande during that first evening in her company was the beginning of friendship. The thought came to him that she would be a dependable, loyal friend. In her presence, listening to her talk or ask remarkably intelligent questions, it did not strike him as odd that he should so regard a woman, when he had never considered a female as a friend before. Only years later did he understand why he felt that way. It was because something within himself had recognized her at once for what she was.

Chapter Ten

It was near to midnight and a full moon lit the Tyrrhenian Sea with silver, touching the terrace outside the home of George of Antioch with a luminescent white glow. There Yolande found her guardian standing beside the carved balustrade.

"Are you dreaming again of ships and the sea?" she teased, linking her arm through his.

"I thought you had retired." When she leaned her head against his shoulder George pressed an affectionate kiss on her forehead. "I should have known you would want to discuss our guests before you sleep."

"Will they stay in Palermo?"

"I believe so. I have offered Father Amrose the use of my own library, as well as introductions to the Greek and Moslem scholars I know. He seems to be remarkably tolerant for a Latin priest, unlike most Northerners I have known. As for Alain, I like that young man."

"Because he is interested in your ships," Yolande said with a little laugh.

"Because he has a mind open to new ideas, because he is willing to learn what he does not know, a trait sadly missing in many Norman nobles," George correctly gently. He added in a dry tone, "And because he is interested in my ships."

Silence lengthened between them until Yolande, knowing he expected her to speak, asked, "And what of Sir Piers?"

"He is *not* interested in my ships." Still the same dry voice.

"Oh, Theo Georgios, that's not what I meant!"

"I noticed your interest in him," said George, and he waited to hear her next comment. He showed neither surprise nor disappointment at what she said.

"I could love a man like that," Yolande murmured. "Married to a man like that, I could be happy all my life."

"You appear to have made a serious decision based on remarkably short acquaintance," he noted. When she did not answer at once George spoke again. "*Poulaki mou,* my dear little bird, you know I want your happiness, for you are my niece in my heart, if not by blood. But have you never heard the rule that no man appreciates good fortune if he has not earned it by his own efforts?"

"I know you too well to take that for an idle

remark. What are you suggesting, Theo Georgios?"

"The Norman nobles in Apulia who hold land from Roger are conspiring among themselves once more," George told her. "Of all Roger's vassels, they are the most disruptive. This time they seek to play Roger against the Holy Roman Emperor, hoping to weaken Roger and thus increase their own powers. I suppose we will have to teach them yet another lesson in respect for their liege lord. And so, *poulaki mou,* if the reports my spies send me from the Italian mainland are confirmed, both Alain and Piers will soon have an opportunity to do great things."

Yolande thought about the possibility of war. It did not frighten her. Every year or two King Roger found it necessary to travel to the mainland to put down another revolt and either execute or forgive the leaders. She thought it was strange that his Norman subjects in Italy, the people in all his kingdom most beholden to Roger for their lands and wealth, should be the most treacherous, continually thwarting Roger's attempts to create a united and peaceful kingdom, while in Sicily the non-Christian Saracens were the most loyal of all his subjects, with the schismatic Greek Christians ranking close behind. George had told her this peaceful situation in Sicily existed because Roger would interfere with no man's religion so long as he was loyal to the king, and that all of Roger's subjects were treated with fairness according to their own customs.

"Do you believe," Yolande asked, "that Piers and Alain will win honors if there is fighting to be done this coming summer?"

"Honors indeed, for brave men," George said, kissing her forehead again, "and, for the most fortunate, treasures beyond price."

The following day George's three guests accepted his invitation to stay with him for an extended visit.

"I shall begin my work this very morning," Ambrose said to him. "I have seen your library, and I've had a note from a Greek friend of yours, who says he will call on me this afternoon." With that, Ambrose took himself off to the library, from which, in the weeks to come, he was seldom to emerge, though he was not lonely there, being frequently joined by a steady stream of visitors from among George's contacts in the community of scholars in Sicily. Even Abu Amid ibn Amid came to call; he and Ambrose were soon on close terms.

"Alain, if you will join me today," George said after Ambrose had left the room, "we will begin your education in naval matters at once."

"I would like nothing better," Alain replied, pleased to find a distraction from his constantly tormenting thoughts of Joanna, incarcerated and believing he had willingly deserted her. "What about Piers? He has not the taste for a sailor's life."

"I think Piers would do well to attach himself to King Roger," George replied. "But, because the king is in seclusion, it will take a few days for me to arrange an interview with him. Piers, perhaps in the meantime you would like my niece Yolande to show you the city and the countryside near Palermo?"

"I would be honored to have so lovely a guide," Piers responded. "I guarantee Lady Yolande every protection while she is with me." Having quickly discerned that there were many levels of meaning to most of George's comments, Piers understood that he was being given a rare opportunity to know Yolande better, but he believed he was also being tested, to discover if he would dare to take advantage of the chance to be private with the girl to press his attentions on her. The idea intrigued him, making him look at her with greater interest.

On that first day she led him on a tour of the city, from George's palatial home on its western side to the docks, the markets, the heavily built Norman churches, the more delicately constructed mosques, the numerous gardens.

"I have never seen any city like this before," Piers exclaimed in wonder. "It is so rich—I can tell as much from the buildings—so clean, and so peaceful. I haven't seen a single street fight all day," he finished, recalling sailors' brawls in Bordeaux and a knife fight he had witnessed in Toulouse.

"There is violence now and then," Yolande said, "but it is always quickly put down. The king watches over every detail. Even now, though in seclusion, he receives reports each day from his ministers. Roger is a great king, as you will learn when you meet him."

Believing Yolande's comments about Roger were influenced by George's opinion of the king, Piers did not respond.

That evening, George offered Alain a permanent assignment as his aide. With protestations of gratitude, Alain asked for a day or two to think over the proposal. Later, in their own chambers, Alain and Ambrose came near to quarreling over what his answer should be.

"I cannot accept the offer," Alain said. "As soon as possible, I must return to England, to Joanna."

"Alain, Alain," sighed Ambrose, "when will you accept the truth? Now that Joanna is a widow, Radulf will marry her off again. Any father would do the same. Radulf will wait just long enough to be certain she is not with child and then he'll chose another husband for her. Or, if she is with child by Crispin, he'll wait until it's born before he sees her marry again. Either way, Joanna is not for you, Alain. She never was, and in your heart you must know it."

"I do *not* know it! I will never stop loving her. Never!"

"We cannot return to England yet," Piers put in. "If we do, the instant we are recognized, we will be killed. Much good our return will do Joanna then."

"We?" Alain stared at him.

"Do you think I would let you go alone?" Piers put a hand on Alain's shoulder. "Uncle Ambrose is right. For the present, at least, we must stay away from England. So, while we are in Sicily, seize this opportunity. Take the commission George offers. You know you will enjoy the shipboard work."

Alain pulled away from him to stand at the window, looking out toward the harbor in the distance. When Piers would have followed him Ambrose shook his head. After a while, without turning around, Alain spoke.

"I have always found your advice to be good, old Sir Piers. You are right once again." Now he did turn, looking toward Ambrose. "I am sorry I was so sharp with you. I know you want only good fortune for me. But nothing, *nothing*, will ever make me stop loving Joanna."

"I do not ask you to stop loving," Ambrose responded. "Only to be sensible about it."

"I will promise you this much," Alain said. "I will stay in service to George of Antioch until I have made myself too powerful to be crushed by Radulf."

"I am glad to hear you say it," Piers told him, "for I intend to remain in Sicily myself. I like this land better with every day that passes."

On the next morning Piers and Yolande rode out of the city and along the coast, following a track that wound through prickly pear and fragrant pine, stopping on a little rise above the sea to eat their midday meal. Yolande had brought a rug for them to sit on and a basket of food that was as mixed as the cultures of her homeland.

They ate the familiar bread and cheese, but there was also a concoction of cold mixed vegetables and rice, aromatic with mint and garlic, packed back into the oval purple vegetable shell, the whole carried in a special ceramic dish. They ate this with spoons, and Piers found it remarkably tasty when washed down with the local red wine.

"The dish is called *melitzanes yemistes,*" Yolande said in answer to his question about the unfamiliar vegetable. "Theo Georgios says the Arabs brought *melitzanes* to Sicily from India."

They ended their meal with the inevitable honey-and-nut pastries that Yolande so obviously loved, and dried fruit.

"Don't you ever eat fresh fruit?" Piers asked, selecting a plump date.

"Of course we do." Yolande licked honey off her fingers, laughing at him and sending a warm glance from her dark eyes. "It is still early in the season, so we are eating fruits dried last year. Wait until summer, when the new fruits ripen. Then we have fresh apricots and peaches, and wonderful figs. Have you ever tasted melon? So sweet, so juicy, like the food of paradise."

At that instant it seemed to Piers that the taste most resembling the food of paradise would be Yolande's lips. How sweet it would be to kiss her, to taste the honey from the pastry she had eaten, a drop of which still lingered at one corner of her mouth; how lovely to inhale the fragrance and the sweetness of the dried apricot upon which she was now nibbling.

He was surprised at his reaction to her, and a

little shocked. Where women were concerned, he had enjoyed whatever favors were offered, while at the same time maintaining his self-control, even in the transports of heated passion. He had never fallen in love in the same way in which Alain loved Joanna, and he hoped he never would. Longing for his lost Joanna had destroyed Alain's spirits and his good sense, robbing him of his zest for life. Even now, half a world away from Joanna, love for her still tortured Alain, keeping him wakeful at night, ruining his appetite, making him solemn before his time. Considering Alain's sorry condition, Piers decided he never wanted to love a woman. And yet, Yolande was so charming.

"This is the way I like the sea," she said, flinging out one hand in the direction of the glistening blue waves. "I like it best when it is there, beyond the beach, and I am here, safe on high ground."

"Don't let your uncle hear you say that." Piers chuckled, sharing her feelings.

"Ah, he knows; he knows." She turned to him, her dark eyes sparkling, her pearly teeth showing when she smiled. She wore her red-brown hair in a single thick braid that swung against her shoulder when she moved. "You may kiss me if you like."

"I would like to very much," Piers said, taken aback by the innocent invitation. "But I won't do it. You are too innocent, too trusting, and I will not betray your uncle's confidence in me, that I would prove an honest escort and a firm protector of his niece."

"I refuse to be ashamed of wanting you to kiss me, so don't try to make me feel that way." She thrust out her lower lip, whether to pout or to keep herself from weeping in embarrassment Piers could not tell. He caught his breath. She was adorable, with her eyes open wide, her cheeks slightly flushed, and her mouth—heaven help him, that tempting mouth! How could any man resist her? Before he could make a move, either to touch her as he wanted to do, or to flee from her as he knew he should, she was on her feet, shaking out her skirts.

"We may as well return to Palermo," she said briskly.

"Is that why you brought me here?" he asked. "To entice me into kissing you?"

"I had hoped you would want to kiss me without enticement on my part," she told him, her sudden display of youthful hauteur making him smile.

"Has no one ever warned you how dangerous it is for a maiden to lead a man into a secluded spot and then offer such an invitation? Are you so naive that you don't know what a man might do to you?"

"But you would not harm me," she said with perfect confidence. "You are my friend."

"Yes, I am, and it's our friendship I don't want to betray. Heed me, Yolande." He meant to issue a stern warning that she should never behave with any other man as she had with him, but before he knew what he was about, he had pulled her into his arms. Her hands slid around his waist and up his back until they rested on his shoulders. A woman of more experience would at once have lifted her face for his kiss, but Yolande nestled her head beneath his chin. He held her gently, as if she were some dark, exotic bird whom close confinement might damage. He felt her sigh and stir against him, and press closer. With one hand he brushed back the hair that had come loose from her braid. The skin of her cheek was soft and perfectly smooth. He touched her cheek again and let his fingers stray toward her lips. Now she did raise her head from his chest to look into his eyes, and he knew she hoped he would kiss her after all.

He almost did. He was shaken to discover how much he wanted to put his mouth on hers and take the sweetness she offered. He bent his head. What stopped him was the reaction of his own body. He stood with one arm around her, with his mouth just a breath away from hers and his thumb gently caressing her lower lip—until he felt himself harden in a surge of desire and knew that if he kissed her he would not stop at kissing. His ever-active, too-clever mind warned him that he could not afford to despoil the niece of the man who had the power to condemn him and his friends to severe punishment—or to guide them toward a brilliant future. He could not be responsible for Alain's downfall, and certainly not for Ambrose's. He had more to consider than one innocent girl's lovely body, or his own physical response after months of abstinence.

"I'll help you pack the dishes," he said, dropping his arms and moving away from her. Under his breath, he added sarcastically, "You've just spoiled any chance you might have had with her, old Sir Piers. Tonight you take Alain, and both of you find women down by the docks." But when he looked at Yolande, on her knees, her head averted, stuffing the remains of their meal into the basket, he knew with frightening certainty that even if he went to another woman, it would be Yolande's face he saw and Yolande's name he would whisper into the darkness.

"What, is George's niece not with you?" teased Alain. "Not hiding behind a corner, waiting to tempt you with some new dish prepared especially for you?"

"For a man who pretends to work from dawn to dusk, you seem to notice the most unimportant details about other men's lives," Piers responded, only half in jest.

"Yolande, unimportant? I don't think so." Alain threw an arm across Pier's shoulders, and they stood for a while, looking out the window of the chamber they shared, at the third day of drizzling rain. "She's the reason you wanted to find a brothel the other night, isn't she? But a whore is no substitute for the woman you really want. That's why I refused to go with you. It's also the reason why you did not go either, in the end." Alain regarded him with a knowing look. "Of course, if you're feeling desperate, George could probably provide a nice, clean woman for you. They have strange customs on this island. It must be the Saracen influence."

"Which is remarkably strong, yet not evil." Ambrose had come into the room in time to hear the last of Alain's remarks. "Unless, of course, the evil lies in my finding but few faults in the hearts and minds of the non-Christian scholars I've met. How are you, Alain? I've not seen you for several days."

"George is driving me hard," Alain said, "but I enjoy every moment of my work. I have hope of witnessing a sea battle before long."

"Do not wish for such a thing." Ambrose crossed himself. "I remember warfare all too well."

"Which is why you will appreciate the strategy of George's most recent battle." Alain launched into a detailed description. When he had finally left them, saying he needed to ask George a question, Piers and Ambrose smiled at each other.

"I knew," Ambrose said with a satisfaction he did not trouble to conceal, "that if Alain could only set his thoughts on some subject other than the lady Joanna, he would begin to recover from his devotion to his lost love."

"I do not think he *has* recovered," Piers said. "Nor will he ever forget the lady. I know Alain too well to imagine that Joanna has been completely banished from his thoughts."

Chapter Eleven

The reports that George was receiving from Roger's mainland domains were soon proven correct. The ever-restive Norman nobles who held lands in southern Italy in vassalage from Roger had once more risen in revolt against their overlord. Worse, in an attempt to escalate the strife and thus encourage the Holy Roman Emperor to take their side in the current dispute, the insurgent nobles concluded a treaty with the northern Italian city of Pisa, which was under the emperor's rule. Emboldened by this advantage, the Norman nobles attacked Naples by land and, on the twenty-first day of April, the Pisan fleet appeared off Naples, blocking the sea approach to the city.

The news roused Roger of Sicily from the torpor of mourning into which he had been sunk since the death of his queen in February. He called his most trusted advisers to the royal palace, foremost among them George of Antioch. George took advantage of the occasion to introduce his guests to the king.

Having grown used to the luxury of George's house, the three Englishmen were not as astounded as they might otherwise have been by the oriental opulence in which the king of Sicily lived. The royal palace was built on higher ground than the city of Palermo, a mile and a half to the west, where it was cooler and much quieter. The Norman rulers of the island had taken an old Saracen fortress and enlarged and altered it, adding courtyards, gardens, fountains, and even a tower topped by a copper-domed observatory, from which the royal astronomers watched the sky each night. On the outside still a strong fortress guarded by three hundred specially chosen men, on the inside the palace had become, during the reigns of Roger and his late father before him, a treasure trove of silk hangings and gold-enhanced mosaics, of carved woods and filigree and intricately patterned carpets, of vases and delicate objects from far-distant lands, the whole made even richer and more alien by the lavish use of perfumes and incense, so the air was filled with the scents of sandalwood and patchouli and with the fragrances of roses and lilies wafting in from the gardens.

The chamber into which George and his guests were ushered had a high, honeycombed ceiling, gilded and painted with fanciful scenes of clouds and birds. A wide mosaic frieze in a geometric pattern ran around the upper wall, and below it a series of murals showing birds and palm trees and a garden crowded with multicolored flowers. Against one wall a fountain splashed, its water trickling into a marble-lined channel that ran down the center of the room. Silken cushions padded the benches set in niches around the room, and the whole was lit by indirect sunlight that came from the garden court just outside, where yet another fountain played and real flowers bloomed to match the painted ones on the inner walls.

In the center of all this splendor, clad in a glittering red-and-gold brocade robe cut in the Moslem style, stood Roger II, King of Sicily, dark of hair and beard and gray-eyed, his noble, handsome face still touched by the shadow of grief.

After Yolande's remarks about Roger receiving his ministers' reports every day in spite of his mourning seclusion, Piers was not at all surprised to discover that Roger knew about the Englishmen who were staying with George. After welcoming Ambrose in the warmest of words and bidding him to make use of all that his kingdom held in the way of books or fellow scholars, Roger turned to the two younger men.

"George says you are willing to take service with me and help to fight my rebellious vassals," Roger said.

"I would like to accept George's offer to continue to work under him," Alain announced. The look Roger and George exchanged at his words convinced Piers that Alain's future assignment had been decided before ever he had entered King Roger's audience chamber.

"I have no objection to your decision," Roger told Alain. Turning to Piers, he said in a joking way, "What about you, sir? Would you be a sailor, too?"

"No, my lord." Piers spoke up promptly and firmly. "I prefer to stay on land. If you will allow it, I would fight ashore by your side or wherever you wish me to be. I am a fair swordsman, my lord."

"I know many men who can fight well," Roger said, "first among them my recalcitrant vassals in South Italy. What I value most is what those vassals sorely lack—loyalty. Can you give me that, Sir Piers? Can you pledge your oath to me and keep it?"

"I can, my lord," Piers said, and meant it, for he had liked Roger on sight.

"I also pledge myself to you," said Alain, going down on one knee and putting out his clasped hands in the old Norman way.

Roger took Alain's hands between his own while Alain swore fealty to him. Afterward, Roger did the same with Piers.

"Welcome to my kingdom," Roger said, embracing each of them. "For my part, I swear to use you hard and reward you well."

The rebel lords captured Naples, but they were soon trapped within its walls. When Roger's army appeared outside the walls and his fleet chased the Pisan ships homeward and then, on the fifth of

June, barricaded the Neapolitan harbor, the rebels settled down for a long siege. Alain had thoroughly enjoyed the excitement of chasing the enemy ships northward, but he found the blockade tedious and boring. He yearned for action.

Ashore with Roger, Piers was anything but bored. After years of contention with his too-powerful vassals, Roger's patience was exhausted. From late summer to early winter he swept through his South Italian fiefs, ousting the current governments from every city and town and installing his own sons as rulers in the most important fiefs of Apulia, Bari, and Capua.

"I'll have done with those rebel wretches for good and all," he said to Piers, who had become a trusted, if still junior, lieutenant to the king.

"They won't give up easily, because they believe they will soon have help," Piers noted. "The latest reports from your spies say the Emperor Lothair is planning to leave Germany and cross the Alps to come against us next summer."

"Us?" Roger grinned at him, clapping one hand on his shoulder. "George was right about you; you are one of us now."

"So I am, my lord," Piers said, thinking that Yolande, too, had been right. Roger of Sicily was a fine military commander, always hiding well his distaste for the violence of war, and from what Piers had seen of him, Roger was also a remarkably able ruler. Piers had no second thoughts about having pledged himself to the man.

By mid-January both land and sea forces were weary and, at George's suggestion, Piers was given leave to return to Palermo with himself and Alain. Once more, even on the smoothest of seas, Piers was violently ill.

"I swear to you," Piers said to his companions, once they had rounded the breakwater into Palermo harbor and he had recovered enough to speak, "I swear I will not leave Sicily again until Roger builds a bridge over the strait at Messina."

"What a marvellous idea." George burst into laughter. "Only tell him how it can be done and he'll see to it, I'm sure. And your fortune will be made. You will feel better, Piers, once you are back in your old room and have enjoyed a bath and put on fresh clothing."

Soon Piers did feel better, and was delighted to see Ambrose again. But throughout the relaxed afternoon of catching up with each others' news, Piers knew he was only waiting, passing the hours until evening came and George and his guests would gather on the terrace. There he would see Yolande again.

In fact, they gathered in the long narrow room next to the terrace, for the wind off the sea was cold and an icy rain was falling. Piers realized with a rueful inward laugh that he had been expecting this evening to be like all those earlier nights, when the air had been warm with advancing spring. But the season had changed, and he had changed, too, had grown older and harder. Having seen the horrors of war, he did not laugh so much now, and he bore two scars. The one along the left side of his jaw was barely a nick, the result of not deflecting an enemy's blow until almost too late. But he had deflected it, and the wound had healed, and now he seldom thought about it. The second scar was on his right hip, a shallow puncture wound that miraculously had not festered. Other men had suffered far worse. He was lucky.

Yolande came into the room after the men had gathered. She went first to George, kissing him on both cheeks.

"I will tell you again, Theo Georgios, how happy I am to see you home safe and well," she said. "And you, Sir Alain. Sir Piers, welcome back." She gave a little gasp when she saw the scar on his jaw, but she recovered quickly and put out her hand. Piers clasped her fingers in his, feeling a delicate trembling that she quickly brought under control.

She, too, had changed in the eight months since they had parted. She was no taller than she had been in the previous spring, nor any heavier. She wore her dark hair in the same style, the knot at the crown of her head laced with pale blue ribbons to match her blue silk gown. Earrings of gold and pearls on thin wires swung when she moved her head. She watched him with a serene and level gaze.

He had left her a girl, eager, open, innocent. In his absence she had matured into a young woman. A remarkably attractive young woman, but, on the surface at least, cool and distant. He wondered if her self-possession was but a disguise for her true feelings, or if while he had been away she had found someone to kiss her as he had refused to do. The thought sent a curious sinking sensation into the pit of his stomach. Surely not; surely she was too well-guarded for any man to take advantage of her. But she had not been well-guarded when he was with her. He could have done anything he liked to her. Who was to say that someone else had not taken what he had scrupulously refused? Did she love another now? Was that the reason for her apparent coolness toward him? What he wanted in that moment was for Yolande to look at him with her warm and melting gaze of the previous year.

"Welcome back, Baron Piers of Ascoli. Congratulations on your new title. I feel certain you earned it well." Her voice was soft, a little husky. Her hand was still clasped in his. "Were you seasick?"

"Most horribly." Thanking heaven for the glint of familiar humor she had shown, he tucked her hand into his elbow. "Would you like me to tell you all about it?"

"Not at the table, sir. Perhaps later." She sounded so distant, so perfectly controlled and polite. She must love someone else. But why should that trouble him so sorely when he did not love her himself? His usual wit having deserted him, Piers said the only thing he could think of.

"Will you ride with me tomorrow?"

"It will rain tomorrow," she said, her eyes lowered.

"The day after, then. Or the day after that," he persisted.

"We shall see. Sometimes in winter it rains for a week or more without stopping."

They dined on roast kid with leeks and a many-petaled, flowerlike vegetable that Yolande called *anginares,* and they drank a fine red wine. They ended with the honey-and-almond pastries Yolande like best, with trays of dried fruits and bowls of nuts set out for those who wanted to nibble on something less sweet. Of all that rich feast, Piers could swallow only a bite or two.

They talked about the war and the invasion expected in the summer, to be led from Germany by the elderly Emperor Lothair. Alain had much to say on the subject, usually in agreement with George's opinions. Ambrose contributed a few thoughts to the conversation, and even Yolande said a word or two from her place beside Piers. Piers sat silent, turning his wine goblet round and round by the stem, wondering what in the name of all the saints was wrong with him that he should feel unwell now, when he had finally reached solid, steady land.

"Theo Georgios has kept me well informed about you and Alain," Yolande told him. "I know how bravely you fought for Roger and how indispensable you have become to our good king. You and Sir Alain are both to be commended."

"It was nothing." Piers brushed aside the compliment, then cursed himself for being so brusque with her.

"It grieves me to see your wound," she said in a voice just above a whisper. "From the look of it, it might have been a killing blow."

"Would you have missed me?" He tried to keep his voice as low as hers had been to avoid drawing notice to them, but he sounded bitter because he feared her answer would be that she would scarcely have known the difference if he had died.

"That is a foolish question, as you well know." Her eyes met his, and in her soft and melting glance Piers saw for a moment the Yolande he had first known.

"Perhaps," she said, just before George and Ambrose claimed her attention, "perhaps it will not rain tomorrow after all."

But on the morrow it did rain, and Yolande proved remarkably elusive, keeping to her own room except for the evening meal, when it was impossible to have a private conversation with her. George had new guests—a group of scholars from Alexandria—and the talk during dinner was lively and erudite, but Piers heard little of it. He could not bear to sit still, and excused himself as soon as he decently could, to wander about the house, ending his prowling on the damp, windswept terrace. Alain found him there.

"Are you avoiding her or waiting for her?" Alain asked, leaning casually against the balustrade.

"Who?" Piers sounded so angry, even to his own ears, that he immediately apologized. "Sorry; my mood is foul these days."

"It's understandable. You are battle-weary. So am I, but I was more fortunate than you. It wasn't quite so bloody where I was stationed. And I'd guess that you haven't had a woman recently."

"I'd guess that you haven't either, my friend." Piers saw Alain's teeth flash white in the evening darkness. "I seem to be *old* Sir Piers in truth. I felt the urge a few times—all right, don't laugh, more than a few times, especially when I was afraid the night before going into battle—but whenever I considered the women available to me I found myself praying or cleaning my weapons instead. Those are an old man's actions, and I am but recently turned three and twenty."

"Perhaps you aren't old at all," Alain said. "Perhaps you have just grown up."

"I grew up two years ago, on the day I was knighted," Piers said in a voice that allowed no dissent to that statement.

"Do you want her?" asked Alain, the question eliciting a sound from Piers that might have been a snarl, or a growl, or even a rude laugh at his own confusion.

"I honestly don't know," Piers replied. "Her body, yes; I'd take her in an instant. But the rest of it? She's not a woman to be used and then discarded, forgotten like one of those creatures who follow the army, who move on to another man as soon as one man has finished. *She* will accept but one man in her life. I knew that much about her as soon as I met her. She is kind and sweet and intelligent. And strong. I detest weak and whining women, but she is the sort who would hold her husband's castle safe in his absence, if need be against overwhelming forces. She is an admirable woman."

"And then there is George," Alain said softly.

"I am not unmindful of the advantages of allying myself with George of Antioch," Piers said. "I like and respect the man, equally as much as I admire Roger himself. Thanks to my ready sword and Roger's generosity, I have accumulated a fair amount of treasure in these last months, a small estate in Apulia to go with my title of baron, but that's nothing compared to George's holdings. If I asked for her he might refuse me. Or *she* might."

"*She*. You have not spoken her name." Alain's voice was still soft.

"Yolande. *Yolande.*" Piers paused, letting the word blow away on the wind. "I want her, I admit that much, but I do not think I love her, certainly not in the way you love Joanna.

"When you return to England I will go with you," Piers went on. "Never think I won't. Clearing your name means clearing mine, too, and both are important to me, as is finding Crispin's real murderer. But I do not think Yolande could survive such a terrible journey. I would have to leave her behind."

"We cannot return for some time yet," Alain said. "I'd take wing and fly to Joanna's side tomorrow if I could, but I have come to understand the wisdom of Ambrose's contention that the best way for me to arrive in England is with lands and wealth and a notable title, perhaps even as an ambassador from Roger to whoever is king of England. That way I'll have a better chance of proving myself innocent of murder. But it will take years until then, and in the meantime you must decide about Yolande. George has her interests always in mind, and he won't let her languish unwed much longer."

"I know." Piers stared out at the storm-tossed,

heavy seas and felt his stomach twist into an all-too-familiar knot. "She is seventeen, well past the age for a girl to marry. I'm sure George has had offers for her."

"If you plan to ask for her," Alain advised, "you ought to do it promptly."

"But do I want to marry her or not? Damn!" Piers pounded a clenched fist on the white stone rail. "I have never been so uncertain of anything. She deserves a husband who will care for her and treat her with kindness and respect."

"And you would *not* treat her as she deserves?" asked Alain. "Do you know of another man who would be as kind to her as you would be? More importantly, can you think of her in another man's arms and not feel your blood turn cold within you, and your heart stop beating? Can you bear to think of her carrying another man's child?"

"Dear God in heaven." Piers grabbed the railing with both hands, raising his face toward the dark, cloudy sky, as if he expected to find there an answer to his dilemma. They stood side by side on the terrace, Alain safe behind the careful barricades he had built around his heart to keep himself from any further pain, and Piers lost in turmoil as stormy as the roiling sea or the wind-blown clouds. After a while Alain put out his hand and rested it on Piers's shoulder. And Piers, still looking seaward but grateful for the steady friendship that had lasted since they were lonely children together in a strange castle, lifted his own hand and placed it on Alain's shoulder.

*   *   *

Behind the two men, in the long and narrow room that opened onto the terrace, Yolande stood in one of the arches, watching them. She had heard part of their conversation; enough to confirm what she already knew, what she had known for nearly a year. Piers liked her, but he did not love her the way she loved him. How young and incredibly innocent she had been to give her heart to him within a day of meeting him, and how hurt and betrayed she had felt when he had departed from Palermo after declining to kiss her, and without telling her what he felt for her. She had nursed her injured pride all through the summer and into winter with promises to herself to be cruel to him when he returned. But she had needed only the sight of his scarred jaw, the tightly drawn skin around his eyes, the hard line of his mouth, to understand that she would never cease to care for him.

As Alain had guessed, there were other men who either had made application to George for her hand or who would do so soon. If she refused all of them, George would tell her she should have been married and a mother by now, and only his deep affection for her had kept her a maiden in his house for so long. One way or another, Yolande believed she would be wed before the summer campaign began. It was up to her to make certain that the man she married was the man she loved and wanted. She knew of only one way to accomplish what she desired. She would give to Piers her most treasured gift. She would give him her maidenhood.

*   *   *

The sun could not banish the chill, and the wind was still strong after the storm, billowing out the cloaks of the man and woman who rode away from the coast and into the hills, where it was warmer.

"We've gone too far," Piers called, reining in his horse. "George expects us to return by midday, and I have no wish to explain an overlong absence to your nurse. Lesia did not want you to come out with me at all."

"Pay no heed to Lesia," Yolande said. "She fusses no matter what I do. Let us rest our horses here for a while before we turn back."

Giving Piers no time to object, Yolande dismounted. She found an icy little spring and let her horse drink; then she seated herself in the sun, on a rock well sheltered from the wind.

"It's warm here, Piers. Come and sit with me. Oh, do come here. You look ridiculous sitting there so sternly on your horse."

She heard him muttering as he dismounted, and she bit her lip to curb her impatience. Piers was such an honorable man. Having once refused even to kiss her when they were alone in this way, would he now resist what she planned to offer him? She looked around the fold in the hillside where she sat, noting the scrubby bushes and the withered grasses, the yellow earth and jutting rocks of the place where she had chosen to give herself to him. She did not mind the barrenness of the scenery. Piers would make it beautiful.

"In the summertime it would be too hot here,"

she said as he sat down beside her, "but now it's just right, don't you think? Like a little room, away from the wind, out of the cold."

"What you call cold feels like spring to me," he said.

"Will you talk to me of nothing but the weather?" she cried, her nerves on edge over what she planned to do. "Or the battles you have fought, or the battles to come, or Theo Georgios's ships, or Roger's generosity? Piers, have you no feeling for me at all?"

He drew up his legs, wrapped his arms around his knees, and sat staring into the distance until she thought she would scream with irritation and nervousness and a breathless anticipation. He had to want her, just a little. He had to!

"I am ambitious," he said at last.

"I'm glad to hear it." She bit off the words, wishing he would say something about the two of them. But any conversation was better than none at all. She seized the opening he had given her. "I can help you advance yourself."

"That's just the problem." He looked at her, his dark eyes moving from her gleaming red-brown hair to her beautiful face, to the soft swell of her bosom revealed by the thrown-back cloak, to her fine, pale hands. "Is it right for me to take advantage of you for the sake of my ambition? I think not, Yolande."

"Last spring I asked you to kiss me," she said, shaken by fear that he would rise and remount his horse and leave her sitting there alone. "Now I tell you that if you do not kiss me, I will kiss you."

"Another man would not hesitate," Piers murmured, almost to himself. "Why do I?"

"Yes, why?" she demanded, praying her words would not make him too angry for tenderness. "Why do you fight so against the thing you want to do when you know it is what I want too?"

"Because I have a habit of considering the consequences before I act." Consequences or no, he caught her chin, tilting her face toward his. "You are remarkably lovely."

"Will you force me to ask again?" she whispered. "Or will you kiss me?"

A faint smile lit his eyes.

"Having come this far, how could I not?" he asked, and put his mouth on hers.

After all his hesitation she did not know what to expect from his kiss. Certainly she had never imagined anything like the fire that blossomed and grew between them. She knew her arms were around his neck, her fingers winding through his black hair. She knew his arms were clasping her ever more tightly against him, knew she was on her back with Piers's muscular thighs straddling hers. She was aware of the sudden delicious hardness and heat of his desire. But all of her being, every tumultuous thought, was centered upon her mouth, and his mouth, and his tongue, seeking entrance, touching her tongue, stroking, stroking, until thought ended in the sweet delight of Piers devouring her, branding her, making her his. The kiss left her gasping for air, whimpering with a new, unexplained need. She could not get close enough to him; she wanted to be part of him.

He was kissing her throat, his hands were on her breasts, and she was moaning with every breath.

"Piers," she cried, pulling him back to her mouth, "I've waited so long, so long for you. Oh, Piers, touch me, touch me."

She hardly knew what she meant by that cry, but Piers knew. He did not think she had ever been kissed by a man before, and now he watched the first bloom of desire grow in her with remarkable swiftness, saw her eyes large and unfocused while her cheeks blushed rosy red each time he stroked his hand across her breasts. Through the wool of her gown he could feel her nipples rise when his fingers brushed against them. Eagerly she pressed her breasts against his searching hands and pushed her hips toward his hardness.

He could have her. She would open herself to him and offer her sweetest, most priceless gift. Even now she lay quivering beneath him, her body ripe and ready for the taking.

"Piers." Never had his name sounded so lovely. Her voice trembled on a quick intake of breath. "Piers, I ache. I burn. I don't know what—help me. Oh, Piers, please, please, help me."

Aching himself, he understood what she wanted. He lifted her heavy woolen skirts, his hand skimming along sleek legs encased in fine stockings topped by ribbon garters. He moved his hand upward to soft, warm thighs, to a dark tangle of hair. He touched her where she was moist and hot and she cried out and pushed herself against his fingers. Probing deeper, he found the tight barrier of her maidenhood. Her legs falling apart, she offered herself to him in wild, innocent abandon.

He could not do it. He could not harm her, not when she trusted him so completely. He was experienced enough with women to know there was a way to relieve her need without taking what was not rightfully his. Moving his fingers, he found what he sought and rubbed gently. She rose to meet his hand, growing rigid and then suddenly erupting into a series of violent pulsations.

Watching her, Piers nearly went mad from the pressure of containing his own desire. It was all he could do to keep from tearing away his hose to free himself so he could plunge into her. He did not think of consequences then, not when Yolande was experiencing her first joy as a woman, not when he wanted to be inside her at that instant, riding the crest of passion with her, sharing it with her, letting her know what tenderness and true affection could mean.

But he denied himself, trying to think of Yolande and what she needed, using his fingers gently and carefully until she was no longer soaring among the stars but lying on a rocky hillside, in his arms, with her head upon his shoulder.

"Oh, Piers, how lovely, how exquisitely beautiful. I never dreamed—no one told me. But you, do you not wish to—?" She stopped, blushing furiously, then went on in a determined way. "My nurse Lesia did explain to me what it is that men need to do at such moments, and you have not done it. Piers, if you wish, I have no objection. In fact, I think I would like it, but only if you do it. I don't think I could bear to let another man touch me in that place."

"Stop it!" He gritted his teeth, fighting the almost unstoppable urge to roll on top of her and take what she offered. He knew he ought to stand up, to put distance between them until his racing pulse had slowed. But she was clinging to him and he did not want to let her go. She was so soft and delicate in his arms. Another man, touching her, putting his hands where Piers's hands had just been? No, never! *Never!* He shook her, attempting to silence her tumbling words and make her stop trying to explain that she had wanted him to do what he had just done to her, that she need not feel embarrassed by what had passed between them. "Yolande, stop it. I cannot defile you by using you in such a way when we are not wed. You are no serving girl, no tavern wench to be taken lightly on a hillside where anyone passing could see us. What I have already done to you is bad enough, for though you are still a virgin, you are no longer an innocent girl. I *am* embarrassed, and ashamed of myself, too, and rightly so. This should not have happened."

Disengaging himself from her arms he sat up, and she rose too, leaving her skirts crumpled around her thighs so he could see the soft white flesh he had stroked. Still dazed and awed by what she had experienced, she gazed into his eyes for a long, silent time until Piers spoke again.

"When I take you for the first time," he told her, "we will be in our marriage bed, after we have been blessed by Father Ambrose, after George and Roger and all the other nobles and ladies of Palermo have acknowledged that we are man and wife."

"Are we to wed then?" Her voice broke. Now that she had the promise of what she most wanted, she felt as frightened as he looked.

"I will speak to George this afternoon," he said.

"Are you sure you want to?" she asked, mindful of the fact that he did not love her. The knowledge gave her pain, but because she loved him she said what she thought was right. "If I am still a virgin, then you are not obligated to marry me. I do not want you to be unhappy, Piers."

"If I do not marry you soon," he said with wry humor, "I will indeed begin to treat you like a tavern wench, and then I will hate myself. That would truly make me unhappy." Standing, he held out a hand to her, to help her to her feet. Once she was standing he let go of her hand, touching her again only long enough to lift her into the saddle.

"Piers," she said when they were mounted and the flushed look had left his face, "*do* you lie with every tavern wench you meet?" She tried to sound indifferent. After all, the gossip she heard from young women she knew who were already married suggested that many men were habitually unfaithful, and the wives had nothing to say about it. She did not think she could bear it if Piers found pleasure elsewhere than in her bed. But she thought he must have understood what was in her heart, that she would never be silent about any affair he might have.

"Why, no," he said, giving her a searching look. "No tavern wenches for me. I only choose the best."

And she knew, without needing to ask or to hear him say the words aloud, that once they were wed he would be faithful to her. She thanked him for his silent pledge in the only way she could.

"After you have most properly taken me in our marriage bed," she told him, "one sunny day we will ride this way again. And when I once more lie upon the ground with my skirts around my waist, and you touch me until I cry out in joy, then you will not have to stop until you, too, are filled with the same joy. Then I will give you in return all that you have given me today."

Piers found George of Antioch surprisingly amenable to the idea of his niece marrying a relatively unimportant, newly made baron. George was also disconcertingly honest.

"Roger and I have discussed your future, which is assured so long as you remain loyal to him," George said. "I have no fear that your wife will live in poverty. However, I am concerned about Yolande's happiness. Though several other men with high titles and greater wealth than yours have asked for her, because you are the man she wants and because I love her too much to forbid her what she most desires, I will allow your marriage. Thus far I have given you great freedom with Yolande because I believe you are an honorable man who would not use her badly. Let me warn you now: Do not betray my trust in you once you are wed. If ever you mistreat Yolande, you will answer to me."

"I assure you, I have nothing but respect and admiration for her," Piers responded.

"You do not speak of love." When Piers would have answered the accusation George raised a hand to silence him. "I have too often seen wise men made fools by love. I have watched some men led into paths of corruption they otherwise would not have taken, then heard them excuse their villainies by claiming it was all for the sake of love. The happiest and most fortunate men I have known were not passionately enamored of their wives, but held them in the same respect you appear to have for Yolande. Allow me one word of advice: Do not stifle or destroy Yolande's love for you. Let it enrich both your lives. That will make her happy and give me no cause for complaint against you."

"I want her happiness, too," Piers said, "for I regard her as a dear friend."

"Then I have no objection to your marriage. In fact," George said, a twinkle coming into his eyes, "I think it is past time for me to change the ordering of my household. Since my wife died some years ago I have kept a rather strict decorum for Yolande's sake. But there are certain adjustments that would make my life . . . more interesting, shall we say?

"First, there is the matter of Yolande's nurse, whom you will certainly not want in your household. Lesia is a good and honest woman, but she would interfere between you and Yolande. There is a cottage on the far side of the gardens surrounding this house. I'll send Lesia there with a servant or two to help her. She and Yolande can see each other when they wish, but it would be better if you begin your new marriage with new servants."

"Thank you," Piers said fervently, eliciting a smile from George.

"Now, as to where you will live," George went on, "I have a property—a small but charming house not far from here. I will give it to you and Yolande as a wedding gift. Decorating and furnishing it should keep her well occupied this summer, while you are in Italy with Roger. Emperor Lothair is most inconsiderate; his invasion will shorten your marital idyll. There is fighting to be done once more, and Roger will be glad of your sword arm in his defense."

Chapter Twelve

The news from Normandy arrived with unusual speed, for it was scarcely two months old when it reached Palermo, but its importance had lent it wings. King Henry I of England had died at Rouen; his nephew Stephen had at once crossed the Narrow Sea to England and there had had himself proclaimed king. Nobles once sworn to support Henry's daughter Matilda as ruler had broken their sacred oaths and gone over to Stephen.

"There will be war in England now," Alain said when he heard of it. "Matilda will not give up the throne without a fight, not after her father promised it to her, not when she has a son to whom to bequeath it after she's gone. I should be there, at Wortham, with my father. Piers, we both should be there."

"We cannot go back," Piers said. "Not yet. We are sworn to Roger now, and our first duty lies with him. Instead of heading toward England we are obligated to go to Italy, I with Roger and you with George."

"I know it." With a sigh, Alain put aside his own wishes. "Unlike the nobles of England, I will not break my oath once it's spoken. But I will never relinquish the hope that one day we will return to England." Nor would he give up his dream of seeing Joanna again, that perfect woman with her golden hair and her sapphire blue eyes and her delicately chiseled features. The memory of Joanna put to shame all the Sicilian beauties he had met, making him refuse George's offer of a cousin's daughter for a wife with the statement that he had sworn never to wed.

However, Roger's offer of a titled wife as reward for Alain's services required a fuller explanation than the one he had given George. In a private interview, Alain told Roger about Joanna and how she had been wed to Alain's dear friend and cousin. Roger, still despondent over the death of Queen Elvira, understood Alain's feelings.

"My advisers insist that I should remarry, possibly to a Byzantine princess, in order to make a strong alliance against the Holy Roman Emperor," Roger said. "But I want no other woman. Forgive me, Alain; I did not know about your lost love. It appears that we have something in common. As I do not want to be pressed to marry, so

I will not press you. But if you should change your mind in the future, you have only to tell me and I will do for you what I can, for I expect you to continue to be valuable to me and to George."

With the immediate issue settled, Alain made in his own mind a reluctant peace with the necessity to remain in Sicily for the present. He did not find it an unbearable situation. There was much for him to learn from George, and his eager, questing mind was enthralled by the culture the Norman rulers encouraged on the island. In his year's stay he had already made friends, Roger and George of Antioch foremost among them, but there were other friends, too, including Abu Amid ibn Amid, the royal commissioner who had interviewed him on his first day in Sicily and who had become Ambrose's friend, too. Alain no longer thought it strange to call an Arab his friend, and enjoyed Abu Amid's company.

There were, occasionally, women; only a few of them. Dark tresses and eyes could never entirely eclipse the remembered beauty he carried in his innermost heart, but he was a healthy young man with a young man's needs. He treated his rare mistresses kindly, paid them well, and gave them no part of himself beyond what was necessary for a pleasant bedding.

Piers, having brought a whole heart with him into Sicily, was more fortunate. His long talk with George had eased Piers's conscience. Piers no longer cursed himself for a calculating fool, but instead made up his mind to appreciate the benefits of allying himself to the family of George of Antioch. Yolande's open and buoyant happiness gave Piers great pleasure. Thinking the temptation would be too great for both of them, he promised himself not to be alone with her until after they married. He might have saved himself his concern for her virginity; she was frantically busy and had little time to spare for romantic dalliance.

"Theo Georgios has decided the wedding should take place in two weeks, before Lent begins," Yolande told him. "There is so much to do. I must have new clothing and linens, so there is endless sewing, and the seamstresses cannot possibly finish all of it in time. Nor can I have our new home ready before the wedding, but do you want to spend our first days together here, in someone else's house?"

"Hush, my dear; don't worry." He caught her fluttering hands and brought them to his lips, then kissed her mouth, quickly, ever mindful of Lesia and the other attendants who constantly hovered about her of late. Where had her old nurse and the tiring woman and the seamstresses been when he had found it all too easy to be alone with her? Had their absence been Yolande's doing, or her uncle's? He did not greatly care who had been responsible. He did not love Yolande, but he liked her very much and he was going to marry her, and that was that. Considering how most nobles married, sight unseen, their contracts arranged by their parents, and too often finding themselves bound to spouses with whom they had nothing in common—considering all of that, Piers thought he had no reason to complain about his own arrangements. "Yolande, my sweet, don't worry about the house. I will see to it."

What he did was talk to George, who, in spite of his many duties for Roger, seemed to have endless time to deal with any problem that might arise in Yolande's life or the lives of his numerous other relatives who made their homes in Palermo. George lent to Piers some of his own servants to clean the new home, and then announced that he was giving his niece and her betrothed their marriage bed. It would be delivered to the house several days before the wedding.

Assured that the housecleaning was progressing as it should, Piers took himself to the market, where he purchased a round table inlaid with marble and multicolored woods and two chairs with comfortable backs and arms, to which he added blue silk cushions. He bought an Arab rug patterned in shades of red and blue on cream. Having sent all of these items to his new house, he next found a jeweler and bought several gifts for Yolande, to add to the necklace of large pearls and the assorted other jewels that were part of his loot from the previous summer's battles. Those battles seemed far away now. He had pushed them to the distant fringes of his memory, so he could enjoy the rewards of battle without thinking about the pain. It was a good feeling to be Baron of Ascoli, a man of substance, to have a house of his own and gold coins in his pockets so he could buy whatever he wanted. He gave

Yolande the pearls for her wedding gift and kept the other pieces to present to her later.

The wedding of Yolande and Piers was celebrated at George's house with a large crowd of guests in attendance. Roger was still in Italy, but the presence of all the members of his Palermitan Curia, who helped to rule Sicily, chief among them the Emir of Emirs, George of Antioch, made up for the king's absence. Alain, in bright red silk tunic and hose, was Piers's chief witness. Piers himself wore blue silk with a heavy gold chain about his neck and several gold rings. He had learned during the past year to enjoy the luxury of Sicilian fashions and had given up the coarser wools of his homeland with little regret.

On George's arm Yolande entered the large, airy reception room where the ceremony was to take place. Her hair was combed into a slightly more elaborate version of her usual topknot and wound through with narrow silver ribbons. She wore the pearl necklace Piers had given her wrapped twice about her slender throat. Two splendid oval pearls, George's personal wedding gift, dangled from her ears. Her wide-necked, long-sleeved gown was cream and silver brocade, cut so the flaring skirt rippled and whispered when she moved.

Piers had expected to see her radiant with happiness. Instead, Yolande's face was pale, her eyes like those of a terrified deer. Piers wanted to speak to her, to tell her not to be nervous or afraid, to assure her that he would always protect her and care for her, but the ceremony allowed him neither the time nor the privacy for a word with her.

The marriage contract was lengthy; although Roger had taken back the Italian lands once held by Yolande's late father, he had given her property in Sicily in return so she would have a suitably large dowry. George had been managing this property for her, but now it passed into Piers's control. The details were complicated and the official reading of the contract to the guests, who served as witnesses to it, took some time. While George's secretary droned on and on, Piers sat in his high-backed chair, watching Yolande out of the corner of his eye. He saw how she was gripping the arms of her chair so hard, her knuckles had turned white. Thinking only to allay her very natural nervousness, Piers reached across the few inches separating their chairs to cover her hand with his own. She gave a startled gasp, loud enough to make the secretary look up from the parchment scroll he was reading. The sound also made George, who was standing next to the secretary, glance at Yolande with raised brows, and it caused Father Ambrose to smile encouragement at the young couple.

Piers did not think Yolande noticed any of those reactions. She was staring at Piers's hand on hers, watching him pry her stiff fingers off the chair arm so he could fold them into his. Then she clutched at him hard, holding tight, and he pressed her hand to reassure her. She seemed to relax a little after that. Her hand did not shake when she signed her name to the marriage contract, nor did she tremble when Piers took her arm to help her kneel for Father Ambrose's blessing and the prayers for the contentment and fruitfulness of their marriage. When they were on their feet again he grasped her lightly by the shoulders and pressed a soft kiss upon her unresisting lips. Then it was done; they were man and wife, and the guests pushed forward to congratulate them.

The feasting began, accompanied by a wide variety of wines, more good wishes, laughter and loud talk, constant music and, fortunately, only a few lewd jokes. Yolande was frequently whisked away from Piers's side by guests who wanted her to talk to some group or other, and during one of those intervals Piers found Alain.

"I want to leave quietly," Piers said, "without noisy guests following us to our new house and into the bedchamber. I can see that Yolande is near to fainting from nervousness, and I'd like to spare her the usual rowdiness. I've ordered a carrying chair for her, so if we can smuggle her out of the house, we should be safe enough."

"Go to the entrance and find the chair and the bearers," Alain said. "I'll take care of Yolande."

Alain was as good as his word. It was not long before he appeared around a corner of the house, leading Yolande.

"He told Theo Georgios that he was kidnapping me," Yolande informed Piers. Looking at Alain, she said, "I thought no one but Theo Georgios and I knew about that private door."

"You would be amazed to learn just how much I know about what goes on in this house," Alain said. Not commenting on Yolande's sudden blush, he added, "Old Sir Piers, you are a fortunate man. May I give your lady her last kiss before she truly becomes your wife?"

Yolande blushed even more furiously at this hint of what was soon to come, but at Piers's consent she offered her cheek to Alain.

"Ah, no," he said. "I have your husband's permission for more than that." Catching her about the waist, he kissed her lightly on the mouth, then hugged her, saying, "Be happy, sweet girl. And now I give you into your husband's good keeping. Love each other well."

"Alain, you sound like Father Ambrose," Piers chided, laughing. But so quickly was Alain gone, disappearing back around the corner of the house, his hasty exit made Piers wonder if perhaps Alain was recalling another wedding at which he had not been the bridegroom. Piers saw Yolande into the carrying chair and closed the curtains. At his signal the bearers lifted the stout bars that supported the chair and began to move forward. With Piers beside the chair, they walked the short distance to the house George had given them.

"I sent the servants away until the morning," Piers said, latching the front door securely to prevent any mischievous guests from intruding on them. "There is furniture only in the master's chamber, but at least it is well supplied. Come, I'll show you."

Because Yolande now looked paler and more frightened than she had during the ceremony, Piers made no attempt to touch her. Instead, with an exaggerated gesture of his hand, he ushered her ahead of him up the stairs and through several empty rooms until they reached the largest chamber on the upper floor. In this room was the bed her uncle had provided, along with the rug, the chairs, and the inlaid table Piers had bought. The unshuttered windows along one wall looked inland toward the rolling hills and the distant mountains.

"I chose this room for us so we would not have to look at the sea and feel ill," Piers said. "From the balcony you can see down into the garden."

"It's lovely." She clasped her hands tightly together. "I am very pleased."

"Then why do you look terrified?" he asked, moving toward her.

"I wanted this so badly," she said, "to be married to you, to be alone in our bedchamber with all our lives ahead of us. I dreamed of the night when you would make love to me at last. But now that it's happening, I am afraid."

"There is no need for fear." He took her clasped hands, pulling them apart and drawing them around his waist so she was forced to come closer to him. "Yolande, you know what will happen, and how you will feel when I touch you. We have done most of it already."

"Not the most important part." She looked as if she would cry, and Piers's heart ached for her. He knew what she wanted of him, but he could not say he loved her. He could not lie to her. Taking her face between his hands, he began to kiss her, gently at first, tenderly, trying to ease her fears and her nervousness. When she began to relax and leaned against him with a throaty little cry he gathered her closer, kissing her more deeply, letting his tongue fill her mouth, refusing to release her until she began to respond. He had known she would. She was too warm-blooded to resist his desire for long.

And he did desire her. There was no wild, throbbing passion—thankfully, not on this night, when he needed to be slow and careful and in full possession of his wits so he could treat her as she ought to be treated—but he felt a strong and steady urge to enter her body, to make her permanently his own.

It was the work of but a few moments to remove her gown, her slippers and stockings, and her fine linen shift, until she stood before him wearing only the pearl necklace and earrings and the ribbons in her hair. She blushed and tried to cover herself with her hands, but he stopped her.

"Let me look at you," he said, taking her hands away from breast and thigh. Small and delicately made, she would have seemed like a perfect little doll were it not for the color staining her throat and cheeks. Her shoulders were square, matching the firmness of her strong jaw. Her breasts were high and round, with rosy tips that stood up tautly when he touched a finger to one and then the other. Her waist was narrow, her hips in goodly proportion to her shoulders, and her thighs—ah, he knew her thighs: he had touched them weeks before and caressed her in places where he now had every right to put his hands.

She said nothing while he looked at her. She stood quietly, running her tongue across her dry lips and waiting for his next action.

"You are still partly dressed," he said, touching the pearls. "Your skin is more translucent, more radiant with life than these paltry things."

He unclasped the necklace and drew the long string of gleaming pearls away from her neck, then held out his hand so she could remove and give him her earrings. He laid the jewels on the table, and when he turned back to her, her hands were tugging at the ribbons in her hair.

"No, let me," he said, brushing her fingers aside. "I have wanted to do this since the first night I met you."

"Have you?" She bent her head, letting him loop and pull on ribbons and pins until her hair came undone and spilled downward to her hips. "I did not know that."

"This is what I wanted to see." He stood with silver ribbons laced through his fingers, staring at her. "Dear God in heaven, but you are beautiful."

Flinging the ribbons down on the table, he took her into his arms, lifting her high and carrying her to the bed. He tore off his own clothing and got into bed beside her. As he pulled up the linen sheet, he saw her staring at his rigid manhood.

"I have seen statues but never a real man before," she said, running her tongue across her lips again. "It's very large, isn't it? That terrible hardness and redness must be painful for you."

"It is tolerable," he told her dryly. "For the moment at least."

"You must instruct me in the best way to ease your discomfort. Would it help if I were to rub it? Or would you prefer that I not touch the swollen part?"

"I am glad to know you aren't nervous anymore," he replied, chuckling at her concern. "But I am not one of your wounded animals, and this discomfort is oddly pleasurable. Don't look so surprised, my dear; from what I know of you, I am convinced that you will soon understand my meaning. Yes, you may touch whatever you like. Here, give me your hand. Let me show you how."

Obediently, she knelt beside him, her luxuriant hair veiling her upper body except where one shoulder and a small, perfect breast peeked through the shining darkness. Piers wrapped her hand around his manhood, then released her to follow her own impulses.

She was a little shy at first, but, with his hoarsely whispered comments to guide her, she learned quickly, her fingers stroking him in the same delicate way in which she had once caressed a bird's broken wing. Soon she was intent on her efforts, her tongue caught between her teeth, her breath coming faster.

"Stop," Piers ordered, knowing he could not endure much more.

"Have I done something wrong?" She sounded

bewildered, as if she had been wakened from a lovely dream.

"It's because you are doing it correctly," he said, pushing her down onto the sheet. "You have done all you safely can for me. It's my turn to please you."

Having successfully eased her initial fear of his size and his hardness by teaching her familiarity with his flesh, he now began a sweet assault on her lovely body. Her mouth was a delight to kiss, her skin unbelievably soft to his touch, her response to his caresses all any man could hope for. When he kissed her breasts she gave a sigh of contentment and closed her eyes.

"Like the afternoon in the hills," she murmured, "but so much nicer without any clothes on."

"Nicer still not to have to stop," he replied, sliding downward across her body. Indeed, he could not have stopped: not if she had begged him to desist at once, not if someone had entered their bedchamber and threatened his life. His tight control was rapidly slipping away. All he could think of was Yolande's soft and willing body, and his own driving desire.

He moved against her, pushing into the moist place where previously he had only allowed his fingers to stray. The barrier he expected to find was still present, unbroken by his earlier explorations. It proved a flimsy impediment, and his steady pressure against it elicited only a soft wince from Yolande. It was quickly breeched and he was buried in her sweet, pulsating warmth.

Instinctively she moved her hips, drawing him deeper into her, and the sensation was so deliciously erotic that Piers thought it would end right then, with one hot thrust. He drew back, warning himself not to react too quickly or too forcefully. He did not want to frighten her. He wanted her to enjoy what they were doing. Gritting his teeth, he made himself wait until her hands circled his waist and slid upwards along his spine in a long, slow caress. Then he eased carefully into her again and heard her sigh in response.

"How strange and beautiful this is," she whispered. Then, "I love you, Piers."

Her soft voice finished him. He could not stop what happened next; it was completely beyond his control. He pushed as deep into her as he could possibly go, and when she moved on him, welcoming him, he poured into her all the physical frustration of waiting for this night, all his unspoken, too well repressed grief for his lost homeland, his repugnance and anger at the terrible things he had seen done in battle, his horror at torn and severed limbs and wasted young lives, and his guilt that he had during the past year emerged all but unscathed from too many battlefields. Along with his seed he spilled into Yolande all the aching, empty loneliness of his carefully controlled emotions and his hungry soul. And Yolande received it all and turned it around and gave it back to him as love.

He heard her cry out and felt against the part of his body that was intimately connected to her the soft paroxysms of her release. An instant later he slipped into a place beyond the present moment that held them both to a safe haven where he and Yolande were one in sweet and tender joy.

When he returned to himself again he was lying beside her and she was stroking his face with gentle fingertips, wiping away the tears that still coursed down his cheeks.

"I never dreamed what a precious treasure you would prove to be," he whispered.

"I love you, Piers." The simple, beautiful words broke open the gate of his carefully guarded heart as nothing else could have done. He knew he could trust this woman with his deepest secrets.

"Except for Alain and poor, dead Crispin, and Father Ambrose, I have never loved anyone," he confessed. "I was a third son, an encumbrance to my parents, who made it plain to me that they much preferred my older brothers. When I was a little boy my mother was so cold to me that I early learned not to depend upon a woman for real affection."

"You can depend on me," she said, her own eyes shining with unshed tears to match those still filling his eyes. "I will never betray you or hurt you, and I will always love you."

"Yolande, I am not certain that I can love you in return, not as you ought to be loved."

"I will teach you how to love. You need not say it until you want to. When you say it—and you will, Piers, in time, for you have a tender heart— when you say the words to me, mean them.

Never lie to me about your feelings. That is the one promise I would have from you."

"How can you know so much of love?" he asked, believing the promise she required would be the most difficult to keep of any oath he had ever taken.

"Perhaps I know about love because I have always been loved," she said. "My mother, my stepfather, Theo Georgios, my nurse Lesia, so many kind people have loved me. Because of their love I am stronger than I might appear to you."

"From lack of love I am weaker than I ought to be," he responded. "Will your love make me strong?"

"Mine, and the love of our children."

"Children." Piers swallowed hard, suddenly comprehending the importance of what he had done that day by marrying, and the true significance of the act they had just completed. Yolande had faced the nervousness and apprehension of a virgin bride and had lived through her long wedding day and her first night of marriage with love and bravery. While Piers, fool that he was, had refused to acknowledge his own fears or his true responsibilities.

"I do not deserve you," he whispered.

"I think you do." She smiled at him, his beautiful, gentle bride, with her red-brown hair strewn across the pillow and her dark eyes shining with love.

"I never thought to find happiness," he said, stunned by the raw emotion filling him. "But here happiness is. What shall I do now?"

"Accept it," she said, putting her hands on his shoulders to pull him down to her again. "And you might enhance it with a kiss—so—or a caress—like this—or even by—yes, Piers, do that again. Oh, Piers, I love you so."

The Emperor Lothair delayed his invasion of southern Italy, not crossing the Alps until late summer, and there was no change at all in the situation at Naples, where the long siege continued. The lack of any serious events that might have called Piers back to Italy gave him the spring and most of the summer with Yolande. The arranging of their new home was completed with surprising speed, thanks in large part to the many wedding gifts they received.

"The presents do make our task easier, though I love to go into the market with you," Yolande told her husband. "It is such fun to find a piece that pleases both of us, and you do bargain well, Piers. What a good price you got for the fountain, and how handsome it looks."

They were sitting in the garden, which Yolande had in a matter of weeks changed from a forest of overgrown weeds into a pleasant refuge of flowers and shade, with the tile-encrusted fountain at its center.

Piers smiled indulgently, enjoying the soft evening air and his wife's sweet presence. Life was good. The carnage of war seemed far away, though he did occasionally wonder how Alain was faring, at sea once again as captain of one of the ships presently guarding the entrance to the harbor at Naples.

"My dearest, we have a small problem," Yolande announced, breaking into his relaxed mood. "It is about Uncle Ambrose. He told me to call him uncle, as you and Alain do."

"He's not sick, I hope? I should have gone with you when you visited George this afternoon, but I did have business at the royal palace. I assume you saw Ambrose as well as George. What's wrong, and why didn't you tell me at once?"

"I wanted to think first about what we might do to help him," Yolande said. "No, Uncle Ambrose is not ill, but he *is* somewhat upset. Theo Georgios's house is large enough for privacy, but still, the situation must make him uncomfortable, especially at night."

"What situation?" Piers stared at her, wondering why she was taking so long to come to the point when she usually spoke frankly and with directness. "Tell me at once, Yolande."

"If I hesitate, it is because I am a little embarrassed myself," she explained. "In my memory, Theo Georgios has never done such a thing before."

"Done what?" Piers demanded with growing impatience.

"Theo Georgios has taken two mistresses," Yolande said. "He is keeping them at his house."

"Two? When he's almost fifty years old? Good lord, he'll exhaust himself and be no use at all to Roger." Piers burst into laughter. Seeing Yolande's affronted expression, he sobered almost at once, to offer his explanation. "When George and I talked about him giving us this house he said something about changing his living arrangements, so I'm not really surprised. He is a widower, Yolande, and he did keep that part of his life completely separate from his household while you lived there. He has a right to a little personal happiness now that he is no longer responsible for a young maiden. Still, *two* women at once?" Piers ended on a chuckle that turned into a full-throated laugh when Yolande swatted at his arm.

"My love, will you be serious?" Yolande cried. "Uncle Ambrose is living in that house. He has no contact with the women, but he knows they are there and for what purpose, and their presence offends him. I am sure he would never complain to Theo Georgios, and he said nothing to me, but I could tell what his feelings were. I think Uncle Ambrose wants to move elsewhere, preferably to a priestly residence, but that will be difficult because Roger does not allow the Latin church to build large establishments in Sicily."

"With good reason," Piers said. "Roger claims the Latin priests are so intolerant of other faiths that if he gave them free entrance into Sicily to build monasteries or abbeys, they would insist upon all the Greek churches being demolished and the rubble swept out to sea, along with every mosque and synagogue, and Latin churches raised in their stead. It would mean the end of Roger's peaceful kingdom. If Uncle Ambrose wants to leave George's house, except for the

Latin cathedral at Cefalu, there are precious few places where he can go and feel at home."

"Which is what I wanted to discuss with you," Yolande said. "Uncle Ambrose does have a place. He could come here. We have enough room. I do not think he would object to the discreetly conducted romantic activities that take place between husband and wife, do you? And, Piers, consider this: When you return to Italy, as you must do soon, Uncle Ambrose would be wonderful company for me."

"You would be willing to do this? To take him in?" Piers asked.

"What is this business of 'take him in'?" Yolande cried, angry now. "How can you say such a thing? Uncle Ambrose is part of your family, and therefore part of mine. There is no question of 'taking him in,' as if he were seeking sanctuary from persecution. Of course I want him to come here. He can easily use Theo Georgios's library during the daytime, while at night he will not have to pray constantly in order to put out of his mind what Theo Georgios is doing with his two mistresses. Piers, stop laughing at me!"

"I am not laughing at you. I am laughing in sheer delight. What an admirable woman you are. Uncle Ambrose shall come to us. I'll speak to him tomorrow. Now, tell me," he asked, reaching out to lightly cup her breast, "what was that you just said about discreet romantic activities between husband and wife?"

217

Chapter Thirteen

The days began to shorten, signaling the approaching end of the hot Sicilian summer. In Italy there was still no sign of the long-expected invasion by Emperor Lothair and his army, but, peace or no, the time had come for Piers to travel to the mainland and visit his fief at Ascoli. On his last night at home he and Yolande dined with Ambrose as usual. Ambrose excused himself as soon as the meal was over and retired to his own room, saying he had work to do.

"The dear man." Yolande looked after him with affection. "He wants to give us this time alone."

"Then let us make the most of it." Piers rose from the table, extending his hand. "Come, sweet wife, it's time for bed."

"Piers, the sun has not set." She directed a mis-

A Special Offer For
Leisure Romance Readers Only!

Get
FOUR
FREE
Romance
Novels
A $21.96 Value!

Travel to exotic worlds filled with passion
and adventure —without leaving your home!
Plus, you'll save $5.00 every time you buy!

Thrill to the most sensual, adventure-filled Historical Romances on the market today...

FROM ◼◼ LEISURE BOOKS

As a home subscriber to Leisure Romance Book Club, you'll enjoy the best in today's BRAND-NEW Historical Romance fiction. For over twenty-five years, Leisure Books has brought you the award-winning, high-quality authors you know and love to read. Each Leisure Historical Romance will sweep you away to a world of high adventure...and intimate romance. Discover for yourself all the passion and excitement millions of readers thrill to each and every month.

Save $5.⁰⁰ Each Time You Buy!

Each month, the Leisure Romance Book Club brings you four brand-new titles from Leisure Books, America's foremost publisher of Historical Romances. EACH PACKAGE WILL SAVE YOU $5.00 FROM THE BOOKSTORE PRICE! And you'll never miss a new title with our convenient home delivery service.

Here's how we do it. Each package will carry a FREE 10-DAY EXAMINATION privilege. At the end of that time, if you decide to keep your books, simply pay the low invoice price of $16.96, no shipping or handling charges added. HOME DELIVERY IS ALWAYS FREE. With today's top Historical Romance novels selling for $5.99 and higher, our price SAVES YOU $5.00 with each shipment.

AND YOUR FIRST FOUR-BOOK SHIPMENT IS TOTALLY FREE!

IT'S A BARGAIN YOU CAN'T BEAT! A Super $21.96 Value!

◼◼ LEISURE BOOKS   A Division of Dorchester Publishing Co., Inc.

GET YOUR 4 FREE BOOKS NOW—A $21.96 Value!

Mail the Free Book Certificate Today!

4 FREE BOOKS

A $21.96 VALUE

Free Books Certificate

YES! I want to subscribe to the Leisure Romance Book Club. Please send me my 4 FREE BOOKS. Then, each month I'll receive the four newest Leisure Historical Romance selections to Preview FREE for 10 days. If I decide to keep them, I will pay the Special Member's Only discounted price of just $4.24 each, a total of $16.96. This is a SAVINGS OF $5.00 off the bookstore price. There are no shipping, handling, or other charges. There is no minimum number of books I must buy and I may cancel the program at any time. In any case, the 4 FREE BOOKS are mine to keep—A BIG $21.96 Value!

Offer valid only in the U.S.A.

Name _____

Address _____

City _____

State _____ *Zip* _____

Telephone _____

Signature _____

A $21.96 VALUE

If under 18, Parent or Guardian must sign. Terms, prices and conditions subject to change. Subscription subject to acceptance. Leisure Books reserves the right to reject any order or cancel any subscription.

4 FREE BOOKS

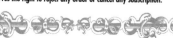

Get Four Books Totally FREE – A $21.96 Value!

▼ Tear Here and Mail Your FREE Book Card Today! ▼

PLEASE RUSH
MY FOUR FREE
BOOKS TO ME
RIGHT AWAY!

Leisure Romance Book Club
65 Commerce Road
Stamford CT 06902-4563

AFFIX
STAMP
HERE

chievous glance toward his crotch. "What a ravenous man you are."

"Will you come with me or no?" He anticipated a positive response, but he was uncertain just what form the response would take. Yolande had a delightfully seductive way of teasing him right up to the moment when they lay unclothed upon their bed, at which point she invariably turned fiery hot and eager for his embrace. And not always in bed, either. There had been the afternoon when she had arbitrarily decided their bedchamber was too far away, so she had simply sat down upon him on the garden bench, claiming her voluminous skirts would hide what they were doing. Or the memorable day when they had ridden into the hills and she had drawn up her horse at the exact spot where once he had refused to take her. There, saying she had a promise to fulfill, she had with perfect calm removed all of her clothes and lain down upon her cloak and opened her arms to him. The memory of that passionate, sun-drenched day made him grow even harder in anticipation of the next few hours.

Piers knew he was blessed beyond the lot of most men. Yolande was the loving, healing foundation of his new life. Oddly, on this evening she made no teasing reply to his question. She only put her hand in his and mounted the steps by his side.

The setting sun shone into their bedchamber, turning their bodies to gold as they undressed each other and setting Yolande's hair aglow with reddish light. She returned his caresses with the same quickly roused interest she always showed, but he knew her moods well enough to sense that there was something on her mind. She waited until she was lying in his arms on the clean white linen sheets, with the covers pushed down to the foot of the bed because the air was so warm.

"Piers, I have hesitated to tell you this. I didn't want you to worry about anything while you are away, but I think you ought to know. If I want honesty from you, then I should keep no secrets, either."

"What have you done, purchased some dreadful piece of furniture for the house?" he murmured, his lips on her throat. "Or have you invited the pope to live with us? The Romans are currently causing the poor man such trouble that he will probably accept your invitation at once. But how shall we explain his presence to Roger?"

"Piers, I am serious."

"Hmmm." He wasn't overly concerned about what she would say next. She had some new announcement every day—that she had taken in a stray cat, or brought a beggar home to be trained as a servant, or invited some bewildered foreign traveler to stay with them for a while. He had grown accustomed to what he still called her wounded birds. The loving heart that cared for him so tenderly included the rest of the world, too. He could not begrudge her that caring, nor could he be jealous of it. He knew her deepest, most passionate love was reserved for him alone.

"I am going to have your child."

It took a moment for her unexpected words to sink into a brain befogged by rising desire. When he finally understood what she had just said he lifted his face from her shoulder and took his hands off her breasts.

"What?"

"Why do you look so surprised? When a man and woman make love every day it is bound to happen."

"Are you sure?"

"Haven't you noticed that I've had only one monthly bleeding since we married? Or did you think it was an arrangement made for your convenience?" She was teasing him, and he knew it was because he was so dumbfounded by her news. "Perhaps you thought my breasts were enlarged for your pleasure, too?"

"And you were going to let me make love to you and perhaps harm the child?"

"If our making love last night, or the night before, or every other night since we were married has not harmed the child, why would making love tonight harm it simply because now you know about it?" she asked.

"Yolande." He cradled her face between his palms, looking into her eyes. "Oh, my dear, how happy you make me. But are you uncomfortable?"

"Not at all. In fact, that is the real reason why I haven't told you before this. I was unsure about my condition because I haven't been sick in the mornings. But I went to see Lesia today and told her my symptoms. She says it's true: I will have a child soon after Christmas."

"I'll send a messenger to Roger at once." Piers sat up, preparing to pull on his clothing. "I cannot leave you now."

"Don't be silly." Yolande caught at his arm to stop him. "You have promised to meet Roger at Ascoli and you will do so. Leave tomorrow, Piers, as you planned to do, and then come back to me for Christmas and stay until our child is born. Lesia warned me there will be a time toward the end when I will be too large and ungainly for lovemaking. You may as well be in Ascoli then."

"I don't want to leave you." Relaxing back onto the bed, Piers leaned on one elbow and put a hand on her softly rounded belly, touching her with a sense of wonder verging upon the reverent. "Our child lies here. Considering how well I know your body, I should have noticed."

"Piers." She stroked his cheek and touched his lips with gentle fingers. "Make love to me now. Love me all night long, so I can remember your wonderful manliness while you are gone. Oh, Piers, after tonight is over it will be so long before we can lie together again. I shall miss you."

"But not yet," he whispered. "I haven't gone yet."

Still overcome by her news, he gathered her close and put his mouth on hers. She opened her lips at once, teasing him with her tongue until he surrendered to the passion that flared so readily between them. When her hands touched his manhood he took them away, raising them above her head and holding them there.

"No," he said, "don't touch me. Later you may do to me whatever you want, but this first time is for you. Keep your hands here, where I have put them." He placed a kiss in the palm of each hand, then began to kiss his way along the inside of her arms. He had almost reached her armpits when she cried out in protest.

"Piers, I want to put my arms around you."

"Stay as you are," he ordered, "or I'll be forced to punish you." He followed up this threat with a long, tender kiss on her parted lips, silencing any further protest from her. A short time later he reached her throat, her shoulders, her breasts, raining kisses upon her flushed skin, with a bit of tasting and licking to cool her rising fever. Writhing beneath his hands, she begged again.

"Piers, please let me touch you."

"Later," he commanded, knowing that if she was to lay one finger on him he would explode at once, for everything he was doing to arouse her had its effect on him. He had not half finished what he planned to do to her, and already he was aching to find his release in her honeyed warmth. But on this night above all others he wanted her to find a deep and complete fulfillment. He drew his tongue down across her belly, circling her navel, caressing her with both hands, fully conscious that beneath her ivory skin their child rested. Somehow the knowledge made what they were doing together even more beautiful and more sacred.

"How precious you are," he whispered, overcome by tenderness, knowing he spoke to mother and child both.

As he moved lower in his continuing worship of her body, her thighs fell apart. He pressed a kiss on each of her rounded knees, then kissed his way along her inner thighs to the tangle of dark curls that was the entrance to their personal paradise. Gently he eased a finger into her.

"Please, please." She thrust against his hand. Her eyes were closed, her lips parted, her face intent on the pleasure now beginning to flood every portion of her body. Piers experienced her pleasure as though it was his own. Which it was. *It was.* His own body was so hard, so tight, so incredibly hot. Never had he felt such searing desire. He knew he could wait no longer; if he tried, he would only embarrass himself and spoil Yolande's release. Even as he realized this, Yolande went rigid with the approach of her climax. Piers chose that moment to thrust himself into her. Her eyes went wide at the force of his entry. It was then, when he was deep inside his wife's body, with her warmth and her love enveloping him and her arms at last encircling his shoulders, it was then that Piers finally admitted what he now knew had been true for months.

"I - love - you," he groaned, the saying of it almost physically painful for him. The second time was easier. "Yolande, I love you."

"Oh, Piers," she gasped. "Oh, Piers."

There was no time for either of them to say more. At the moment when he felt his own release begin to overtake him he was aware that she was melting and throbbing beneath him, and then they were swept away together into a place of heat and ecstasy beyond anything Piers had ever experienced before.

"I do love you," he said to her the next morning. "I should have told you long before last night. You are my heart and my life. If anything should happen to you, I would die, too."

"I will be careful. I will do everything the midwife tells me to do." She lay back against the pillows, watching Piers yawn and stretch in preparation for rising. "Must you leave so soon? Could we not make love just once more?"

"Even if there was time," he said, smiling down at her, "I doubt if I would have the strength for it. After last night I am completely drained. You, dear wife, have a most inventive imagination." He stopped, recalling some of the things she had done to him.

" 'Tis you who tired me," she murmured, snuggling into his arms. "I have never stopped hoping you would learn to love me. Knowing you do made last night wonderful. You were wonderful." She let her hand stray downward, and to his own surprise, Piers felt his flesh harden.

"There, you see," she whispered. "It is possible, after all. You only needed a little encouragement."

"Yolande—" But her mouth was on his, stopping his cautious words, and Piers could not resist the touch of her tongue against his, or the way she leaned over him, letting her breasts rub

225

across his chest. And when she straddled him and took him inside her he was as hot and eager for her as he had been the first time they had made love the night before. Lying beneath her, he watched her climax come upon her, softening her lovely features, and he heard her wild cry. Then he rolled her over and thrust hard into her, letting himself go, giving to her all the hot, youthful passion of his manly soul.

"I love you," he whispered over and over, the words like a charm, like a refreshing breeze, like the breath of life itself. "Oh, Yolande, I love you, love you, love you. . . ."

Yolande's baby was born on the Feast of the Epiphany, a daughter as delicately made and as beautiful as her mother, with a cap of straight black hair like her father's.

"You must have her baptised Epiphania, for the feast," said George of Antioch, who had come to the house immediately upon learning that Yolande was in labor, and who had waited with Piers and Alain through a long night. "Since you have asked me to be a godfather I ought to have some say in the choice of name.

"So should I, if I'm to be a godfather, too," Alain put in, looking at the tiny creature nestled in her mother's arms. He poked a finger at the miniature hand, and it opened and closed like some fragile sea star. "What name would you like, little one?"

"Alain, you might choose Maria for the name you give her, in honor of the Blessed Virgin,"

Father Ambrose suggested.

"Yolande and I were thinking of Samira," Piers said.

"But isn't that a Moslem name?" Father Ambrose shook his head. "Still, I suppose it would not be inappropriate for a child born in Sicily, so long as she has a proper Christian name as well."

"I shall please all of you." Yolande was almost as pale as the bedlinens, and she had dark circles beneath her eyes after her long ordeal, but her smile was brilliant and her face was alight with happiness. Piers had told her several times that he did not care if their first child was a girl. Piers loved her so well that she could not doubt they would have other children, sons and daughters to fill their home with laughter and love. Smiling at the men who surrounded her bed, she held up the baby so they all could see the little face. "Good sirs, may I present to you Epiphania Maria Samira."

"A long name for so small a child," Alain said, smiling.

"But a good name. Yolande learned diplomacy at my knee," George confided to Ambrose.

Epiphania Maria Samira was baptised the next day by Father Ambrose, with George and Alain as godfathers and three noblewomen, all wives of highly placed Palermitan officials, as godmothers. Once the celebrations were over, her parents ignored the long official name and called their daughter Samira. She was a happy and naturally sociable baby and soon had both George and Alain, as well as all the members of Piers's household, wound about her tiny fingers.

"She has Norman eyes," Alain said when Samira was six months of age. "Yolande, have you noticed how they've changed from blue to a lovely shade of gray-green? How could that happen when you and Piers have dark eyes?"

"If you did not spend so much time at sea, you would have heard the discussion long before this," Yolande told him. "My father was a Norman baron and my mother often told me about his beautiful gray-green eyes. We have concluded that Samira inherited the color from him."

"I believe she must have inherited her grandfather's Norman tenacity, too," Alain said, laughing. "See how she clutches my finger and won't let go. I do believe she remembers me from the last time I saw her four months ago."

"You ought to have children of your own, Alain." Sitting on the garden bench beside him while he tried to pry his finger out of Samira's grasp, Yolande looked hard at him. "You ought to have a wife. I know several lovely young girls of good parentage."

"No." Alain let Samira pull his finger into her mouth and suck on it. He met Yolande's glance with fierce eyes. "I will take no wife in Sicily. This sweet infant will be my daughter. You and Piers will be my brother and sister. You are all the family I need."

Samira grew bright and healthy, a joy to her doting parents. Unhappily, after her first child Yolande's future pregnancies ended in miscarriages or stillbirths. Her inability to give Piers strong sons was a continuing sorrow to Yolande, but never did he speak a word of blame to her. Instead, they grew closer with each sad loss, their love never wavering.

Their lives settled into a pattern, with Piers away for part of each year, on the mainland with Roger. The danger there from the armies of the various holy Roman emperors who invaded South Italy with disturbing regularity, coupled with Yolande's dislike of the sea and her fear of seasickness, kept Piers from asking her to accompany him. She had never seen the lands or his castle in Ascoli that he held in fief from Roger.

Piers did not mind if Yolande stayed at home. Palermo provided a far more luxurious environment than Italy, and it pleased him to think of his wife supervising his household or tending to her garden, with Samira sleeping in her padded basket or, when she was old enough to walk, playing near her mother. It was a picture he could conjure into his mind when he was lonely, or when he was preparing to go into battle. Knowing they were safe gave him peace; the desire to return to them inspired him with greater courage than he otherwise would have shown. Soon he had new titles and more grants of land in reward for his devotion to Roger.

Alain, too, fared well during the bright afternoon of Roger's long reign. He held the title of emir now, and had his own lands in Italy, as well as property in Sicily at Trapani and near Taormina. From contacts he made through George, Alain invested in businesses with several Greek merchants who shipped goods throughout the Middle Sea. Both Alain and Piers were becoming richer than they had ever dreamed of being.

After spending nearly ten years in Sicily, eight of those years living with Piers and Yolande and acting as their private chaplain while he pursued his studies, Father Ambrose was called home to England.

"I have been elected to lead the Abbey of St. Justin, where I lived before I came to Sicily," Ambrose told his friends. "I suspect the choice devolved upon me only because I have been away for so long that I am not involved in any of the quarrels that have divided the abbey in recent years. It seems even monks and priests cannot prevent themselves from taking sides in a dispute between rulers, and of course, we have all heard the tales of the civil war now tearing England apart. The abbacy of St. Justin's is not a position I can welcome, but I feel called to do what I can to bring peace to that house of God."

"I am sure you will succeed," Yolande said, "but how can we manage without you here? What other priest can so completely rejoice with us in our happiness or grieve with us in our sorrows? Dear Uncle Ambrose, who will hear my confessions?"

"I know one or two priests who have come to Palermo to study Greek and Arabic as I once did," Ambrose told her. "I will find someone to minister to your needs before I go."

"St. Justin's Abbey," Alain said thoughtfully, "is not very far from Banningford Castle."

"It is nearer to Haughston," Ambrose said. "I will be certain to send you word of my arrival at St. Justin's and I'll tell you how our old friends fare."

"And our enemies," Alain added.

Ambrose left Sicily in the early spring of the Year of Our Lord 1144. It was two years later when his first letter from England reached Alain.

I arrived safely in time for Christmas, but with the abbey in sad disarray there was little to celebrate, Ambrose wrote. *On my way here I saw how much of England has been laid waste by this terrible war between Stephen and Matilda. Villages in this area are destroyed with such regularity that the inhabitants have no desire to rebuild. Farmers fear to plant crops, for the contending armies steal the food before it can be harvested, leaving the peasants to starve. I pray constantly for peace.*

Baron Radulf still rules at Banningford, and at Haughston, too. I have learned that the lady whose name is ever in your heart remains in her tower room, confined by her father's orders. More than that I have not been able to learn, for Radulf's lands, though not distant in miles from St. Justin's, are completely self-sufficient and thus separate

231

from the surrounding countryside. Radulf entertains few visitors; his wife never leaves the castle; the villeins who live on his lands do not speak to outsiders. Somehow, through all the vicissitudes and shifting loyalties of this war, Radulf has maintained his independence and, if anything, has grown steadily stronger and more entrenched in his own lands, as well as in the bordering lands that once belonged to Crispin.

Ambrose ended his letter with affectionate prayers for the well-being of all his friends in Palermo, and especially for Alain, Piers, Yolande, Samira, and George of Antioch.

Not wanting to add to Piers's present burdens, Alain did not mention England or show the letter to him. Yolande was recovering from yet another stillbirth and Piers was seriously concerned about her health. Piers himself had been ill, of an infected battle wound.

During that summer, while at sea, Alain often thought about returning to England. Joanna, kept in a tower room by her father, called to him across half the known world. In his mind her bright image had faded somewhat during the years since he had last seen her, but he felt duty-bound to carry out his promise to return to her. He even went so far as to suggest that Roger might send him on an embassy to England.

"To what end?" asked Roger. "Can the king of England support me in my constant battles against the holy Roman emperors? Or against the Byzantines, who would also like to unseat me from Sicily? No, my friend, there is nothing your countrymen can do for me and, therefore, no need for an embassy to whoever may presently be ruling that unhappy land. But if you are in the mood for a delicate task, I'll send you to Rome to speak with the pope, whose support I do need."

Thus, once more, the return to England was delayed. The years passed and, ever obedient to the oath of fealty he had sworn to Roger, Alain sailed with the navy to Italy under George's command, to Corfu, even to the Greek mainland, on successful campaigns. His honors and his wealth accumulated. When he was at home in Palermo Alain often visited Piers and Yolande. Samira called him Theo Alain. Had it not been for his nagging sense of guilt over Joanna, he would have been happy.

And then everything in Roger's kingdom began to change. Roger had at last paid heed to his advisers and agreed to remarry.

"You ought to think of marriage, too," he said to Alain. "You aren't getting younger, you know, and men were not meant to live out their years alone. No one can ever take my dear Elvira's place in my heart, but Sibyl of Burgundy is a good woman and I will be content with her. Alain, you should do as I am doing, and marry for the sake of convenience."

But Alain could not reconcile himself to a marriage of convenience, and more and more often

233

he wished his sworn duty to Roger did not keep him in Sicily.

Once married, Roger stayed in Palermo more than he had done in the past, and George, too, remained at home. Both were aging, and George in particular was often unwell, suffering from painful kidney stones and from a wasting disease that slowly sapped his once great strength. Yolande tended George during his ailments, often staying at his house for days at a time.

On Easter Sunday in the Year of Our Lord 1151, in the cathedral at Palermo, Roger had his eldest surviving son, William, crowned as co-king of Sicily, a sure sign that the old warrior understood how badly his own health was failing. The event was attended by anyone of note in the kingdom and by many foreign dignitaries.

Shortly after the coronation, with its attendant exhausting social activities, George of Antioch became seriously ill. Yolande spent long days by his side, but neither her loving care nor the skills of his doctors could save him. George lingered painfully through the summer and early autumn, dying as the old year moved toward its end. They buried the great Emir al-Bahr on a rainy, wind-swept December day, with Yolande shivering between Piers and Alain.

"You should not have come to the cemetery," Piers said to her. "You are wet and chilled."

"Of course I should be here," Yolande responded. "And now I'll see to the reception at his house. I was hostess for Theo Georgios often enough in my youth; today I will be his hostess one last time."

When she moved away from her husband to speak to a member of the Curia, Piers and Alain exchanged worried glances.

"I can see to it that she does not get with child again," Piers said in a low voice. "There are enough different ways of loving to make certain of that, and I would not put her into such danger after the last time. But I cannot stop her from tending to the needs of everyone she loves; it is her nature to care for others, and so she overtires herself, as she has done for George."

"Perhaps now that George is gone you can make her rest," Alain suggested.

But Piers's concern was well-founded. Shortly before Christmas, worn out by the long hours she had spent with George, Yolande fell ill. And grew steadily worse.

"I have explained your absence from court to Roger," Alain said early in the new year. "He understands that you don't want to leave Yolande. How is she today?"

"No better." They were in Piers's private study, a pleasant room that Yolande had furnished for him with a large writing table and chairs well padded with cushions for comfort. Shelves on one wall held rolled-up scrolls, maps of southern Italy and Sicily, and a few bound books. Two tall windows looked out to the garden. Piers rubbed his hands across his face. "Samira is with her. We take turns, so she is never alone. Dear God, Alain, what am I going to do if—? No, I won't think about it. I can't. Yolande will get better. When the spring comes, when the sun is warm again, we'll ride up into the hills and eat almond and honey pastries and laugh and make love, just as we've always done."

There was nothing Alain could say, no comfort to offer to a man facing the loss of a beloved woman. But there was the friendship that always lay between these two men. Alain put a hand on Piers's shoulder in silent sympathy, and they stood that way for a while.

"Papa." Samira appeared in the doorway. "Mama is asking for you."

"Excuse me, Alain." Piers was out the door before Alain could speak.

"Theo Alain." Samira came toward him, her bright young face shadowed by worry. There was an odd catch in her voice. Alain heard in it the sound of new maturity. "I think you should go to Mama, too. She loves you like a brother."

"Is she worse?"

"I have sent for the priest. He is with her now." Samira's lips trembled. She swayed on her feet, and Alain put an arm around her. She leaned against him, and he could feel the struggle she underwent to exert her will so she would not cry. After a while she straightened her shoulders and tried to smile at him. "Come with me, Theo Alain. Please. She would want you there, and Papa will need you."

They found Piers sitting on the bed, holding his wife up in his arms so she could breathe more easily. Alain had seen enough of death over the years to deduce from Yolande's chalk-white face and fevered eyes that the end was near. In the corner of the room the priest knelt in prayer at a bench Yolande had placed beneath a crucifix hung on the wall.

"Alain. Dear friend." Yolande's voice was a breathless whisper, the movement of her fingers barely discernable. Alain took her hand and bent to kiss her cold cheek.

"I am here," he said. "I will stay with you and Piers for as long as you want me to be here."

"Don't—don't go," Yolande whispered.

But he did make way for Samira, who sat on the opposite side of the bed from Piers and held her mother's hand. Alain moved to the foot of the bed, where Yolande could see him and know he was there. And there he waited, while Yolande's breathing grew ever more shallow and tortured, while Piers whispered words of love to her and repeatedly caressed her face, while Samira held her mother's hand to her warm cheek as if to infuse her own life into the dying woman.

Alain prayed as he had never prayed before, though not for Yolande's life; he could see clearly that it was ending and there was nothing any man could do to save her. He prayed instead for Samira, who was the closest thing to a daughter that Alain had ever known. He prayed for Yolande's soul, which, judged by her goodness and the love in her heart, ought to ascend directly to heaven at the instant of her death. Most fervently of all he prayed for Piers, for strength and courage for his dear kinsman and friend.

It was just after midnight when Yolande took a long, obviously painful breath.

"Oh, Piers," she said, very clearly, "I love you so." She let out her breath and nestled her head onto Piers's shoulder and closed her eyes.

There was silence in the room, each person in it listening for Yolande's next breath. It did not come, and it did not come. Alain clenched his hands into fists, holding his own breath.

"No," Piers said, gathering his wife more closely into his arms. "*No.*"

"She has gone from us, my son," murmured the priest, moving to the bedside. "It is time to send for her women to prepare her for burial."

"Alain." Piers's eyes were dark pools of agony. "Take them all away. Let me have a few moments alone with her."

"But, my son," began the priest. He stopped when Alain took his arm in a firm grasp.

"Do as he asks," Alain commanded. "Wait outside. You, too, Samira."

Alain tried to help Samira stand, but at once realized she was too overcome to move. He put his arms around her, lifting her to his shoulder like the child she still was. He carried her into the next room, where she clung to him, weeping bitterly, a child's tears, copious and unrestrained, until she fell asleep in his arms and he gave her over to the servingwomen who bore her away to her own chamber. Then he waited once more, achingly aware of the empty silence in the room where Piers was. Another hour passed before Piers came out of the room, dry-eyed and composed.

Calmly Piers made all the funeral arrangements, refusing to let Alain or Samira help him. With grave dignity and not a single tear, he moved through the next days, until Yolande was buried. Once the funeral was over and all the mourners had left his house, he closed himself into his study and, claiming he wanted to observe a period of quiet mourning, refused to see anyone. Knowing how much he and Yolande had loved each other, most of Piers's friends did as he wished and left him alone. Alain went to the house several times, only to be told that Piers did not want to see anyone. After being repeatedly refused admission he ceased to knock on the door of the building that had once been like a second home to him. He decided he would give Piers a bit of time, and then he would insist on seeing him.

Six weeks after Yolande's death, on a rainy February night, Alain sat in his own house, reading the document that had been delivered to him earlier that day. He had expected it; indeed, he was surprised that it had not come sooner. Upon the death of George of Antioch, Roger had appointed Philip of Mahdia to lead the Sicilian navy. Philip was an excellent choice as the new Emir al-Bahr, an honest and intelligent man, one of Roger's most able ministers, and Alain heartily approved of Roger's decision. Nor could Alain find aught to dispute in Philip's wish to have his own men as aides and high officers. In Philip's place Alain would have felt the same way.

And so on that rainy evening Alain sat reading for the third time, with very mixed emotions, the document that sent him into honorable retirement. There was no disgrace in the wording of the letter, no hint that he ought to go into exile. Alain still held all of his lands and honors and fine-sounding titles. Except for those pertaining to the Sicilian navy; he was no longer a part of the navy.

"So, at the age of thirty-eight, when most men are at the height of their power, I have lost my career," Alain muttered to himself, thinking that wealth and empty titles would mean nothing without the activity that had filled his life for seventeen busy years. Never again would he sit with Roger and the other captains to plan strategy, nor insist to a junior officer on the right kind or the right amount of ship's stores. There would be no more pacing on deck while he searched the horizon for the enemy's sails. No more starry nights at sea, no gut-wrenching terror before a battle. No victories. "I am an old man now."

There was a small mirror on the wall of his private sitting room. Alain went to it, to stare at the reflection of a handsome man with tanned skin that crinkled into lines around his gray eyes, with curling dark brown hair just beginning to turn white around his temples. His carefully trimmed beard and mustache were lightly sprinkled with gray.

"An old man," he repeated to himself, "with

honors and wealth and nothing to do."

"My lord." At the sound of his personal servant's voice Alain turned from the mirror. "My lord, there is a woman at the door who insists on seeing you. She is too well-covered for me to discern if she is young or old, so I cannot tell if she speaks the truth, but she claims to be the daughter of the Baron of Ascoli. She has no attendants with her, so she may be lying."

"I'll soon find out who she is." Picking up the scroll, Alain began to reroll it. "Bring her to me."

The figure the servant conducted into the room a few moments later was small and heavily cloaked and hooded. With a tug at his heart, Alain recognized the cloak.

"Samira," he said, "why are you wearing your mother's clothing? More importantly, why have you come to my house without a maidservant?"

"Because I do not want anyone but you to know where I am," Samira answered, removing the cloak and shaking the raindrops from it before laying it over a bench. "Most particularly, I do not want my father to know I have come here. You must promise not to tell him."

"I think if Piers were to learn that you have come to my house alone so late at night, even our old friendship would not save me," Alain said in a stern voice, deliberately trying to impress upon her the seriousness of what she had done.

"I have a good reason for coming here." Samira brushed aside Alain's concern. "Aren't you going to offer me any wine?" She moved into the pool of light cast by the candle Alain had been using.

Her hair was smooth and shining black, pulled into a single thick braid that hung halfway down her back. Her skin was the color of rich cream, her cheeks lightly touched with rose, and her gray-green eyes behind the dark fringe of lashes were cool and intelligent. She was one month past her fifteenth birthday, on the threshold of a glorious, as yet unawakened beauty. She glanced down at the scroll Alain had tossed onto a small table, tapping the parchment with one slender finger.

"The wine, Theo Alain? I am chilled."

"Serves you right for coming out on a night like this." But he gave her the wine in a fine silver goblet, and she sipped at it as if she really believed it would warm her. "Well, child? Why are you here?"

"I am not a child," she said with exaggerated dignity.

"You are to me and always will be. Now, if you do not want me to turn you over my knee, explain yourself at once. Then I can see you safely home."

"Theo Alain." Samira set down the wine goblet beside the scroll. "I need your help."

"For what?"

"For my father. Since Mama died he has locked himself into his study."

"I know. He won't see me. I have tried, and he refuses." Alain thought with some guilt that he ought to have tried harder and more often.

"He sits at his writing table all day, staring out at Mama's garden as if it was in full bloom," Samira said. "At night he goes upstairs to the room they shared, but I do not think he sleeps. He does not look as though he sleeps."

"He loved your mother very much. Perhaps he needs more time to recover from her death."

"Do you think I do not grieve for Mama? I cried myself to sleep every night for weeks. But then I began to understand that she would not want me to withdraw from life and waste my days and nights in sorrow. I have begun to take over her duties in the house. I go to church every day. I ride; I visit friends. Even when I do not want to do these things I make myself do them, because Mama would want me to, and because with each day that passes it does grow just a little easier to do them.

"But Papa makes no effort to shake off his grief," Samira said. "He is not at all like my loving father anymore. He will not talk to me. He does not eat. I am afraid he will die, too, of a broken heart. Theo Alain, I cannot lose both parents. I cannot!"

"Work is the best remedy for a broken heart," Alain said, speaking out of his own experience. "Perhaps if Piers took up his duties for Roger again, that would help. I can speak to Roger and ask him to send Piers on a new assignment. I understand there has been some fighting near Ascoli; that ought to interest him."

"Don't you dare suggest such a thing to Roger! Or to Papa," Samira cried. "If my father goes into battle in his present mood, he will let himself be killed. Please, Theo Alain, can't you think of something to rouse him out of his grief? Something exciting and challenging, perhaps even something far away from Sicily, to distract him and occupy all his mind and his energies?"

"You do present an interesting proposition," Alain said, his hand resting on the scroll from Philip of Mahdia. "Your plea comes at a time when I am myself in need of distraction."

"Do you have an idea?" Samira looked at him with such an expression of hope that Alain could not help but smile at her.

"Indeed I have," he said. "But I want to think my plan through before I speak of it. Samira, would you be good enough to invite me to eat with you and your father tomorrow evening?"

"Of course." Samira looked almost happy again. "You are always welcome. I don't think Papa will eat, though. He will not even join me at the table to sit with me."

"He will eat after he hears what I have to say," Alain promised.

Chapter Fourteen

"I never thought you would prove to be a coward, Piers, but you have." With the blackest scowl he could muster and the aggressive stride that made men under his command watch him in fear of his next move, Alain advanced into Piers's study, holding in one hand a rolled-up and tied piece of parchment. Samira followed him into the room, looking first hopeful and then apprehensive when she heard the way Alain was speaking to her father.

"Are you going to sit there sulking forever?" Alain rounded the end of the writing table to position himself in such a way that he blocked the garden view. "Roger tells me you have sent him a letter in which you resigned every post he has ever given you. Is that what you worked so hard for during all of these years? For the chance to slink away like the spineless coward you are? Do you really believe that is what Yolande would have wanted you to do?"

"Oh, Papa, tell me you have not!" Samira threw her arms around Piers's neck. "How could you? Mama was so proud of you, of the way you came to Sicily empty-handed and yet you achieved so much. She would be so disappointed now."

"Ashamed would be a better word for what Yolande would feel tonight," Alain said in his coldest voice. Surely this attack ought to rouse Piers out of his apathy. Any moment now he would be out of his chair and reaching for the sword that stood propped in a corner, daring Alain to call him a coward just once more.

"You don't understand, either of you." Shaking off Samira's arms, Piers rose and tried to walk around the table and past Alain's firmly planted form so he could look out at the garden again.

"Do I not?" Alain moved to block Piers's way. "Have you forgotten why we left England?"

"That was different. Joanna lived. She lives yet, for all we know." Again Piers tried to step to the window, but still Alain stood solidly in his path.

"Who was Joanna?" asked Samira. Neither man answered her.

"For eighteen years Joanna has been as lost to me as Yolande now is to you," Alain said with peculiar intensity. "But I did not turn the world away from my door or forsake my friends or lock myself into a lonely room because of it."

"As I recall, you got drunk," Piers said. Samira saw in his eyes the first glimmer of life he had shown for weeks. Giving up his attempt to get to the window, Piers perched on the edge of the table and looked from Alain to Samira and back again. "What do you want of me, Alain?"

"I need your help."

"To do what?" Piers sounded bored and weary, making Samira believe he expected to be told of some task set for him by Roger.

"Read this." Alain held out his hand, offering to Piers the scroll he had been carrying.

Piers took it, unfastened the ribbon that tied it, and began to read. While his attention rested on the parchment, Alain looked toward Samira and gave her a long, slow wink.

"So," Piers said, dropping the scroll carelessly onto the table, "Roger refuses to relieve me of my titles and grants me only a temporary retirement, until my personal affairs are all in order once more. It means nothing. My affairs will never again be in order. My life is over."

"Well, mine isn't!" Alain shouted at him. "I don't want to spend the rest of my years staring at a garden or at the sea while I grow old and feeble. And neither should you. That scroll, which I wheedled out of Roger only after much effort, means you will have the time to help me and, by God, I demand that you do."

"Help you to do what?" Piers sounded distinctly uninterested.

"To return to England and solve a mystery that has been left too long," Alain said. "To finally clear my name of the charge of murder still lodged against me."

"Murder?" Samira cried. "Oh, Theo Alain, not you!"

"Thank you for your confidence in me, child." Over Piers's bowed head, Alain smiled at her, winking again. "Did you know your father was named as my accomplice?"

"Never! Not Papa! I knew nothing about this. How could anyone ever think—?" Samira stopped, grinning at Alain. "Of course. I understand. Honor demands that both of you prove your innocence. It will be a difficult and challenging task, especially after so many years have passed, but it is a quest that cannot be denied."

"Exactly." Alain grinned back at her. "Well, Piers, what say you to my challenge?"

"England?" To Samira's delight, Piers actually seemed to be thinking seriously about the idea. "A long sea voyage from Sicily to Provence? God, how I hate being seasick."

Taking heart at what she saw as a slight improvement in her father's mood, Samira hurried to the door to summon the servants she had previously stationed outside the study.

"Just put everything on the writing table," she said, scooping up the document from Roger. "Papa isn't using it right now."

"What are you doing?" Piers demanded.

"I invited Theo Alain to eat with us," Samira informed him. "Since you refuse to leave this chamber, we will just have to serve him supper in here."

"I'm talking about being seasick and you have the servants bring in food?" With loathing Piers regarded the trays of fruits and baskets of bread, the platter of roasted chickens and the pitchers of wine now being arranged on his writing table.

"You don't have to eat if you don't want to, Papa," Samira said, "but don't deny our guest a meal. Theo Alain, may I offer you a piece of chicken?"

"I'll carve it," Alain said, sending the servants away with a gesture. "Samira, you pour the wine." Quickly, he sliced the breast of one chicken. Then, with a glance toward Piers, who had finally reached the window and was standing with his back to the room, Alain cut off two chicken legs, leaving the thighs attached, and laid them on one side of the platter.

"If I remember correctly," he said to Samira, "you and I both prefer the breast meat."

"Thank you, Theo Alain. Will you tell me more about this proposed trip to England?"

"Yes, Alain, do tell us more." Piers loaded the invitation with sarcasm, but he did turn from the window when Alain spoke again.

"What better time for us to go than now?" Alain said, speaking more for Piers's information than in answer to Samira's question. "With George dead and Philip of Mahdia commanding the navy, I am no longer assistant to the Emir al-Bahr. Philip is polite to me, and I think if I were to offer an opinion on a naval matter, he would at least listen to me, but it's clear he thinks I am too old to be of any further use. Did I tell you that I am now officially retired from the navy?"

"You are not old," Piers said.

"Then neither are you, for we are the same age," said Alain, the gleam in his eye suggesting to Samira that Piers had just walked into a carefully laid trap.

"Philip ought to value your experience instead of retiring you," Piers said, no longer sounding bored or uninterested in the conversation. He had not looked at the food since the servants had set the platter down, and he did not look at it now. His eyes were on Alain, but he picked up one of the chicken legs and took a bite of it. "A man of your age, or mine, is not useless. We are as strong as we ever were." When Piers began to prowl about the room, gnawing at the chicken leg, Alain smiled at Samira and nodded his head, as if Piers had already made his decision.

"You know, Alain, there have been too many changes here in Palermo recently, and most of them for the worse. I saw Roger every day before"—Piers stopped to take a deep breath—"before Yolande became ill. I noticed how Roger is much altered since that attack of brain fever he suffered last year, when he could not talk or move his right side for a week. There were days when he treated his dearest friends as if they were his enemies. He was not always kind to Queen Sibyl, either, or to his own son. Now he has in effect released you and me from our oaths to remain here and serve him." Piers took another bite of chicken.

"This is good. I always did like the leg and thigh." He stopped by the table to pour himself a cup of wine. "Yes, Alain, we might do well to leave Sicily for a while. I will consider your suggestion."

"There is no need to think about it, Papa," said Samira, overjoyed to see her father eating and talking in his usual way. "I know the voyage will be just what you need. As soon as we can find a place on a ship, we will go. How exciting it will be. I cannot wait to see England."

Piers and Alain both stared at her.

"You will not go to England," Piers declared, tossing the cleaned chicken bone back onto the platter. "*If* I decide to go, you will stay in a convent in Italy during my absence."

"Never! I'll run away and follow you."

"Samira," Alain put in, "the sea voyage is long and can be dangerous. Overland travel is almost as bad. We cannot subject you to such a trip."

"What if you decide to stay in England? Will I then never see either of you again?" Samira demanded. "Will I spend my life in some dreary convent because you have forgotten all about me?"

"I could arrange your marriage before I go," Piers threatened, breaking off a piece of bread and popping it into his mouth.

"Aha! So you *are* going! I knew Theo Alain would convince you to come to life again. But, mark my words, Papa, until I meet a man I can love as Mama loved you, I will not marry. If you try to force me to it, I will stand before all the assembled guests and announce that you are charged with murder in another land. That ought to keep any reputable family from allowing a son of theirs to wed me."

Observing Piers's horrified face, and the second large chunk of bread arrested halfway to his mouth, Alain saw a chance to reach his friend's sense of humor. Furthermore, he saw the logic in Samira's argument.

"Piers, I warned you and Yolande time and again that you were too indulgent with this girl," Alain said while Piers continued to stare dumbfounded at his rebellious daughter. Alain began to laugh. "You could always take her to England and consign her to a convent there."

"*We* were overindulgent?" exclaimed Piers, offended by Alain's attempt at humor. "What of you, with all your gifts and special treats? What of George? Thanks to the two of you, see the kind of daughter I have now."

"The most loving of daughters," Samira declared. "A daughter who will go with her father anywhere, even into that cold, dark, northern land. Even as my mother would have gone with you."

"You cannot deny it, Piers," Alain said. "Yolande would have gone with you, even across the sea for all her fear of the water, and well you know it. We dare not leave Samira behind. If Roger suffers yet another change of his recently clouded mind and decides to strike out at you for some reason, no Italian convent will be strong enough to keep Samira safe. She must go with us. Furthermore, we ought to go soon."

"I will be of great help to you," Samira promised. "And I won't delay you. I'll be a good traveler; you'll see, Papa."

"Alain?" Piers frowned, shaking his head. "Do you really feel so strongly about this?"

"I do." Alain's glance was level and straightforward. "We cannot know what will happen in Sicily while we are gone. We may be away for years. Samira will be safer, and far happier, with us."

"To leave all of this, leave everything that is left of Yolande." Piers looked around his study. "I don't think I can do it."

"I am putting my affairs here in Palermo and the care of my house into the charge of a Greek merchant I know, who is a relative of George's," Alain said. "I trust the man completely. If you like, he could do the same for you. That way, the house will be waiting for you undisturbed when you return. Your lands in Italy, like my own, are well managed by the seneschals we appointed, so there's no need to worry about them while we are gone."

"As for Mama," Samira spoke up, "you will not leave her, Papa. She will be in your heart, and in mine, wherever we go."

They left Palermo on the morning tide three weeks later.

"Theo Alain, how can I thank you for what you've done?" Samira caught his arm, slipping her hand into his elbow as they walked along the deck. The sea wind made her blue cloak blow out around her, and her eyes sparkled with excitement. "Papa is so much better now. All the activity of packing, all the immediate decisions he had to make helped, but it was your insistence that he go with you that started it all. In these last few days he has come to life again."

"Don't expect too much of him, too quickly," Alain warned, his eyes on the lone figure standing at the rail, looking backward toward Palermo. "It took Piers a long time to learn to love Yolande. It will take him an equally long time to learn to live without her."

"But he has taken the first step," Samira replied. "And so have I. So have you, Theo Alain. The first steps toward a great adventure and a new life."

Part III

Rohaise
England, 1152-1153

Chapter Fifteen

The cold December wind howled about the walls of Banningford Castle, blowing open the shutter covering one of the windows in the western tower. Icy rain spattered onto the cushions padding the ledge below the unglazed window. Joanna hastened to close the shutter, but paused with one hand on the latch. From her high room she could see a section of the road stretching along the other side of the moat. The builders of the castle had deliberately planned that those approaching by road would encounter first the forbidding, unbroken stone curtain of the western wall, and then would be forced to travel halfway around the outside of the castle until they reached the drawbridge at the center of the eastern wall. At every step of the way anyone nearing the castle was under the observation of the guards, who always stood watch upon the battlements.

The castle was built in the shape of a square, with a tower at each corner and only two openings in the outer walls. There was the main entrance across the drawbridge over the wide moat. Those entering this way went beneath the portcullis and through a narrow, crooked passage in the twenty-foot-thick outer wall. At intervals along this tunnel-like entrance metal gratings were set into the ceiling so flaming oil could be poured through the grates onto unwanted intruders. The second opening to the castle was an exit rather than an entrance. It was the postern gate near the western tower where the lord's family lived, and was intended for quick escape in time of emergency. Never in the history of Banningford had there been such an emergency; the postern gate was opened only when the captain of the guard inspected it to be sure the hinges were oiled and working smoothly.

Banningford had been beseiged once during the war between Stephen and Matilda, but it had not been taken. Joanna believed it was impossible for anyone to take the castle. She knew the strength of its high, wide walls all too well. For every day of her life she had felt the oppressive weight of those stone walls confining her, imprisoning her spirit and her hope until she believed that only death would free her.

Hearing a sound borne upward on the wind, Joanna smiled sadly, recognizing her son's voice. She tilted her head to hear it better. But the sound she loved was overridden by another voice, almost equally as dear to her.

"Joanna, close the shutter. I cannot bear the cold. My fingers turn white." Rohaise wrapped her arms across her chest, tucking her hands into her armpits to warm them. "Joanna, *please.*"

"There is a party of travelers on the road." Here, so high in the tower, the arrow slits of lower levels gave way to narrow twin windows in this room and in the lord's chamber directly above. Joanna leaned out of the window, trying to get a better look. "Six of them; four men and two women, I think. They are so bundled up against the cold that it's hard to tell. They must be mad to seek shelter here."

"Will you kindly come out of that window?" Rohaise stood as close to the charcoal brazier as she could get without singeing her clothes. "Joanna, we will both freeze."

"They've reached the south tower where the road turns. There is nothing more to see." Joanna latched the shutter and came to the brazier, shivering. "Poor travelers, abroad on such a day."

"They will find no warmth or comfort at Banningford," Rohaise said. "Baird will send them away. He always does."

"I don't like this one bit," Piers muttered to Alain. "We should not use Samira in this way. It's too dangerous for her. I should have insisted that she stay at St. Justin's. She would be safe with Uncle Ambrose."

"The task ahead of us is vitally important to

me, too, Papa." Samira had heard him. "We agreed, it is up to me to keep attention focused on myself, so you and Theo Alain can pass into Banningford unrecognized."

"We aren't likely to be recognized after all these years," Piers grumbled, still not reconciled to the part Samira was to play. "Not when we have wrinkles and beards, and certainly not when no one expects to see us here. Radulf may have forgotten all about us by now."

"Never think so," Alain warned. "Samira, be sure always to remember our new names. Your father is Spiros, and I am Lucas. A mistake about our names could be costly."

"I will not forget, guardsman Lucas." Samira flashed a smile at him, then looked toward Banningford Castle. "Heavens, what a gloomy place it is." She drew hard on her reins, bringing her horse to a halt at the edge of the moat, where the road ended. Her companions stopped also, Piers and Alain on either side of her, the others ranged behind. Samira pushed back her hood so any watching men-at-arms could see she was indeed a female. She sat proudly upon her horse, refusing to let herself shiver, ignoring the long strands of her glossy black hair when the wind pulled them free from her single braid and whipped them about her face. Across the moat a mailed and helmeted figure appeared on top of the wall, and a heavy masculine voice flung out the guardsman's well-known challenge.

"Who goes there?"

"I am the lady Samira of Ascoli." They had

agreed not to mention Sicily, in case some rumor of Alain's or Piers's life there had reached England and Radulf's ears. "I claim the traveler's right to food and lodging until this storm abates. Good sir, lower the drawbridge and let us in."

"Go away."

"We are weary and badly chilled," Samira called back. "There is no other suitable place nearby where we can take shelter for the night."

"That's your concern, not mine."

Now there appeared beside the guard on the wall a taller, bareheaded man whose fair hair was ruffled by the strong wind. This man leaned over the battlement, looking at the party below, counting their number.

"Let down the drawbridge!" the newcomer ordered in a clear voice that carried beautifully to Samira's ears.

"But, my lord . . ." objected the guard.

"Would you let a lady freeze to death? Lower the drawbridge. At once!" In a less commanding voice, the young man called out to Samira, "I will meet you in the outer bailey, my lady, and conduct you to the great hall." He disappeared from sight, and the drawbridge began to come down.

"There, you see, Papa, you do need my help. Left to yourselves, you could never enter Banningford so easily." Samira urged her horse forward to the wooden bridge. Piers pushed his mount in front of hers.

"I go first," he said to her. "Stay between me and Alain at all times. It won't look strange; we are your guards, after all."

There was just room enough for them to ride single file through the long, narrow entrance that turned first to the left and then to the right, until they finally reached the outer bailey. Here the high castle walls sheltered them from the wind, but icy rain and sleet still fell upon them. And here, at the foot of the staircase that led upward to the guards' walkway at the top of the wall, stood the blond young man upon whose orders the travelers had been admitted. He came toward them at once, smiling in welcome with one hand extended.

"Holy God in heaven!" Alain swore, catching his breath.

"Sweet Jesus!" Piers uttered at the same instant.

If they had been attacked at that moment, neither man would have been capable of offering any aid to Samira. Alain and Piers could do nothing but sit upon their horses, gaping at the man approaching them. He seemed the ghost of their long-dead, murdered cousin, a reincarnation of Crispin's youthful form.

"Welcome to Banningford Castle, Lady Samira." The young man caught at the reins of Samira's horse. "I am Lord William Crispin, and your most devoted servant, my lady. We are not accustomed to guests, but I shall see to it that everything possible is done to make you comfortable."

"I thank you, sir. Are you the baron of this castle?" Samira knew full well he was not, but her mission was to keep people looking at her, so she gave the young man her most brilliant smile and remained on her horse, where she could easily be seen by all the men-at-arms in the bailey and on the battlements.

"My grandfather, Baron Radulf, rules here," said William Crispin. "He is away from home just now. Allow me to see you to the great hall."

Still holding on to the reins of Samira's horse, William Crispin led it diagonally across the outer bailey to a second stone wall.

"How well defended you are," Samira murmured, ducking her head so she could fit through the low, sharply angled passage in the wall. "I believe it would be impossible for any army to swoop down upon Banningford and take it."

"It was built for warfare," William Crispin said. "You may be familiar with more luxurious castles, but I was born at Banningford, and my mother lives here, so it is home to me."

"Your mother?" They were out of the passageway now and well into the inner bailey, where there was plenty of room for her to move, but Samira did not dare to look backward at either Alain or Piers. She kept her eyes on William Crispin's face. When he held up his arms she set a hand on each of his shoulders and let him lift her off her horse. He was strong; in his hands she felt light as a spring blossom drifting toward the ground. Dear heaven, how handsome he was, his blue-eyed fairness so different from the darker men of Sicily. Samira stood trying to catch her breath, with his hands still at her waist and her face raised toward his. She heard her father clear his throat and at once recalled her duty. "I look forward to meeting your mother, my lord."

"You cannot." William Crispin's face changed, becoming closed and distant. "By her own choice, my mother sees no one except close family members. But my step-grandmother is here, so you will have a chaperone for your visit."

William Crispin held out his arm, and Samira placed her fingers upon it. With a courtly gesture of his free hand, he started toward the entrance to the west tower, taking Samira with him. They were stopped at once by the sheer bulk of the tallest, brawniest, ugliest man Samira had ever seen. Beneath a fringe of gray-streaked brown hair, a pair of shrewd brown eyes glared at her. The man's nose looked as if it had been broken more than once, and his face was seamed by exposure to the elements and more deeply furrowed by several long scars.

"Baird," said William Crispin, "we have a guest."

"Guest?" Baird repeated, frowning until his face cracked into even greater ugliness. "I've had no order from Radulf about any guest."

"The lady is a traveler in need of shelter," William Crispin explained. "We could not turn her away."

"I would have." Baird did not move.

"But it's not your castle, is it?" William Crispin looked at Baird with raised eyebrows and a hard expression, until Baird moved aside, allowing the younger man to conduct Samira toward the tower entrance.

"Who are all these people?" Baird demanded, watching as Samira's company dismounted.

"They are my servants," Samira said. "Two knights who are my personal guards, their two squires, and my maidservant. Surely, in a castle as strong as Banningford, you do not find four men and two women to be a threat?"

"Baron Radulf does not allow guests," Baird insisted.

"I will take full responsibility for admitting Lady Samira to Banningford," William Crispin told him.

"Well, then," said Baird, most ungraciously, "it's on your head, not mine. You can explain this woman's presence here to Radulf when he returns. What of the men? Where are they to be quartered? You there; that's not the way to the stables," he yelled at one of the squires.

"The servants do not understand your language at all, though the guardsmen do speak a little Norman French," Samira said, as she had been instructed to do. "My maidservant will sleep in the chamber with me. My guards will sleep outside my chamber door, as they always do. The two squires will be content in the stables with the horses, if you will be good enough to show them where to go."

Every member of their company did, in fact, speak perfect Norman French, but no one at Banningford was to know it. Thus, they hoped the inhabitants of the castle would talk freely in the presence of the servants, while Samira, Alain, and Piers could ask questions of their hosts.

The entrance of strangers where no unknown people ever came had brought servants and men-at-arms to gape at the beautiful young woman being escorted into the great hall. And the whispered news had brought Lady Rohaise from the upper levels of the western tower.

"Will," she cried, hurrying toward the young man with Samira, "my dear boy, what are you doing?"

"Only what I was taught to do while I was fostered at Bolsover Castle," said William Crispin. "I am showing respect and generosity toward a lady who was close to freezing. Banningford ought to be a more hospitable place."

"Hospitable? Oh, Will, you have been away for too many years," Rohaise said. "And you have returned too recently to understand Radulf's wishes in such cases."

"So I told him." Baird had followed Samira's party into the great hall. "But he would not listen."

"If my presence here is inconvenient for you," Samira said, putting on her loftiest manner, "then we will depart at once and spend this frigid night in the forest."

"It would be best," said Baird, who, ten years before, had been promoted to captain of the guard and who took seriously the responsibilities of his position. "We have to obey Baron Radulf's orders."

"But how can we ask them to leave now?" murmured Rohaise. She rubbed at her chapped fingertips. "It is much too cold to send anyone away."

"You certainly will not leave," William Crispin declared to Samira. "Rohaise, I want the small chamber in the western tower prepared for our guest."

"The western tower?" Rohaise said, looking frightened. "Surely some other room would be more suitable."

"Not at all," said the young lord. "The chamber that was my mother's when she was a girl will be exactly the right accommodation for an honored guest. Rohaise, I want hot meats, fresh bread, and spiced wine for the evening meal. And a clean cloth on the high table. I want you to sit there with us, to keep Lady Samira company."

"But, Will, you know I always eat with—" Rohaise shut her mouth, looking desperate.

"Baird, don't you have something to do on the outer wall?" asked William Crispin.

"Aye, my lord, but first I'll send my woman to tend to your guest."

"There is no need to disturb Lys." Rohaise's voice was unnaturally high and tense. "I will personally see to Lady Samira's comfort. You know I can be depended upon, Baird."

"I hope so, for your sake," Baird said rudely. With a last annoyed look in Samira's direction, he stamped out of the hall. He apparently ignored Rohaise's declaration and located his woman at once, for by the time Samira and Rohaise reached the assigned chamber in the western tower, Lys was already there, directing the cleaning of the room.

Lys was a short, square woman, pretty in an overblown way, but with a tightly drawn mouth that looked as if it could not soften into laughter or even the slightest smile.

"We will need a brazier, Lys," said Rohaise. "This room is much too cold for our guest's comfort."

"In winter no one is comfortable," Lys responded sourly. "The best an unexpected traveler can hope for is a room to herself and clean linens."

"I fear I am greatly inconveniencing you," Samira murmured, glancing from the narrow bed to the arrow slit that provided all there was of fresh air or natural light. The chamber smelled of dampness and dust. It had obviously not been used for many years.

"Not at all." Rohaise wrinkled her nose in distaste at the pile of dust being swept out the door by the servant under Lys's instruction. "It is just that my husband has never encouraged his friends to visit here, preferring to see them when he goes to court each year."

"Perhaps, once this dreadful war ends, you will have guests more often," Samira suggested.

"I do not think so." Rohaise looked sad. Noticing her expression, Samira waited until Lys and the serving woman had left before she spoke again.

"It must be lonely for you, with just yourself and Lord William Crispin's mother." When Rohaise did not answer, but went to the bed and began to fluff up the mattress, Samira persisted. "Is she terribly ill?"

"What makes you say that?" Rohaise seemed startled by the question—almost frightened, in fact. Samira began to feel sorry for her, and a bit shamed by the need to obtain as much information as she could from her hostess. But it was necessary, so she steeled herself against sympathy and pressed on with the questions she had to ask.

"Lord William Crispin said his mother sees only family," Samira explained, "so I assumed she must be ill. I have some skill in healing. Perhaps I could be of help to her."

"Joanna is in excellent health. She simply prefers to spend her time in solitude."

"But where in a castle can one possibly be alone?" Samira exclaimed with a laugh. "Men-at-arms everywhere, swarms of servants, no privacy even for the lord and his lady—oh, I know the life well, Lady Rohaise, and I find it difficult to imagine anyone living a solitary life behind castle walls."

"Are there castles like Banningford in Ascoli?" Rohaise regarded Samira with a peculiar intensity.

"Ascoli itself is much like Banningford." Samira had never been to Ascoli, but Piers had described it to her often enough for her to pretend she knew it well. "There is not one private corner in the entire castle except, sometimes, for the chapel." Still Rohaise kept her eyes upon Samira's face, until the younger woman began to feel uneasy.

"If solitude is required, it can be found," Rohaise said, speaking so quietly that Samira had to step closer to hear her. "In the chamber directly above this one, a lady need only retire behind a locked door."

"You mean, when you go to the lord's chamber at night, there you can be private?" Samira asked, still probing for information.

"The lord's chamber is on the second level above this room," Rohaise said, in the same low voice. "Between the lord's chamber and this one lies another room."

Samira understood that for some reason of her own Rohaise was deliberately providing the information Samira sought. Samira would have asked more questions, but they were interrupted by Lys, who came in with a servant carrying a brazier and a bucket of charcoal. A maid with the bedsheets followed, then Samira's maid Nena, and lastly, Alain and Piers with Samira's baggage.

Rohaise waited until the bed was made up and the charcoal had begun to heat the room. She watched Samira and the little, dark-eyed maid. Most particularly she watched the two bearded guards who took such great care with their mistress's boxes and baskets and saddlebags.

"If you are truly determined to sleep outside Lady Samira's door," Rohaise said to the one called Spiros, "I will have straw pallets brought to you."

"Men-at-arms are used to discomfort," Lys said. "They won't mind sleeping on the floor."

"You may go now, Lys," Rohaise said. "Take the other servants with you."

"You will be needed in the kitchen," Lys said, looking at Rohaise and not moving from her position by the door. With a jerk of her head she indicated that the man who had brought the charcoal and the maid who had brought the sheets should leave. "I will wait and go to the kitchen with you, Lady Rohaise."

"Of course." Rohaise sighed, looking toward her guest. "If you have need of anything, Lady Samira, don't hesitate to ask. I will order hot water sent to you so you can bathe."

"Thank you." No matter how she tried, Samira could not think of a way to keep Rohaise in the room while at the same time getting rid of Lys.

"And you, good sirs." Speaking slowly and distinctly, Rohaise looked from Alain—Lucas—to Piers—Spiros. "Is there anything else you require?"

"Nothing, my lady," said "Lucas," affecting a heavy Greek accent. After a nod to Rohaise he walked across the room to look through the arrow slit.

"I would like a bath," "Spiros" said, using the same accent. "We have ridden long, and I for one am saddle-sore. Do you have a bath house, Lady Rohaise?" He let his tongue stumble over her name.

"It is next to the kitchen," she replied. "You should find hot water there, ready for your use."

"Then I shall take advantage of it as soon as possible. Thank you, Lady Rohaise."

Wondering at the careful way in which both were speaking, Samira noticed that her father was smiling at Rohaise. She saw Rohaise's eyes warm and her mouth begin to curve into an answering smile, a response cut short by Lys's sharp voice.

"Lady Rohaise, are you coming?"

"Yes." Rohaise tore her gaze from Pier's face. "I will see you at the evening meal, Lady Samira."

Piers followed her to the door, to hold it open until he was sure Rohaise and Lys were too far away to overhear anything said in Samira's room.

"Do you think you can learn anything from her?" Alain asked Piers as soon as the door was latched.

"I will do my best," Piers answered. "Rohaise is not treated respectfully by Baird or by Lys. Any noblewoman would resent such insolence. Nor, as I recall, was Radulf a fond husband. Rohaise may be ready to welcome a friendly ear."

"I think she's lonely, and eager to talk to someone," Samira said. "She volunteered information as soon as I began to question her." Samira went on to relate all that Rohaise had revealed.

"So Joanna is just above me." Alain looked toward the ceiling. "This arrow slit is too narrow for me to climb through it and up the outer wall to her chamber, but I could mount a few stairs and be at her door in a moment."

271

"You'd be killed before you got that far," Piers responded. "Didn't you notice the guard on the stairs just above this level? Radulf isn't taking any chances on Joanna escaping. Or on the possibility of someone trying to get to her."

"Why?" Samira asked.

"What do you mean?" said Alain.

"Why has Radulf kept his daughter locked in that room for eighteen years?"

"I wonder about it myself," Alain admitted. "On the surface it doesn't make any sense."

"From what I once knew of Radulf," Piers put in, "keeping Joanna isolated *did* make sense, at first. Radulf may have feared that whoever killed Crispin would try to kill Joanna, too. Added to Radulf's fears for his daughter's life must have been concern that she could be carrying Crispin's child. Which she was. No one seeing William Crispin could doubt whose son he is."

"When I first saw him I thought he was Crispin's ghost," Alain said. "I almost called to him by name. Thank God I stopped myself in time. Crispin's son. Piers, this changes much in our plan. We cannot do anything to put Crispin's son in danger."

"Indeed not," said Piers.

"You men are missing my point," Samira told them. "I can understand why Radulf would keep his daughter well guarded until her son was born, and perhaps for some time afterward. But William Crispin spoke of being fostered at another castle, which means he probably left Banningford when he was seven years old. So at some time Radulf must have decided his grandson was no longer in danger, or he would never have let the boy go. Presumably Joanna is now safe from the murderer, too, yet she still remains in that room. Again I ask you, *why?*

"Here are some other questions for you," Samira went on when no one answered her. "Why does the lady of this castle permit her servants to treat her so rudely? Why is she afraid? And why did she so quickly tell me, a complete stranger, where Joanna is? For that is what Rohaise was doing, though she did not say the exact words."

"If you knew Radulf," Piers told her, "you would not ask why Rohaise behaves as she does. Let us make you as comfortable as we can in this cramped and cold room, and then, while you bathe and change your clothes and prepare to spend the evening charming young William Crispin into telling you everything he knows about his father's murder and his mother's situation, and while Alain stands guard outside your door, I shall visit the bath house and see what I can learn there."

"What we need to know," Alain said, "is how I can get into Joanna's room. Once I have seen her and talked to her we can better plan how to rescue her while keeping her safe—and keeping her son safe."

"Because he must be kept safe," Samira said in a fierce voice. "No matter what happens to us, we cannot allow William Crispin to come to harm. If he is hurt in any way because we are at Banningford, proof of your innocence will be meaningless."

Chapter Sixteen

The bath house was little more than a shack built between the castle kitchen and the laundry. Because of its location and the constant fire over which iron cauldrons of water were heated, the house was always warm and usually filled with steam. The light from the oil lamps set about the room gave the place an eerie, cloudlike effect. The tub was wooden, shaped like half a giant barrel, with strips of coarse linen draped over it to protect bathers from splinters. A bowl of semi-liquid soap sat upon a wooden shelf and next to the bowl was a neatly folded pile of small, rough cloths to use for washing.

There were no towels. Deciding to try the laundry first and then the kitchen in search of something with which to dry himself after his bath, Piers stepped from the overheated bath house into the cold darkness of the inner bailey. It was late afternoon and the sun had set, but Piers discovered his memory had not failed him. He had visited the bath house several times on his previous visit to Banningford, so it was easy enough for him to locate the door to the laundry. He had just put out his hand to open it when the door swung outward and a woman appeared, carrying a pile of folded white fabric.

"There you are, Sir Spiros," Rohaise said. "I have the towels you will need."

He did not point out that she could easily have sent a servant to get the towels and take them to the bath house. Instead he watched with growing interest while she lifted the ring of keys that dangled from her girdle, selected one, and locked the laundry door.

"Is it necessary?" he asked, remembering to use his false Greek accent. "Who would want to steal towels and clothing? There would be no point to it. Such stolen goods could easily be found."

"It's not from fear of losing the linens, or even the clothing," Rohaise said. "Radulf once discovered a man-at-arms and a kitchen wench in there together, dirtying the sheets intended for Radulf's bed. He had them both whipped, and since then I have held the key to the laundry."

"I noticed the large collection at your girdle," Piers remarked with studied casualness. "Do you have all the castle keys?"

"Oh, no," Rohaise told him. "There are keys that only my lord Radulf carries; when he is from home Baird has them. Those have to do with the outer defenses, certain weapons, the dungeon."

"But you have the keys for the inner castle," Piers murmured. "For the wine cellars, the food storerooms, the chambers in the western tower."

"Why do you ask?"

"Curiosity about English customs, my lady."

"No, it's something more than that." Her face was a blur in the darkness. "Someone is coming. You have your towels. I must go back to the kitchen. Lys will wonder where I am."

Piers could also hear the approaching footsteps. It sounded to him like two men, and they were talking amiably. Sensing that Rohaise had considerable information that she might with a little persuasion impart to him, Piers decided he could not let her leave. But neither, for many reasons, could he allow her to be seen talking to an unknown man.

He did the only thing he could think of: He pushed Rohaise against the laundry wall, letting his cloak fall around them so her gown would be hidden. When she gasped at what he was doing and would have protested he brought his mouth down over hers to silence her. With a bit of luck the men now almost level with them would think it was but one of their comrades they saw, dallying with some serving wench, and they would pass by, leaving Piers and Rohaise alone.

In the eleven months since Yolande's death, Piers had not touched a woman. He had not wanted to, and he did not want to kiss Rohaise now, but kissing her seemed the only way to keep her quiet. He expected her to fight him and she did, though only for a moment. He kept her firmly against the wall, but he was not rough with her, knowing she was at a disadvantage when pitted against his greater strength. Rohaise had only one hand free to use against him, her left arm being wrapped around the pile of clean linen towels. Still, she could have slapped him or scratched at his face with her right hand. She did not. She stood quietly, letting him cover her mouth with his. Then, very slowly, she opened her lips.

Piers felt the first faint warmth of masculine interest. He became aware of her hand twining into his hair. After a while she pulled back a little, and at once he let her go. The talking men were well past them now and had not noticed the embracing pair, nor paused in their stride.

"I beg your pardon," Piers whispered, forgetting to use his accent. "I thought you would not want to be discovered here, alone with me."

"Did it not occur to you that if we had been discovered with you kissing me, it would have been far worse than if we had merely been seen talking?" The words should have been angry. Instead, they were spoken in a dreamy voice that made Piers think she might be ready to talk freely.

"Rohaise, I have a few questions. Will you answer them?"

She hesitated, and he sensed the tension and the fear in her. But she nodded her head. They were standing so close together that her forehead rubbed against his chin. Before she could change her mind he opened the bath house door and pushed her inside.

The cold winter air stirred the steam into whorls of movement pierced by the dim yellow light from the oil lamps. Rohaise put the clean towels down on the shelf next to the soap and the washing cloths. She picked up one of the oil lamps and held it near Piers's face so she could see him better. She moved the lamp this way and that, and Piers began to be anxious.

"Put down the lamp," he said in a low voice.

"I will not." She moved the lamp again, casting the light directly on his face. He heard her catch her breath and saw her hand tremble. The yellow light wavered, then steadied. To his great relief she did not cry out.

"Sir Piers. It is you."

He did not answer, hoping she would decide she must be mistaken.

"The man with you, the one you call Sir Lucas: Is he Sir Alain?"

Still Piers did not reply to her questions. He waited, fully expecting her to give the alarm, wondering if he could bring himself to kill her before she did so and knowing he could not.

"Lady Samira is much like you," Rohaise said. "She has your hair and kind eyes. Her questions made me suspicious, but it was your eyes that gave you away, Sir Piers. After all these years I still remember them."

"Lady Rohaise." He got no further. She raised her right hand and brushed her fingers along his cheek, across his beard to his lips. There she lingered, looking at his mouth and touching it with her fingertips while her own lips parted.

"Never has anyone kissed me so sweetly or so gently," she said, taking her hand away from his face. "Was it your intent to seduce me into betraying Radulf?"

"I only wanted to protect you from those men walking by, lest they recognize you and report to Baird that you were talking to me. Lady Rohaise, I must ask you not to reveal my presence here."

"Why have you returned?"

"To find justice," he said.

"From Radulf?" She gave a bitter laugh. "You will never have justice from him."

"Do you know anything about the night when Crispin was killed?" Piers asked.

"Only that Radulf did not stab him, because Radulf was sitting at the high table until he was called to the entry hall and told that Crispin had been attacked," Rohaise said. "I have never believed either you or Alain had anything to do with Crispin's death, though I have no information that would prove you innocent. I know nothing more about that night, but I think Joanna may know what really happened."

"Why do you say that?"

"Because she will not talk about it. At first she would weep when Crispin's murder was mentioned, and it seemed natural enough for her to do so. But after William Crispin was born her tears ceased, and whenever her husband's death was mentioned she grew very still and would not speak. Again, it seemed natural that her grief should end when her child was born, and natural, too, that she would want to put that terrible night behind her and think instead of her son's future.

"Sir Piers, I believe you and your friends are here not only for justice's sake, but also to rescue Joanna from her confinement."

"If that was true," Piers asked, "would you help us?"

Rohaise looked hard at him, holding up the oil lamp again so it illuminated not only Piers's face but her own. In her eyes, on her face, he could see the struggle within her, and he knew it when she made her decision. She swallowed hard, pressed her lips together, and nodded.

"There was a time when I was completely loyal to Radulf," Rohaise said. "I had been raised to submit myself to the man who would be my husband, and I believed if I could but turn myself into the kind of wife Radulf wanted, he would learn to love me. I thought if I gave him a son he would care for me and treat me kindly, so I permitted indignities from him that I will not describe to you. Now I know Radulf will never love me—no, not if I were to give him ten sons. Radulf does not know how to love."

"I am sorry for your unhappiness," Piers said. His conscience was prodding him for the way he was using her to obtain the information he sought, and for tempting her into betraying her husband. If Radulf learned what she was doing, Rohaise would be in grave danger.

"Men are often unkind to their wives," Rohaise went on. "There is nothing exceptional about it. But even the most ruthless of men care about their own offspring. Radulf has been cruel to Joanna. She does not deserve to be locked away, to waste her life in that tower room. For Joanna's sake more than for my own, I will help you, Sir Piers. How shall I begin?"

"By not telling Joanna that we are here."

"Not tell her? I must! Think what hope it would give her to know that there is someone trying to rescue her."

"Which is exactly why you cannot tell her," Piers said. "Give her hope of freedom and she will look happier and speak with renewed confidence, and the change in her will give her away. And us. Who does she see each day?"

"Myself, Lys, and Baird," Rohaise answered. "Radulf when he is here. Her son, of course. In good weather she is allowed to walk upon the battlements for an hour while the midday meal is served in the great hall, so she is seen by the guards on duty then, though she never speaks to anyone."

"She leaves her room?" Piers asked, delighted by this information.

"While most of the castle folk are in the great hall," Rohaise said, her next words dashing Piers's hope of an easy rescue. "We seldom have company at Banningford, but when we do Radulf does not allow Joanna to leave her room. Nor do I think Baird will let her walk while you are here."

"Then we must find some other way for Alain to reach her."

"Not by the stairs," Rohaise cautioned.

"I know, I've seen the guard outside her door," Piers said. "He could be overpowered, but he would probably give the alarm, and then we'd have the entire castle down on us, and we'd be no help to Joanna."

"Her door is fastened by both lock and key and a heavy wooden bolt," Rohaise told him. "If Sir Alain were a bird, he could fly in the window to his love. It's wide enough to admit a man willing to squeeze himself through. Sir Piers, I must leave you now. I have been gone too long, and if Lys becomes suspicious at my absence, she will report it to Baird. I can deal with the questions Lys will ask, but I am afraid of Baird."

It occurred to Piers that Rohaise needed rescuing every bit as much as Joanna did, but he did not say so. He did, however, do something utterly unforgiveable, and not just because he thought it might induce her to continue to help him and Alain. He caught her face between his hands and bent his head and kissed her again, very gently, letting his mouth linger on hers.

"Go, then," he whispered. "I'd not put you in danger. We will talk again, Rohaise."

"I will help in any way I can," she said, her eyes soft and shining. Then she was gone in a breeze of cold night air, and Piers stood looking after her.

"It's your fault, Yolande," he murmured into the drifting steam. " 'Twas you who taught me to respond to a kind and loving heart. But somehow I do not think you would blame me for kissing her once to keep her safe from discovery and scandal—nor the second time, either, because I wanted to feel her lips on mine again."

Having finished her bath and dressed for the evening, Samira sent her maid, Nena, to the kitchen to listen and learn what she could while pretending she could not understand a word that was said. When Nena had gone Samira called Alain into her room.

"I have been thinking," she announced.

"I've noticed that you do it quite a lot," Alain teased. "You are just like your father. What is it this time, child?"

"I wish you would not call me a child." But she was too interested in her new idea to remain annoyed with him for long. "Theo Alain, I have been trying to imagine why Baron Radulf would keep his daughter confined for so long."

"And what have you concluded?" Alain appeared amused by her earnestness, but he soon sobered as he listened to her.

"Have you considered the possibility that witnessing her husband's death might have permanently affected Joanna's wits?" Samira asked. "Radulf might have been forced to lock her up to protect her from herself. She might have been confined out of love."

"You have been raised too gently, Samira. You have never met a man like Radulf. Whatever his reason for keeping Joanna in that room, it was not love; of that I am certain."

"Nevertheless . . ." Samira paused when her chamber door opened. Seeing it was Piers, she smiled at him and waited until he had closed the door again before she continued. "Theo Alain, you do not know what you will find when you finally gain entrance to Joanna's room. You ought to be prepared for a woman who will not know you, even after you have revealed yourself to her. Or a woman who does recognize you and begins screaming for help and calling you a murderer. Or even a woman who is chained to her bed to prevent her from harming herself. You must consider the possibility that Joanna is kept in that room because she is mad."

"Though I am forced to admit that Samira's theory is not terribly farfetched," Piers said to Alain, "I can tell you that Rohaise has a far more pleasant assumption to suggest—if pleasant is the correct word to use in this case."

"I would be very glad to hear Rohaise's opinion," Alain responded, "since I find Samira's idea profoundly disturbing. What does Rohaise have to say on the subject?"

"She thinks Joanna may have information Radulf does not want spoken in public." Alain greeted this pronouncement with a long whistle. He thought for a moment after Piers had spoken.

"If Rohaise is right," Alain said, "then Radulf may be implicated in Crispin's death. I know Ambrose has always believed it might be so, but he had no proof."

"Rohaise insists that Radulf could not have

done it; he was sitting in the lord's chair, in full view of all his guests, until he was called out of the hall after Crispin was stabbed," Piers said.

"Radulf could have ordered someone else to do the killing for him," Samira noted.

"Earlier today you asked me why Joanna has been confined," Alain said to her. "Now I also ask why—why would Radulf want Crispin dead when his purpose in arranging the marriage was to get himself a strong ally who would see to it that Joanna produced the grandchildren Radulf wanted and needed for heirs? It would make no sense for Radulf to kill Crispin, or to have him killed."

"For the last hour I have been thinking about the marriage contract," said Piers. "Crispin mentioned to me that Radulf asked for a last-minute change in it, but I cannot remember exactly what the change was; only that Crispin said Father Ambrose approved of it. So much happened shortly after Crispin and I talked about it that the conversation was driven right out of my thoughts."

"Perhaps Uncle Ambrose can remember." Within one day of meeting the abbot of St. Justin's, Samira had begun to call him by the familiar name her father and Alain used for him. They had spent a few days at St. Justin's, resting after their long journey and discussing their plans with Ambrose, and Samira had grown fond of him. "He might even have a copy of the marriage contract. It may have been given to St. Justin's for safekeeping."

"You are almost as clever as your father," Alain told her with approval. "We can ask Ambrose when next we see him."

"What would you do without me?" Samira asked, her gray-green eyes dancing with humor.

"I would sleep more soundly," her father replied. "Knowing you were safe would greatly relieve my mind."

"Well, dear *Spiros* and dear *Lucas*, my beloved guardsmen," Samira bowed to each in turn, "we must not keep Lord William Crispin waiting when he has commanded a feast for our evening meal. I daresay the ordinary folk of this castle will be glad to have us as guests. Something tells me they usually get only dry bread and moldy cheese at night."

"A moment, please, Samira." Alain raised his hand to stop her from opening the door. "Piers, did Rohaise give you any information on how to get into Joanna's room?"

"She suggested you fly in through the window, which is wide enough to admit a man," Piers replied. "I thought it was rather a good idea."

"Fly?" cried Samira. "What does that mean? No man can fly." She broke off, gazing in astonishment at Alain, who was grinning.

"Clever Piers," Alain said. "Will Rohaise help us do it?"

"She has most of the keys for the inner castle at her girdle," Piers replied. "All I have to do is convince her to give that particular key to me."

"What are you talking about?" Samira demanded.

"Scaling the outer wall," Alain said, still grinning at Piers.

"Scale the wall?" Samira repeated. "Theo Alain, to do that you would have to leave the castle, go halfway around the castle wall to the western tower, and swim the moat. You cannot think of it. You would freeze to death in the cold water or in the wind after you left the water. And how could you get up the wall without help from the inside? Anyway, the guards on the battlements would soon see you."

"Perhaps not, if I climbed up on a moonless or cloudy night," Alain said. "As for the inside help, you and your father and Rohaise will provide it."

"You could be killed!" she protested.

"So could we all," said Piers, "which is why I did not want you to come with us. Therefore, the sooner we finish what we have come to do and get out of Banningford Castle, the less likely we are to lose our lives. Now, if Rohaise is correct, and Joanna knows who killed Crispin, one of us has to talk to her, and the best person for the job is Alain."

"You will have to get out of the castle without being seen," Samira said to Alain.

"Easy enough to do if I go through the postern gate," Alain told her.

"I begin to understand." Samira nodded her approval. "That's the key you want Rohaise to give you, isn't it, Papa? But will Rohaise have it, or is it in Baird's keeping?"

287

"When a castle is attacked," Piers said, "the duty of a captain of the guard is to direct the resistance on the outer walls, which puts him far away from the inner bailey. It would be only sensible for Rohaise to have the postern key so she can quickly let family members escape if attackers should reach the inner bailey."

"Would Radulf trust Rohaise with the key?" Samira asked. "He sounds like an overly suspicious man to me. Does he trust his wife?"

"Now that is a very interesting question," said Alain. "Piers, you had better find the answer to it tonight. We need that key. Without it, I'll have to leave the castle through the main gate, as Samira pointed out, and if I'm not seen going out, you may be sure my absence will soon be noted and embarassing questions asked of you and Samira. Possibly *painful* questions, if you understand me."

"I understand perfectly." Piers regarded his beautiful daughter and thought of Baird questioning her. "I will get the key from Rohaise this evening."

Chapter Seventeen

Except for the twin pools of light around the silver candelabra that Rohaise had set at each end of the high table, the great hall was as gloomy as it had ever been. There were spots of color to be seen during the evening meal; Samira's dark-haired beauty was enhanced by her gown of vibrant blue, Rohaise had put on a wine silk dress, young William Crispin wore a green tunic. They were the brightest figures at the high table, for Alain and Piers wore simple dark tunics that fitted well their disguises as Samira's guards, and Baird had not troubled to change from his spotted and soiled leather garb. Servants and men-at-arms were clothed in their drab everyday wear, and away from the high table the hall was barely lit by the few smoky torches set into sconces along the walls.

Alain had lived for so many years in the warmth and sunlight of the lands of the Middle Sea, and had grown so accustomed to buildings open to light and air that adjustment to the shadowed, damp world of an English castle was difficult—and in this particular castle there were searing memories. Looking around the hall, he could see it in his mind's eye not as it was at present, but the way it had been during the last meal he had eaten at Radulf's table, when Joanna had belonged to Crispin and Alain's heart had lain in painful pieces within his bosom. Still, he could not completely imagine himself back in that vanished time. He had changed and experienced too much ever to wish himself to be twenty-one again. Nor could he entirely escape the brutish realities of the present.

"This is not a banquet ordered by Radulf. I see no need for such nonsense as those silver candlesticks or for this," Baird complained, waving away the servant who presented a silver basin and a ewer for him to wash his hands. "I have no wish to smell like a flower."

" 'Tis but the sign of a gracious host," said William Crispin, "to see to it that his guests are treated with courtly manners. You should have changed your clothes, Baird."

"I am no noble lord," Baird replied. "I am but the captain of the guard and a busy man. Lady Rohaise, I'll thank you to tell your lazy servants to hurry with my meal and not dawdle over these foolish niceties. I have work to do."

Apparently deciding the best way to deal with

Baird's unrelenting surliness was to ignore him, William Crispin leaned forward, looking across Samira on his right hand to speak to Alain, who sat between Samira and Baird.

"Sir Lucas, Lady Samira has told me that you are among her father's guardsmen at Ascoli and that you are a great fighter. I wish you would entertain us by describing some of your battles."

"Aye," said Baird. "At least it would be interesting conversation. Tell us about the battles you have fought and the weapons you use in that foreign land."

Not knowing how much either Baird or William Crispin might know about the constant warfare in Italy, Alain spoke carefully, keeping his remarks brief and mentioning only the most familiar weapons and their use. While he talked, he was aware of Baird's watchfulness, and he began to wonder if Baird had recognized him, or, failing that, if Baird was thinking that he had met Alain in the past but could not remember when.

"My grandfather would find your stories most interesting," William Crispin said when Alain had finished. "It is too bad you must leave on the morrow and cannot wait for his return."

"One night in a place is enough when you are traveling," said Baird, picking up his wine cup. "What I would like to know is why you are here. Why did you chose to stop at Banningford?" Over the top of his cup his shrewd eyes challenged Alain.

"It was because of me." Samira spoke up before Alain could respond. "I was so severely chilled and so weary that my good servants here feared I would fall ill if I tried to go much farther."

"So I have been told." Baird had grown very still and watchful. Beside him Alain took a tighter grip on the hilt of the knife he used to carve his meat. It would serve just as well as a weapon, if he needed one. Like a hound with a bone, Baird persisted in his questioning, worrying the subject over and over again. "Why were you traveling past Banningford? What is so attractive here?"

"If you will forgive my saying so," Samira responded with one of her quick, dazzling smiles, directed first toward William Crispin and then at Baird, "there was nothing particularly fascinating about this castle. It was simply on our way."

"On your way to where?" Baird demanded, and Alain hoped Samira would remember the story they had agreed upon.

He should have known she was too clearwitted to be frightened into saying the wrong thing. "My late grandmother was a Scottish princess," Samira announced, "a descendant of King Duncan of hallowed memory. Before she died at Ascoli, where she lived for many years after marrying my grandfather, this noble lady made me swear to make a pilgrimage to King Duncan's grave at Iona. That is why we are in England now. We are on a sacred pilgrimage." She said those last words in so fervent a voice that William Crispin looked at her in reverent admiration, and even Baird nodded his approval. But he would not be silenced.

"I wonder you do not stay at the religious houses along your way instead of at castles," Baird said.

"In fact," said Alain, thinking the time had come for him to intervene, "we have been doing just that. We planned to spend this night at St. Justin's Abbey."

"You should have gone there," Baird told him. "It's not so far."

"I would not risk my lady's health when she was feeling unwell," Alain replied blandly.

"Hummph." Baird's derisive snort told Alain all he cared to know about the man's concern for any lady's health. After that Baird applied himself to his food and asked no more questions. Alain could hear Samira talking quietly to William Crispin, who was insisting that she should call him Will, as did those who knew him best.

"Only my mother always calls me William Crispin," he said.

Knowing Samira would do her best to pry out of the young man any information he might possess that could be useful to them, Alain did not interrupt their conversation. He did listen to what was being said, and it soon became clear that young Will believed a version of the events of long ago far different from Alain's recollection.

"I only know," Will said, in answer to a delicately probing question from Samira, "that my father was most foully murdered by a man who claimed to be his friend but who lusted after my mother."

"Oh, dear," Samira murmured sympathetically, "how frightening it must have been for Lady Joanna."

"She was there at my father's death," Will said. "Afterward she withdrew into isolation out of grief, for she loved my father dearly. I believe she loves him still. When I visit her I often find her in prayer, and I am certain she prays for him."

At that point Alain made himself stop listening. He had no way of knowing for certain who had taught Crispin's son the false story, though he thought it must have been Radulf. He could only hope Joanna did not believe it. But if she did not, why did she allow her son to continue to believe such lies?

So many questions, he thought. *Why, and why, and why? Who has the answers? Joanna? Radulf? Baird? Has Baird recognized me? Is he clever enough to hide it if he has?*

Will and Baird, and Rohaise, too, assumed their guests would leave Banningford on the following day. But the visitors, having succeeded in entering, planned to remain for a second day and night, hoping by then to learn what they needed to know in order to ferret out Crispin's real killer. And to free Joanna. The unraveling of the true story would begin with Joanna.

Alain lifted his half-full wine cup, then set it down untasted. The work before him later that night would require steady hands and a clear mind. Without them, he and his companions might be dead by sunrise. With luck, he might see Joanna before the night was through. If only Piers could convince Rohaise to hand over the key to the postern gate. . . .

On Will's left side sat Rohaise, and on her left, Piers.

"Sir Spiros," Rohaise said, remembering to call him by his assumed name, "is there aught I can do to make your stay at Banningford more pleasant?"

"Just one small thing," Piers responded. "However, I am not certain I ought to ask it of you."

"As I told you earlier, I will do anything I can to help." Her voice was a breathy whisper, and Piers knew she was frightened. She took a sip of wine. "Tell me what you want of me before Lys or Baird or someone else interrupts us."

"What I must have," Piers said, his voice as low as hers, "is the key to the postern gate."

She went white at his words. She said nothing; she just picked up her wine cup and drained it. Thus fortified, she spoke in a perfectly normal voice.

"If you will excuse me, Sir Spiros," she said, loudly enough for anyone to hear, "I must just see to one small matter in the kitchen. I will return in a few moments."

She left the table, and no one around her seemed to think anything of her going. Piers waited, believing he could trust her, yet praying that he had not misjudged her, that she would not give them away to Baird. He could not touch his food until she returned.

After what seemed like a very long time she slipped into her seat again, smiling at Will's questioning look.

"Sometimes Lys forgets to bring in the pudding at the right time," she explained easily. "Tonight she is ready. It will be served next, Will. I know how much you like it."

When Will had thanked her and returned his attention to Samira, Rohaise slid her left hand beneath the table. Piers felt her press upon his thigh, and when he put his own hand down she placed a small metal object into his palm.

"I could not take it off my girdle while I was at the table," she said. "Someone would have noticed."

"Thank you." He hid the key in the purse at his belt.

"You should know," she whispered, "that Baird has a second key, which he uses when he tests the gate. 'Twas last tested two days ago, so the hinges are newly oiled and should be silent."

"My thanks again for the information."

"Please be careful." She spoke with her eyes on Lys, who was serving a large oblong pudding set upon a silver tray.

"It's not I who will use the key," Piers said. "But thank you for caring."

"Truly, Sir Spiros," Rohaise said in a normal voice as Lys approached with the pudding, "if you continue to thank me for such a simple meal, I shall not know how to reply to you. Lys, do give Sir Spiros a large square of the pudding. The recipe is said to come from Lombardy, so the dish may be familiar to you, sir."

The pudding was baked in a pastry crust and contained chopped prunes, dates, and dried figs in a mixture of eggs and heavy cream, flavored with cinnamon and orange peel. Piers had tasted lighter, more delicate versions in Italy.

"Excellent," he said, smiling at Lys. She looked back at him with cold, hard eyes and moved on to pass what remained of the pudding to those at the lower tables.

Because of the premature darkness of winter the inhabitants of the castle retired early. It was well before midnight when Alain, Piers, Samira, and her maid, Nena, gathered in Samira's room.

"Here's the postern key." Piers gave it to Alain. "Don't lose it; we have to give it back to Rohaise before anyone discovers it is missing."

"If Baird has another, as you say, keeping it for a day shouldn't prove too risky," Alain replied. He let Samira attach the key to a leather thong and then fasten the thong around his neck. This precaution completed, he looked toward the maid. "Nena, have you talked to our squires recently?"

"Yes, sir. They have learned that in this cold weather the guards on the walls don't walk about as often as they should. They look busy when Baird appears, but when he's not there, they try to stay inside as much as they dare."

"Baird drank a fair amount of wine tonight," Alain remarked, pulling a loose black woolen tunic over the one he was already wearing. "Let us hope he sleeps well and doesn't waken the guards too often."

297

"The kitchen maids were teasing Lys," Nena told him, blushing. "They said when Baird drinks a lot, he wants his woman. Lys didn't look too happy about it."

"I could almost feel sorry for Lys," Alain murmured.

"Let us hope her charms keep Baird well occupied," Piers said. "Are you ready, Alain?"

"I only need my knife." Alain belted the weapon at his waist.

"Theo Alain . . ." Samira had been a bit distracted during the preparations, and now she put out a hand to keep Alain where he was. "You heard Will talking to me tonight. He believes his mother loved Lord Crispin. How can we break his heart by telling him otherwise? And what will he think of us when all of this is over?"

"He's a fine young man, isn't he?" Alain interrupted her questions. "I don't want to break his heart, either. Why don't we let Joanna decide what to tell her son?"

"I suppose that would be best," Samira agreed.

"Alain, for God's sake get moving, and get this job done," Piers said. "Every moment we stay here increases the risk that we will be discovered. If we are found out, we will have no other chance to prove our innocence. We have to get the information we need and then leave Banningford at once."

"I know, old Sir Piers." Alain clapped him on the shoulder. "Yours is the harder task this night, to lie outside Samira's door and pretend you are asleep when you would much prefer to be with me. I understand how much depends on my actions in the next few hours. I promise you, I will not fail."

"Theo Alain, where is the rope Nena and I are to let down for you?" Samira asked.

"Here." Alain opened his saddlebag. Along with Piers's bag, it had been tossed with apparent carelessness into a corner of Samira's room. Grinning at her and at Nena, hoping to dispel their seriousness for just a little while, Alain pulled out the rope and showed them the four-pronged metal hook attached to one end.

"I was afraid I would have to sleep on this grapple and pretend it was a pillow," he said. "You are to give me a little time to reach the spot below this arrow slit. Imagine me creeping down the stairs to the entry hall and then out to the inner bailey. Perhaps I will stop for a word or two with someone who notices me, or possibly I will go to the stables to check on our squires, which is my purpose for leaving the tower if anyone should ask me. When no one is looking I'll unlock the postern gate and slip through the wall and then out onto that narrow ledge of land between the wall and the moat. On tiptoe, because there won't be much room, I'll stroll around to this side of the tower. When I get here I would very much like to find this rope awaiting me."

"You make it sound so easy." Samira looked doubtfully at the coiled rope and at the hooked grapple. "There is scarcely a toehold at the base of the castle wall, and the wall itself is so steep and smooth."

"It *will* be easy," Alain assured her. "I will be climbing to heaven, to see my love. All you have to do, ladies, is let the rope out of the arrow slit. Do it slowly, so it doesn't tangle or knot. Just let it fall straight down."

"The arrow slit is so narrow and the wall so thick," Nena protested. "We won't be able to put our heads out to watch the rope go down."

"You couldn't see it anyway, goose," Samira told her. "The night is dark and cloudy."

"If you can't see the rope, Nena," Alain said, "then neither can the guards on the wall. But I will find it because I know it will be there. Now, Samira, the two of you will have to hold the grapple as the last of the rope plays out. It is too large to fit through the arrow slit, but we don't want it to make a loud noise when the prongs hit the stone wall, or damage the wall for that matter. Chips in the stone around an arrow slit can raise questions in the minds of men determined on complete security for their castle."

"I understand, Theo Alain."

"Once the rope is let down," Alain said, "then comes the difficult part. You will have to stay awake until I climb down to the ground again after I've talked to Joanna."

"I will not sleep at all," Samira promised.

"Nor will I," said Nena.

"When I reach the ground and I'm ready to go back to the postern gate," Alain said, "I'll pull on the rope twice. Then you are to haul it up and hide it in my saddlebag again. After you've finished you may sleep. In the morning I'll tell you what happened."

"Be careful," Samira urged, kissing his cheek. "I will pray for you."

"It will be all right," Alain promised.

It was bitterly cold climbing up the rope, and the leather gloves Alain wore did nothing to keep his fingers warm. The climbing was not hard for him; he had always been an active man and had climbed into the rigging of many a ship, or swung from ship to ship on a rope. He had scaled the walls of a few castles, too, in Italy and Greece. He knew he could reach Joanna's window as long as he was not spotted by the guards on the walls, and as long as his hands did not grow so numb with cold that they refused to work.

When he reached the arrow slit outside Samira's room he sensed the stillness of the two women inside, listening for the sound of his passing. He did not waste breath or energy speaking to them. The most difficult part of his climb lay ahead of him, and he needed to conserve his strength, for the cold was sapping his ability to move as easily as he usually did. He hooked his right arm inside the arrow slit, holding himself securely so he could angle his upper body backward and look toward his goal.

When it had been built seventy years previously the castle wall had been as perfectly smooth as workmen could make it, but heat and cold, rain and ice, had all taken their toll, and now there were rough spots on the surface. There were not enough irregularities to allow a massive scaling of the walls by an army, but a single determined man might climb to the top of the western tower, or to the window about ten feet above Alain's present position and approximately four feet to his left. Feeling with his left hand, he found a spot where his foot could fit, and a hand-hold at the right level above it. Pulling his arm out of the arrowslit, he began to work his way upward again.

When he reached the double windows at Joanna's room the shutters were securely latched. He hung by his fingertips, with one toe slipping out of the notch in the wall where he had placed it, and for the first time considered the possibility that his plan might fail.

"No," he groaned. "I won't give up. She's there, just a few feet away from me."

He could see a faint light around the edges of the shutters, which he assumed meant she was still awake. He could hear no sounds to indicate she had company. He decided to chance calling out to her. He had no other choice.

"Joanna." He prayed the guards on the wall would be warming their fingers over a brazier or huddled against a distant tower for protection against the wind. *"Joanna."*

Now he did hear a sound from within. The latch was being opened and one of the shutters was drawn back. He slid his hands over the width of the windowsill, seeking a better purchase. When he got his arms inside as far as the elbows he hung there, catching his breath before he started to lever himself across the sill.

"Who are you?" He would have known her voice anywhere, that sweetly modulated sound, now filled with amazement and just the faintest thrill of fear. "How did you reach my window?"

"My love, it's Alain. I'll tell you in a moment how I got here. Just let me get inside."

"*Alain?* Is it really you?"

"Yes. *Oomph.*" He fell through the window, tumbling across the padded seat below it and landing most ungracefully on the floor at her feet. He shook himself, preparing to rise, and got to his knees. "Joanna, my love."

"*You bloody bastard!*"

He did not see what she hit him with, but he knew it must be a pitcher of wine because suddenly the wet, sticky stuff was cascading over his head and shoulders and he had to wipe it out of his eyes. He licked his lips, tasting cinnamon and cloves and the honey used to sweeten the wine.

"Joanna, what—?"

"Bastard! You left me—left me! And after you promised to come to my aid if I should need you," she shouted at him. "Liar! Liar!"

He reacted as he would have done in the midst of battle, which was where he imagined he was, because while she yelled at him she kept hitting him about the head and shoulders with a heavy object. He knew he had to silence her before the guard on the tower stairs demanded to know what was going on inside her room.

He surged off the floor in a lightning-swift movement, clamped one hand over her mouth and with the other hand grabbed her by the hair. The wine pitcher fell out of her hand, dropping to the floor with a loud thud. Before Joanna had time to react or try to protect herself from him, Alain threw her onto the bed. Since he had to keep his hand over her mouth he landed on top of her, his weight knocking the air out of her lungs. She lay beneath him, the brilliant blue eyes he remembered so well blazing at him with a raging anger.

"I have to talk to you," he whispered fiercely. "Will you be quiet if I take my hand away?"

For answer she bit him hard, sinking her teeth into the side of his hand with an expression of ferocious glee. Acting on instinct, Alain tore his hand away and raised it, ready to strike her. Joanna opened her mouth to scream, and would have, if there had been enough air in her.

"Lady Joanna?" A rough male voice sounded from the other side of her chamber door. "Lady Joanna, is something wrong? I heard a noise."

Joanna took a breath, filling her lungs. From the look on her face Alain knew she was going to call for help. His hand ached where she had bitten him. He wasn't going to sacrifice his other hand to her teeth, and he had the distinct feeling that if he tried to kiss her to keep her quiet, she would bite his lip. He'd leave a trail of blood all the way down the western tower to the ground— if she didn't have the guards in to slice him into pieces before he got that far.

"Lady Joanna?" the guard called again.

"He'll kill me," Alain said, very low.

"I'd like to watch that," she told him sweetly.

"You do, and you'll never get out of this room," he responded. "Send him away and you'll have at least a slight chance at freedom."

"Lady Joanna, if you do not answer me at once, I am going to get the key from Baird." The door rattled as the guard banged on it.

"It's nothing," Joanna called. "I stumbled when I got up to latch the window shutter. My shin hurt so much that I couldn't answer you at first."

"I know I'm not supposed to speak to you, but I am concerned. Shall I call Lady Rohaise?"

"No need to trouble her," Joanna replied. "It's only a bruise. It'll be fine by tomorrow."

"As you wish." They could hear the sound of footsteps moving away, descending the first five or six steps below Joanna's chamber.

"What's he doing, watching Samira's chamber door, too?" asked Alain. This supposition was confirmed by a sleepy question poised in Piers's voice and a laughing reply from the guardsman. Alain fervently hoped that Piers would leave the matter alone and go back to his feigned sleep instead of trying to come to his aid.

"Get off me, you brute," Joanna ordered.

"Not just yet." Hearing no further comments from either the guard or Piers, Alain let himself relax a bit. As he did, he became intensely aware of Joanna's body beneath his. Her room was warmed by braziers set at either side of her bed, and after his precipitous entry the open shutter had swung back until it nearly covered the window again, thus blocking the inflow of cold out-

305

side air. Alain's fingers were warmer; he could feel his nose and cheeks again, and in the center of his being there was a lively stirring in response to Joanna's closeness. She felt it, too.

"You disgusting man," she hissed, trying her best to push him off her. "How I hate you."

"You loved me once," he said. "I love you still."

"You do not. If you did, you would have rescued me long before this."

"It was impossible. I've been away from England".

He saw her eyes blaze blue fire, saw her mouth open to shout at him. This time he risked it. He brought his mouth down on hers, claiming the kiss he had wanted for so many years.

She fought him. She pulled his hair and pounded her fists on his back and thrashed her legs about until he clamped his thighs over hers and held her still.

He paid no attention to her muffled cries of outrage or to the sobbing moans that came later. These were the lips he had dreamed of, this was the body he had ached for, this was Joanna, his beloved, in his arms at last, and he did not let her go for a long, long time.

"Have you finished?" she asked coldly.

"I will never be finished with you. That was but a kiss. I want all of you, everything you have to give me."

"If you want anything from me, you'll have to take it by force," she snarled.

"If that was true, you'd have called the guard in here when you had the chance."

"Oh, I'll call the guard," she said, "but not until I've heard the wonderful excuse you must have for leaving me here to rot, after you promised to come back and save me." With that, she began to struggle again.

"Have done, woman," he growled. "I'm not a boy any longer, and it was hard work climbing up the tower wall."

"It's too bad you didn't fall and break your neck," she told him, trying to get her wrists out of his grasp.

"The Joanna I once knew would never have said such a cruel thing to me."

"I am much changed, my lord." She drew a long, sobbing breath. "Did it never occur to you to take me with you when you fled?"

"Would you have gone with me?" he asked, beginning to be angry at her continued rage. "Or would you have stayed to weep over poor Crispin?"

"He was a better man than you," she declared. "*You* left me to my father's kindness. Crispin gave me a son."

"I've met him. The resemblance is terrifying."

"You left me." Her voice cracked and broke. "You ran away and never came back for me."

"I'm here now. Joanna, I never stopped loving you, or thinking about you, but I had to wait to return until the time was right."

"*Eighteen years?* A long wait, my dear, dear lord."

The sarcasm in her voice lacerated his tightly controlled emotions. This was not the way he had imagined their reunion. He looked at the woman lying beneath him, lying so still that he began to suspect she was planning some new trick to bring the guard back to her door. Still holding her wrists at each side of her head, he moved, stretching his full length on her, thigh to thigh, breast to breast, all of her, soft and curving and infinitely desirable, all of her beneath him.

"I have dreamed of your mouth for every day of those eighteen years," he said, and kissed her again. This time she did not fight him. In fact, she lay inert, letting him caress her mouth with his.

"Joanna," he whispered. "My dear love."

"I hate you," she murmured. "Don't do this to me. Let me go on hating you. It gives me strength."

He would not stop. He kissed her until she began to respond, until he dared to release her wrists and her hands crept around his back to hold him closer to her. He kissed her until her lips opened and she took his tongue inside her hot sweetness.

"You did that once before," she said afterward. "You kissed me in the herb garden and put your tongue in my mouth and I thought my heart would stop beating."

"Joanna," he said, most reluctantly leaving her and sitting up. "I would gladly spend the whole night making love to you, but that's not why I've come."

"Then why are you here?" she asked, with a return to her earlier coolness toward him.

"I have much to tell, and much to ask of you," he said. "Will you listen?"

"I will, but only because you said I might have a chance at freedom." She rose from the bed, smoothing her skirts. She gave him an odd, considering look, one side of her mouth tilting upward in a half smile. "Think well, Alain. Do you really want to free me? I am no longer the innocent, meek creature you once knew. What I have endured has changed me, and I cannot revert to what I once was."

"I did notice the change," he said ruefully, rubbing the back of his neck where she had hit him and looking at the wine pitcher on the floor.

"You have changed, too," she said, her eyes still on him. "You've grown a beard, there's grey in your hair, and your shoulders are so broad that I'm surprised you were able to get through the window."

"It wasn't easy," he admitted.

"Will you go back the same way?" There was just the shadow of a smile in her eyes.

"If I live long enough," he told her.

The humor went out of her. She sat beside him on the bed, folding her hands in her lap.

"Tell me what you want to say, Alain. I will listen without interrupting."

Quickly he recounted all that had happened since he and Piers had fled Banningford, leaving Crispin dead in his young wife's arms. He described their careers in Sicily under King Roger, Piers's marriage and his wife's death, his own refusal to wed because of his love for Joanna. He finished with an account of their return to England and their hopes of discovering the identity of Crispin's murderer.

"So Piers has a daughter," she said when he was done. "I am surprised he would bring her here, into such danger."

"She is a strong-minded and resourceful young woman." He smiled, thinking of Samira. "I don't think he could have prevented her from coming with us."

"And you say you never married. But I presume there were women."

"A few. None of them was you."

"Well, I need not protest my fidelity to my dead husband," she said, an edge of bitterness in her voice, "or the purity of my affection for a young man who kissed me once. I have had no opportunity to sin. It's too bad, really. There were children I would have liked to have. Children . . ." Her voice trailed off into a sad silence.

"I'm sorry." His hand rested on hers.

"Do I look much older to you?"

"You appear to be remarkably young. You have no gray hair; there are only a few tiny lines around your eyes; your skin is as soft and smooth as I remember."

"That's what Rohaise says, but I wanted to hear it from you. I suppose it's because I haven't done much living. I have been like an insect trapped in amber, immobilized, frozen in time." She removed his hand from hers and refolded her own hands in her lap. "You said you have much to ask of me. Tell me what you want."

Taken aback by her coolness, he did not respond at once.

"You spoke of a chance for my freedom," she prompted.

"To prove that I am innocent of Crispin's death," he said, "and that Piers is innocent of complicity with me, we have to discover who the real murderer is."

"I see." There was no sign of emotion on her part.

"There is also the question of why your father has kept you here, in this room, for so many years."

"It's perfectly obvious," she said.

"Do you know who killed Crispin?"

"Oh, yes. I've known since the beginning. The problem was, I forgot some of the details. I suppose it was because I was so upset by seeing Crispin all covered with blood. And then he died in my arms. Living through something like that makes small incidents seem unimportant, and so I forgot part of that night." She rose, to walk about the room. "But, confined here for so long, I have had more than enough time to remember and to work it all through."

"Tell me everything," he demanded.

"I require a promise from you first."

"Joanna, I will give you anything you want." He went to her to take her hands and hold them against his chest, over his heart. "I love you. I have never loved anyone else."

To his dismay, she took her hands out of his, folding them in front of her in the same way in which she had folded them in her lap. Alain wondered if she did so to keep them from trembling. In her dark gown with her hair pulled back into a tight braid she looked like a nun, severe and unapproachable. He felt a chill in his heart as he began to understand just how different she was from the girl he had once known.

"I want justice," she said.

"You shall have it."

"More than justice, I want revenge."

"Joanna—"

"A good man was deprived of life," she went on as if he had not spoken. "My son was made fatherless, and I—I have lost eighteen years of my life. My youth is gone. All that I might have been, or seen, or done during those years was taken from me. I want to see the guilty punished."

"You have my word on it."

"You don't understand. I want to participate. I will not sit here, alone, waiting patiently while someone else does what must be done. You will include me in your plans or I will not tell you what I know."

"Your silence won't get you out of this room," he reminded her.

"Until an hour ago I thought only death would get me out of this room," she replied. "If you will not do as I want, then nothing has changed for me. Well, my lord, am I to help you, or are you to leave Banningford at first light and never look back?"

"Your strength of will and your courage shame

me," he murmured. "You will not relent, will you?"

"No." She met him with a look he knew well. He had seen it often enough in men about to go into battle. He could not refuse her.

"All right," he said, adding, "Joanna, there isn't much time. I have to get down that rope and through the postern gate before sunrise."

"I understand."

"I wish you would be a little more emotional," he said.

"As I was when you first arrived in my room?" She allowed herself a smile. "Perhaps after I have emptied my heart and my thoughts of the knowledge of foul villainy that has fermented inside me for so many years, perhaps then I will find room in myself for some gentler feelings. But first, the story as I know it. This is what happened."

It took her a while to tell everything. Alain interrupted, asked questions, made her repeat portions of the story.

"My God," he said when she was finished. "I have no doubt that you are right about this, but how terrible. How twisted, and stupid."

"It's the result of madness," she said. "Telling it to you, I began to realize that something must be done at once; otherwise my son will become involved. I am glad you have come back, Alain."

"Unfortunately, I have to leave you now," he said. "I have stayed much too long."

"You promised I could play a part in your scheme," she reminded him.

"So you shall. If I possibly can, I will return

tonight. Will you be good enough to leave the shutter unlatched for me?"

"Not only that, I'll give you wine in a cup instead of straight out of the pitcher," she said, letting the corners of her mouth tilt upward.

"One day soon, I hope to hear you laugh again," he murmured, touching her face. He went to the window niche, then stopped with one knee on the padded seat. "If anything should prevent me from coming to you this way, we will make an attempt to get you out by the stairs. If someone you do not know opens your door and says, 'Alain sent me,' go with that person without fear."

"The guard outside my door tonight is Owain," she said. "He's Baird's man, yet I think he is sympathetic to me. He is the only man-at-arms who dares to break the rule against speaking to me. He might prove useful to you."

"It's good to know you have someone among the men to care what happens to you," he said, adding, "I must go."

"Do not forget, Alain, you promised I could be part of your plan. You gave your word."

"You are a part of everything I do." Seizing her in his arms, he kissed her, a quick, hard meeting of their lips. "Until tonight, my love."

"Take my hands," she said. "I'll ease you across the sill."

It was still too dark for her to see much, but she leaned far out of the window, waiting until she heard a bird call from the direction of the moat straight below her. Only then did she latch the shutters and remove her gown and go to bed.

In the inner bailey Baird was making his predawn rounds of the castle defenses when he heard the postern gate swing open. He crept closer to the gate, hugging the castle wall, his dark gray cloak making him all but invisible against the gray stones. He had just come down from inspecting the battlements and he knew full well there was no invading force threatening Banningford. Thinking to catch one of the castle servants or men-at-arms returning from some romantic nocturnal excursion, he peered through the gray half light.

Baird smothered an exclamation when he recognized the foreign guardsman, Lucas, who closed and locked the gate behind him and then headed toward the western tower. Baird caught the smell of wine and spices as the man passed him.

"Now, what the devil has he been doing, and how did he get the key from Rohaise?" Baird muttered to himself. "And where outside these walls did he find wine, that he should reek of it? Did he take the wine with him? Did he meet someone and share it? Not Rohaise, for she's safely abed in the lord's chamber and I'd have been told if she stirred out of it. Is someone planning to capture Banningford by treachery? Damn! I knew that foolish boy should not have let those strangers in. It's a good thing I sent for Radulf as soon as they got here."

Chapter Eighteen

Rain and sleet began again shortly after sunrise, the icy wetness drenching anyone who ventured out of doors. In her room in the western tower Joanna peered out at the gray landscape and shivered, thinking of Alain trying to climb the tower wall to reach her.

"Good morning." Rohaise came in, followed by Lys, with a tray of food. They both stopped short, seeing the partially dried wine on the floor and wrinkling their noses at the smell of it. "What happened?"

"I stumbled and dropped the pitcher, and there is nothing in this room that I could use to clean up the mess." Joanna frowned at Lys. "Send someone to scrub the floor. I want clean sheets, too. The wine spattered onto my bed."

"Later I will send the woman who cleans here."

Lys banged the tray down on a small table. "You ought to be more careful." With Joanna's food delivered, Lys planted herself by the door, folding her arms across her buxom chest.

"You may go," Rohaise said to her.

"I may not," Lys returned. "Baird told me not to leave you alone with Joanna this morning, and to report to him everything you say to each other."

"*Lady* Joanna to you," Joanna informed her. "Mind your manners, woman. By what right does Baird presume to monitor my conversations?"

"So he can report them to your father," Lys replied, a flicker of some indefinable emotion lighting her dull eyes.

"And precisely why does Baird imagine my words today will be especially interesting to Lord Radulf?" Joanna demanded. Well aware that her every reaction would be reported, she used haughty coldness to cover her fear that Baird had learned about Alain's presence at Banningford.

"Baird probably imagines that I will be coerced into carrying messages to or from you," Rohaise said. "We have visitors in the castle."

"Aye," Lys put in, "there's a heathen princess in the great hall, making a fool out of your son."

"She is not a heathen." Young Will came into his mother's room. "Lys, I forbid you to speak disparagingly about Lady Samira. Now, leave us. I would speak privately with my mother."

"Baird says I am to stay." Lys did not move.

"Baird is not the master of Banningford Castle," Will reminded her. "Until my grandfather returns I am master here. Begone!"

317

Faced by the determined young man, there was nothing Lys could do but leave.

"How I loathe that woman," Joanna muttered. "Always listening, always watching, as if I had any secrets Radulf does not already know."

"I suppose Grandfather keeps them because Baird is so loyal to him," Will told her. "Grandfather says loyalty is no small thing, but I wish he would give you some other servingwoman."

"Forget Lys. Tell me about your guests," Joanna invited. "Sit down, William Crispin. Have you broken your fast? Here's bread and cheese and some cold fowl. Rohaise, will you take some wine?"

While the two women sat on the side of Joanna's bed, eating and drinking, Will perched on the windowseat and regaled them with his description of Samira.

"I thought I had seen beautiful women while I was fostered at Bolsover Castle," Will said, "but no one could equal Lady Samira's beauty. Her hair is dark as the night sky, her eyes gray-green as the deep forest on a misty morn. And her conversation! She is brilliantly educated; she has seen so many places that I have only dreamed of visiting. Mother, I wish you would break your rule of not meeting anyone and allow Samira to come to your room. Or, better yet, go to the great hall for a meal so you can talk with her. I want you to meet her."

"I cannot." Joanna leapt to her feet. "William Crispin, do not press me on this. You know I never see anyone but you and Rohaise and your grandfather."

"Also Baird and Lys, though you heartily dislike them," Will noted. "And the woman who cleans this room."

"You do not know what you are asking of me."

"I understand why you first wanted to retire to this room," Will said.

"Do you?" Joanna's voice was bitter. "How can you possibly know what my feelings were months before you were born?"

"Mother, it's time to give up mourning for my father. You have missed so much of life by staying here. It's time to re-enter the world. You are not a prisoner; Grandfather says the guard at your door is there at *your* request, to keep out people you don't wish to see."

"Rohaise, help me!" Joanna stood with her hands clenched at her bosom, looking as if she would burst into tears. "Tell him I cannot leave this room."

"Will, please stop this harassment." Rohaise put up both her hands as if she would physically prevent him from saying anything more. "Do not question your mother. Allow her to do what she believes is best."

"But she's wrong," Will insisted. "She does not have to stay here in this room. I asked Grandfather about it once, and he said it was entirely her decision.

"Mother, you won't have to go to the great hall, if that is what frightens you. Lady Samira is in the room just below this one. I fear she will not leave it today, for her guards report that she is ill, but you could meet her there."

319

"Samira is ill?" Joanna cried, wondering what was really happening in Samira's room. "Of what? Rohaise, have you been to see her?"

" 'Tis but a slight chill, nothing to cause concern," Rohaise said with a strange look at Joanna. "Her guards are overprotective and insist she cannot travel in bad weather. I believe they will leave on the morrow."

"I hope to convince them to stay," Will announced. "I want Lady Samira to meet Grandfather, too."

"Why?" Joanna asked, horrified by this idea.

"Because," her son informed her, "I want Grandfather to arrange for me to marry Lady Samira."

"Oh, sweet, merciful heaven." Overcome by a sense of impending doom, Joanna sank onto the windowseat beside her son. "He will never allow it."

"Because her dowry will be in foreign lands and not in England?" Will laughed at her concern. "What difference will that make? Other knights marry foreign ladies all the time."

"Your grandfather has definite plans for you," Rohaise cautioned. "Radulf does not like to have his arrangements disrupted."

"All the same, when he comes home I am going to speak to him," Will said. "I'm sure I can convince him to give me what I most want."

"He will never change his mind," Joanna declared. "William Crispin, I beg you, *do not ask him.*"

"Don't look so frightened." Will put his arm

around her. "Mother, I'm sorry if I upset you. Perhaps you are right and you ought to remain here, where you feel safe. It's plain to me that the prospect of facing the world outside this room is too much for you. But will you consider receiving Lady Samira here, in privacy, before she leaves Banningford?"

"I will consider it." Joanna knew it was a promise she would have to break. There could be no question of openly admitting a stranger to her room.

"When you meet Samira I'm sure you will understand why I want to marry her," Will said, kissing his mother. "I'll leave you with Rohaise. I only stopped in to say good morning. Until later, Mother."

"He believes I am safe here," Joanna murmured when he had gone. Wearily she rested her head against the stone windowframe. "There is no safe place, not for me. And now, not for him. Rohaise, I have much to tell you."

"What is it, Lys?" Rohaise's warning voice cut across her words, stopping what Joanna would have said.

"Now that Master Will has left I'm back to do my duty as Baird instructed me," Lys declared. "I am to stay here while you are in the room, Lady Rohaise."

"In that case, Joanna, we will talk later," said Rohaise. "Since all we have to discuss is this day's menus and the beauty and intelligence of our lady guest, what we have to say can only bore Baird when it's repeated to him. We wouldn't want to do that, would we? Come along, Lys; let's see to the kitchen chores."

Rohaise left behind her a stepdaughter who wanted to scream from fear and frustration. Joanna wanted her son to marry a woman he could love, but she knew Radulf would never allow the boy to wed someone whom Radulf had not personally chosen. Unknown to his grandson, Radulf's trip away from Banningford was for the purpose of arranging William Crispin's marriage to a girl whose dowry included extensive lands, some of which bordered on William Crispin's barony of Haughston. Joanna could not bear to think of the consequences of her son informing his grandfather that he wanted to marry elsewhere.

Her only hope lay in Alain. If, together, they could expose Crispin's murderer, if she could but attain her freedom, she would have some say in the choice of her son's wife. If Samira was all William Crispin said, and all Alain claimed she was, then Joanna would gladly consent to the marriage.

Now she had to wait for Alain to come to her again. He had promised to return that night. Once more she would trust in him to help her, this time not because of a girlish love but because it was in his interest, too, that the truth should be revealed.

The long day dragged on. Joanna paced back and forth in her chamber, counting off the endless minutes with each step. Her nerves stretched near to breaking, and she snapped at Lys and the cleaning woman when they appeared to change her bed linen and mop the wine off the floor.

Just after midday the sky cleared and the sun came out. Disregarding the cold, Joanna flung the shutters wide and leaned out of her windows to check on the condition of the tower wall. She was relieved to see that the wind had dried any ice that might have clung to the surface. Alain would be able to climb up to her again.

"What are you doing?" Baird had come into the room. Behind him, Lys appeared with Joanna's midday meal.

"The weather has cleared," Joanna said. "I want to take my usual walk."

"Not while there are outsiders in the castle," Baird said. "You know the rule. Don't ask for what I cannot allow."

"You despicable man." Joanna wondered, as she had done many times over the years, how she was going to keep her hatred of Baird under control.

"Here, now," Baird said with a vicious grin, "treat me with courtesy, Lady Joanna. You know who I am."

"Indeed," she told him, "I know just who, and what, you are."

"Aye," Baird returned. "That you do. I am captain of the guard at all times, and master of this castle in Lord Radulf's absence. Remind your son of that, Lady Joanna. He tends to forget it."

"You leave William Crispin alone!" she screamed at him. "Touch one hair on his head and my father will have you drawn and quartered."

"If Radulf doesn't order it done to young Will first, once he hears the boy is set on marrying a stranger." Baird gave a chuckle that sent terror to Joanna's heart.

"Get out, you eavesdropping witch!" she shouted at Lys. "Get out, both of you!"

"Yes, come along, Lys." Baird's fist buffetted Lys's shoulder, knocking her toward the door. "It's plain to see Lady Joanna is about to suffer a fit of madness, and I wouldn't want you to be hurt, now would I?" Pushing Lys ahead of him, Baird went out and locked the door, leaving Joanna ready to fly out the window on the wings of her rage.

Still it was only midday. There were long hours to endure until Alain came to her. She ate the meat and bread and leftover pudding Lys had brought. She paced the floor for a while, then threw herself onto the bed and actually slept. When she wakened the sun was setting. Lys returned, thankfully without Baird, to bring warm water so Joanna could wash. Lys would not speak to her, but Joanna did not much care. When the woman had withdrawn, taking with her the dirty dishes, Joanna resumed her impatient waiting.

Radulf returned just after nightfall. With Baird, who had been at his side since the moment he had entered the castle gate, Radulf strode into the great hall and right up to the high table, where Will sat talking with Piers and Rohaise.

"What's this I hear of you, young man?" he shouted at Will. "In these dangerous times you welcome unknown guests in my absence?"

"Grandfather, it's only a lady on a pilgrimage

and her two guards," Will replied, sounding calm and reasonable in comparison with Radulf's ire. "How can there be any danger in so few guests?"

"Where is this lady?" Radulf stared at Piers, who looked calmly back at the tall, heavyset man with the florid face and cold blue eyes. "Answer me, fellow!"

"Lady Samira is ill." Piers spoke in his heaviest Greek accent. "That is why we are remaining for a second night of your hospitality, sir. We hope that by resting all day, our lady will be able to travel in the morning. I do thank you for your excellent wine, sir." With those words, Piers lifted his cup in a graceful, slightly effeminate gesture, smiling and toasting Radulf, whose expression promptly changed to one of disgust.

"Hummph, it's not even a man." Radulf turned to Baird. "Was it for this you called me home before my business was concluded? Where are their squires?"

"In the stables," Baird said.

"Set a watch on them. See that they remain in the stables all night. And put your best man on guard on the tower steps. Those precautions ought to prevent any trouble from our guests," Radulf ended on a sneer of contempt for the creature who sat drinking wine with a most unmanly flare.

"Aye, my lord." Baird went to give the orders.

"Rohaise, I want food and drink," Radulf said. "Not here. In my own room. I've ridden hard all day and I'm too tired to deal with the likes of him tonight." He jerked his head toward Piers, who again saluted him with the wine cup.

"I'll see to it at once." Rohaise left the high table.

"And I, good sir, shall inquire of my lady," Piers said to Radulf, "whether she will be able to travel on the morrow. So terribly tiresome, this business of ladies falling ill. Shall I go to your chamber, dear sir, and inform you there what she says?"

"You stay out of my chamber," Radulf ordered. "Tell Rohaise what your mistress says. She can report to me. And you see that you remain where you are supposed to be this night. My men will be watching all of your company."

"Dear sir, I do assure you we have nothing to hide." Piers gave Radulf a fetching smile, which Radulf chose not to return.

"If you are telling the truth, then we'll all sleep well, and I'll punish Baird tomorrow for taking me away from important negotiations," Radulf said. Dismissing Piers from further notice, he turned his attention to his grandson. "Will, get to your bed. I'll talk to you on the morrow, too. A few lashes with a birch rod ought to impress some sense into you. When I say no one is to be admitted to Banningford without my permission I mean it."

"Yes, Grandfather." The flush staining Will's face showed how humiliated he was by Radulf's treatment of him, but he was too well-mannered to argue with his grandfather while Piers was present.

"This civil war isn't over yet, you know," Radulf went on. "There's plenty of trickery on both sides. It has taken all my wit and cunning to keep my lands through these past years, and I'll not chance having them lost to me because you can't resist some girl's smile."

"It was only common courtesy, Grandfather, to invite chilled and weary travelers to rest in our great hall," Will said.

"Oh, get to bed," Radulf ordered curtly. "Courtesy be damned. You're too soft, boy. I'll start tomorrow, teaching you to be a real man. I should have done it years ago."

By that time Piers was too far up the tower stairs to overhear anymore. He found Alain standing guard outside Samira's door.

"What the devil's going on?" Alain demanded.

"Come in and I'll tell you," Piers said, opening the door. "Alain, I think you ought to postpone your climb to Joanna's window."

"If I don't go to her tonight, she will believe I have deserted her for a second time," Alain objected.

"Nor can we stay here another day," Piers went on. "Not with Radulf at home. He could recognize us at any time."

"I could divert him so that he doesn't notice you," Samira suggested. "I would like to do something more to help you than just spend a boring day in this room pretending to be sick."

"Except to bid him farewell, you are to stay out of Radulf's sight," Piers directed with all the force of a deeply concerned father. "Alain, if you are determined to chance that climb again, leave the tower at once before Baird posts more guards, but beware the stables."

A short time later Piers returned to the great hall, looking for Rohaise.

"Take the hot water and the food up at once," Rohaise ordered two servants. "Tell Lord Radulf I will soon join him. Yes, Sir Spiros; do you have a message for my lord from your mistress?" She stepped closer, so Piers could lower his voice.

"Can you keep Radulf so well occupied that he won't hear any unusual noises?" Piers asked, hating himself for the use he was making of this good woman and sickened by the thought of her in bed with Radulf.

"If you are asking what I think you are asking," Rohaise said, looking straight into his eyes, "I must tell you it has been nearly fifteen years since Radulf has shown any such interest in me. He drinks too much, and the drink makes him incapable. Perhaps his disinterest is also the effect of the herbs I frequently put into his wine. He likes the taste, you understand, and the herbs help him to sleep. The wine I just sent to his room is liberally laced with them. Radulf will sleep heavily tonight. I will stay in the lord's chamber with him, to be sure he does sleep, and I will call out loudly to him if he leaves it, so you can hear me and be warned.

"Here comes Baird," Rohaise said under her breath. More loudly, she said, "I will give Lord Radulf your mistress's message, Sir Spiros. We will expect to bid her farewell in the morning. Good night to you, sir. Good night, Baird."

"Lady Rohaise." With a thoughtful expression, Baird watched her until she disappeared up the tower steps. "Where are you going now, Sir Spiros?"

"To sleep outside my mistress's door, which is my post for this night," Piers replied.

"Where is your friend, Lucas?"

"I believe he was going to the bath house, and then to the stables to check on the squires," Piers said.

"See that you stay where you are supposed to be," Baird ordered. "That means all of you."

Joanna was waiting by the window when Alain reached it. She caught at his arms to help him over the sill and into the room.

"Whatever you are planning to do," she said before he could speak a word to her, "you must do it quickly. My son intends to marry Samira."

"Now, there's an interesting idea." Alain brushed off his knees and tugged on his tunic, straightening it. "By the by, your father returned this evening."

"Then why did you come to me?" she cried, terrified. "You must flee. All of you must go at once, before he discovers who you are."

"We can do nothing until the castle gate is opened in the morning," Alain pointed out. "As I understand the situation, Rohaise has undertaken to keep Radulf well drugged with wine until then. Which gives us time to spend together."

"You have involved Rohaise, too? Heaven help her." Joanna swallowed hard, fighting back fear. "Ah, well, perhaps it will be for the best, if only we can end these long years of deception. About your plans, Alain; tell me what you are going to do."

"When I left you this morning, Joanna, it was with your promise of wine in a cup when I returned."

"I do remember." She poured out the wine. When she offered the cup to him he put his hand over hers and stood looking deep into her sapphire eyes.

"Joanna, my love."

"Drink your wine, my lord."

"I was not sure what I would find here tonight," he murmured. "You were so cool the last time I visited you."

"I have had eighteen years to learn self-control," she said. "I have hidden my true feelings for every day of that time. Even from Rohaise. Especially from Rohaise."

"Does she know who killed Crispin?" he asked, sipping at the wine while he watched her closely, trying to find some chink in the emotional armor she wore so well that it seemed to be part of her natural character.

"I would not put Rohaise into danger by telling her," Joanna answered. "If she knew, and inadvertently revealed what she knew, she would be killed at once."

"I told Piers and Samira," he said, putting down his wine cup. "In case something happens to me, I wanted someone else to know the truth."

"Very sensible of you."

"I am done with being sensible," he told her. "Whatever may happen on the morrow, for these few hours at least, we have each other."

"Have we?" She edged away from him.

"I have wanted you since the first moment I ever saw you," he said, closing the distance she had put between them. "There was a time when you wanted me, too."

"Perhaps that time is past." She backed away again.

"I don't believe it," he said, matching her step for step.

"Before you go any further," she was still retreating and sounding ever more desperate as he followed her across the room, "before you say anything you may regret, I am obligated to tell you that I did not dislike what Crispin did to me in our bed. In fact, on several occasions I enjoyed it very much."

"I'm glad to hear it. Crispin deserved the best of women, which you were, and are. What was between you happened long ago. It's in the past and I have made my peace with it. I cannot be jealous of a dead man; certainly not of one as dear to me as Crispin was.

"Joanna, I also have a confession I feel obligated to make. I hated your father, and hate him still, for giving you to Crispin when I wanted you so badly I thought I would go mad from my need of you. I could have killed Radulf for arranging your marriage to Crispin. But never did I hate Crispin, and never did I wish his death because of you."

Alain's next step brought him to Joanna's side. With her back against the stone chamber wall she could go no farther. Alain moved so his body was pressed along hers. He put a hand on the wall at each side of her head.

"No, don't." Her voice quavered. "Perhaps another time, Alain."

"The only time there is," he said, "is now."

"I have withstood evil and cruelty," she whispered, closing her eyes against the sight of his face, so close to her. "It's only love that terrifies me. Love almost destroyed me once. It may destroy me yet."

"Do you think I'm not afraid?" he asked. "After so many years of dreaming about you and wanting you, the reality of you, so near to me, has all but undone me. The only thing in this life I fear is that you will say you don't love me anymore, or that you don't want me. That is why I am afraid."

"Alain . . ."

"Let me love you. If these next hours are all we are meant to have, then let us have this much at least. Let me know, just once, how it feels to make you mine."

She did not answer. He could feel her trembling; he could hear her soft, sobbing breath and see the quiver of her lower lip. He had spent that day in an agony of expectation, remembering all too vividly the sensation of her soft body against his. More than anything else it was his driving desire for her that had propelled him up the tower wall a second time, when common sense dictated that he should remain at Samira's door beside Piers.

"We should wait," she pleaded. "This is unsafe. Someone may come."

"I cannot wait. Not any longer." He began to rub his hardness against her, gently but insistently. She whimpered, stiffened, and tried to push him away. His lips touched her throat, her ear, her cheek, moving ever closer to her mouth.

"Please," she begged. "Don't. If Lys comes to the door, or my father . . ."

He ignored her faltering whisper. When her weak efforts to get away from him failed she stopped fighting him. He kissed her eyelids, her cheek, the corner of her mouth.

"Alain." Her arms moved around him, her lips opened to his kiss. After a while she tore her mouth away to make one more protest. "It has been too long, too many years. Too much has happened."

"I know, I know." He caught at the skirt of her dress, pulling it upward. "None of it matters. Only this matters."

She began to weep when his hand stroked along her thigh and into warmth and dampness. He kept his hand were it was, letting her grow used to his tender invasion, until her tears stopped and she lifted heavy eyelids. Her eyes were a clear, pure sapphire, and there was no more fear in them. Her face was so radiant that his heart nearly stopped.

"Yes," she said, very clearly.

So great was the rush of his desire that he almost took her there, against the wall. With difficulty he restrained himself. But his hands were shaking violently.

"Help me," he whispered, laughing softly at his

own boyish weakness. After a moment's hesitation she recovered enough to help him get her dress over her head and then to assist him in removing his own clothing. It was her turn to chuckle when she discovered he was wearing two tunics.

"I had to keep warm for you," he said, struggling to remove the second tunic and kiss her at the same time. "A cloak would get in the way."

"In the way of what?" she teased. She looked at him with a playful expression that he felt certain masked a serious attack of trepidation. He was certain she was nervous because he was quaking inside himself. He wanted her so much, and he wanted to please her, and he was afraid he might fail.

They stood, finally, unclothed, two lovers middle-aged by the standards of their own time, and yet oddly untouched by the passage of years. His hair and beard might be threaded with gray, but his broad shoulders and his arms were as heavily muscled as those of a much younger man, his hard belly was flat, his thighs and calves still strong and well fleshed.

Motherhood had given her a fuller figure, and she was taller than she had been at fourteen. She was almost as tall as Alain. Her breasts were heavier than the current ideal of beauty, just the size to fit perfectly into Alain's cupping hands. He traced the glorious curve from bosom to slender waist, to gently rounded abdomen to hip, and then caught her buttocks, pulling her against his hardness. With a long, deep sigh she wound her arms around his neck and held on to him.

The wonder of having her naked in his arms blazed through Alain, immobilizing him until she threw back her head to look at him. He saw her tongue come out and move slowly around her parted lips; he saw her smile a slow, seductive smile.

"Alain," she commanded in a hoarse whisper, "take me to bed."

He lifted her and carried her the few steps necessary, then laid her upon the new linen sheets. She drew his head downward.

"Put your tongue in my mouth again," she whispered. "Kiss me, Alain. Teach me what to do with my tongue."

"Gladly." He did not stop with kissing her mouth. He drenched her in kisses, from her forehead to her toes and back again. He touched her in places where, from her astonished response, he knew she had never been touched before. He took her hands and put them on himself, showing her how to give him pleasure and, by so doing, to increase her own delight. He was a little surprised at how innocent she still was. Then, later, he was even more surprised at her eagerness.

"Alain," she whispered when he knelt between her thighs, "come to me."

Uncertain if their coming together would hurt her after so many years of abstinence, he tried to be slow and careful. Nor did he want to rush his own pleasure. He had waited so long to have her, and now he wanted it to be perfect for both of them. He touched her, probing lightly with one finger. She cried out and closed around him, lifting her hips to him, protesting when he withdrew his hand. Her reaction was all the encouragement he needed. He entered her slowly, easing into her warmth. She was tight, and sweet, and moist with delicious longing. He pushed deeper.

"Alain." Her voice was a sigh, a moan of erotic delight, a fulfillment of all his dreams, a consolation for the long years that had so cruelly separated them.

Looking into her eyes, he saw there the reflection of his own soul's longing and knew that though she might try to hide it, she loved him with the same unalterable passion that he felt. They smiled at each other, hearts and bodies joined at last. Tenderly they kissed, and looked into each other's eyes again, marveling at the wonder of their coming together.

And then she moved on him, and he lost all hope of containing his boiling passion. He rode her hard, with a fiery, desperate need. She matched him, meeting every firm thrust with her own eager movements, harder and ever harder. Alain was by that time aware only of his clamoring, incredible desire to have all of this woman, to make it impossible for any other man ever to take her in this way. She was his—*his*—and he had waited so long for her. He could not stop the triumphant shout he uttered at the final moment. His body seemed to explode into exquisitely sensitive fragments that only slowly came back together again, leaving him still deeply embedded in Joanna's yielding flesh, still hard and moving, but more slowly now, and fully conscious of the lovely pulsations of her innermost body.

The intense pleasure he felt did not stop; it went on and on, and she was melting beneath him, sobbing and gasping, and still the tremors inside her continued until he was sobbing, too. In the end, when at last they lay exhausted on the damp sheets, he could only pray that Rohaise had given Radulf extra herbs to make him sleep soundly, and that the guard on the tower steps was also fast asleep, so that neither of them had heard the sounds of lovers coming together in a place where lovers should not be.

"Baird," Owain, the lieutenant of the men-at-arms called softly, "you had better come at once."

"What's wrong?" Baird kicked Lys out of his way and rose from the pallet they shared. In the same quick movement he took up his sword, girding it at his waist. "Is it an attack?"

"I don't think so," Owain replied. "It's something strange, and you said to call you if we noticed anything out of the ordinary. Sir, there is someone climbing *down* from the western tower."

"Is there, by God?" Baird was on his way toward the inner bailey, with Owain following him. "What have you done about it?"

"I set an extra man on the western wall, and another on the northern wall, to watch him and discover where he goes, while the other guards on duty look for signs of impending attack."

"Well done. Rouse the second contingent, but be quiet about it. There's no sense in letting an enemy know when we're aware of him." Leaving Owain to carry out his orders, Baird went up the outside steps to the western battlements. Upon finding the man Owain had set to watch the tower, he demanded in a low voice, "Where is he?"

"The climber? There." The man pointed. "One arrow will take him."

"Aye, and silence him, too," Baird growled, squinting into the shadows. "Radulf will want information, not a dead body. Don't let him out of your sight, and let me know at once if he goes anywhere but around toward the northern wall."

"D'you believe he'll come in by the postern gate?" the man asked.

"Why not? It's how he got out. For the second night." Baird scanned the outline of the western tower, though he knew its exact conformation. "There are just two places he could be leaving: the lord's chamber or Lady Joanna's room."

"Mayhap he's done murder," the man gasped.

"Be silent, you fool." Baird cuffed the man. "If he's done murder, then it's too late to help the victim. All we can do now is catch the killer, if that's what he is. Stay at your post and inform me of his movements when he reaches the ground."

Baird returned to the inner bailey, where the sleepy men he had ordered called out were assembling.

"A fine lot of good you'd do in a surprise attack," Baird told them. "Pull yourselves together and form up in two lines on either side of the postern gate. And be quiet about it!"

While the men followed his orders, Baird

sprinted up the steps to the northern wall.

"Nothing yet," the guard there replied to his question. "Hah! Wait, see there."

"I see." Baird peered over the edge in the direction where the man-at-arms was pointing at a figure skulking along at the base of the wall. "Watch him. Don't let him out of your sight. Tell me at once if he doesn't use the postern gate."

By now it was light enough to see more clearly, and Baird noticed the guards on the western wall, signaling frantically to him. With a wave of his hand to let them know he understood, the captain of the guard once more descended to the bailey and positioned himself beside the postern gate.

"Don't move or make a sound until I give the signal," he told his men, aware that none would dare to disobey him.

The first rays of the midwinter sun were just gilding the roof of the western tower when the postern gate opened silently. Down in the bailey there was still not a lot of daylight, and the man entering had emerged from the narrow passage before he saw the guards awaiting him.

"So, I was right; you are a spy," Baird said. Alain went perfectly still at the sound of his voice. "Owain, take our guest to the great hall. I will rouse Radulf and, by God, Lucas, if I find you've murdered him in his sleep, I'll see you unmanned and disemboweled before I let you die, and I'll do the same to your friends."

Chapter Nineteen

When Rohaise got to the great hall she found Piers and Alain there before her, with Baird's lieutenant Owain guarding them. Baird met her at the entrance to the hall.

"Where is Radulf?" Baird demanded. "By God, woman if you've harmed him—" He left the threat unfinished.

"I have done nothing to hurt Radulf," Rohaise said. A single glance at the guests who were now prisoners told her it might be well to play for time. Any delay in whatever Baird intended would give Piers and Alain a chance to think of a way to save themselves. She gave Baird a conspiratorial smile and then let the men-at-arms see it, too. Walking into the hall, she drew Baird after her by speaking to him as she moved. "You know how it is when a man returns home after an absence from his wife. We were awake far into the night, and I fear we both drank a bit too much wine. Radulf was still sleeping when I left him." To emphasize her suggestion that her night with Radulf had been a passionate one, Rohaise slowly stretched her shoulders and gave a sensuous yawn.

"Do not fret yourself, Baird," she said. "Radulf will rise when it suits him. Indeed, he has already risen several times since his return."

The men-at-arms began to laugh, and even Baird was diverted enough to give her a knowing look. But the horror on Piers's face shook Rohaise. Surely, after their conversation of the previous night, Piers would understand that she was only pretending?

"Pleasant night or not," Baird said, "we need Radulf here, to judge these spies and tricksters and to decide upon their exact punishment."

"Punishment?" Rohaise cried. In her alarm for Piers's sake she forgot to try to look like a well-loved wife. "What harm could these good folk possibly do to us?"

"For one thing," Baird announced, pointing to Alain, "that slippery fellow got into the upper tower last night. And the night before."

"What's amiss here? Baird, what are you saying?" Will came into the hall. Seeing Piers and Alain with their guards, he asked, "Baird, are you preventing these men from leaving as they planned to do?"

"Oh, they'll leave," Baird told him, "with their bodies in a cart and their heads on pikes above the gate." Stalking across the hall to where Alain stood, Baird added, "How did you get the postern key?"

"I stole it from you," Alain said, laughing in the man's face.

"Impossible," Baird growled. "I still have my key. You either stole Rohaise's key or she gave it to you. Which would make Rohaise a traitor to her lord."

At this, Rohaise felt a thrill of fear and knew her own life was hanging from the same thread as Alain's and Piers's. If Radulf believed Baird's accusation, he would have no compunction about punishing her, too. But Alain did his best to remove her from suspicion.

"It might have been Rohaise," Alain responded to the glowering Baird with a sly smile, "or it could have been the lovely Lys. Are you sure your key never left your possession, Baird? Can you be certain it's not your woman who's the traitor?"

While Baird stared wordlessly at Alain, Rohaise decided the time for action had come. Praying no one would notice what she did, she returned to the entry hall. There, hiding the movement of her hands by turning to one side and taking advantage of the heavy folds of her woolen skirts, she hastily pulled a key off her girdle. Back in the great hall she caught at Will's arm, pushing the key into his hand.

"No one knows I have this," she whispered urgently. "It's an extra key to your mother's room. Tell her she must come to the great hall."

"She will not," Will said. "You know as well as

I do that she won't leave her room."

"If you want Lady Samira to live until sunset," Rohaise whispered fiercely, "then you will do as I say. Free Joanna! Hurry, Will, and don't let Radulf or anyone else stop you."

"Owain," Baird ordered, breaking off his angry contemplation of Alain's mocking face, "watch Lady Rohaise. Don't let her leave the hall. And you, Garth, find Lys and bring her here so I can have the truth out of her. I will rouse Radulf myself, and I had better find him in good health." With that, Baird left the hall.

"Lady Rohaise," Owain spoke to her more politely than Baird had done, "I must ask you to join these prisoners so I can more easily watch all of you."

"Of course." Rohaise stepped to Piers's side. "Good day to you, Sir Spiros. I do regret this imposition on your patience and hope it will end soon so that all of you may continue your journey."

"Be quiet, please, my lady," said Owain. "No talking allowed."

But Owain could not stop Piers from looking at Rohaise, and what she saw in his face gave her the courage to smile at him as if their sudden captivity was unimportant. She was relieved to find, on glancing around the hall a few moments later, that Will had disappeared.

As he went up the tower steps, Will could hear Radulf, two levels above, cursing at Baird and demanding to know why his rest should be disturbed so early in the day, though it was by now midmorning. Almost immediately, two pairs of booted feet rang on the stairs, coming downward. Not wanting them to see him, Will knocked on the nearest door. It opened at once and he ducked into Samira's room.

The maid Nena was pressed against the far wall with both hands over her mouth as if to stifle a scream of terror. It was Samira who had opened the door.

"Where are Spiros and Lucas?" she asked, her voice trembling just a little. "If that dreadful Baird has harmed them, he will answer to me. He had no right to take Spiros away so roughly."

"Your men are safe below," Will told her. He was filled with admiration at her calmness and her courage. That she was in danger he did not doubt, but he did not know why. He was about to ask her the meaning of what was happening and why her guards were being held, when he heard Radulf and Baird passing by her door. Will, Samira, and Nena all stood as if frozen until the footsteps had faded.

When the men had gone by Will took a deep breath, inhaling air filled with Samira's scent, a blend of southern flowers and tantalizing spice that suggested a world far different from the one he knew. Looking around the room, he saw that she must have dressed in some haste. The bedcovers were tossed to one side, pieces of clothing were strewn here and there, and in one corner of the room saddlebags were piled in an untidy heap. An odd shape protruding from one of the bags caught Will's eye. He went to the corner and pulled out the metallic object, then stood holding it while his heart sank and his hope for a future with Samira vanished. In his hands he held the proof of Baird's accusations against the man known as Lucas.

"You brought this here," he said, holding up the four-pronged grapple with the remarkably long piece of rope attached to it. He tugged at the rope, uncoiling part of it. "Good saints in heaven, there's enough rope here to reach from the tower to the ground. There's no room in the saddlebag for anything else. Samira, how could you?"

"You don't understand," she said.

"Will you tell me that your servants brought it into the castle and left it in your room and then used it without your knowledge?" he asked.

"I knew about the grapple," she said, "but we had good reason for what we did."

"Who are you really?" he muttered. "Why are you here? Were you only pretending to like me?" That was the hardest question of all to ask, and he was not certain if he wanted to hear her answer.

"I was not pretending," she said.

"Then I will hear your explanation."

"Later I will tell you everything," she promised. "Will, it is essential to free your mother as quickly as possible. She is the only one who can save me and those good men whom Baird is holding in the hall."

"Rohaise said something similar. But my mother is not a prisoner." Will held up the key,

345

looking at it as if it could answer his question. "Is she?"

There was a loud shout from below, followed by the sounds of many voices. Moving quickly, Will stuffed the rope and grapple back into the saddlebag and pushed it against the wall so it would be as inconspicuous as possible.

"There's no point in taking unnecessary chances," he said. His heart lifted at the grateful look Samira gave him. "I will await your explanation with interest."

The voices below grew louder. Will opened the door a crack to hear better.

"What are you doing here?" It was Radulf speaking, and though he sounded irritated, he did not seem to be terribly angry.

By clinging to the wall side of the steps Will was able to inch his way downward without being seen by either the guard outside his mother's door on the next level up from Samira's room, or by the men in the entry hall directly below. Samira was right behind him, moving on silent feet. When he motioned to her to return to her room she shook her head and put one finger to her lips. Then she touched his shoulder and pointed toward the hall.

Radulf was there, with a few of his men-at-arms and at least half a dozen monks in black-hooded robes. More monks crowded into the doorway from the inner bailey. One of the monks, with a large gold cross hung upon his chest, had thrown back his hood to reveal a bald pate with a fringe of white hair and a kindly, wrinkled face. He spoke with a voice remarkably strong and youthful for one so elderly.

"We are on our way to Lichfield," this apparent leader of the monks said, "and as darkness falls early when the weather turns so foul, we are forced to beg lodging for the night. Radulf, you cannot refuse a man of God, who is also an old acquaintance and who was once related to you by marriage for a short time."

"You and I were never friends, Ambrose," said Radulf. "You once stole three of my best horses."

"No, we were not friends," Ambrose agreed, "but the debt of the horses I *borrowed* has long been repaid. Remember, Radulf, it was I who blessed your daughter's fruitful marriage to my nephew, the marriage that gave you your grandson and heir. Now, what is this I see beyond us in your great hall, but other kinsmen of mine, with your men set about them as if they are prisoners. Radulf, what does this mean?"

"Your kinsmen?" exclaimed Radulf.

With perfect serenity Ambrose brushed past Radulf to enter the hall, and Radulf's men made no move to stop him. Nor did anyone stop the monks who filed into the entry hall and then to the great hall after Ambrose.

"Twenty of them," Will whispered, counting.

"Exactly right, and on time," Samira whispered back, her words adding to Will's growing confusion.

Will waited until his grandfather and all of the men had gone into the great hall before, with Samira behind him, he turned around and started up the steps to his mother's room. There he boldly faced the guard, a burly fellow with a blank, unintelligent face.

"My grandfather has sent me to take my mother to the great hall," Will said.

"Not so," the guard declared. "I have instructions from Baird not to let anyone in or out of this room unless he or Baron Radulf personally tells me to."

"Who else would give this key into my hand if not Radulf, or Baird with Radulf's permission?" Will demanded, showing the guard the key Rohaise had passed to him. "Would you dare to disobey your liege lord?"

"I'm not sure about this." The guard hesitated, frowning and shaking his head, as if thinking was a great effort for him.

"But, good sir," Samira put in, "you are to come with us."

The guard stared at her with a stupid expression until Samira gave him a coaxing smile.

"Well, then, if I'm still to guard Lady Joanna, I suppose it's all right," the man said, his eyes on Samira.

"Of course it is," Samira said. "What is planned for the next hour promises to be most interesting. You won't want to miss it."

"Stand aside," Will ordered, "and let me unlock that door."

He prayed the guard would offer no more objections, nor run down to the hall to ask Radulf about the change in orders. Will thought the best course would be to act as if he had complete authority, as if he knew what was going on. "I said, stand aside."

The guard obeyed, and within a moment Joanna's door was open. Joanna stood in the middle of her room, wearing a dark blue wool gown, with her hair falling loose down her back and a comb in one hand. She looked from her son to the young woman with him.

"Are you Samira?" she asked, sounding not at all surprised by the sudden arrival of visitors.

"I am, my lady. I have a message for you."

"Mother," Will broke in, "Rohaise sent me to take you to the hall. There is something going on down there, and Samira and her friends are in great danger. Do you know a monk named Ambrose?"

"Ambrose is here?" Joanna asked.

"My lady," Samira said, "I was told to say, 'Alain sent me.'"

"Alain?" Will gaped at Samira. "Will someone please tell me what is happening?"

"The end of my imprisonment," Joanna said, smoothing her hair and tossing the comb aside, "or the end of all of us. And Ambrose here, too, just as Alain promised. He has not failed me; now I shall not fail him. Come, Will, Samira, let us not keep them waiting."

"Do you mean you are actually going to the hall?" cried Will.

"My darling son." Joanna patted his cheek, then rested her hand on his shoulder. "I will not deny the danger that awaits us there, but I promise, before this day is over, you will have answers

349

to all your questions. Shall we go?"

She did not wait for him to answer. Her chamber door stood wide open; the guard outside it had drawn respectfully to one side to let her pass. With her head high, Joanna led the young couple out of the tower room, down the curving staircase . . .

. . . and into the great hall just as Radulf was loudly proclaiming Alain's guilt in Crispin's murder. Radulf saw them come in. His eyebrows went up at the sight of Joanna, but he did not prevent her from entering the hall to hear his attack on Alain and Piers.

"You fled my justice once," Radulf declared to Alain, "but you won't escape it a second time. I'll have you hanged from the castle wall, you and your accomplice here."

"Grandfather." Will left Joanna and Samira and hurried to Radulf's side. "I heard the last part of your accusation. Is this so? Did Sir Lucas and Sir Spiros kill my father?"

"False names for false men," said Radulf. "From this priest's own lips I heard him confess them his kinsmen, and then I, too, recognized them. Aye, Will, these are Alain of Wortham and Piers of Stokesbrough, returned to the scene of their crime."

"Grandfather." Will's youthful face was pale, his mouth set in a hard line. He put out his right hand toward Radulf. "Give me your sword. It is my right—no, more than a right, it is my duty to execute the men who murdered my father. Give me leave, Grandfather. Do not turn them over to Baird."

"So, you are my true heir after all." With glittering eyes Radulf regarded his grandson. "These past weeks since you returned from fostering, I have feared you might have grown up too soft. Aye, my boy, it's but your own right you've claimed. No one here will deny you your vengeance. Go to it, lad. Let justice be done at last. Stab them in the belly as they once stabbed your father. Guards, hold those killers still for their execution." After a triumphant look in Joanna's direction Radulf drew his sword and put it into Will's right hand.

Two men-at-arms took Alain, pulling his arms out from his body and holding him so he was immobilized from the waist up. Two other men-at-arms took Piers in the same way.

"I considered you friends." Will advanced on them, lifting Radulf's sword. "I invited you into my home and made you welcome. You sat at table with me and ate the food I offered. Liars. Murderers! Thieves! You stole my father's life from me before ever I was born." He pointed the sword at Alain and stood poised to strike.

"*No!*" Joanna's scream tore through the hall. She flung herself upon Alain, covering his body with her own. "If you want to kill him, you must kill me first."

The men-at-arms were so surprised by Joanna's sudden forward rush that they loosened their hold on Alain. He pulled his arms free, caught Joanna in a tight embrace, and thrust her behind him.

At the same time Piers also pulled free from the startled men holding him, and when his right arm dropped from their grasp Rohaise put a sword into his hand.

"No one saw me pick it up," she whispered. "Use it well."

"I'm going to need it." Piers started forward to where Samira stood alone in the center of the hall. Radulf also moved toward her, one hand outstretched to capture her wrist. Samira saw him coming and sidestepped his reach, just as Piers placed himself between them.

"Lay one finger on my daughter and you die," Piers said in a low, dangerous voice.

"Daughter?" cried Will and Rohaise in unison.

"It's true," Samira said. Ignoring the men-at-arms with drawn swords who were menacing her and Piers, she went on, "I am the daughter of Piers, Baron of Ascoli, a title my father won by his great valor. And now it is time for the whole truth to be told. Uncle Ambrose, will you convince Lord Radulf here to allow those who want to speak to do so?"

"Not I," said Ambrose, moving to her side, "for I have not touched a weapon since I became a priest, but I believe these men-at-arms will convince Radulf more readily than I ever could."

"What men-at-arms?" shouted Radulf, looking about. "I see no one save my own dozen men, and they will not listen to you, priest."

Ambrose had only to move his head a little and

the men who had come in with him threw off their priestly robes to reveal chainmail and swords beneath the covering. When Radulf spun on his heel to head for the entrance and there call for reinforcements he discovered two pair of the newcomers standing back to back, preventing anyone from entering or leaving the great hall. Radulf's men looked about uncertainly, as if awaiting orders. Baird stood alone with one hand on his sword hilt, watching Radulf.

"What the devil is this?" Radulf shouted at Ambrose.

"They are my men," Alain said. "Men of Alain, Emir of Trapani, First Assistant to the Emir of Emirs of the Kingdom of Sicily." He continued rattling off the list of all his titles and honors, while the hall grew ever quieter as the men in it began to realize that they were not merely dealing with a condemned outlaw. When he had finished with his own titles Alain recited all of Piers's as well. Finished at last, and with one arm around Joanna, he walked across the hall to join Piers and Samira at its center.

"Mother?" Will approached her, and Joanna put out her hand, catching her son to her side.

"Stay with me and be quiet," she ordered.

Radulf, however, would not be quiet. He began to bluster.

"Seize them!" he roared. "That man will do harm to my daughter. Stop him, I say!"

No man of Banningford moved, in part because Alain's people stood among them with swords at the ready, in part because Baird did not speak. In the confusion, Lys had been brought into the hall, and she stood behind Baird, watching and listening with all the tenseness of an animal who has sighted its prey and is preparing to strike.

"Do be seated in the lord's chair, Baron Radulf," Alain said in mocking tones. "Ambrose, will you lead the discussion?"

"There is nothing to discuss," Radulf shouted, refusing to move from where he stood. "These men are murderers, outlaws by royal proclamation. Anyone may kill them."

"You lie!" Joanna broke away from Alain's protecting arm and dropped Will's hand so she could step forward to confront her father. Her eyes blazed with the accumulated wrath of eighteen years of injustice, but her voice was steady. "Alain did not kill Crispin, and Piers did not help in the murder, and you know it. You have always known it."

"Mother," Will cried, coming to her, "you are overwrought. Let me take you to your room and then we men will see justice done."

"I will never set foot in that room again," Joanna declared. "I will die rather than go back there. Nor will there be justice done in this hall without my testimony. William Crispin, you have been told lies all of your life, lies about me, about your father, and about these two good men who stand here falsely accused. I have been forced to remain in that room by threats of harm against you and Rohaise if I ever spoke a word of what I know. For I know how your father was killed, and by whom, and why."

"Rohaise, take her away," Radulf ordered. "My daughter is mad, poor thing. It's why I have protected her for all these years."

"I am not mad," Joanna declared, "though there was a time when I imagined I *was* losing my wits."

"Let Lady Joanna say what she wants," Ambrose broke in, forestalling another protest from Radulf. "I have a certain personal interest in the events of which she speaks, since it was my nephew who was murdered. I want to hear Joanna's story."

"She will say nothing worthy of belief," Radulf told him.

"I shall decide whether to believe her after I have heard her," Ambrose said. "Radulf, if you will not sit, I will. I am older than you, and my bones are weary." He went to the high table and sat in the chair Rohaise usually used. His action forced everyone in the hall to face the dais, so that Ambrose assumed the position of a judge, while those one step down from the dais, standing on the floor of the hall, now appeared to be petitioners.

"Radulf, I invite you to join me," Ambrose said.

"I'll stay where I am," Radulf said with a sneer. "I have no liking for the pretensions of the clergy and the church."

"So I have noticed." Ambrose smiled a little. "Very well. You may speak, Lady Joanna, and I hope no one will interrupt you until you have finished."

Joanna took a few steps toward the dais, until she stood within the light provided by a pair of torches hung in wall sconces. With her dark gown blending into the shadows of the hall, her illuminated face and halo of golden hair took on a shining clarity that added to the forcefulness of her words, for she told her story calmly and well.

"At first I was too shocked and grief-stricken to understand the meaning of what I saw and heard on that terrible night when Crispin was killed," Joanna said. "Later I was forced to accept my father's decree that I should be isolated in my tower room. When I knew that I was carrying Crispin's child I believed it was for the best that I continue to stay there. Even then, William Crispin, even before you were born, I loved you so well that I would not risk any harm coming to you. By then Alain and Piers were gone, vanished, and at my father's instigation they were proscribed outlaws. By then I knew that anything I might say about that night would not be believed. I understood that I could rely only upon myself.

"During those months before my son was born," Joanna went on, speaking now directly to Ambrose, "I had time to recover from the shock and to think. I began to remember bits of conversation and little things I had seen. By the time William Crispin was born I knew who had really killed my husband. I have lived with that knowledge for all the years since."

Here Joanna paused, looking around at the

faces in the hall, at beloved relatives, friends, strangers, and at her lover, before she returned her full attention to Ambrose.

"For those who were not here at the time of my marriage, let me say that my father arranged for me to wed Crispin of Haughston so that our lands would be joined, and in the hope that Crispin would become a trustworthy ally in the civil war my father foresaw taking place after King Henry's death. In that decision, my father was wise, for there was a war, which is not yet ended, and Crispin would have proven a reliable ally. My father wanted one thing more from my marriage: an heir to all these combined lands.

"But Crispin also held lands in Normandy, and he announced on his first night at Banningford that as soon as our wedding festivities were over, he would take me there, to stay for several years. He also spoke of a pilgrimage to Compostela, which would have kept him absent from England for an even longer time.

"It was Crispin's desire to go abroad that caused his death," Joanna said. "My father would permit no interference with the plan he had so carefully constructed: to have a dependable ally living on lands that bordered Banningford and to have a grandson whose education he could direct."

"What baron would not want the same?" scoffed Radulf. "This madwoman's ranting is ridiculous."

"Is it?" Joanna gave him a cold, dark look. "Father Ambrose, do you remember how the terms of my marriage contract were changed the day before the wedding?"

"The incident is clear in my mind," Ambrose said. "I thought of the contract, too, although, unfortunately, not until after Alain and Piers had left St. Justin's Abbey for Banningford. I ordered the contract brought to me from the vault where important documents are kept. I read the contract again just yesterday. According to it, if Crispin died, Radulf was to become guardian of his lands, holding them safe for any children of the marriage. Which Radulf has done; those lands have been his to rule since Crispin's death. Radulf also became guardian of Crispin's child."

"The contract further stated that Crispin should hold my lands in a like manner if I should die before he did," Radulf said.

"So it did," Joanna agreed. "But that part of the contract mattered nothing to you, because Crispin had already declared his intention to leave England, and thus you had decided to have him killed."

"This is preposterous!" Radulf shouted.

"You gave him a few nights with me, hoping he would get me with child," Joanna went on, as if Radulf had not spoken. "But you could not afford to let me pass out of your control because I was your only hope for an heir."

"When Crispin was killed," Radulf sputtered, "I was sitting in the lord's chair, in full view of all my guests. In fact, Father Ambrose, you were also at the high table and saw me there."

"I did not say you did the deed," Joanna told

him. "I said you ordered it done."

"Tell them," Alain urged. "Tell everyone who murdered your husband."

"Baird did it," Joanna said.

"Not so," Baird responded, laughing at her. "I was passing wine to Radulf's guests, at his special request because the wine was too expensive to let the servants handle it. Everyone in this hall on that night saw me."

"You did serve the wine," Joanna replied. "You carried the tray while Lys poured out the wine. She used one pitcher for most of the guests. The second pitcher, containing wine drugged with herbs and poppy syrup that Lys had stolen from Rohaise's stillroom, you personally poured into the cups of Crispin, Alain, and Piers."

"Nonsense!" Baird laughed again. "There was no drugged wine. Radulf, I fear you are right: This poor woman is mad. With your permission, I'll take her to her room."

"Will you fling me down the stairs on the way, to break my neck and thus silence me? And then claim I did it myself out of madness?" Joanna asked. "It took me a long time to remember what happened, Baird. Don't stop me now. After they drank the drugged wine Crispin and Alain got sick and rushed out to the entry hall and then into the garderobe. Piers went with Crispin, to help him. When I followed them I saw someone leaving the entry hall, hurrying out the door to the inner bailey. It was you, Baird, you with blood on your hands and your new green tunic. But when you later returned to the entry hall with my father, and when you carried me up to my room, you were wearing your old brown tunic. The shock of finding Crispin dying drove those glimpses of you out of my mind for months."

"Baird?" Radulf rounded on his captain of the guard. "Is this true? Was it you? And all this time I trusted you. How could you betray me like that?"

"What I did was done by your orders," Baird grated. Looking wildly about, he spied Lys, standing behind him. He grabbed her by the hair and dragged her forward. "Tell them, Lys. Tell them what Radulf's orders were on that day."

"Ow! Let me go!" Lys screeched. Baird threw her to the stone floor and raised one booted foot, preparing to kick her.

"Stop this!" Ambrose did not raise his voice by much, but it cut through Lys's wails and Baird's curses. "Stand up, woman, and tell us what you know."

"Baird's right," Lys said, pulling herself to her feet. "Radulf wanted drugged wine given to the three young men. He wanted to make the murder seem like a quarrel among them. Sir Alain's interest in Lady Joanna had been remarked by many of the wedding guests, and it was common gossip among the servants, so it was easy to blame him for the killing."

"Not true," Radulf declared stoutly. "If these two servants of mine conspired together to kill my son-in-law, I'll have them hung at once. Moreover, I will apologize to Alain and Piers and see to it that the writ of outlawry against them is rescinded."

"I'll not die for your crime, Radulf." Baird's sword was in his hand and he faced his master with a snarl. "I've done everything you ever asked of me, but not this. *You* devised the plan to kill Crispin after he insisted on traveling to Normandy and would not change his mind. It was your decision to do away with him before you could even be sure he'd gotten Joanna with child, because you didn't want her and her useful womb taken away from Banningford, out of your control. It was you who kept Joanna in that tower room and threatened to kill the boy and Rohaise if she ever told what she knew. And it was you who convinced young Will and anyone else who questioned the arrangement that Joanna had isolated herself in prolonged mourning for Crispin."

"You fool!" Radulf yelled at him. "Be silent!"

"For what reason should I be silent now?" asked Baird, baring his teeth in a mirthless grin. "These folk have found out the truth. You are already condemned, Radulf, and so am I. But where I kept faith with you and believed you would reward me, you betrayed me to save yourself. That betrayal ended my loyalty to you. I renounce you as my liege lord."

While he spoke those last words, Baird hefted the sword he held. Then, moving so swiftly that no one could stop him, he lunged at Radulf, stabbing him. Radulf doubled over and fell to the floor, clutching at his middle.

At first no one moved. Baird stood with his

dripping sword in hand, looking down at his dying master.

"Father!" Joanna went to her knees, gathering Radulf into her arms as she once had held Crispin.

"Joanna, leave him," Alain said, trying to lift her.

"I cannot. In spite of all he's done, he is still my father," she replied, her voice perfectly calm, her eyes dry. "I can still hold him until he dies."

"My lord." Rohaise knelt on Radulf's other side and took his limp hand. "Radulf, speak to me."

Radulf opened his eyes, looking first at his daughter and then at his wife.

"Damned women," he said, and breathed his last.

Chapter Twenty

There was deep silence in the hall. Joanna let her father's body down onto the stone floor. She rose, pulling Rohaise up with her. Behind the high table, Ambrose did not move, though it was his duty to perform the necessary rites over Radulf. Only Baird was quick enough to take advantage of the general bewilderment at what had just happened.

"Now," Baird said, pointing toward Will with his bloody sword, "you'll all dance to my tune. Owain, Garth, seize the boy."

"No," Owain said. "With Radulf gone, young Will is our new baron. We will take our orders from him."

"Do you dare to defy me, your superior? Then I'll do it myself." Within the blink of an eye Baird had knocked Radulf's sword out of Will's hand

and held the young man with one arm around his throat. "Come near me and he dies."

Whether Baird would have carried out his threat no one would ever know, for Lys picked up Radulf's sword and ran at him. Unused to wielding such a heavy instrument, she managed only a clumsy slash at Baird's sword arm. She did little real damage, but she did hurt Baird badly enough to make him drop his weapon and release Will.

In the uproar that followed Baird went down beneath the blades of Alain's men-at-arms. Lys dropped Radulf's sword on the floor and walked away from Baird's body like someone in a dream, not stopping until she reached the high table. There she paused, looking straight at Ambrose.

"Do what you want to me," Lys said. "It doesn't matter now. This day I, too, have had my vengeance."

"Woman," Ambrose replied, "I thank you for what you have done. Attacking Baird that way was an act of courage. He could easily have killed you, and I believe the chance was good that he would have killed young Will."

"Courage? Not from me." Lys gave a bitter laugh, then began to speak in a low, angry voice. "To look at me, would you think I am the bastard daughter of a nobleman, that while my father lived I was petted and indulged and even loved? Radulf captured me after a battle at my father's castle, and when he had finished with me he gave me to Baird. Since that day I have spent my life in fear. Each time Baird took me, he did it by brute force, or by threatening to use force. Everything I have done to aid him and Radulf was done through fear.

"I am sorry, Lady Joanna, Lady Rohaise," Lys said, turning to the women now approaching the high table, "but I feared for my own life. I knew, all those years ago, that Radulf and Baird planned to kill Baron Crispin, but I was too cowardly to tell anyone who might have stopped them. I was too frightened to speak out afterward, and again my cowardice brought great pain.

"But no matter what I did for Baird, it was never enough, and his brutality toward me never ended. I hated him more and more as the years passed, but I was trapped, until these strangers came," Lys went on, indicating Alain and Piers. "Soon after they arrived I began to suspect what they had come to do, and I did not give them away to Baird or Radulf. It is because I did nothing that these men are still alive and the truth is known today."

"It is because you did nothing long ago that I was forced to flee England," Alain said angrily, joining the group before the high table. "Thanks to your silence, Piers and I were declared outlaws. One word from you would have saved us. But you kept silence."

"Who would believe a servingwoman with Baird and Radulf calling her a liar?" Lys cried. "That's all I have ever been at Banningford, and if I had dared to utter one word against them, either man would have killed me at once, and my efforts would have come to naught. But you don't understand the position I was in, do you? None of you understand what it is to be so afraid for so many years."

"I do," Rohaise said. "There were times when I would have put a knife in Radulf if only I had been able to overcome my fear of him enough to act. And there were many times when I could cheerfully have killed Baird for some of the things he did.

"Please." Rohaise looked toward Ambrose. "Please judge Lys gently, remembering how her action prevented Baird from harming Will."

"This is not an ecclesiastical matter. It is not for Father Ambrose but for me to judge Lys." It was young Will who spoke, and all eyes turned to him. "I am heir to Banningford and Haughston and your new baron, as only Owain has had the wit to comprehend."

"Will, she did save your life." Rohaise refused to be daunted by the severe look of the young man whom she had known since the day he was born. But it now appeared that none of them knew Will as well as they had imagined.

"Lady Rohaise," Will said sternly, "if you can feel no honest grief, then you will at least show respect for your dead husband. See to his body at once. He will be buried tomorrow morning, after an all-night vigil in the chapel. I feel certain that Father Ambrose will be happy to conduct the funeral service."

"But, Lys," Rohaise objected, putting a protective arm across the servingwoman's shoulders.

"Take her with you. I will decide her fate later," Will said. "I will consider your plea, Rohaise. As for yourself, I expect to see you dressed in full mourning within the hour.

"Owain, you are the new captain of the guard," Will informed the man-at-arms. "Garth, you are to take Owain's place as lieutenant. Delegate six men to carry my grandfather wherever Rohaise wishes, and find someone to prepare a coffin. Clear these other men out of the hall. Find stabling for the horses of the visiting men-at-arms and places for the men to sleep for the night. And see that the floor is scrubbed."

"Aye, my Lord." Turning to his men, Owain began giving orders with a huge grin across his face. Within a surprisingly short time the hall was empty except for Alain, Piers, Ambrose, Joanna, Samira, and Will himself.

Alain and Piers stood with Ambrose, talking quietly and observing Will, who was with the women.

"Though the boy handles himself well, he won't be eighteen until the spring," Ambrose said. "I doubt if he will like to hear me say it, but he will need a guardian until he's old enough to be made a knight."

"Many another lad has been knighted before he turned twenty-one," Alain remarked. "From what I've seen of Will in the last hour, I'd say he is his father's true son and will do very well as baron here, and at Haughston."

"I was Crispin's guardian once," Ambrose reminded them, "but I was a younger man in those days. I would not take up the task again without assistance."

"Is there some baron or knight in the neighborhood who could live with Will and guide him until he comes of age?" Alain asked.

"Actually, there are two such men," Ambrose said. "Since Will now holds two baronies, subject always to King Stephen's confirmation of his titles, I think both the men I have in mind could be useful to Will. What say you, my friends?"

"Us?" exclaimed Piers. "No, that's impossible."

"I have other plans for the immediate future," Alain murmured, his eyes on Joanna. "She has endured too much darkness. I am going to take her out of the gloom of an English castle in winter to a place where she can live in bright sunshine for the rest of her life."

"I recall a time when you were in serious difficulties and I helped you," Ambrose said, "I am but asking you to repay my good deed."

"Uncle Ambrose, you are shameless," Piers said, chuckling.

"Amazing, isn't it? But if you were leader of a poor abbey with few endowments, you, too, would quickly learn to survive by shamelessly asking great favors of any who might grant you what you most need. Besides," Ambrose went on in a more serious tone, "while what has happened here today removes the onus of murder from you, there are still official requirements to be met. Someone will have to travel to the royal court to present your petition to King Stephen, asking him to rescind the writ of outlawry against you. Allow me to point out to you that a priest who is also a respected abbot will make an admirable advocate."

"Especially one who is prone to offer bribes," Alain said, winking at Piers. "The man is outrageous."

"As I said, shameless." Piers's eyes were twinkling. "To think a priest would voluntarily do a good deed, which, after all, priests are expected to do every day, and then, eighteen years later, try to make the recipients of that deed feel guilty about it."

"From all I've heard," Ambrose went on, unperturbed by this teasing, "petitioning Stephen for anything takes months, and a writ of outlawry is a complicated business. Couple that with our king's notorious indecision, and it ought to be clear to you that you will need a place to live until the matter is settled."

"I do believe," Alain said to Piers, "that he's offering us a home."

"I will visit you often," Ambrose promised, "so you needn't feel overwhelmed by your new responsibilities."

"He's going to advise us on castle defenses," said Piers to Alain.

"I know as much about defending a castle as you do," Ambrose told them, "and I must confess there are times, particularly when I am called upon to settle quarrels between the brothers at St. Justin's Abbey, or when lack of supplies to feed the hungry villagers weighs heavily upon my heart, that I sorely miss the days when I was but a simple knight."

"You were never a *simple* knight," Alain declared.

369

"Well?" Ambrose looked from one to the other. "Will you do it? For Crispin's sake? For Will's? For mine?"

"We owe Crispin that much," Alain said, looking toward Joanna again.

"And we owe you even more," Piers added, laying a hand on Ambrose's shoulder.

"Thanks be to God and all His saints for honest men," Ambrose murmured.

A short distance from the three older men, Samira approached the new baron, stretching out her hands to him.

"Will, when I saw Baird grab you like that, I was so frightened for you," she said. Instead of welcoming her, Will drew back, glowering at her.

"Since I try to be honest," he told her, "I dislike falsehood in others. From the moment you first came to Banningford you have lied to me with your words and by the things you did not say."

"But now you know why you must understand that some deception was necessary in order to discover and then reveal the truth."

"I despise falsehood, especially in women."

"How else are women to get along with men except by falsehood, when men are so unreasonable?" she demanded. Swallowing her exasperation with his attitude, she added, "Will, you asked me earlier if I only pretended to like you. Liking you was the easiest part of what I had to do, and it was not feigned."

"William Crispin," Joanna said to him, "I lied to you, too, every day that I saw you, for all of your life until today. I did it to keep you safe."

"I was Radulf's only heir," Will replied scornfully. "He would not have harmed me."

"Not after he realized that you would grow up strong and healthy and a credit to any baron. I will admit, my father did have some scruples. He would not have had me killed, either—at least not while I might still be useful to him. But he grew to enjoy the power he held over me; he liked threatening to harm you or Rohaise unless I obeyed him. Will, my point is, I lied to you for many of the same reasons that Samira did, and all of them for your own good. Think about what I've said, and don't judge Samira too harshly."

"That's twice in one hour I've been asked to show leniency to a woman. Mother, I will tell you what I have told Rohaise. I will consider your plea. Now you must excuse me. I have my duties." Will stalked away from them, heading toward Ambrose and his friends. When Samira would have followed him Joanna stopped her.

"Give him a day or two to grow used to being the new baron," Joanna advised. "He's no fool; he'll soon see that we intended only good."

"Perhaps you are right." Relaxing a little, Samira smiled at Joanna. "Theo Alain has told me so much about you. On our journey to England he explained to me what happened when he first met you. I have always thought of him as a remarkable man, and since he never stopped loving you I believe you must be an equally remarkable woman. I hope we can be friends."

"I know we will be." Joanna said nothing about

her son's previously stated intention to marry this woman, but having met Samira she agreed completely with William Crispin's choice. She decided it was time to begin Samira's training as lady of the castle.

"For the rest of the day Rohaise will be occupied with the details of Radulf's funeral," Joanna said. "Isn't it sad that I can't seem to think of him as my father anymore? He's just the late baron now, and instead of sorrow I feel only relief that he's gone.

"Samira, I will need your help. I am unfamiliar with all of the servants except for Lys and one cleaning woman, and as we have guests there is a lot to do. Alain and Piers ought to have rooms of their own instead of sleeping on the floor outside your chamber. I refuse to sleep in my old room anymore, so I'll need a new one. The Lord's chamber has to be cleaned and prepared so William Crispin can move into it, Rohaise will need another room, and we'll have to find a place for Father Ambrose to sleep, not to mention all of Alain's men-at-arms. And we have to feed them all." Still talking, she led Samira out of the hall, toward the kitchen.

Piers caught up with Rohaise just as she was leaving the chapel where Radulf's body lay in its coffin, a tall candle at its head, another at its foot. Piers took Rohaise by the arm, drawing her aside.

"There is something I must know," he said to her. "Is what you told Baird true? Did you lie with Radulf last night?"

"No." Rohaise's gray eyes were clear and only

slightly shadowed by the happenings of that day. "What I said to you yesterday was the truth of it, Sir Piers. For years Radulf has been unable to perform his husbandly duty toward me. What I told Baird was merely a poor attempt to keep him from calling Radulf into the hall. I hoped to give you and Sir Alain time to think of a way to escape. But my attempt at delay failed. I am not very good at that sort of thing."

"There you are wrong, my lady." Piers breathed a sigh of relief. "You are remarkably good."

"Does it matter whether I lay with my late husband or not?" she asked, and narrowly observed his reaction to her question.

"It matters a great deal," Piers said. "Though why it should, I cannot understand. I scarcely know you. It should not matter to me."

"But we are old friends," she told him. "I marked you well when I met you at Joanna's wedding. It's how I recognized you so quickly when you returned. I never could forget your dark eyes or the way you were so polite to me when Radulf was always so coarse."

"Rohaise." He let his hand glide softly along her cheek, and she turned her face into his palm, relishing his touch.

"I would very much like to hear the true story of your wanderings after you left England," she said. "I imagine it would be a long and interesting tale, and a most romantic one. Will you tell me all of it?"

"At the moment I do not feel like talking." He let his thumb rub across the lower margin of her lips.

His voice sank to a level just above a whisper, but soft as it was, still Rohaise could hear the wonder in his next words. "Once, love sought me out, but for almost two years I refused to see it. I am older now, and wiser, and I know how brief life is. I shall not be so blind a second time."

"I have never known love from a man," she murmured. "Nor gentleness, nor kindness, either, until you kissed me that first night."

"I did not mean it then."

"I know. I knew as much when you did it," she said, smiling at the memory.

"If I were to kiss you now," he whispered, "I would mean it." To his surprise, she stepped backward, so that his hand dropped from her face.

"Not here," she said. "Not with Radulf lying in there, unburied, and not in this place where I lived so unhappily with him. Joanna has expressed a wish to visit Crispin's tomb, and to leave Banningford as soon as possible. When we are at Haughston, my lord baron of Ascoli, I am certain I will feel—" she paused, searching for the right words "—I will feel more receptive."

"I will be patient," Piers promised, "though it will be difficult."

"Will it, my lord? How flattering." She gave him a bright smile, entirely at variance with her sober widow's dress. The smile was quickly smothered when Will appeared, leading his mother to the chapel to pray at Radulf's bier, with Alain behind them. No matter that Rohaise's heart was singing at her sudden freedom from Radulf's harsh rule, there were formalities to be observed, and she knew they were important to Will. The boy had entirely too much to absorb at the moment. She would do what she could to make his path easier, which meant disguising her feelings for Piers while Will was present.

"My lord baron," Rohaise said to Piers, "will you join us in the chapel, or would you prefer not to go in?"

"I'll go with you," Piers said. "Radulf will need all the prayers he can get."

"That's generous of you, sir," Will said, pausing at the chapel door, "considering what you suffered at my grandfather's hands."

"It's over now, and continued anger on my part will only hurt me. It's time to forgive." Piers put out his arm, and Rohaise laid her hand on it. They walked into the chapel together, behind Will and Joanna and Alain.

During the rest of that day and the evening Rohaise kept a discreet distance from Piers. She centered her attention on Will, who was making decisions and issuing orders as if he were a much older man. Because she was watching him so closely, she noticed how little Will ate, either at the midday meal or in the evening, and he disappeared from the hall before the other inhabitants of Banningford had begun to think of seeking their beds. Rohaise thought she knew where he would be.

As she expected, she found him in Joanna's old room. He had opened the shutters and now he knelt on the windowseat, staring out at the darkness. The room itself was lit only by star shine and the pale light of a half moon. Rohaise went to Will and stood behind him without speaking at first. He acknowledged her presence by a slight movement of his head.

"I always believed she stayed here by her own decision," he said. "How cruel my grandfather was, to allow her only as much of the world as she could see from these two windows."

"He did let her walk on the walls whenever the weather was clear," Rohaise said, seating herself beside him.

"Under guard, so she could speak to no one," Will replied, his voice filled with bitterness, "and only after you insisted on that one concession. How terrible for her to know she was constrained to return here after every walk. And to think I admired Radulf and wanted to be like him."

"You left Banningford when you were but seven years old," Rohaise reminded him. "After that you only saw him when he visited the Earl of Bolsover, or when you all met at court. During those short reunions I am sure Radulf was as charming as he knew how to be. There was no way for you to know his true character."

"I've been home for seven weeks," Will insisted. "I have been told I am no fool, so why couldn't I see the truth of my mother's situation?"

"Because all of us pretended that what Radulf claimed was true," Rohaise said. "We gave you no reason to doubt him."

"You lived in fear, too." Will moved a little, settling himself more comfortably on the windowseat. In the dim light Rohaise could just barely make out his face. "What a monster the man was."

"On the subject of having an heir, I believe he was mad," Rohaise said. "Perhaps he brooded too long on his lack of a son. Who can tell how such a mind works? Certainly, once your father was dead, Radulf felt he had to protect himself from exposure of his crime and ensure that he would keep the lands he had gained by his wicked plotting. At least it's over now, and we can all begin anew. Will, you have done very well today. Your father would be proud of you."

"I know so little about him. All any of you would tell me was that he was a good and honest man."

"So he was. I think you are very like him." Struck by inspiration, Rohaise leaned forward to touch his hand. "If you want to know about your father, ask his best friends and kinsmen. Talk to Piers and Alain."

"My new guardians?" Will's irritation at the arrangement Ambrose had insisted upon sounded in his voice. "I am perfectly capable of managing my own estates."

"Indeed you are, if what we saw today is any indication," Rohaise said. "It's only for a few months, Will. Piers thinks you ought to be knighted on your eighteenth birthday. Surely by then King Stephen will confirm you as baron. Use the time until that day to make friends with your father's friends. You liked them well enough when they first came here."

"Perhaps I will."

"It's the sign of a wise man to change with

377

changing circumstances." Hearing his low laugh at her comment, Rohaise went on, asking the question that had remained in her mind for the greater part of the day. "Have you decided what to do with Lys? Because if you haven't, I have a suggestion."

"Which is?" He sounded more amused than angry at the mention of Lys. Encouraged, Rohaise spoke quickly.

"I always thought it was remarkable for Lys, who was first presented to me as a mere serf, to be so expert at her duties. Now I know why. She was raised to be mistress of a manor house. She and I talked while we prepared Radulf's body, and Lys told me her father had arranged her marriage to one of his tenants. As his wife Lys would have had the running of the man's manor house. But her betrothed and her father were killed when Radulf took her father's castle in some baronial war long before I married Radulf. Since that time the poor woman has lived in constant fear, as she explained to Ambrose earlier today. She told me some of the things Baird did to her. I won't repeat them; they are too awful. Baird broke her spirit with his brutality. If you punish her, she will never recover. But I believe if you were to give her useful work to do, she will in time regain some measure of self-respect."

"What kind of work?" Will asked.

"I want you to make her your chatelaine. With Lys managing domestic matters and Owain in charge of defenses, Banningford will be well run, leaving you free to live here or at Haughston, whichever you choose."

"What?" Will exclaimed. "You expect me to elevate that woman after all her petty cruelties to my mother? She was never properly respectful of you, either."

"The way Lys treated Joanna and myself was largely Baird's doing and, to some extent, Radulf's. All three of us were Radulf's victims. Joanna and I are free now. I'm asking you to free Lys, too."

"Free Lys," Will said softly into the darkness. "And my mother wants me to forgive Samira for her deception. I will never understand women."

"Give it time," Rohaise advised. "You aren't even eighteen yet."

On his side of the windowseat Will began to laugh again. The laughter ended on something that sounded suspiciously like a sob. Rohaise reached out and pulled him to her, letting him rest his head on her shoulder.

"I'm frightened," he whispered, sounding like the boy he still was. "My world is turned upside down in an hour; everything I believed about my family was wrong. And now so much responsibility, so many lives depending on me—and will depend on me until the day I die. How am I to do it, Rohaise? How can I make the right decisions?"

"You won't be alone," she said. "Piers and Alain, Samira and your mother and I will all be with you. For what it's worth, considering that I only knew him for a few days, I think your questions are the very ones you father would have asked in your place. I believe he was a deep thinker, too."

"When I was a little boy you always knew how to make me feel better. I'm glad there's one thing that hasn't changed since this morning." Will sat up and cleared his throat. When he spoke again he sounded like the true lord of the castle. "Thank you, Rohaise. I knew you would give me good advice. I shall follow it. All of it."

The crypt at Haughston Castle was built of unadorned gray stone. Heavy, rounded arches supported the low ceiling, which was also the floor of the chapel, directly above. The party from Banningford paused on the steps, waiting for the servant with the torch to advance into the crypt so they could see more clearly.

"There are five barons of Haughston interred here," Ambrose said, leading the way. "My grandsires lie there on your left. Here is my father's tomb. This one is my older brother's resting place." He paused to lay a hand on the smooth stone. "My dear brother, who was Crispin's father. And this one is Crispin's tomb."

They gathered around, looking at the marble effigy of a young man in armor and helmet.

"Crispin." Joanna went to her knees. "My father would never let me come here. He wouldn't even allow me to attend Crispin's funeral."

"You are here now, my dear." Rohaise knelt beside her stepdaughter.

Then the rest of them—Alain, Piers, Will, and Samira—were on their knees, too, and Ambrose was praying aloud for peace for Crispin's soul, for the comfort of his widow and son, and for those men wrongly accused of his murder but after so many years proven innocent. Lastly, Ambrose prayed for mercy and forgiveness for those who had taken Crispin's life, who now had gone on to face eternal justice. When Ambrose had finished and the others had begun to edge toward the stairs Joanna lingered at her husband's tomb. Lightly her fingertips traced the cold sculpted face.

"This looks nothing like the Crispin I remember," she said.

"It does not," Alain agreed. "Very likely the sculptor never saw Crispin, alive or dead. But I see him again every time I look at his son."

"So do I." Glancing over her shoulder, Joanna made certain the rest of their party was in the process of departing the crypt. "You knew Crispin better than I, Alain. Tell me, do you think he would mind that we are lovers?"

"Crispin had a generous soul. I think he would be happy for both of us."

"I hope so. I would never do anything to sully his memory, or to hurt his son."

"Crispin's spirit might be happier," Alain said, "if we were husband and wife. And if, as I have begun to suspect, Crispin's son resembles his father in his feelings about the way men should treat women, it would be advisable for us to betroth ourselves before Will discovers what I have done to you. Under no circumstances do I want to have to meet that young man with my sword in my hand."

"What you have done to me?" Joanna cried.

"I've done the same to you, and with equal joy, as well you know."

Alain put his hand on the marble shoulder of Crispin's effigy in a gesture Joanna had seen him use toward Crispin when he lived, and toward Piers, too. Alain put out his other hand and Joanna took it.

"Crispin," Alain said, "I do here make my solemn vow upon your tomb, that I will love and protect Joanna with my very life. All that I have is hers. Rest easy, old friend, dear cousin. Your murder is avenged, your widow is free, your son is in possession of his full inheritance, and you are remembered with love."

At a sound on the steps they turned to see Piers standing there. He came forward at once and laid his hand on Alain's shoulder.

"I heard," Piers said. "I am the witness to your vow, before God, and Crispin, and the world."

They remained that way for a time, with Alain's hand on Crispin's shoulder in the familiar, casual gesture of friendship, with Piers's hand on Alain's shoulder in the same way, and Joanna's hand in Alain's. When they finally left the crypt was illuminated only by the faint light filtering down the stairs from the chapel above. It was quiet in the crypt, too, except for a brief stirring of air that hovered for a moment above Crispin's tomb, like a contented, peaceful sigh.

Chapter Twenty-one

Toward the end of the evening meal Will announced he had decided to remain at Haughston indefinitely.

"Our years at Banningford were tainted by Radulf," he said to Joanna. "Because of that I do not wish to live there for a while. Let us begin again in a new place."

"An excellent idea," said Alain.

"I am glad you approve." Will had still not entirely adjusted to the idea of having two guardians, so his affronted pride tinged his remark to Alain with sarcasm.

"I shall depart tomorrow morning," Ambrose said into the uncomfortable silence. "I will take with me two of your men-at-arms, if you will spare them, Alain, and I'll head directly to court. I will do my best for you, but don't expect a prompt reply from King Stephen. From all I've heard of him he never makes a decision if he can put it off until another day."

"The Earl of Bolsover used to say," Will broke in, "that if Stephen would only make a decision and stick to it, this long war might have ended ten years ago."

"I think the earl was not far wrong," Ambrose said. "At least England is relatively peaceful at the moment. With Matilda and her son Henry returned to Anjou, and no battles or sieges to deal with, perhaps Stephen will not be too distracted to see me. Thank you for mentioning the Earl of Bolsover, Will. I'll speak to him, too, and since he knows you well he can put in a word for speedy confirmation of your titles.

"Now, Alain, Piers, since we have let it be publicly known that Radulf was the true villain in Crispin's death, and since gossip travels quickly, I do not think you two need fear too greatly for your lives until I return."

"I have also sent out word that they are under my protection," Will said. "No one will dare to harm them if the heir to Haughston and Banningford guarantees their safety."

"Thank you, Will," Alain responded. "That is just the sort of generous gesture your father would have made."

"Would he?" Will looked from Alain to Piers and back again, open curiosity filling his young face. "I wish you would tell me everything you can remember about my father."

"It will take a long time," Alain said, wondering

whether to start with the day when three lonely young pages had met and innocently decided to be friends, or if he ought to tell about some amusing youthful scrape instead.

"Perhaps," Piers suggested, "we can talk about Crispin each evening as we sit together over meat and wine. Or if some event during the day raises a memory, we can tell you as we work together."

"Yes," Will replied with the first enthusiasm he had shown toward either Alain or Piers since they had come to Haughston. "I would like that."

Alain knew what Piers was doing. He was arranging a way for Alain and Will to learn to know each other gradually, while talking about a subject dear to all of them.

Alain and Joanna had not told Will of their plan to marry. The lovers and Piers were scarcely out of the crypt where they had pledged their troth before they had come close to quarreling over Joanna's insistence on waiting.

"Will thinks he is too old to have guardians," she said, "and I think he still believes that I bear an immortal love for Crispin. Let him grow used to your presence, Alain. Let him learn to know and like you. I am certain it won't take long. Then, when we do tell him, he will be more accepting of our love."

"I don't need anyone but you to accept my love for you," Alain responded. "The boy has had enough of lies and evasions. I think we ought to tell him at once, and let him deal as best he can with our intention to marry. Let it be now, while he has other changes in his life and new responsibilities to distract him, so he won't be thinking only of us."

"I will not upset him!" Joanna cried. "Not when he has just learned terrible things about his grandfather. We will wait until I am prepared to tell him or I will not marry you at all."

Taken aback by this unexpected threat, Alain agreed to wait for a while to announce their betrothal.

"But in nothing else will I wait," he said, not caring that Piers stood beside them. "You are my true love and we have been separated for too many years. See to it that you have a room to yourself, for I plan to visit you every night."

"Alain, hush, please." Joanna blushed, her throat and face and even her ears turning bright pink.

"We are betrothed; we have a witness to our vows, so there is nothing wrong in our lying together," Alain said. "You belong to me now, and I will never allow us to be parted again."

"What will Piers think?" Joanna cried.

"That he's glad to see you happy," Piers said, grinning at them. "If you will excuse me, I really ought to have a long talk with my daughter."

"Well, my lady," Alain said when they were alone, "will you see to it that you have a private chamber? Until Will marries you are the lady of this castle. How will you dispose your guests?"

They were still standing at the top of the crypt steps, which emerged aboveground behind the chapel altar. Apparently deep in thought, Joanna walked around the altar, down two steps, and into the nave before she stopped to answer his question. She looked backward at him over her shoulder.

"I shall dispose them conveniently," she said, her eyes dancing. "Which I suppose means I'll have to situate Rohaise near Piers. Perhaps you and he could share a room, since neither of you intends to sleep there."

"Piers and Rohaise? You must be joking."

"Perhaps Piers will sleep in his own chamber for a while yet. Rohaise is behaving with all the somber propriety expected of a new widow, but I think it is done largely for Will's sake, and I'd wager it won't last long." Joanna looked amused. "Haven't you noticed how much Piers likes my stepmother?"

"But he loved his wife," Alain protested.

"Does that mean he can never love anyone else? Alain, I want you to tell me about Piers's wife. Was he kind to her?"

"He claimed to be marrying her for purely practical purposes," Alain replied. "At the time he spoke to me as if he had serious reservations about the arrangement. Piers is entirely too clever for his own happiness and sometimes for his own safety, and he continually questions his own motives. I think he secretly loved Yolande from the beginning of their marriage, yet for some reason he couldn't admit it to himself or to her. But once Samira was born there was never any question about his devotion. Everyone who knew them knew they loved each other deeply. When Yolande died Piers was so heartbroken that Samira became afraid for his life and begged me to think of some way to bring back his interest in living. My attempt to do so resulted in our return to England at this particular time."

"Would he treat Rohaise well?"

"Without a doubt. But he loved Yolande so much that I wonder if he could care for Rohaise enough to make her happy."

"Alain, I do not know if you are blessed or cursed because you can love only one woman," Joanna said. "Some of us can love more than once. I was extremely fond of Crispin, though it was a far milder emotion than what I feel for you. There are different kinds of love. And there are people who marry several times and live contentedly with each spouse. Perhaps Piers is one of those. I do know," she added, moving closer and turning the full power of her sapphire eyes on him, "that once the heart is opened by a great love, there is room in it for more beloved people, not fewer. If Piers truly loved his wife, it may well be that he can love Rohaise, too."

Haughston was a larger castle than Banningford, so it was easy enough to give each person of the three couples now in residence private, if small, rooms. Because no woman had lived there since the death of Crispin's mother some thirty years previously, the castle lacked comforts.

"There is so much to do here," Joanna said to the other women as they inspected unused bedchambers and an inadequately stocked stillroom. "I will need both of you to help me make this dreary castle livable again."

Rohaise had long years of experience and Samira had been well trained by her mother. Under Joanna's supervision they set to work the day after their arrival. Soon the castle was engulfed in a bustle of domestic activity. Rooms were cleaned. Seamstresses were called in from the village to help in making cushions and coverlets and bedcurtains. Old linens were darned and laundered, quilts and moldy pillows beaten to remove the dust and then aired in the winter sunshine to freshen them still more.

Meanwhile, the men reorganized the administration of Radulf's baronies, replacing many of his officers with men of Will's own choosing. When the weather was fit the men and women rode out together on hunting parties intended to bring in fresh meat to supplement the adequate but boring supplies of dried or salted meats available in the castle kitchen. The long winter evenings were filled with talk and laughter, for Will was beginning to unbend toward Alain and Piers.

"By now he must know everything there is to know about Crispin," Alain said to Joanna one evening. They were sitting at the high table, and he glanced toward where Piers was talking to Will while Samira and Rohaise listened.

"And almost everything about you and Piers," Joanna added. "For every question about his father he asks one about the two of you."

"I've noticed. My love, now that he knows me better, I think we should inform him of our plans to marry."

"Not yet," Joanna said. "Wait until after Twelfth Night."

"While I will admit to a certain extra excitement each time I secretly creep into your bedchamber," Alain replied, "still, I would rather go openly and boldly, as your husband."

"It's not so long to wait. Christmas is only three days away," she noted.

"After my extreme patience in this matter you will probably expect me to be an indulgent husband," Alain teased. Catching her hand, he pressed a lingering kiss on her fingers. "For you, Joanna, I would wait until the end of time if I had to. But, please, I implore you, let us tell him sooner than then, so that when we are finally wed we will not be too aged to enjoy our married state."

They kept the holy day quietly, as Will insisted they ought to do that year, but they could not deny holiday pleasures to the servants, men-at-arms, or villagers of Haughston, who had scarcely known Baron Radulf and who had no reason to mourn his death. From the day after Christmas to Twelfth Night there was a feast every midday, with entertainments lasting well into the night. All who lived in or near Haughston were invited. When a wandering minstrel appeared at the castle gate offering music and fanciful stories in return for food and lodging, Joanna hired him at once. For those who liked rougher entertainment there was no shortage of wrestling matches between the men-at-arms belonging to Alain or Piers and those men attached to the castle.

On the third night after Christmas, while everyone else listened to the minstrel's songs, Piers pulled Rohaise out of the hall and into a shadowy corner.

"What are you doing, sir?" she demanded. "What are you holding? It's too dark here for me to see clearly."

"A mistletoe berry." He held it up between two fingers.

"I believe it is used," she informed him. "I saw you a while ago, kissing one of the kitchen maids."

" 'Twas she who captured me," he said, laughing. "I had nothing to do with it, and I fear she was greatly disappointed by my lack of enthusiasm. This berry, lady, is fresh and pure as the snow falling outside, and with it I claim a kiss." He put his arms around her, but she pushed against his chest, holding him off.

"Will you mean it this time, Sir Piers?" She sounded like a frightened young girl.

"Rohaise, there is nothing I want more at this moment than to kiss you."

"That's not to say you'll mean it. Have you been drinking too much?"

"I am not Radulf!" He flung away, turning his back on her. "You have been so distant since we came to Haughston that I begin to think you dislike me."

"That's not it." She was quiet for a moment, until she moved around to face him. "Piers, I don't know how to respond to a man who treats me kindly, who does not order me about or say coarse things to me in front of others."

"I can be coarse when the occasion is right. For me such an occasion will always be private." He caught her face between his hands. "Shall I kiss you, Rohaise? Do you want me to?"

"Only if you mean it, my lord." She stood very still, with her hands resting on his chest, waiting, until Piers bent his head and put his mouth on hers. It was a gentle kiss, but one full of promise. When he drew away she sighed, reluctant to have it end.

"If you would like," he said softly, "I believe I could find another unused mistletoe berry."

"That won't be necessary." She let her hands slide upward along his chest and around his neck. He pulled her closer, enfolding her in his warmth and strength. This time when their mouths met hers was slightly open. He took immediate advantage, touching her lips with his tongue, then moving into her mouth. Rohaise, who had never been kissed so deeply or so thoroughly before, felt as if she were sinking into a vat of warm, sweet honey. All of her limbs felt boneless. The least movement was an effort, while deep in the core of her delicious sensations disturbed and thrilled her very soul. Piers put his hands on her hips, holding her against him. She did not mind; she was not afraid of him, and she wanted more of what he was doing to her.

"Come with me," he whispered. "Come upstairs."

"I'm not sure how I'll get there," she whispered back. "Perhaps I'll fly. I feel as if I could."

"I'll help you." After another brief kiss he put an arm around her waist to guide her, and side by side they ascended the stairs, quickly, before anyone could see or question them. Rohaise did not think her feet actually touched a single step.

They went to her room, where with a pounding heart she watched Piers bolt the door. He must have heard her catch her breath at the motion that elminated any possibility that she would change her mind and refuse him. He came to her at once and lifted her chin, holding her so she could not avert her eyes from his burning gaze.

"I promise I will do nothing to hurt you," he said.

"I know. I'm not afraid, not with you."

He helped her to remove her clothes and take down her straight brown hair. When she was naked he stepped back to look at her, a smile softening his sharp, narrow features.

"You are lovely," he whispered.

She did not tell him how Radulf had always complained about her thinness and said her breasts were too small. Piers had no criticism about her body. Instead, he kissed her breasts and shoulders, caressed her, and murmured that her skin was soft as fine silk. He eased her down onto the bed, and there he touched her breasts again. He touched her in other places, too, in ways that made her tremble and ache to hold him inside her.

When he removed his own clothes and knelt

next to her she opened her arms and took him to her with a tenderness and need she had never experienced before. She closed her eyes when she felt him pushing into her so she could relish the sensation with no distractions. She could feel him so far inside her that she knew she was going to shatter and disintegrate from a penetration that was hard and gentle at the same time.

"Look at me, Rohaise." She obeyed his tender command, to find him gazing at her as if she were something miraculous. All her apprehensions gone, she found she could smile back at him. The smile ended when he began to withdraw from her. She gave way to panic. Radulf had done this to her innumerable times, had too often left her aching and miserable. She clutched at Piers's back, digging in her nails, daring to cry out what she was feeling. "Don't go. Please don't leave me."

But this was not Radulf holding her, and Piers knew exactly what she needed.

"I leave only to return," he murmured, and surged into her again. He repeated the movement several times, withdrawing almost completely and then filling her, while she grew steadily more heated and her moans increased in intensity with each stroke.

"Don't tease me," she begged, still not entirely sure she could trust him not to leave her desolate.

"I tease myself, too," he whispered, "and it's time to stop." With that he plunged deeper still, displaying a new and sudden urgency, the action turning her moan into a cry of pleasure. She began to understand that this was what she had desired all her life, this tender affection, this hot, continuing motion of a man inside her, this building certainty that something wonderful was going to happen, something only Piers could create, and she comprehended at last that she could trust him to stay with her until her need was fulfilled.

"Rohaise," he whispered. "Lovely Rohaise."

The words ended in a groan, and Piers went rigid, straining against her. She knew what was happening to him; what she did not understand was her own reaction. She could not breathe; her heart seemed to stop beating and a strange, half-strangled cry tore from her throat. An incredible heat swept over her. An instant later Rohaise discovered that, just as she had always imagined, lying with a man who cared about her was indeed the most beautiful thing in the world.

Chapter Twenty-two

The midday feast was well underway before Piers and Rohaise entered the great hall and walked hand-in-hand toward the high table. They stepped onto the dais, Piers's happy grin and Rohaise's shy smile and shining eyes providing fair warning to all seated there. With an elaborate flourish Piers pulled out a chair so Rohaise could sit. By this time everyone in the hall was looking at them.

"My lords and ladies," Piers said, "I have the honor to inform you that Lady Rohaise has consented to be my wife."

"No, you can't." Against the noisy background of applause and cheers and a few raucous whistles erupting at Piers's announcement, Will's angry cry could only be heard by those nearest him. "Rohaise, you cannot do this. Grandfather has not been dead for even a month."

"Will, I am sorry if our plans upset you," Rohaise told him, "but you know as well as I do that widows with large inheritances are frequently married off very quickly."

"You don't have an inheritance," Will objected.

"No, I have not, thanks to Radulf. He married me for the lands I brought him, and he saw to it that those lands became entirely his once our marriage was consummated. Save for my small widow's portion, I am a pauper since Radulf's death."

"You will always have a home with me. I'd never put you out," Will said. "You don't have to remarry in order to survive."

"You are kind, Will, and I thank you for caring what happens to me. I want to marry Piers, and since I have no great holdings for men to quarrel about, I am free to do as I please."

"We plan to wait until Uncle Ambrose returns," Piers added. "I want him to bless our marriage."

"It's too soon," Will insisted. "You scarcely know each other. We have no real proof that these men are great lords in Sicily as they claim to be."

"Ambrose has known Alain and me since we were boys," Piers said. "He has sworn to the veracity of our story. Do you doubt a priest, Will?"

"I question this unseemly haste. I cannot approve of the marriage." Nor would Will be moved by Piers's calm assurance that he would treat Rohaise well. He was similarly unaffected by Rohaise's insistance that she had known and liked

397

Piers before Will was born, or that her marriage to Radulf had brought her no happiness and, considering the terrible things he had done, she could not truly mourn his death.

"You are too old to wed," Will told her in a desperate attempt to end the argument in his favor. He succeeded in stopping the argument, but not in the way he expected. Rohaise burst into laughter, and Piers's shoulders began to shake.

"I can tell you honestly," Rohaise said between bouts of giggles, "that at this moment I feel no more than sixteen, and as happy as a young girl in love for the first time. Which, in truth, is what I am." She took Piers's hand and smiled into his eyes with such adoration that Will pushed back his chair and stood up.

"This is disgusting," he said, and left the dais, striding out of the hall with his face set and grim.

"Now, that is much like his father," Alain remarked. "If you remember, Piers, Crispin could be stubborn, too."

"He will not stop us," Piers answered, putting a protective arm around Rohaise.

"It pleases me greatly to see you happy again, *old* Sir Piers," Alain said. Turning to Joanna, he asked, "When Will returns to the hall why don't we tell him our news, too, and have done at once with the decisions that will upset him?"

"Certainly not," Joanna cried. "Why would you suggest such a thing? Let him learn to accept Piers's and Rohaise's betrothal before we distress him with yet more bad news."

"Bad news?" Alain was tired of being patient,

weary of keeping his love for this woman a secret from her son. At her words his temper flared into real anger. "As baron, your son will have a fair amount of bad news, I assure you. The revelation that his mother intends to marry a man who has loved her for the better part of his life does not fall into the category of *bad news*. Castle walls undermined by sappers during a siege, villages burned and sacked, crops destroyed in warfare, loyal servants hanged by invaders, a wife dead in childbirth, a beloved child slaughtered—those are bad news. I say we tell him now and be done with it. When he does learn the truth he won't thank you for keeping it from him."

"Don't you dare give me orders!" Joanna was on her feet. "I am no longer the biddable girl you once knew. I have had enough of obedience to last me *two* lifetimes. I will decide what, and when, and how, to tell my son. *I*, not you or any other man!" Before Alain could reply to her outburst she left the table, hurrying out of the hall. Alain went after her, their hasty passage causing little stir among the revelers, who were at that moment entranced by a juggler's attempts to toss into the air and catch four flaming torches without setting himself or his audience on fire.

"I do hope she's not going after Will," Rohaise remarked. "Samira followed him as soon as he left, and I really think she can bring him to a reasonable state of mind before his mother could."

"Do you think we will ever quarrel like that?" Piers seated himself and pushed a plate of sliced venison in sauce toward Rohaise.

"Possibly," she said, "if we had a son and did something to shock him."

"A son. What a lovely thought." Piers picked up a piece of the venison on the point of his knife, offering it to Rohaise. She bit into it, her teeth slicing it neatly in half. Piers popped the remainder into his own mouth, then bent forward to kiss the juices off her lips.

"Well, at least you didn't run after your precious son, to coddle him." Alain shoved at the door of Joanna's room, shutting it with a resounding slam.

"Go away. I don't want to see you right now."

"Joanna, you are being unreasonable. Will is a strong young man and is maturing rapidly. He can accept the truth when he's told it. Consider the way he has dealt with the events at Banningford."

"I won't listen to this." Joanna began pacing back and forth, but she didn't have much space in which to move. Her room at Haughston was half the size of her chamber at Banningford. She reached the bed, turned, and came back toward him.

"I think it's you who cannot accept what has happened." Fists on hips, eyes narrowed, Alain watched her distracted movements. "It must be difficult to find yourself completely free after so many years."

"It is not difficult at all. It's wonderful. Do you know what it was like during those years, Alain?"

She paused, taking quick, panting breaths, staring at him with eyes that did not see him at all, but focused instead on a room miles away at Banningford, a room she could not leave except briefly and by her father's permission, a world circumscribed by four walls and two narrow windows. "Everything was decided for me: when I could walk upon the battlements and for how long, what I would say to my son and how long he might visit me. Every detail of my life was decided by someone else—someone who ought to have cared about me, should have loved me, and did not. Have you wondered how I survived with my wits intact? I'll tell you, Alain. I made a vow to myself. I swore that if I was ever released, I would never again allow anyone else to make decisions for me. No, not even you."

"All the same, Will must be told," Alain insisted. "If you wait much longer, you will have to begin lying to him again, and that will only make him more angry when he does learn the truth. It might be easier for him if another man tells him. Tomorrow morning I can lead him into a discussion of Piers's intentions toward Rohaise, and while we talk I can tell him we have two marriages to plan, for I intend to wed you as soon as possible."

"No! You can't do that. You won't let you hurt William Crispin when he's suffering so much pain over what his grandfather did. You haven't been listening to me, Alain. You are trying to do to me just what Radulf did. You are trying to control me. This is my decision to make. Mine! Why can't you understand?" Her eyes were wild, and she was close to tears.

Alain recognized the look and braced himself. When she sprang at him, raising her hands to scratch at his eyes, he was ready for her. He caught her by the arms and flipped her backward onto the bed, where he held her down with the weight of his body. Her outraged scream he muffled with his mouth, kissing her hard.

"Are you going to rape me?" she demanded, still not entirely subdued. Alain was beginning to understand that Joanna would never be subdued. He found the realization remarkably exciting.

"I would never rape you," he whispered, his mouth on her throat. "However, I do plan to make you want me enough to plead with me to take you." His hands were in her hair, pulling out the pins to release the golden waves and spread them over her shoulders.

"I am very angry with you," she said, but she did not try to stop what he was doing.

"Good. I'm angry with you, too. And both of us are still angry with Radulf." He paused to look into her troubled eyes. "Anger released can easily turn into passion. Let your rage and your desire loose on me. No, don't try to push me away. I won't be denied, Joanna, and if you were honest with yourself, you'd admit you don't want me to stop."

While he spoke he was tearing off her clothing and his own. She did not resist, but she did not help him, either. When he had finished, he sank down beside her on the bed. Seeing him already fully aroused, her eyes widened.

"Yes," he whispered, his hand on her breast, "you remember the last time we lay together, don't you? And the very first time we made love, how wonderful it was."

"Alain, please, about William Crispin—" He kissed away whatever else she might have said. His hands worked their magic on her body, his kiss was deep and long, and before it ended she was moaning. "Alain, Alain."

"Say it," he commanded. "Tell me you want me."

"I want you."

"Where?" He teased with his fingers, knowing full well where she wanted him and intending to deny her until she was writhing with ecstasy and begging him to take her. He would wait until she was throbbing with her own climax and he was bursting with need of her. Then, and only then, would he thrust into her as hard as he could to seek his release in her hot, dark depths. Making love to her had been his dream for so many empty, lonely nights, and this time he was going to do it the way he wanted.

"I want you to lie on top of me." Her whispered request surprised him.

"I am much too heavy," he protested.

"I don't care. I want you inside me, and on me, too. I want to feel all of you at once. Please, Alain."

He removed his hand from between her thighs. She cried out, looking at him with such longing that he gave up his wish to master her. Whatever demons haunted her after her long imprisonment, however changed she might be from the innocent fourteen-year-old girl he had first desired, she was still Joanna, and he loved her with all his heart.

She grabbed at his shoulder, tugging at him until he shifted position. Still pulling him downward, she spread her legs, inviting him. He entered her with a smooth, hard thrust and then let his full weight settle over her. He rested there, his body pressed against hers from toe to forehead, with her arms around his waist to hold him tightly to her.

"You were right," she breathed, "I am still angry with you, I'm furious, and I want you so much . . . so much."

Alain groaned with the effort of controlling himself. Every part of his body was responding to the touch of her skin. It was an incredible sensation. Then she was tightening herself around him and moving with a wild, demanding heat that seared his mind until he could no longer think at all and self-control was out of the question.

"I love you," she whispered, and with those sweet words in his ears he sailed with her into an ecstatic union that lasted so long it finally left him weak and drained and unable to move.

He did not know how much later it was when he was able to gather enough strength to roll to one side and hold her in a loose embrace. Later still, she spoke again.

"You must promise me you won't tell William Crispin until I decide it is time," she murmured. "If you love me, if you truly want to marry me, then you will agree that I, and I alone, shall be the one to decide when to inform my son about our betrothal. If you love me, you will try to understand how much it means to me to be able to arrange my own life in the way I want."

"Will it always be like this?" he asked. "Will you continually insist upon having your own way?"

"Perhaps not every time we disagree, but often enough to irritate you, I am sure." She touched his face with tender fingers. "If we had wed while I was still an unformed girl of fourteen, I might well have become the obedient wife a nobleman expects. I have told you several times, I am that girl no longer. If you want me for your wife, you must learn to deal with the woman I am now."

"How can you question my wanting you when I have waited so long for you?" Alain sighed, wondering who had bested whom in their passionate contest of bodies and determination. Then humor lit his eyes as he thought about the future they would have together. "Of one thing I am certain: You and I will never be bored with each other. When we are old and feeble you will still be able to surprise and delight me, my dear and only love."

Up on the walkway at the top of the castle wall, Samira found Will staring into the blowing snow and gray skies of a winter storm.

"Here's your cloak," she said, holding it out to

him. "You'll freeze without it." When he did not take the garment she stood on tiptoe to lay it over his shoulders.

"Did you know about their plans?" he asked, not looking at her.

"Rohaise called me to her room this morning. She and my father told me then." Samira paused, biting her lip, then revealed the rest of it. "They spent last night together, Will."

"What do you expect me to say to that?" he demanded. "Did you think that piece of information would convince me to approve of this proposed marriage? Rohaise is a *grandmother!* It's shameful!"

"Only a step-grandmother," Samira said with wry humor. "Rohaise is just a few years older than Joanna. But I know how you feel, Will. I was shocked at first, too."

"I don't suppose there's a thing we can do to stop their marrying?"

"Not unless you lock Rohaise up the way your grandfather did Joanna. I don't think you have the stomach for that kind of prolonged cruelty. Let me warn you that if you try to harm my father, you will have me to contend with, not to mention Theo Alain and all his men." Samira let the threat sink in for a while before she asked, "Would it really be so terrible, to see Rohaise happy? You do love her, don't you?"

"I suppose I'll have to accept their decision," Will said after a long silence.

"I think it would be wise."

Will withdrew his gaze from the snowy landscape to look at the girl beside him.

"Alain says Piers is clever. I think you have inherited his cleverness, Samira."

"My father claims that I more resemble my mother. Have you forgiven me yet for deceiving you when we first met?" she asked. "If you will but listen, I can explain, and perhaps also make you understand why I will raise no protest over my father's decision to remarry."

"I already know more than I care to know about the events at Banningford." Obviously he thought that would be the end of their conversation. He turned one shoulder toward her in dismissal. Samira would not allow it.

"You don't know everything you should about our reasons for what we did. You see, Will, it all began when my dear mother died and I feared my father would die, too, of grieving for her." She went on, telling him her version of the events that had brought her to England, omitting only the story of Alain's love for Joanna. That portion of the tale was Alain's to tell, not hers.

At first Will seemed indifferent to her words, and Samira wasn't sure he was paying attention to her, but soon he gave up his expressionless contemplation of the falling snow. Leaning an arm on the edge of the wall, heedless of cold or wind or snow, he listened with growing interest, even asking a question now and then. He was particularly interested in the details of her life in Sicily and in the exploits of Piers and Alain while they were in service to King Roger. So engrossed in Samira's story were they that they noticed nothing beyond the spot where they stood on the high walkway along the battlements.

"Why, it's almost dark," Will exclaimed when Samira had stopped talking.

"You are covered with snow." She began to brush the white flakes off his shoulders.

"So are you. It's in your hair." His hand glided over the top of her head and downward to her shoulder, then around to the nape of her neck, showering snow away from her. They grew still at the same moment, with her hand resting on his upper arm and his fingers grasping the thick braid of dark hair that hung down her back.

"I'm sorry I was angry with you," Will said. "I should have heard everything you had to tell me before I judged your actions."

"I am sorry it was necessary to deceive you," she replied. "Before we met you none of us knew how trustworthy you are." In the swiftly gathering dusk she could just make out his face and see the snow collecting on his fair hair. She took her hand off his arm, intending to remove the white dusting, but he caught her fingers in his.

"Your hand is like ice. Samira, you must be half frozen."

"I don't mind, so long as you believe me."

"I do. Every word. Now come inside and let's find a fire and some hot, spiced wine to drink while we talk some more."

On the morning after Twelfth Night, just as the inhabitants of Haughston Castle were rousing themselves to aching heads and indigestion, and

swearing never again to eat or drink so much—
no, not even when rowdy Twelfth Night came
round again next year—a single horseman bearing a royal pennant rode up to the castle gate. He
was admitted at once and taken to the great hall
by one of Alain's men-at-arms, where he was met
by Alain and Will.

"I am sent with a summons from King Stephen," the newcomer announced. "Matilda's son,
Henry of Anjou, has returned to England with an
army. King Stephen calls upon all nobles who
are loyal to bring troops and join him. Our royal
lord is determined to defeat young Henry and
thus end this long war once and for all."

"We must go," Will said to Alain. "The Earl of
Bolsover used to say that for all Stephen's faults,
he is our annointed king and we owe him our
fealty. We have to defend him against Matilda's
son."

"I never had the opportunity to swear my oath
to him," Alain replied, "but I will go with you all
the same, and take my men-at-arms to fight beside your men."

"Somehow I knew you would." Will put out his
hand and Alain took it, appreciating that Will
was offering his friendship.

"What's happening?" Piers walked into the
hall. Upon being told the news, his response was
similar to Alain's. "Only a few of the men who
came with us are mine, but we will all go with
you, Will."

They made their plans in haste, sending a messenger to Banningford with orders for Owain to

send a group of men from there to a meeting-place along the road. Owain was to prepare Banningford to withstand a siege if it should prove necessary. The same orders were given to the captain of the guard at Haughston. The king's messenger was well fed before he was sent on his way, to the other castles where he was to deliver the royal summons to arms.

By then everyone at Haughston had heard the news, and the ladies of the castle were deeply distressed.

"William Crispin, I wish you would not go," Joanna said. "Under the present circumstances, surely you can be excused. You are needed here."

"We leave at dawn, and I ride at the head of my men," her son responded. "Forgive me, Mother, but I cannot stay to talk with you. I am busy."

Joanna had no more comfort than Will had given her from Alain. She lodged her protest when he joined her in her bedchamber after most of the castle was quiet for the night.

"If we join Stephen and give him what support we can," Alain said, "he will feel obligated to withdraw the writ of outlawry against us. Piers agrees with me that taking our men to Stephen can only help our case."

"You swore we would never be parted again," she cried, distraught with fear for him and for her son.

"I am doing this for us," he declared. "For my honor's sake, so you won't have to marry an attainted criminal. Joanna, I don't want to leave you, but I must. I beg you to understand."

"I think I do," she said, trying to smile, though her eyes were filled with tears. "If I want you to respect the decisions I make, then I must give your choices equal respect. Go then, my dear love, and I will pray for your safety every moment until you return to me."

"How brave you are, and how much I love you. What I do in battle, I'll do for love as well as honor," he vowed. "I will shed no more blood than I absolutely must."

He caught her to his heart, and while he kissed her she promised herself to spend the rest of the night proving to him that he was everything to her.

Rohaise did not protest at all. She understood Piers's manly nature too well to object to something he felt he had to do.

"I will miss you every day and every night," she told him.

"Think of the happy homecoming we'll share." He kissed her once, then grew serious. "If I do not return, I want you to know that you have re-made my life and given me great joy. I have written a document, giving you a property in Sicily. Samira has the parchment. I want you to see my girl safely home if I am unable to do it. Will you promise me, Rohaise?"

"I promise gladly, but I'd rather have you in my arms."

"So I will be, God willing. You are precious to me, Rohaise. You are worth the long journey to

England, worth all the danger we faced, and more."

Samira knew she had no right to say anything to Will to try to change his mind. And where Joanna and Rohaise could say their farewells in private, Samira had to be content with a few hasty words in the inner bailey. After embracing Piers and Alain she gave her hands to Will, who stood holding them and looking down at her as if he wanted to say something but could not. Unlike the older men, he was not wearing chainmail. Will, not yet knighted or confirmed in his titles, wore only his squire's sword, with the baldric that held it fastened over his blue wool tunic. His dark cloak was still slung over one arm.

"God keep you safe, my lord," Samira whispered.

"And you, my lady." His hands tightened over hers.

With a soft cry, Samira rose on tiptoe to kiss his cheek, Will turned his head just in time, so it was his lips she touched—and lingered upon.

"My lady, I will win every battle for your sweet sake," Will promised. He dropped her hands to swirl his cloak in a circle and settle it upon his shoulders. Walking away a pace or two, he vaulted onto his horse's back. With a wave of one hand, he wheeled the horse toward the castle gate.

Samira could not bear to watch the three men ride away. She fled indoors, seeking the quiet of her own chamber, where she could weep without being seen.

Chapter Twenty-three

The men did not return until late March. Ambrose came with them, and it was he who recounted the end of nearly twenty years of civil war. This he did while they all sat at a feast to celebrate the homecoming.

"Stephen's army and Henry's faced each other from either side of the Thames at Wallingford," Ambrose said. "It was bitterly cold that day, with deep snow on the ground and the river partially frozen, truly a terrible time and place for a battle. Then a few of Stephen's nobles and some priests went to him and told him the war was destroying the country. The long strain of it has destroyed Stephen's health, too, and I believe he was eager to find peace by any honorable means. He and Henry held a conference and came to an agreement. Matilda will not become queen, which re-

413

lieved those nobles who do not want to be ruled by a woman. Instead, Stephen will remain as king for his lifetime, and Matilda's son Henry is to inherit England after Stephen's death. There were other points discussed, but the royal succession was the most important item. And so, at last, the war is over, and no battle was fought to end it."

"How foolish," Samira cried. "After so many years, after countless lives lost, villages and castles destroyed, after a fair country has nearly been ruined beyond repair, now they come to terms? Why couldn't they have been so sensible twenty years ago?"

"Because the circumstances have changed over time," Ambrose said. "Stephen's own son is dead now, so it is all the same to him if Henry inherits the kingdom. And in those earlier years Matilda was still a vigorous and arrogant woman, determined to have her own way and be queen as her father had promised. The difference to her now is that her son is grown into a man who can easily rule this land, so she, too, will probably be content when she learns of the final resolution. All England must be rejoicing today."

"We have our own private reasons for rejoicing," said Piers. "Thanks to your efforts, Uncle Ambrose, Alain and I are now free men in England."

"But landless," Ambrose added. "Unfortunately, when Alain's father died, Wortham escheated to the crown because a criminal cannot inherit. Stephen gave the land and title to one of his nobles years ago and has refused to take it back."

"I do not care about the land," Alain said. "All I wanted was to clear my name and Piers's, and to discover and punish Crispin's murderer. That we have accomplished. As for Wortham, I have not seen it since I was seven years old. I scarcely remember it. I am sorry for my father's sake that the title has passed out of our family, but the honors I have earned for myself in Sicily mean more to me."

"Since as a younger son I never had lands to lose," Piers added, "I also am content to have my honor restored and ask no more than that of England's king. I will always be grateful to you, Uncle Ambrose, for what you have done for Alain and me."

"Will has been officially confirmed as baron of both Haughston and Banningford," Ambrose told Joanna. "Stephen himself knighted your son."

"I know we have you to thank for that, too," Joanna said. "William Crispin has changed since he's been away. He's more grown up. He's tougher."

"These months with Alain and Piers, and then his time at court, have all been good for him," Ambrose agreed. "Will is a man now, with no more need for guardians."

"A man. Yes, he is." Joanna looked along the table toward her son. "William Crispin, there is something I want to tell you. I intend to marry Alain."

There was an abrupt silence at the high table. Everyone turned to look at Joanna.

"Well?" she said to her son. "Aren't you going to say anything?"

"Mother, I already know about it," he said.

"How could you know?"

"I am young but not blind," Will told her. "I noted the way you and Alain looked at each other. Then, one night when we were away, while we sat drinking and talking, I demanded to know what Alain's intentions toward you were, and he told me the whole story of his long love for you. He also said he would marry you as soon as you are ready."

"The moment seemed right," Alain added.

"I am sorry you didn't feel you could tell me yourself," Will said to Joanna. "But Alain explained you needed time to decide when and how to tell me."

"Did he?" Joanna slanted an appraising look toward Alain. "I recall an earlier decision I made about a wine jug. I assure you, my lord Alain, I am prepared to make the same decision again."

Rohaise began to laugh. Piers looked at her as if he expected some explanation, but she held her sides and leaned against his shoulder and kept on laughing.

"You men," she gasped, wiping her eyes. "You think you are so clever, arranging everything for your women. You planned to surprise Joanna with this news, didn't you? But she has a surprise for you that I'll wager none of you expects." She went off into more gales of laughter.

By this time Samira was giggling, her eyes bright, with one hand held over her mouth to contain the sounds. Then Joanna began to laugh, too.

Bewildered by this behavior, the men looked at each other, shaking their heads at the vagaries of women.

"Joanna, enough of this. Explain yourself," Alain commanded.

"You may not order me," she said. "I have told you more than once, I will never again be ordered by any man. However, if you ask me politely, I may decide to tell you."

A slow grin spread across Alain's face. "Very well, my dear lady; will you be kind enough to disclose your mysterious secret?"

"I would be delighted, my lord. I am glad to know my son has no objections to our marriage, because you will have to wed me as promptly as possible. I am carrying your child."

"A child?" Alain stared at her. "A child. Joanna, my love!"

"Rohaise and I have counted as best we could, and we believe it occurred the very first time we made love. Your climb up the tower wall to my room was most opportune, my lord," Joanna informed him with a teasing smile.

"*Mother,*" Will chided, rolling his eyes, "lower your voice, please. You needn't tell everyone in the entire castle of your condition.

"Wouldn't you think," Will added to Samira, who sat on his other side, "that at their ages, they'd show a little more restraint?"

"I think it's lovely," Samira replied, looking at Will without the hint of a blush.

On Samira's other side, Piers leaned toward Rohaise.

"Is there any chance that you might be following Joanna's example?" he asked.

"No, my lord, I regret to say I have no such hope."

"In that case," Piers murmured, "I shall take immediate steps to change your condition."

"I hope so, my lord," Rohaise murmured. "Oh, I do hope you will."

Later on that starry spring night, when the castle was finally quiet, Alain stirred in Joanna's arms. She moved her head, giving him a questioning look. The light of the single oil lamp showed a woman flushed and happy from lovemaking. Alain raised himself on one elbow to look at her.

"My task in England is done," he said.

"My lord?" A faint crease appeared between her brows.

"Don't look so worried," he said, kissing the tip of her nose. "I remember a young girl who spoke with shining eyes of traveling abroad. By now I know better than to command you, Joanna, so I'll ask instead. Will you go with me?"

"I have always wanted to see the world," she murmured. "I convinced myself to marry poor Crispin with a cheerful face because he promised to take me to Normandy and Compostela. Do you remember?"

"I remember. And your father was angry. . . . "

"Yes, well, all of that is finished now. Take me to Sicily, Alain. I want to see brilliant sunshine on turquoise waters. I want to see palm trees and eat dates and talk to Saracen lords."

"I will have to fight off the Saracen lords," he teased. "They'll want to kidnap you for their harems."

"No, not me. I'll soon be too fat, and I'm much too old. I am almost thirty-three."

"Not too old for me," he whispered, "or for love."

"Oh, no, not too old for love at all." A moment later, wrenching her mouth from his, she asked, "May I have a sapphire silk robe and long golden earrings?"

"I am breathless at the thought of you with your hair down and nothing on beneath a silken robe," Alain said. "You may have anything you want. I told you before, I am a rich man. Now, concentrate, my dearest, and stop interrupting. I am trying to make love to you."

Epilogue

Lady Samira of Palermo and Baron William Crispin of Haughston and Banningford were married in early April of the Year of Our Lord 1153. Because the lands in Normandy that Will had inherited from his father had lain untended for many years he decided to travel there immediately after his wedding to inspect them and see to their restoration.

"I want you to go with me," he said to Alain and Piers. "I will value your advice, and since you insist on returning to your own lands you can rest in Normandy after the crossing from England."

"Thank you," Alain responded. "We plan to travel slowly, so as not to tire Joanna."

"It's I who ought to thank you," Will told him. "You freed me as well as my mother, and through you I now know my father. I am glad we can be friends."

"You and Samira are always welcome in my home," Alain said.

"Piers has told me the same. Our farewell will not be a final good-bye, of that I am sure," Will replied.

In the first week of September, Joanna gave birth to a daughter, whom they named Eleanor for Joanna's mother. Two weeks later, Joanna and Alain, Piers and Rohaise, left Normandy en route to Sicily.

Author's Note

Roger II of Sicily died in 1154, and was succeeded by his son, William I. With Roger's death the most brilliant days of a glorious, albeit brief era in the history of a tragic island were over, though relatively peaceful Norman rule continued in Sicily for another forty years. On December 25, 1194, Emperor Henry VI Hohenstaufen, the husband of Roger's daughter Constance, was crowned King of Sicily in Palermo Cathedral. Thus, the Holy Roman Emperors at last took possession of the island they had for so long coveted. Their rule was fatal to the tolerant and enlightened blend of Greek and Roman Christianity, Islam, and Judaism that Sicily's Norman kings had so carefully cultivated.

The title held by George of Antioch, Emir al-Bahr, in Arabic, Ruler (or commander) of the Sea, found its way into modern languages. In French it is *amiral*, in Spanish, *almirante*, in English, admiral.

SPECIAL SNEAK PREVIEW FOLLOWS!

Madeline Baker writing as Amanda Ashley

Cursed by the darkness, he searches through the ages for the redeeming light, the one woman who can save him. A creature of moonlight and fancy, she fears the handsome stranger whose eyes promise endless ecstasy even while his mouth whispers dark secrets. They are two people longing for fulfillment, yearning for a love like no other. Alone, they will face a desolate destiny. Together, they will share undying passion, defy eternity, and embrace the night.

**Don't miss *Embrace The Night!*
Coming in August 1995 to bookstores
and newsstands everywhere.**

Embrace The Night Copyright © 1995 by Madeline Baker

He walked the streets for hours after he left the orphanage, his thoughts filled with Sara, her fragile beauty, her sweet innocence, her unwavering trust. She had accepted him into her life without question, and the knowledge cut him to the quick. He did not like deceiving her, hiding the dark secret of what he was, nor did he like to think about how badly she would be hurt when his nighttime visits ceased, as they surely must.

He had loved her from the moment he first saw her, but always from a distance, worshiping her as the moon might worship the sun, basking in her heat, her light, but wisely staying away lest he be burned.

And foolishly, he had strayed too close. He had soothed her tears, held her in his arms, and now he was paying the price. He was burning, like a moth drawn to a flame. Burning with need. With desire. With an unholy lust, not for her body, but for the very essence of her life.

It sickened him that he should want her that way, that he could even consider such a despicable thing. And yet he could think of little else. Ah, to hold her in his arms, to feel his body become one with hers as he drank of her sweetness. . . .

For a moment, he closed his eyes and let himself imagine it, and then he swore a long vile oath filled with pain and longing.

Hands clenched, he turned down a dark street, his self-anger turning to loathing, and the loathing to rage. He felt the need to kill, to strike out, to make someone else suffer as he was suffering.

Pity the poor mortal who next crossed his path, he thought. Then he gave himself over to the hunger pounding through him.

She woke covered with perspiration, Gabriel's name on her lips. Shivering, she drew the covers up to her chin.

It had only been a dream. Only a dream.

She spoke the words aloud, finding comfort in the sound of her own voice. A distant bell chimed the hour. Four o'clock.

Gradually, her breathing returned to normal. Only a dream, she said again, but it had been so real. She had felt the cold breath of the night, smelled the rank odor of fear rising from the body of the faceless man cowering in the shadows. She had sensed a deep anger, a wild uncontrollable evil personified by a being in a flowing black cloak. Even now, she could feel his anguish, his loneliness, the alienation that cut him off from the rest of humanity.

It had all been so clear in the dream, but now it made no sense. No sense at all.

With a slight shake of her head, she snuggled deeper under the covers and closed her eyes.

It was just a dream, nothing more.

Sunk in the depths of despair, Gabriel prowled the deserted abbey. What had happened to his self-control? Not for centuries had he taken enough blood to kill, only enough to assuage the pain of the hunger, to ease his unholy thirst.

A low groan rose in his throat. Sara had happened. He wanted her and he couldn't have her. Somehow, his desire and his frustration had gotten tangled up with his lust for blood.

It couldn't happen again. It had taken him centuries to learn to control the hunger, to give himself the illusion that he was more man than monster.

Had he been able, he would have prayed for forgiveness, but he had forfeited the right to divine intervention long ago.

"Where will we go tonight?"

Gabriel stared at her. She'd been waiting for him again, clothed in her new dress, her eyes bright with anticipation. Her goodness drew him, soothed him, calmed his dark side even as her beauty, her innocence, teased his desire.

He stared at the pulse throbbing in her throat. "Go?"

Sara nodded.

With an effort, he lifted his gaze to her face. "Where would you like to go?"

"I don't suppose you have a horse?"

"A horse?"

"I've always wanted to ride."

He bowed from the waist. "Whatever you wish, milady," he said. "I'll not be gone long."

It was like having found a magic wand, Sara mused as she waited for him to return. She had only to voice her desire, and he produced it.

Twenty minutes later, she was seated before him on a prancing black stallion. It was a beautiful animal, tall and muscular, with a flowing mane and tail.

She leaned forward to stroke the stallion's neck. His coat felt like velvet beneath her hand. "What's his name?"

"Necromancer," Gabriel replied, pride and affection evident in his tone.

"Necromancer? What does it mean?"

"One who communicates with the spirits of the dead."

Sara glanced at him over her shoulder. "That seems an odd name for a horse."

"Odd, perhaps," Gabriel replied cryptically, "but fitting."

"Fitting? In what way?"

"Do you want to ride, Sara, or spend the night asking foolish questions?"

She pouted prettily for a moment and then grinned at him.

"Ride!"

A word from Gabriel and they were cantering through the dark night, heading into the countryside.

"Faster," Sara urged.

"You're not afraid?"

"Not with you."

"You should be afraid, Sara Jayne," he muttered under his breath, "especially with me."

He squeezed the stallion's flanks with his knees and the horse shot forward, his powerful hooves skimming across the ground.

Sara shrieked with delight as they raced through the darkness. This was power, she thought, the surging body of the horse, the man's strong arm wrapped securely around her waist. The wind whipped through her hair, stinging her cheeks and making her eyes water, but she only threw back her head and laughed.

"Faster!" she cried, reveling in the sense of freedom that surged within her.

Hedges and trees and sleeping farmhouses passed by in a blur. Once, they jumped a four-foot hedge, and she felt as if she were flying. Sounds and scents blended together: the chirping of crickets, the bark of a dog, the smell of damp earth and lathered horseflesh, and over all the touch of Gabriel's breath upon her cheek, the steadying strength of his arm around her waist.

Gabriel let the horse run until the animal's sides were heaving and covered with foamy lather, and then he drew back on the reins, gently but firmly, and the stallion slowed, then stopped.

"That was wonderful!" Sara exclaimed.

She turned to face him, and in the bright light of the moon, he saw that her cheeks were flushed, her lips parted, her eyes shining like the sun.

How beautiful she was! His Sara, so full of life. What cruel fate had decreed that she should be bound to a wheelchair? She was a vivacious girl on the brink of womanhood. She should be clothed in silks and satins, surrounded by gallant young men.

Dismounting, he lifted her from the back of the horse. Carrying her across the damp grass, he sat down on a large boulder, settling her in his lap.

"Thank you, Gabriel," she murmured.

"It was my pleasure, milady."

"Hardly that," she replied with a saucy grin. "I'm sure ladies don't ride pell-mell through the dark astride a big black devil horse."

"No," he said, his gray eyes glinting with amusement, "they don't."

"Have you known many ladies?"

"A few." He stroked her cheek with his forefinger, his touch as light as thistledown.

"And were they accomplished and beautiful?"

Gabriel nodded. "But none so beautiful as you."

She basked in his words, in the silent affirmation she read in his eyes.

"Who are you, Gabriel?" she asked, her voice soft and dreamy. "Are you man or magician?"

"Neither."

"But still my angel?"

"Always, *cara*."

With a sigh, she rested her head against his shoulder and closed her eyes. How wonderful, to sit here in the dark of the night with his arms around her. She could almost forget that she was crippled. Almost.

She lost all track of time as she sat there, secure in his arms. She heard the chirp of crickets, the sighing of the wind through the trees, the pounding of Gabriel's heart beneath her cheek.

Her breath caught in her throat as she felt the touch of his hand in her hair and then the brush of his lips.

Abruptly, he stood up. Before she quite knew what was happening, she was on the horse's back and Gabriel was swinging up behind her. He moved with the lithe grace of a cat vaulting a fence.

She sensed a change in him, a tension she didn't understand. A moment later, his arm was locked around her waist and they were riding through the night.

She leaned back against him, braced against the solid wall of his chest. She felt his arm tighten around her, felt his breath on her cheek.

Pleasure surged through her at his touch and she placed her hand over his forearm, drawing his arm more securely around her, tacitly telling him that she enjoyed his nearness.

She thought she heard a gasp, as if he was in pain, but she shook the notion aside, telling herself it was probably just the wind crying through the trees.

Too soon, they were back at the orphanage.

"You'll come tomorrow?" she asked as he settled her in her bed, covering her as if she were a child.

"Tomorrow," he promised. "Sleep well, *cara*."

"Dream of me," she murmured.

With a nod, he turned away. Dream of her, he thought. If only he could!

"Where would you like to go tonight?" Gabriel asked the following evening.

"I don't care, so long as it's with you."

Moments later, he was carrying her along a pathway in the park across from the orphanage.

Sara marveled that he held her so effortlessly, that it felt so right to be carried in his arms. She rested her head on his shoulder, content. A faint breeze played hide and seek with the leaves of the trees. A lover's moon hung low in the sky. The air was fragrant with night blooming flowers, but it was Gabriel's scent that rose all around her—warm and musky, reminiscent of aged wine and expensive cologne.

He moved lightly along the pathway, his footsteps making hardly a sound. When they came to a stone bench near a quiet pool, he sat down, placing her on the bench beside him.

It was a lovely place, a fairy place. Elegant ferns, tall and lacy, grew in wild profusion near the pool. In the distance, she heard the questioning hoot of an owl.

"What did you do all day?" she asked, turning to look at him.

Gabriel shrugged. "Nothing to speak of. And you?"

"I read to the children. Sister Mary Josepha has been giving me more and more responsibility."

"And does that make you happy?"

"Yes. I've grown very fond of my little charges. They so need to be loved. To be touched. I had never realized how important it was, to be held, until—" A faint flush stained her cheeks. "Until you held me. There's such comfort in the touch of a human hand."

Gabriel grunted softly. Human, indeed, he thought bleakly.

Sara smiled. "They seem to like me, the children. I don't know why."

But he knew why. She had so much love to give, and no outlet for it.

"I hate to think of all the time I wasted wallowing in self-pity," Sara remarked. "I spent so much time sitting in my room, sulking because I couldn't walk, when I could have been helping the children, loving them." She glanced up at Gabriel. "They're so easy to love."

"So are you." He had not meant to speak the words aloud, but they slipped out. "I mean, it must be easy for the children to love you. You have so much to give."

She smiled, but it was a sad kind of smile. "Perhaps that's because no one else wants it."

"Sara—"

"It's all right. Maybe that's why I was put here, to comfort the little lost lambs that no one else wants."

I want you. The words thundered in his mind, in his heart, in his soul.

Abruptly, he stood up and moved away from the bench. He couldn't sit beside her, feel her warmth, hear the blood humming in her veins, sense the sadness dragging at her heart, and not touch her, take her.

He stared into the depths of the dark pool, the water as black as the emptiness of his soul. He'd been alone for so long, yearning for someone who would share his life, needing someone to see him for what he was and love him anyway.

A low groan rose in his throat as the centuries of loneliness wrapped around him.

"Gabriel?" Her voice called out to him, soft, warm, caring.

With a cry, he whirled around and knelt at her feet. Hesitantly, he took her hands in his.

"Sara, can you pretend I'm one of the children? Can you hold me, and comfort me, just for to-night?"

"I don't understand."

"Don't ask questions, *cara*. Please just hold me. Touch me."

She gazed down at him, into the fathomless depths of his dark gray eyes, and the loneliness she saw there pierced her heart. Tears stung her eyes as she reached for him.

He buried his face in her lap, ashamed of the need that he could no longer deny. And then he felt her hand stroke his hair, light as a summer breeze. Ah, the touch of a human hand, warm, fragile, pulsing with life.

Time ceased to have meaning as he knelt there, his head cradled in her lap, her hand moving in his hair, caressing his nape, feathering across his cheek. No wonder the children loved her. There was tranquility in her touch, serenity in her hand. A sense of peace settled over him, stilling his hunger. He felt the tension drain out of him, to be replaced with a nearly forgotten sense of calm. It was a feeling as close to forgiveness as he would ever know.

After a time, he lifted his head. Slightly embarrassed, he gazed up at her, but there was no censure in her eyes, no disdain, only a wealth of understanding.

"Why are you so alone, my angel?" She asked quietly.

"I have always been alone," he replied, and even now, when he was nearer to peace of spirit than he had been for centuries, he was aware of the vast gulf that separated him, not only from Sara, but from all of humanity as well.

Gently, she cupped his cheek with her hand. "Is there no one to love you then?"

"No one."

"I would love you, Gabriel."

"No!"

Stricken by the force of his denial, she let her hand fall into her lap. "Is the thought of my love so revolting?"

"No, don't ever think that." He sat back on his

heels, wishing that he could sit at her feet forever, that he could spend the rest of his existence worshiping her beauty, the generosity of her spirit. "I'm not worthy of you, *cara*. I would not have you waste your love on me."

"Why, Gabriel? What have you done that you feel unworthy of love?"

Filled with the guilt of a thousand lifetimes, he closed his eyes and his mind filled with an image of blood. Rivers of blood. Oceans of death. Centuries of killing, of bloodletting. Damned. The Dark Gift had given him eternal life—and eternal damnation.

Thinking to frighten her away, he let her look deep into his eyes, knowing that what she saw within his soul would speak more eloquently than words.

He clenched his hands, waiting for the compassion in her eyes to turn to revulsion. But it didn't happen.

She gazed down at his upturned face for an endless moment, and then he felt the touch of her hand in his hair.

"My poor angel," she whispered. "Can't you tell me what it is that haunts you so?"

He shook his head, unable to speak past the lump in his throat.

"Gabriel." His name, nothing more, and then she leaned forward and kissed him.

It was no more than a feathering of her lips across his, but it exploded through him like concentrated sunlight. Hotter than a midsummer day, brighter than lightning, it burned through him and for a moment he felt whole again. Clean again.

Humbled to the core of his being, he bowed his head so she couldn't see his tears.

"I will love you, Gabriel," she said, still stroking his hair. "I can't help myself."

"Sara—"

"You don't have to love me back," she said quickly. "I just wanted you to know that you're not alone anymore."

A long shuddering sigh coursed through him, and then he took her hands in his, holding them tightly, feeling the heat of her blood, and the pulse of her heart. Gently, he kissed her fingertips, and then, gaining his feet, he swung her into his arms.

"It's late," he said, his voice thick with the tide of emotions roiling within him. "We should go before you catch a chill."

"You're not angry?"

"No, *cara*."

How could he be angry with her? She was light and life, hope and innocence. He was tempted to fall to his knees and beg her forgiveness for his whole miserable existence.

But he couldn't burden her with the knowledge of what he was. He couldn't tarnish her love with the truth.

It was near dawn when they reached the orphanage. Once he had her settled in bed, he knelt beside her. "Thank you, Sara."

She turned on her side, a slight smile lifting

the corners of her mouth as she took his hand in hers. "For what?"

"For your sweetness. For your words of love. I'll treasure them always."

"Gabriel." The smile faded from her lips. "You're not trying to tell me good-bye, are you?"

He stared down at their joined hands: hers small and pale and fragile, pulsing with the energy of life; his large and cold, indelibly stained with blood and death.

If he had a shred of honor left, he would tell her good-bye and never see her again.

But then, even when he had been a mortal man, he'd always had trouble doing the honorable thing when it conflicted with something he wanted. And he wanted—no, needed—Sara. Needed her as he'd never needed anything else in his accursed life. And perhaps, in a way, she needed him. And even if it wasn't so, it eased his conscience to think it true.

"Gabriel?"

"No, *cara*, I'm not planning to tell you good-bye. Not now. Not ever."

The sweet relief in her eyes stabbed him to the heart. And he, cold, selfish monster that he was, was glad of it. Right or wrong, he couldn't let her go.

"Till tomorrow then?" she said, smiling once more.

"Till tomorrow, *cara mia*," he murmured. And for all the tomorrows of your life.

Don't miss this haunting romance written in the immortal tradition of *Interview With The Vampire*.

Madeline Baker Writing As Amanda Ashley

Cursed by the darkness, he searches through the ages for the redeeming light, the one woman who can save him. But how can he defile such innocence with his unholy desire?

An angel of purity and light, she fears the handsome stranger whose eyes promise endless ecstasy even while his mouth whispers dark secrets that she dares not believe.

They are two people longing for fulfillment, yearning for a love like no other. Alone, they will surely face a desolate destiny full of despair. Together, they will share undying passion, defy eternity, and embrace the night.

_52041-9 $5.99 US/$7.99 CAN

Dorchester Publishing Co., Inc.
65 Commerce Road
Stamford, CT 06902

Please add $1.75 for shipping and handling for the first book and $.50 for each book thereafter. NY, NYC, PA and CT residents, please add appropriate sales tax. No cash, stamps, or C.O.D.s. All orders shipped within 6 weeks via postal service book rate. Canadian orders require $2.00 extra postage and must be paid in U.S. dollars through a U.S. banking facility.

Name_____
Address_____
City _____ State_____Zip_____
I have enclosed $_____in payment for the checked book(s).
Payment <u>must</u> accompany all orders.☐ Please send a free catalog.

DANCE of the FLAME

ELAINE BARBIERI

**Elaine Barbieri's romances are
"powerful...fascinating...storytelling at its best!"**
—*Romantic Times*

Exiled to a barren wasteland, Sera will do anything to regain the kingdom that is her birthright. But the hard-eyed warrior she saves from death is the last companion she wants for the long journey to her homeland.

To the world he is known as Death's Shadow—as much a beast of battle as the mighty warhorse he rides. But to the flame-haired healer, his forceful arms offer a warm haven, and he swears his throbbing strength will bring her nothing but pleasure.

Sera and Tolin hold in their hands the fate of two feuding houses with an ancient history of bloodshed and betrayal. But no matter what the age-old prophecy foretells, the sparks between them will not be denied, even if their fiery union consumes them both.

_3793-9 $5.99 US/$6.99 CAN

Dorchester Publishing Co., Inc.
65 Commerce Road
Stamford, CT 06902

Please add $1.75 for shipping and handling for the first book and $.50 for each book thereafter. NY, NYC, PA and CT residents, please add appropriate sales tax. No cash, stamps, or C.O.D.s. All orders shipped within 6 weeks via postal service book rate. Canadian orders require $2.00 extra postage and must be paid in U.S. dollars through a U.S. banking facility.

Name _____
Address _____
City _____ State _____ Zip _____
I have enclosed $_____in payment for the checked book(s).
Payment <u>must</u> accompany all orders.□ Please send a free catalog.

An Angel's Touch

Time Heals
SUSAN COLLIER

Tired of her nagging relatives, Maeve Fredrickson asks
for the impossible: to be a thousand miles and a hundred years
away from them. Then a heavenly being grants her wish,
and she awakes in frontier Montana.

Saved from the wilderness by a handsome widower, Maeve
loses her heart to her rescuer—and her temper over the antics
of his three less-than-angelic children. As her angel prods
her to fight for Seth, Maeve can only pray for the strength
to claim a love made in paradise.

_52030-3 $4.99 US/$5.99 CAN

Dorchester Publishing Co., Inc.
65 Commerce Road
Stamford, CT 06902

Please add $1.75 for shipping and handling for the first book and
$.50 for each book thereafter. NY, NYC, PA and CT residents,
please add appropriate sales tax. No cash, stamps, or C.O.D.s. All
orders shipped within 6 weeks via postal service book rate.
Canadian orders require $2.00 extra postage and must be paid in
U.S. dollars through a U.S. banking facility.

Name _____

Address _____

City _____ State _____ Zip _____

I have enclosed $_____ in payment for the checked book(s).
Payment must accompany all orders. □ Please send a free catalog.

PREFERRED CUSTOMERS!

*Leisure Books and Love Spell
proudly present
a brand-new catalogue and a
TOLL-FREE NUMBER*

*STARTING JUNE 1, 1995
CALL 1-800-481-9191
between 2:00 and 10:00 p.m.
(Eastern Time)
Monday Through Friday*

*GET A FREE CATALOGUE
AND ORDER BOOKS USING
VISA AND MASTERCARD*